LOCH NESS II

Curse of the Caoineag

A NOVEL

MATT KUNZ

LOCH NESS II
Curse of the Caoineag
Copyright 2023 Matt Kunz

Twitter: @MattKunz59
www.facebook.com/mattkunzauthor
www.mattkunzwrites.com

Print ISBN 978-0-9976298-8-0
Library of Congress Control Number – Coming Soon
Author Photo: Matt Kunz Milton, GA
Cover Design: Matt Kunz w/ www.canva.com

DEDICATION

To Father Matthew and Father Patrick.

Your love for stories inspired my own.

CHAPTER 1

Police Captain James Anderson's boots thudded as they stepped from gravel to wood. He took his hands out of his coat pockets, took off his police cap, and rubbed his fingers through his hair. He reset the cap on his head, the white Sillitoe tartan checkered band showing clear against the royal blue material. He bumped his fists against his hips. Before him, the orange tape wrapped around two thick round wooden poles. The tape was supposed to block people from crossing onto the boat dock.

This evening, it didn't work. Two Scottish men had ignored the tape, crossed the barrier, and were climbing aboard a boat.

The sun was setting behind the mountains. The smell of ozone hovered in the air after the afternoon's rain. Emily, his wife, would have supper ready in half an hour. She'd be upset if he came home late.

Anderson huffed. Were the men trying to sneak out to do some fishing? It didn't matter. The events of the past few days were one for the record books. The news reporters had a field day.

It was all so odd; he didn't know what to say when the reporters came to him asking for information. All he said was, "We need tae dig into this tae get ye th' whole story." It was a stall tactic. He knew it. They knew it. But it was all he had.

He stood by the tape. "Crime Scene" was etched in black across the shiny tape's orange. The evening breeze blew the tape as it draped loosely between the two wooden beams that guarded the entrance to the dock.

He squinted, trying to guess who was out there. He couldn't tell. Their backs were to him. He guessed by the location of the boat it was Keith Wallace and his lad, Cameron. They tended to dock there. If they didn't have their fedoras on, he'd notice their bright shiny red hair.

"Oh, enough already." Anderson tipped his police hat. "I'd better get tae work." He stepped over the orange crime scene tape. He marched on the wooden dock toward the boat, his footsteps thudding with each step. He liked the heaviness of his boots. Their solid sound on the wooden boards gave him authority.

As he approached and neared the boat, he studied the situation. One man, younger than the other, was in the boat. The one still on the dock tossed a ring of rope to him.

"Wallace!" Anderson said, half stating, half questioning.

The men raised their heads; the one on the dock lifted his head a moment, revealing his face. Yes, it was Wallace.

"What are ye' doin' ou' here?"

Keith Wallace and Cameron Wallace paused. Keith said, "Just tryin' tae get some fishin' in."

"A' this hour?"

Keith blushed. "Aye. Hopin' tae before th' sun's down."

Anderson frowned. "The sun's goin' down in five minutes. Wha' luck do ye think you'll catch in tha' short amoun' o' time?"

Keith didn't say anything. Cameron tried to answer, but Keith raised his hand.

Anderson said, "Ye wouldn' by chance thin' yer goin' tae catch th' Loch Ness monster, are ye'?"

Keith and Cameron stayed silent. Aye, guilty as charged, Anderson thought.

"And, Mr. Wallace, wha' are ye' teachin' this lad? Ye know we have crime tape a' th' entrance."

Keith lowered his head.

"Bu'—" Cameron said.

Keith interrupted. "Enou', lad. I shouldn' ha' brough' ye'. No th' now, anyway."

"But, Da–"

Keith glared, and Cameron lowered his head.

Anderson grinned. He liked a working authority, even if it was just between a father and a son. "Na' tae worry," he said. "We'll have this dock open in na time."

"Toss me th' rope," Keith said.

Cameron tossed the rope into his father's hands.

"Tha's a good lad," Anderson said.

Cameron shook his head, grunting.

Keith tied their boat to the dock. "So, wha' happened ou' there?" he asked, gesturing towards Saint Michael's Catholic Church.

"Don' rightly know," Anderson said. "We're still tryin' tae figure it out."

"Do ye' think it exists?"

Anderson scratched his neck. "Do I think wha' exists?"

"Ye know. Nessie."

Anderson paused. As the sun disappeared behind the mountains, its last remaining daylight shimmered over the deep dark waters of Loch Ness. So many rumors had surfaced the past few days with the American, Tom Wayne, showing up, chasing after Sean Paterson's girl.

Anderson had helped Tom after he was beaten and bruised by an unusual gang of thugs. After that, the story became outright strange. Three boats had blown up in the loch in the past few weeks. Chairman Briggs had been arrested. Two men were missing, and another was confirmed dead.

And Tom Wayne, Sean Paterson, and his daughter, Marella, were still alive.

That was all he knew.

As for Nessie? Best to leave the name out of the reports, or else the press would go berserk. "I don' know." Anderson said. "Bu' in a day o' two we'll ge' this tape off, and ye both can search fur him."

Cameron jumped off the boat and landed on the dock.

"Are ye' goin' tae write us up?" Keith asked.

"Na. Jus' consider this a warnin'." Anderson tipped his hat.

Keith tipped his fedora, and his bright red hair behind his ear reflected in the waning sunlight. "Let's go lad." He and Cameron moved past Anderson, their footsteps thumping upon the wooden dock.

Anderson stood still, waiting and watching. As the Wallaces threw their legs over the crime scene tape and returned to the parking lot, he thought he'd stay a little while longer and look around.

The boats rocked back and forth, their ropes rubbing against the dock handles as they kept them in place. The soft creaking and the groaning of the boats soothed Anderson's thoughts.

There was a boat missing. McGregor's. It had blown up a few weeks earlier when Sean Paterson and Tom Wayne had taken it out at McGregor's urging - or so they said - to find the Loch Ness monster. Sean Paterson had lost his leg in the explosion, and since then McGregor was arrested for insurance fraud and attempted murder - by higher authorities than Anderson. He had tried to get more information, but those higher authorities weren't so easy to release what they knew.

He moved along the dock, further away from the shore. The boats swayed, and the breeze from the loch cooled his face. He was alone.

He stopped in his tracks. There was a faint singing sound. *Singin'?* It was coming from the loch, out in the water. He walked further, his heavy boots thumping on the wood.

The singing was growing clearer. It was soft and beautiful, like that of a woman. The notes were in minor chords, and the tune was sad. As he marched, he checked the dock between the boats. Was someone else was hiding between them? He inspected each gap, but there was no one there. Yet the further from shore he went, the singing grew more clear, beautiful, yet mournful.

Through the rocking of the boats came the soft lyrics of the woman's song.

Sad is th' spouse

when love goes away
Th' bond must return
'Tis life th' price tae pay

"Wha' *is* tha'?" he said.

He quickened his pace, examining the spaces between the boats. Nothing. One after another he went. He came upon one space. There was no one there, just some black feathers on the walkway left by a blackbird. The singing was further down. He kept going until he came to the end of the dock.

Just beyond McCulloch's boat was a young woman. Her hair was bleached, and it hung from her head over her pale white skin. She was naked. She sat on the wood facing away from him, her feet submerged in the water, her hands resting her shoulders upon the edge of the wooden dock.

Two souls unite in th' presence
o' th' holy priest
When they're torn apart
Th' creatures will feast

Anderson's eyes widened. At first, he thought she was a ghost. But, no, this was a girl. "Lassie," he said. "Wha' are ye' doin' ou' here?"

The woman sang her sad song and paid him no mind.

"Now, lassie, ye ha' tae be cold." He took his coat off and motioned to her. He went to her and draped his coat over her bare shoulders, covering her smooth back and her white arms.

The woman lifted her head. Her face was beautiful, like a model from one of those London magazines. Her eyes shimmered like green embers.

Anderson said, "Wha's yer name?"

The woman didn't answer. Her lips curled like she knew more than he did.

Anderson lowered his hand, suggesting she take it. "Lassie, I'm here tae' help. Le' me get ye someplace warm."

The woman smiled a moment longer, and then her eyes closed shut. She grimaced. Her face contorted. She opened her eyes again, and they flooded with tears that ran down her cheeks. Her green eyes went red from crying. Then she opened her mouth, and a great wail entered Anderson's head.

Anderson lifted both hands and thrust them against his ears, but it was to no avail. The woman's scream filled his brain, like knives penetrating his skull. He stumbled. His legs wobbled. He couldn't get the sound out of his head. He couldn't think. What was happening?

He twisted. A large black smooth head lifted above the water from a long slender neck. Two green glowing eyes peered at him.

Anderson's heart thudded against his sternum. The sight before him filled his limbs with fright. *Was it . . . ? Could it be . . . ?*

A second head surfaced - this one larger. And a third. Six green eyes hovered several meters out of the water, staring him down. Water ran off their powerful muscles and dripped into the dark waters of Loch Ness.

The woman closed her eyes. Tears streamed down her cheeks. She held onto the jacket that Anderson had draped over her shoulders. She wrapped it over her naked body, twisting the cloth not to keep warm but as a reaction to anguish. She closed her mouth.

The wailing stopped.

Anderson fell to a knee, relieved. He lifted his head.

The green eyes showed teeth, and in an instant, as if on cue, all three heads lunged at him. The sharp teeth ripped into his body and pulled him from the dock and splashed him into the water.

He screamed before water rushed into his mouth and his lungs.

In no time, he was several meters below the air. As his flesh was torn from him, the girl sat, her feet below the surface of the water, his coat wrapped over her shoulders, her emerald eyes the saddest eyes he had ever seen.

A dark red liquid spread throughout the water and blocked out the dimming light. Then everything went dark.

CHAPTER 2

Tom Wayne rolled over on his bed, smacking his lips and stretching. The sounds of nature outside his window stirred him. He was feeling better. He had sustained many injuries a few weeks ago, but this morning his joints no longer ached. His arm was now out of a sling, and his ankle had regained its flexibility.

Usually, the church bells woke him, but he didn't hear them this morning. Had he slept in? A small brown and gray songbird sang outside his window. It sat on a branch of the large tree that stood several yards from his room. The song was cheerful. Tom smiled.

He told himself to get up and move. "What time is it?" The clock said 7:45 a.m. What happened to the church bells? He had slept in. He awoke remembering last night's date with Marella. He stretched on the bed, loosening his joints.

He wanted to win Marella's heart, and that meant he had to be a gentleman. Sure, Sean Paterson, Marella's father, was in the hospital, leaving Marella at home alone. He would have loved to spend the night with her, but she would have none of it. She wasn't that kind of girl.

Also, Father Gibson wouldn't approve. Tom's recent decision to attend Mass at Saint Michael's Catholic Church which loomed across the street from his room at Annabel's Bed and Breakfast, placed him in a new territory, with a new philosophy. When Father Gibson spoke with Tom, it was like the priest read his thoughts. That alone made Tom second-guess his behavior. No funny stuff, he had told himself. He wanted this relationship to work long-term.

He stood next to his bed. He cleaned up, got dressed, and went downstairs. Annabel was fixing waffles like she did the past several weeks. "Aye, ye slept in this mornin'," she said.

The smell of the waffles filled Tom's lungs, and he was glad for it. "Yeah. Got in late."

"Better late than ne'er." She popped the waffles from the toaster, and then picked up the butter knife. "The usual?"

"Please." He sat down.

She handed him his waffles. This had become a typical morning routine after the events a few weeks ago. He had once made the attempt to return to America. He tried to keep his job long enough so he could organize his life and move to Scotland for good. Unfortunately, the Scottish investigators and the US Embassy recommended he stay in the country.

Which, for him, wasn't a problem. That meant more time with Marella. He had come across the Atlantic to get to know her and play the hero, helping her with whatever problem she had. Little did he know his love for her would lead him down the path of a curse that obsessed him with the Loch Ness monster.

But that was over now. Sean Paterson was healing, though minus his leg. And Marella was appreciating all of Tom's support, his helping her, her father, and his taking care of odd tasks that came up. If the investigators and the press would leave him alone, it would make things a whole lot easier.

"Yer friend called again this morning," Annabel said.

Tom raised his eyes. "Detective O'Malley?"

"Na'. The other one."

She had to mean Ms. Liz Stevens. A reporter from the London Tribune, she had heard of Tom's adventure and wanted to do a piece on him. Her attractiveness, while nice from a distance, dissipated with her persistence.

"What did she want?"

"She didn' say. Kind of mysterious, tha' one."

"She's strange."

"Aye." Annabel lifted up her newspaper. "I like your other friend, better."

Tom lifted his glass of orange juice. "I'll toast to that." He finished his waffle.

Annabel smiled, happy Tom enjoyed her waffles.

"I want to show you something," Tom said. He reached into his pocket.

"Wha's tha'?" she said.

Tom placed two earrings on the table. They were silver, ending in shiny green four-leafed clovers.

"For me?" she said.

Tom chuckled. "No."

"Who are they for?"

"You know."

11

Annabel grinned. "Marella will like them."

Tom blushed. "Thanks. I needed to hear that."

Annabel folded her hands and rested her chin upon them. "Where'd ye find them?"

"Smith's Store."

"Aye, they have a little o' e'erything in there, don' they?"

"Are you going to grab yourself a pair?"

"Maybe I will," she said, smiling.

Tom put the earrings back into his pocket. "Well, I'd better get going."

Annabel said, "So soon? Wha' are ye doin' today?"

"Sean is getting out of the hospital. He's going home."

"Is he now?"

"Yeah. I've been helping Marella fix up their place so he can use it. You know. Get around in a wheelchair. That sort of thing."

"That's quite a change."

"It will be." Tom stood. "But with a little help, I think he'll adjust."

"Yer a good man, Tom Wayne," Annabel said.

Tom thanked her. He put his plate in the kitchen sink, saluted her, and went out the front door. Annabel said, "Take care!" before the door shut behind him.

Saint Michael's Catholic Church appeared first when he exited Annabel's Bed and Breakfast. It was a large Catholic church across the street at the edge of the town of Thurwick. A mighty structure, Saint Michael's had been built centuries ago. It had once housed several seminarians who were planning on joining the cloth, but today the rooms were empty except for

Father Gibson's, and a guest room that housed a visiting priest or two.

He had gotten in the habit of attending the 8:30 morning Mass, but today there wasn't time. He headed down the road to Sean Paterson's home.

The morning air was cool after yesterday's rain. He strode along, his feet hitting the gravel, and he avoided the sporadic puddles along the way.

The spring blooms were trying to pop open. He had given Marella a bouquet of unopened blooms the first time he arrived at her door, but this time he'd hand her opened blooms. They would signify their blossoming relationship.

He stopped and studied the blooms. They were white and yellow. Most were half open, but others had opened fully. He reached down to break a stem. He paused at the sound of crunching tires on the dirt road.

A horn honked.

Tom flinched. He didn't recognize the car. He let go of the stem and stood tall, waiting.

The car skidded to a stop, and the window rolled down. Mud splashed on Tom's shoes, and Tom jumped back. The driver was Detective Logan O'Malley. He didn't pause to say hello. "Tom. Ye need tae come wi' me."

There was no one else in the area. It was strange for someone to come all this way to pick him up. O'Malley had driven hard to find him like he was in a rush. "What's the hurry?"

"Na time tae explain. If you'll ge' in the car–"

"I can't. Sean Paterson gets home today, and I promised Marella–"

"We have tae brin' ye in fur questionin'," O'Malley said.

"I've told you everything I know," Tom lied. He had gotten used to it, but he would not reveal the secret to the Loch Ness monster.

"Have ye now?"

Tom didn't like his tone. "What's this about?"

"Somethin' happened last nigh'," O'Malley said.

"What happened?"

O'Malley, an older man with graying hair, gripped the steering wheel. For a detective, he didn't have the best poker face. "It'd be best if ye come wi' me tae the station. I can tell ye there."

"Am I under arrest?"

"Fur yer sake, I'm tryin' tae avoid tha' distinction. 'Tis better fur ye if ye come willingly, as a gesture of help."

Sean Paterson's house was a twenty-minute walk away. Marella would be waiting. If he didn't show up, today of all days, that would not bode well for their relationship. "Can I come this afternoon? I promised Marella."

"If ye'd like me tae arrest ye, I can."

"You're not giving me much of a choice," Tom said.

"I'm sorry," O'Malley said. He gestured for Tom to climb into the passenger seat.

Tom didn't like this. Since the events a few weeks ago, he had been hounded by reporters, interrogated by authorities, and suspected of crimes by suspicious locals. At least Detective Logan O'Malley, of all those who questioned him, had an open mind. It was for that reason Tom decided to build a relationship with him if only to get an ally on the inside.

"Okay," Tom said. "But as soon as I get there, I get to use the phone to call Marella."

O'Malley didn't answer. He leaned over and opened the passenger door.

Tom studied the blooming wildflowers for half a second. So much for romance, he thought. He went around the front of O'Malley's car and climbed in. O'Malley gunned the gas and sped back into Thurwick.

CHAPTER 3

O' Malley's car stopped outside the front door of an old brick building between two light blue police cars. The Thurwick police station was very old, without any additions to make it more modern. Tom couldn't tell if they kept it old-fashioned to make the town of Thurwick appear like Mayberry, or if they were hiding ancient Scottish torture devices somewhere in a secret hidden basement.

O'Malley opened his car door. A man in his mid-fifties, his gray head and beard gave him a kind face. If he had not been a police detective, Tom would imagine him more like a monk. "Na' delayin'. Let's go inside."

Tom climbed out of the car and followed Logan O'Malley up the old steps into the police station.

He went inside. There was an empty jail cell to his left, a corkboard full of "Wanted" posters, a few desks with ladies typing on their computers, and a painting of the Loch Ness monster plastered on the far stone wall. Nessie, as the locals referred to the monster, appeared in the most unexpected places. It was a truth he knew far too well.

O'Malley said, "Come wi' me." Tom followed him into a small office on the right, noticing the women working along the way. "Mornin' Felicia. Sandra," O'Malley said as he walked past.

Felicia and Sandra paused from their typing and looked up, watching Tom as he passed.

"Good mornin', Detective," Felicia said.

Sandra huffed and went back to her typing.

Inside the office was a small table and four chairs. The walls were bare except for the blind-covered windows.

"I get a phone call," Tom said.

"Aye, ye will," O'Malley said.

A man in his forties stepped in. Tom thought he recognized the man, but he wasn't sure how. He wore a suit and tie, his hair was combed, and his shoes had been shined. As he entered, he offered his hand. "Mr. Wayne," he said. "I'm Mark Bain. I sit on the Thurwick Council."

Tom raised his eyebrows. It had been several weeks since the Thurwick Council meeting. He had arrived in town, tired from an overseas flight and bus ride when he had agreed to come with Sean and Marella Paterson to the meeting. The meeting had been crowded, and chaotic. That was when he had met Caleb, which was right after the Council voted unanimously, eight to nothing, in favor of rejecting Sean Paterson's request for funding to find the Loch Ness monster. Tom studied Bain's face. He couldn't quite place the man. Still, the vote had been eight to zero. If Bain was on the Council that meant he, too, had voted against Sean. And, he had sat on the Council with Chairman Briggs.

17

And that made Tom suspicious.

"Okay," Tom said. "Why am I here?"

Bain and O'Malley sat down. "We'll get tae tha'. Please," he motioned with his hand. "Have a seat."

Tom sat reluctantly.

A man walked through the door. He was a larger man, with broad shoulders and thick dark hair. His nose was crooked like it had once been broken. Tom didn't want to meet this guy in a back alley. He wore a uniform and a badge on his chest. Law enforcement, Tom thought. The large man closed the door behind him, and the blinds shuddered as the door shut.

"Mr. Wayne," Bain said. "This is Assistant Police Captain Ian Fleming. He wants tae ask ye some questions."

What was going on here? Tom was in a closed room, in a police station, and he was outnumbered three to one. This was not how he planned his day.

"I've told you everything I know," Tom said. "We've been through this a hundred times."

"It's not about tha'," Fleming said. His voice was loud and deep. "'Tis somethin' new."

"New?"

"Aye," Fleming said. "Where were ye, last nigh'?"

"Last night?"

"Aye."

O'Malley dropped his eyes and folded his hands, waiting. Bain studied Tom, watching his every move. Fleming frowned. He appeared worried.

Why was he worried?

"Last night I was with Marella Paterson. We had a date."

"And where'd ye go?"

"Nothing special, I suppose," Tom said. "We had dinner at Guthrie's Pub, then we went by Saint Michael's Church and walked along the loch."

The three men leaned back. Their eyes met, signifying some sort of silent communication. Fleming said, "Tha' was it?"

"Yes," Tom said. He'd been questioned so many times he had learned that short answers were often best, and not to offer more information unless asked.

Bain said, "And people saw ye?"

"Yes. I have a receipt for Guthrie's. As far as Saint Michael's, I don't think anyone saw us there. You'd have to ask Marella."

"I'll see tha' receipt, if ye don' mind."

Tom twisted and removed his wallet from his back pocket. As he put the receipt on the table, he slid it first to O'Malley who gave a faint smile, and then he slid it to Bain.

Bain studied it, shifted his eyes to Fleming, then sat back in his chair.

Tom said, "I get a phone call, remember."

"Na' until we're done."

"What's this about?"

Fleming said, "Mr. Wayne, did ye happen tae walk pas' the boating dock las' evenin'?"

"The boating dock?"

"Aye."

Tom shook his head. "No. That's been off limits since the past several weeks. Why? Have you opened it again?"

Bain and Fleming stayed silent. O'Malley took a deep breath and relaxed his hands.

"What's going on?" Tom said again. "I get to call Marella."

Then, through the thin wall, behind the blinds, Tom heard a familiar voice. "Why'd ye brin' me here?"

Tom's heart melted. "She's here!" He stood up.

Fleming, Bain, and O'Malley remained sitting.

Tom opened the door.

A freckled-faced police officer led Marella past the other women. She wore a brown jacket over a tan skirt and black boots. Her red hair draped over her shoulders. Tom's heart leaped. Marella's entering the room made everything better.

"Wha's this about!" Marella said. When she noticed Tom, she said, "Are ye in on this tae?"

"No, they picked me up this morning when I was on my way to see you."

"Mr. Wayne," Fleming said. "If ye could wait ou' here." He pointed at a nearby empty chair.

"I'll stand."

The officer gestured for Marella to enter the small room. Marella paused. She glared at the officer, the men in the room, and then Tom. She shook her head and went inside. As Fleming shut the door, Marella's voice came through the wall. "Wha' now?"

Tom waited.

One of the women typing on the computer raised her eyes, her lips trying to repress a smile.

Tom listened. Fleming's loud voice mumbled, but Marella's came through the window loud and clear.

"I was with *him!*" Marella said.

The typing woman snorted, her eyes laughing.

Tom blushed. *Yes, Marella was talking about me.*

There was a mumbled voice. Bain, maybe. Probably Fleming, Tom thought.

Through the window, Marella continued, "Na, we were nowhere near the dock las' night."

Another mumbled voice. Likely Bain.

"Why should I trust ye? Yer a politician. The las' one I met blew my father's leg off!"

Tom smiled. Yes, definitely Bain. Tom was so in love with Marella.

The mumbled voices grew agitated.

"Are ye done with me yet?"

Soft voices.

The door flung open. Marella stormed out of the small room.

Tom jumped up from the chair. "Let's go."

"Aye, let's!" Marella said. She marched past the computers toward the front door. The women on the computers watched, their faces hinting that they admired Marella's confidence.

Fleming and Bain stepped from the office, saying nothing. O'Malley followed them and hurried to Tom.

Tom opened the front door to the station for Marella, and they left the building. The cool breeze blew Tom's hair. Marella's swayed, her red curls floating atop her shoulders. In front of them was Thurwick square. Dorlan Hall, Guthrie's Pub, and the museum stood across the old cobblestone road, their wooden signs weathered by the constant highland weather. Marella's dress blew in the cool breeze, but she didn't mind. O'Malley drove him to the station. How would they get back to Sean's cottage?

"Did they drive you here?" Tom said.

"Aye. Didn' give me a choice."

"Me, too."

The door behind them opened, and O'Malley stepped out.

"Ye!" Marella said. "I've had enough o' ye!"

If not for O'Malley's monk-like face, Tom would have decked him.

"Please," O'Malley said. "Something happened las' night, and we ha' tae square things away."

"What happened?" Tom said.

"Did ye notice somethin' strange in there jus' now?"

Marella's face was blank.

Tom shook his head. "No."

"Tis Captain Anderson," O'Malley said. "He's missin'."

CHAPTER 4

A few weeks ago, a gang of locals had attacked Tom. After the gang ran away, Captain Anderson stood over him. Tom opened his black eyes as the captain helped him up.

The captain was an older man, O'Malley's age. Anderson was supposed to send O'Malley to the hospital to get more information after the attack, but when O'Malley hadn't arrived, Tom left.

"The Police Captain?" Tom said.

"Aye."

Marella gasped. Tom understood. While a few pedestrians walked among the Thurwick storefronts, none of them were within earshot of their conversation. "So, you think we had something to do with him?"

O'Malley shook his head. "Na' me. Though considerin' all tha' you've been through since ye've been 'ere, yer name came up foremost by those who're wonderin'."

"You mean Bain and Fleming."

"The politicians on th' Council didn' ge' good press when Briggs was arrested. Some o' them took it personally."

"Like Bain."

"Aye. And others."

"Great," Tom said, his lips pursing. He thought he was done with the local politicians coming after him. "And Fleming?"

"Doin' his job," O'Malley said. "As was I."

"Bu' we were nowhere near th' docks las' nigh'," Marella said.

"And 'tis a good thin' you weren't," O'Malley said. "And a good thin' tha' Tom had yer dinner receipt." O'Malley said to Tom. " 'Cept I canno' believe ye came all this way across th' ocean tae order a hamburger."

"Guess I was homesick," Tom said.

"If yer done wi' us now, we need tae get home. My da's gettin' ou' soon, and he'll need our help," Marella said.

O'Malley opened his car door. Tom opened the rear door for Marella, then climbed in the passenger seat.

As O'Malley backed up, and the car bounced along the cobblestones, he said, "I'm glad Sean is gettin' out. I'd been worried about him while he was in care."

"Tha' makes two o' us," Marella said.

Tom, too, had been worried. While Sean was in the hospital, what were the chances that some goon would come into Sean's room and create an accident? With Vaas and Coffee out of the picture, and Briggs arrested, it was possible the heads were chopped off the snake, scattering the underlings. But there was no telling for how long. "So what happened to Anderson?" Tom said. If others suspected him of foul play, he wanted to know.

24

"We don' know," O'Malley said. "His car was still in the dock parkin' lot this mornin'. His wife, Emily, said she expected him home fur supper. When he didn' come home, she got worried and called Fleming. Fleming went onto th' dock wi' his flashlight last night and looked around, but didn't find anythin' except fur his parked car."

"Did they check the boats?"

"Na until t'is mornin'. Fleming and Sergeant Scott searched th' boats a' first light. They didn' find anythin' in th' boats."

O'Malley hesitated.

Tom waited, but he sensed O'Malley wasn't finished. "So, what did they find?"

O'Malley was driving the car past Annabel's and Saint Michael's Church as he said, "They found Anderson's coat floatin' in th' wa'er on th' far side o' th' dock."

"His coat?"

"Aye."

"Anything else? No cuts or marks on it?"

"Nay. T'was in one piece."

"That's strange," Marella said.

"Well, maybe he'll turn up," Tom said.

O'Malley's car bounced along Mackay Rd., the dirt road that lead to Sean and Marella Paterson's home. The bumpy ride caused Tom to put his hand on the overhead handle for support.

"I hope he does," O'Malley said. "T'would be better fur e'eryone if he did."

"How about you?" Tom said. "Do you think he will?"

"'Tis na' fur me tae make predictions. Only tae find wha' happened."

Tom rubbed the back of his neck. "I want to put the past behind and move forward."

"Our past has a way o' frustratin' our future, Mr. Wayne."

Marella's torso bounced with the bumpy road, her hands on the seat and the door to lessen the jolts. She smiled at Tom, and he smiled right back.

"I'm not going to let that happen, Detective O'Malley. I've got too much I want to do."

"Suit yerself," O'Malley said. The car rolled to a stop. In front of the car was Sean Paterson's home. Sean's old blue sedan sat in the driveway. The windmills and trinkets that lined the front unkempt lawn blew with the highland wind. Tom climbed out and then helped Marella from the back seat.

O'Malley leaned out his driver's window. "Mr. Wayne. If ye do find anythin' suspicious, please reach ou' tae me." He handed Tom a card. "My number's on this."

"What about protection?"

"Same instructions," O'Malley said. Then he stepped on the gas and drove back down the dirt road.

Tom examined the card. It said: Logan O'Malley. Detective. Town of Thurwick. Then it gave his phone number.

"The guy doesn't even have an email address," Tom said. He reached down and held Marella's hand.

"I didn' expect this today." Marella stepped away from Tom and opened the front door.

"Me either," Tom said. He followed her inside.

"We'd better ge' goin'. Da's goin' tae wonder why we're late."

"Need anything before we go?"

"Nay. I was jus' about tae leave tae ge' ye when th' woman officer showed up." She grabbed her set of keys from the keyring on the wall.

"I was on my way, you know." Tom said.

"Right. I bet ye and Annabel were havin' waffles."

"And what if we were?"

"Well, I might have to reconsider our arrangements."

Tom was taken aback. "Reconsider what?"

Marella opened the driver-side door to the sedan. "Oh, somethin' tae keep me from gettin' jealous." She laughed and climbed inside.

Tom opened the door. "I don't know why, but I sort of like the sound of that."

Marella winked and Tom laughed as they pulled out of the driveway and drove down the bumpy dirt road toward the Thurwick hospital.

CHAPTER 5

Tom and Marella entered the Thurwick hospital. It was the one place he had visited far too often since he had arrived in Thurwick. He hoped this would be the last.

"Hi Erin," Tom said to the receptionist. "Are you going to miss him?"

"O' course. Mr. Paterson ha' been a joy e'er since he's arrived."

"Now I know yer lyin'," Marella said.

Tom and Marella hurried past Erin and went down the hall, made a right, and opened the door.

"Ah, Marella! And Tom!" boomed Sean Paterson. He was sitting down in a wheelchair, holding a cane in his right hand, and supporting a prosthetic leg and a bag of treats on his lap. "Am I gla' tae see ye. Where have ye been? They've been tryin' tae kick me ou' o' here o'er an hour ago."

The doctor in the white lab coat raised his eyebrows while resting against a table.

"We'll tell you in the car," Tom said. "Is he ready?"

The doctor rolled his eyes. "He's yers now," he said.

"Wha' else should we do tae help him," Marella said. "After all, we're his family."

"Marealla, my dear," Sean said. He lifted a cane and tapped the metal leg on the nearby table. "Na need tae worry abou' me. I'm goin' tae make me an iron leg, and I'll be as good as new. You'll see me up and abou' in no time."

The doctor said, "We've scheduled physical therapy three times a week, jus' until he gets stronger."

"Bah!" Sean said.

"And he's still takin' pain meds, bu' he should be off those in a week o' two."

"I won' have time fur therapy," Sean said. "I have some catchin' up tae do." He held up his prosthetic leg. "This, this is th' future!"

"Da!" Marella said.

"Well, 'tis better than chasin' after some monster."

Marella closed her mouth.

"He's got a point," Tom said.

"Shall we ge' goin'?" Sean said. He rested his cane on his lap, and with his two hands, wheeled himself toward the door.

"If ye have any questions, give us a call," the doctor said.

"We'll be fine," Sean said as he rolled past Tom and Marella out the door. From down the hallway, he shouted, "Erin, are ye goin' tae miss me, lassie?"

Marella, her eyes sad from Sean's injury, managed to laugh at her father's attitude. "He's glad 'tis o'er, isn't he?"

Tom was sympathetic to Sean, as he carried the same curse that Sean had held for thirty years. "I'm sure he feels a ton of relief. I know I do."

"Ye know, now tha' he's this way, I canno' be goin' back tae th' states. He's goin' tae need me."

"And you're going to need me."

Marella leaned in and hugged Tom.

"Ahem," the doctor said. "If ye two are finished, I have another patient tae see."

Tom and Marella stepped back. The doctor slipped past them through the door and went down the hall. "Come on," Tom said. He and Marella moved toward the front door.

Sean handed Erin a bouquet. "These are fur ye, lassie, fur all th' grief I'd been givin' ye."

"Mr. Paterson!" Erin said, blushing.

Sean's voice lowered. "Now, wha' happened 'ere between us, let's keep it a secre'. I don' want me daughter tae find out."

"Find out wha'?" Marella said.

"Oh, I said tae much. Off I go!" Sean Paterson wheeled himself past the receptionist's desk to the front door. The automatic doors opened for him, and he rolled into the afternoon sunshine. He stopped and lifted his arms as the sun's rays fell upon him. "Ah, freedom!"

Tom and Marella smiled at Erin, who tended to her bouquet. "Let's get your father home," Tom said.

"And let's look tae th' future," Marella said.

Tom agreed. They had survived their previous adventure, and in his mind, the future seemed bright.

CHAPTER 6

L iz Stevens shut her laptop. She had written notes, preparing her column. A young girl in her twenties, she wore a professional outfit that showed off her features.

She reported for The London Adventure, a travel magazine that targeted British millennials. She had done articles about Scotland Yard tours, the alleys of Jack the Ripper, and Big Ben. But her claim to fame was her article interviewing the Duke and Duchess of Cambridge from inside the Queen's Palace. She still could not believe she managed the interview.

It was on a whim. Stevens had waited at the gates to the Palace, wondering if anybody important would drive by.

The guards stood, defending the area.

Stevens's "Press" badge hung down her chest. She walked like a tourist. She batted her eyes, hoping to get a reaction.

The guards paid her no attention.

A car appeared. People gathered around, but security held them back. Aware that royalty was present, they did not treat the vehicle like a crowd at a rock concert but rather with respect and awe.

The car rolled inside the gate. To her surprise, the vehicle stopped. The Duke stepped out of the car. He pointed in Stevens's direction.

There was a tap on her shoulder. "You with the press?" said a voice behind her.

"Yes," said Liz.

"You may go."

Liz had forgotten about her press badge, but today her habit of wearing it paid off. She walked through the gates, a security guard in a suit accompanying her.

The Duke stood still. "Who are you with?" he asked.

"The London Adventure," she had said.

"Great magazine," he said.

"We need to go." A British voice next to her spoke. It was the Duchess. She had leaned into the open car window. "There's rain coming."

"Oh, right." the Duke had said, "Let's do this inside."

Liz said, "Alright," not sure what was happening. They led her into the palace. There she interviewed the Duke and Duchess of Cambridge.

Right place. Right time.

The article gave Liz national recognition among her peers, a tribute to someone so young. Now that it happened, though, the pressure was on. She received a raise, and the magazine demanded more articles, without any skimping on the quality.

She had heard about a strange occurrence in the highlands in a small Scottish town called Thurwick. The ridiculous story centered on the Loch Ness monster. Those involved said it was there, but they didn't know how to prove it.

Or they didn't want to.

The way Tom Wayne and Sean Paterson told their story made her suspicious. Tom was not a good liar. He may have gotten better at it over time, but prior interviews convinced her that Tom knew more than he let on.

She sipped her coffee inside the small Thurwick shop. Through the window, cars bounced as they rolled across the old cobblestone square. A few pedestrians walked between the shops. To her left was Dorlan Hall. Across the way was Guthrie's Pub. There were other small shops, the now-closed insurance business once owned by Chairman Briggs who was in maximum prison. There was a museum, which how a small town like Thurwick managed to fund a museum was beyond her. Then, there was the police station, a nondescript building except for the blue police cars out in front.

To the right, was the hospital. The clouds had opened up, and a man in a wheelchair rolled out. He had a basket in his lap, along with something plastic. One of his legs was missing, and yet the man grinned from ear to ear. He lifted his arms into the sunlight and shouted, which sounded like, "Freedom!" Then he rolled forward.

A second later, a dark-haired man in his twenties and a woman with thick red hair, wearing a brown skirt and coat, exited the hospital.

It was them: Sean Paterson, Tom Wayne, and Marella Paterson.

She put her coffee down. If Tom were alone, she could use her charm to get in front of him. But he and Marella were together every chance they had. If she tried to butt in when Marella was around, she'd get nowhere.

Instead, she had to find a way to get to Tom when he was alone. Then she could bat her eyes, use her looks, and try to get the complete story.

There was more to the Loch Ness monster than what Tom had said. And, now that Sean was out, he, too, might be a source. She hadn't tried to talk with him since he had lost a leg. Perhaps it was best not to use him in his weak state to advance her career. After all, she did have some standards.

But Sean didn't appear weak anymore. In fact, he appeared quite happy.

She made a note of everything. She had to try for Sean, to glean any additional information from him.

But Tom had the secret.

She was sure of that.

He knew everything.

He was on the yacht when it sank. He knew Coffee, and Vaas, both of whom disappeared. He knew about Briggs, and why he was in jail. And he knew the man they called Caleb, the poor soul who crashed his speedboat into Coffee's yacht.

Most importantly, she was convinced Tom saw the Loch Ness monster. He had struggled in interviews to refrain from describing it. Yes, he was a bad liar.

Liz Stevens picked up her coffee and put her laptop into her travel bag. Her Press badge was still on, but she thought, for now, she might want to take it off. Her tactics needed to be more covert.

She walked out of the shop and stood behind her parked car. She watched as Tom and Marella helped Sean into the blue sedan. When they were all inside, Marella backed the car out.

Sean rolled down the window and stuck his cane out the passenger door. With a dramatic swing, he pointed his cane forward, and the car rolled over the cobblestones in the direction of Saint Michael's Catholic Church.

Liz climbed into her own car. She pulled onto the cobblestones and followed them.

CHAPTER 7

Emily Anderson tapped her foot. She hadn't slept since yesterday. She worried about James since he hadn't come home for supper. She sat in her rocking chair, moving back and forth, working her needlepoint but trying not to think. She had finished making a cap out of yarn this morning, having worked on it all night. It lay next to her on the side table under a lamp. She hadn't bothered to put it away. Instead, she picked up her needlepoint and worked on that. Something about the rhythmic threading of string calmed her thoughts. As soon as she stopped, though, the fear of panic, of something wrong, entered her body. It was a feeling she'd rather not have, so she kept threading strings.

Her orange and white cat, Shamus, jumped on the old warn sofa next to her and let out a pitiful meow.

Emily ignored Shamus. She threaded the needle, trying to make the needlepoint landscape image in front of her.

Shamus jumped upon the back of the sofa and rubbed his face into her hair.

Emily moved her head. Keep threading, she told herself. If she stopped, the panic would return.

Shamus bit Emily's hair and pulled.

"Ow!" Emily lifted her arm and swatted.

Shamus disappeared behind a cabinet.

"Ye stupid feline! I already fed ye. One more like tha' and ye'll be eatin' wha' ye catch outside!" She stopped threading, and the fear crept inside her chest. The thoughts raced. What happened to James? He was a loyal police officer. A good man. A Captain no less. No one in Thurwick wanted to hurt him.

He was an officer when they agreed to marry thirty years ago. They were young. She knew it would be tough, that there would be dangerous nights. But day after day, and night after night, James came home. Smiling. He loved his job. He was always happy. He wasn't a tough officer, but people respected him. She loved seeing him come home. He always came home.

Why didn' he come home las' nigh'?

She stood up and paced, back and forth across her red carpet between her wooden furniture. Her shoes thumped on the wooden floor, then mashed on the carpet, then thumped, then mashed.

She passed a picture of their wedding day. Oh, what a lovely day that was, married at St. Michael's all those years ago. They didn't have much. It was a modest home, the best they could afford. They didn't have money, but they made a life together. This home was theirs. And he came home to it. For thirty years, he came home to it. *Why na las' nigh'?*

She stepped around the den table and adjusted the flower centerpiece. It didn't sit right. She tried it again. Still not right. Frustrated, she picked up the centerpiece and threw it in the trash can. Tears welled up in her eyes, but she told herself not to cry. She rubbed her hands on her hips, trying to calm the nerves.

There was a knock on the front door.

She held her breath.

A second knock.

She moved to the door, anticipating the worst. What news was coming? Something terrible, she was certain. When she opened it, Ian Fleming stood before her, his broad shoulders under his blue police officer's uniform.

"Ian," She said. "Any news?"

Fleming's face held disappointment. He shook his head, but his hand motioned he wanted to come inside.

Emily stepped back, and Fleming walked in. His broad shoulders bumped the coat rack as he came through.

"Wha' have ye heard?" Emily asked.

"I'm sorry mum. We haven' go' any leads."

Emily held her breath. The thoughts kept racing inside, the fear, the panic. She wanted this all to be over, but the terror kept creeping inside. "Well, have ye checked the docks again?"

"Aye, this mornin'. Bu' I had to leave. Bain wanted me tae question th' American."

"I'll tell ye, tha' boy and Mr. Paterson are up tae na good."

"Mrs. Anderson, we don' know tha'," Fleming said.

"Well, Thurwick was peaceful until th' lad showed up."

"Mrs. Anderson."

"I'm serious, Ian. How many have died in th' las' few weeks?"

Shamus came out from behind the cabinet and rubbed his fur on Fleming's leg. Fleming stood, letting the cat do its thing.

"We interviewed th' boy and Marella Paterson. Th' boy had a receipt tha' they had dinner a' Guthrie's las' nigh'."

"Bu' wha' abou' after? Were they near th' dock after?"

Fleming shook his head. "They said they were a' Saint Michael's."

"Did anybody see them there?"

"Nay," Fleming said.

"Well, there ye have it. They left dinner and did somethin' wit' me husband!"

Fleming lowered his chin. His large fingers squeezed the bottom of his coat. "Mrs. Anderson, I was good friends wit' yer husband. I want James home jus' like ye. I'm leavin' now tae check the docks again. Maybe there's somethin' we hadn' seen."

Emily's jaws tightened. Her insides were about to explode. Her fear and her rage were getting the better of her, and she knew it. "Wha' am I supposed tae do while yer searching. Jus' wait?"

"I'm sorry," Fleming said. "I'll le' ye know as soon as I find anythin'."

Emily moved to the door.

Fleming tried to muster a smile, but it disappeared. He went out the door and proceeded down the front walkway.

Emily shut the door. She didn't feel safe. The click of the lock echoed like a chapter in her life slamming shut.

Shamus meowed.

Emily ignored her cat. She sat on her sofa, picked up her needlepoint, and threaded her yarn.

CHAPTER 8

Sean Paterson wheeled himself to the side of the house. His eyes widened at the wooden ramp by the door. "Did ye build this yerself?"

"Yes, sir."

"Aye," Marella said. "And he's been handy wi' other things inside. Wai' 'til ye see."

"I hope ye hadn' been tae handy."

Tom said, "No, sir. You can trust me."

Sean didn't answer. He rolled his wheelchair onto the side ramp, studying the boards, listening for creaks and any sign of instability. He approved and rolled himself the rest of the way.

Inside the house, they came into the kitchen. "Will ye loo' a' this." Sean said. There were new green curtains at the kitchen window. The sink and counter were clean and there were no dishes in sight. Pictures of Marella and Sean hung on the walls. A large brown binder sat on the kitchen table. "Marella, my dear. Ye have sure cleaned up th' place."

"Well, Tom helped."

"Did he now?"

Tom didn't respond. He knew this was an important day for Marella. She had been through so much for so long, and she had been distraught over Sean's losing his leg - and almost his life - when McGregor's boat blew up. But Sean's relief - he was no longer obsessed with finding the Loch Ness monster, not even an interest in it - gave Marella hope that things would improve for them. Marella needed hope. Tom decided this moment had to be hers. He would stay in the background while Marella and Sean healed, both physically and emotionally.

"Wha's this?" Sean said, rolling to the kitchen table and picking up the binder.

"I put togethe' some news clippings," Marella said. "The press swarmed Thurwick like flies while ye were in th' hospital."

"I know," Sean said. "Thank goodness Erin kept mos' o' them away." He winked at Sean. "I didn' wan' tae give away our secret while they had me sedated."

Tom hummed the tune "Veni, Veni Emmanuel", the song they had used to lure the Loch Ness monster.

"Lad," Sean said. "We agreed na' tae e'er sing tha' again, remember?"

"No one's around," Tom said.

Sean's eyes flashed at Tom. "I'm serious, lad. We have tae be careful. Na tellin' who migh' be listenin'."

"Understood," Tom said. He leaned over Sean's shoulder as he flipped through the binder. The first headline said, "Nessie Lives!" and it had pictures of Tom, Marella, and Sean. Why did they have to take so many pictures? Too many people in town knew who he was.

Marella didn't like it either, having mentioned it to him more than once on their dates.

Further down the page, there was a headshot picture of Chairman Briggs.

Sean flipped the page. There was another headline: "Briggs Arrested!" The top image of this article was less kind to Briggs. It showed him in handcuffs, being led away by three men: Detective Logan O'Malley, Assistant Police Captain Ian Fleming, and Police Captain James Anderson.

"Serves him right," Sean said.

"Aye," Marella agreed.

"Tha' reminds me," Sean said. "Wha' kept ye two this mornin'?"

Tom said, "Captain Anderson didn't come home last night."

Sean paused. "No?"

Tom shook his head.

"Anderson hadn' missed one of Emily's meals in thirty years. I know. I myself had been o'er there a time o' two fur supper." Sean's eyes lowered. "Except tha' was a long time ago."

"Fleming and O'Malley questioned us abou' it," Marella said.

"Oh? What'd ye tell them?"

"Th' truth. We didn' see him."

"What do ye thin' happened tae him?"

"No idea," Tom said. "It bothers me that Bain was there, though."

"Bain?"

"He sits on the Council. Young guy."

"Bain," Sean said, rubbing his chin. "The one sittin' on th' right?"

"At the meeting?"

"Aye."

"I think so. He never spoke, though he voted against your request for funding."

"They all did."

"Yeah. That's why I didn't trust him."

"I don' blame ye."

"I hope Anderson turns up fur our sake," Marella said. "Tis abou' time our lives get back tae normal."

Sean tapped the floor with his wooden cane. "As close tae normal as can be."

Marella frowned. She still had trouble adjusting to the sight of her father in a wheelchair.

"Ah, lassie," Sean said. "As many times as I've been on th' loch, I'm grateful I only lost a leg. Tom, here, could have lost a lot more."

Tom didn't answer. Marella's big green eyes sparkled at him. He didn't know what to say but thought he'd try to be of help.

Tom stepped behind Marella and tapped her on the shoulder. Her large green eyes glanced at him. He beckoned her to follow him.

"Wha'," she mouthed.

Tom's eyes hinted, "Come here."

Marella left her father while he studied the pictures. Tom led her around the corner into the den.

Marella grinned. "Wha' are ye doin'?"

Tom said, "I got something for you." He reached into his pocket.

"Wha' is it?"

He handed her the earrings with the four-leaf clovers. "I saw these and thought you'd like them."

"These are nice!" She held them in her hands and studied them.

"I thought they'd look good on you."

Marella said, "Thank ye," and she leaned up and kissed Tom on the cheek.

"Since we're going back to normal, what if I run out and get us some barbeque for dinner. We can grill out, the three of us," Tom said.

"Now yer talkin' lad. 'Cept I wan' mine tae be a steak. Remember, Nessie go' me last one."

Marella and Tom both flinched. "Da! Ye been watching us?" Sean had rolled up behind them in his wheelchair.

"Yer me only daughter," Sean said.

Marella showed Sean the earrings.

"Nice," he said.

"So, steak it is?" Tom said.

Marella said, "Me tae."

"And bring me an Old Mortality, as this ol' man still has life in him!"

"Yes, sir."

Tom stretched out his palm, and Marella handed him the keys to the car. "I'll be back."

"Don't be tae long," Marella said. She faced the mirror and held the earrings up to her ear, the four-leaf clovers glinting a bright Scottish green.

Tom smiled and exited the door, stepping on the wooden ramp and double-checking its sturdiness. When he was satisfied, he climbed into the car and drove it out of the driveway. He ignored the car's bouncing due to worn-out shocks, and he imagined a future with Marella.

Everything was working out better than he could have imagined.

He and Marella had come to know each other quite well over the past several weeks. While Sean recovered from losing his leg, Tom and Marella helped where they could, taking care of errands, working on the house, and going to Mass. Normal things. If only he could avoid the investigators, the authorities, and the press. They had been hounding him and Marella for several hours each day. Only recently had they backed off.

Until this morning, when O'Malley picked him up. That was strange. What happened to Anderson? That was a new event. It was the first time someone questioned him about something he didn't know.

As he bounced along Mackay Rd., another car approached in his direction. Tom had been around enough to know Mackay was rarely traveled. He pulled closer to the side to make room for the other car.

The other car slowed down. The driver was a woman.

Tom stepped on the gas.

The woman driver tried to wave him down.

Tom decided to pretend he didn't see her. Today was not the day to be delayed. Not anymore.

As he bounced on the dirt road, he glanced at his rearview mirror.

"Oh, geez," he said. "Damned press."

The other car turned around and followed him.

CHAPTER 9

L ogan O'Malley stepped over the crime scene tape. Ian Fleming was several meters ahead of him, peering in between the boats on the dock. A gull stood upon one of the round wooden posts that held up the tape. The cloudy sky shaded the landscape, which was typical of spring Highland weather.

"Do ye think she'll be okay?" O'Malley said.

Fleming said, "Na tellin'."

Fleming had told him about his meeting with Emily Anderson, and O'Malley's heart went out to her. O'Malley wanted to find James. Yes, James Anderson was a police captain, but he was also a devoted husband.

Fleming had said she was suspicious of Tom and Sean. It didn't make much sense, though. Tom had a receipt showing that he and Marella Paterson had a date. Neither gave any indication of knowing about James's disappearance. They even questioned them separately, as detectives often do, to catch one or the other in a lie. Fortunately for Tom and Marella, their stories matched.

But that didn't mean Councilman Bain or Emily Anderson had to like it.

The gull lifted its wings and soared from the wooden post over the boats toward the water. Fleming searched between a fishing boat and a rowboat.

"Find anything?" O'Malley said.

Fleming shook his head. "Na' sure. Doesn' this fishing boat belong to Keith Wallace?"

"I wouldn' know." O'Malley's boots thudded on the wooden boards. "Why?"

"See the rope tha' ties it tae th' dock?"

"Aye."

"Tis rather loose. Like it was tied down in a hurry."

O'Malley studied the knot. Fleming had a point. The knot was slipping with the gentle rocking of the boat on the water. "Should we redo th' knot fur him?"

"Na. Let's look around. After, we'll call Wallace and have him come and redo it. Then maybe we'll ask him a couple o' questions."

"Where'd ye find th' coat?"

"O'er there." Fleming marched to the end of the dock.

O'Malley followed.

Fleming pointed. "It was floatin' in th' water right here."

The boats floated behind them, tied down with strong ropes. The wood under O'Malley's feet creaked. Under the boards were the deep dark waters of Loch Ness. He shuddered to think that James, his friend for several years, could be somewhere in the waters below.

He lifted his eyes. The scene of Loch Ness was like that out of a painting. The sun's rays broke through the heavy clouds, reflecting off the mist and creating shimmering sparkles in the air and on the water. The hills on the far shoreline were Scottish green. O'Malley wasn't a fisherman, not even close. He had once had a near-drowning accident as a child, and water made him nervous. He wanted to overcome his fear. He liked the idea of fishing, and he was envious of the boat owners and their boats but, try as he might, he couldn't get himself comfortable on the water.

He rubbed his hands together, trying to stay calm.

He knelt down and studied the boardwalk. He touched the weathered wood. Would he find anything unusual - a torn piece of cloth, a hair, even blood? All he found was a small black feather that hooked onto a splinter.

"Stange," O'Malley said. "No sign of violence."

Fleming went left, examining the water around the wooden boards and poles. He shuffled his large feet, his head and shoulders bent over.

O'Malley stood and went right. His reflection rippled in the water and, behind it, so did the light and clouds from above.

Something moved quickly.

He jumped back, keeping his balance but feeling very uneasy being so close to the deep waters of the loch. Mustering courage, he paused and caught his breath. After a moment, he understood what had moved. It had been the sideways twisting of a small fish. It came out from under the dock, hunting for a treat. But when it saw Logan O'Malley's shadow, it darted under the boards.

He made his way to the end of the dock, watching the water, wondering if there were more fish. The wind blew off the loch, blowing his gray hair and beard. Then he noticed something - a piece of cloth. A small piece of fabric was sticking from the water. It was like the color of the water, only a different shade of blue.

Police blue. Thurwick police blue.

He reached down and grabbed it. It slipped in his fingers. Something slimy covered the material. He gripped it tight and lifted it up.

"Oh, criminy!"

The item hung in his hand as he lifted it shoulder-high. Cold water dripped from the soaked material and splattered onto the wood at his feet.

"Fleming, ye'd better take a look a' this."

Fleming lifted his head and lumbered across the walk. "What'd ye find."

O'Malley said nothing. He held the item, his face grave.

Fleming moved closer. When he was a few meters away, he paused. His eyes widened. Then sadness fell over his face. "That's na' good."

O'Malley shook his head, still holding the item at arm's length. The water dropped and splattered onto the wood. It was Anderson's police hat. It was soaked through. The Sillitoe tartan chequers reflected off the royal blue.

"Wha' did tha'?" Fleming said.

O'Malley shrugged.

Something tore Anderson's hat in two, leaving serrated edges put there by large sharp teeth.

CHAPTER 10

Emily Anderson had had enough. She put down her needlepoint. Shamus lept upon the rear of the sofa again and rubbed his face in her hair. The fear grew inside her, like a train on the tracks with nothing to stop it. She stood up and walked on the red carpet and the wooden floors to her wedding picture on the table. She picked it up. She admired the picture, her with her white dress, smiling, and James with his police uniform, grinning.

He had been nervous that day, but once the ceremony finished, he was all fun. They had left St. Michael's to go to Guthrie's Pub - except then it was called MacNee's - where they celebrated with toasts all around, telling stories with friends and neighbors and anybody else who wanted a good time. While the storytelling was at its crescendo, though, she and James had sneaked out of the party to go to their home, where they had completed their wedding ceremonies.

The next day, James got up and went to work. That was his way, to be there. He was always there. Dependable. Give the effort. He may not always have known what to do, but he knew that being there was the first step.

James's not coming home last night told her he was in trouble - or worse. He gave too much effort over the years. She couldn't let him down. He wouldn't want her to sit, stewing, waiting for the bad news. No, she had to go out, to find him, to be there for him.

She didn't sleep last night, but so what. That was unimportant. She had to find him.

She went back to the sofa. The cap she had knitted last night still rested on the side table. She picked it up and put it on her head.

Shamus meowed.

"Ye'll have tae watch th' place fur awhile," she said. She rubbed his back, and Shamus arched it upward as cats do. She went to the small table in the nook, She ignored the scattered books, unfinished letters, and misplaced pens. She opened a drawer and pulled out a notepad. She picked up one of the pens and wrote a note.

Ian.

I can't sit here. James would want me to find him. I went to look. I'll be back at sunset if we don't run into each other.

~ Em

She went to the coat hanger and put on her coat. Fitting her cap against her hair one more time, she grabbed the note and went outside. She shut and locked the door. She stuck the note into the door. If Fleming came by again, he'd see it.

The cool Highland air blew over Thurwick, cooling her cheeks. Her new cap helped keep her warm. She took a step.

Over the cool breeze, her ears picked up a strange sound. Was that a girl? Was she singing? The sound surprised her. It was rare to hear music in Thurwick. But something about the song touched her. The song knew how she felt.

She decided to ignore the song. She had a job to do. She had to go out and find her husband, to help him, to bring him home.

She stepped away from her home toward her car.

The music continued. With each step she took, the wind carried the music into her ears, and into her soul. It called to her. It wanted her to come to it.

She opened the car door. She paused, leaning on the car door and listening to the music. It was soft, mournful, and beautiful. She wanted to go to it.

She shook her head. No th' now, she thought. I have tae find James.

She climbed into the car and shut the door.

The music went away in the cab, the breeze unable to carry it through the windows, but the memory of it rang in her heart. She turned the ignition and listened to the humming of the engine. The engine drowned out the music, or had it? She thought she could hear - no, feel - it from outside. She blinked and thought of James, and the wedding picture on the table. He'd want her to find him. He'd want her to find him, not staying at home, but being there for him. She had to search.

Emily Anderson put the car in reverse and drove it out of the parking space. She held the steering wheel tightly. Should she go to the music?

No, she thought. The dock. James was last seen at the dock.

She shut the music from her mind as she steered the car toward downtown Thurwick.

CHAPTER 11

Tom drove into Thurwick square. He passed Dorlan Hall and parked next to Guthrie's Pub. A few doors down, past the now-closed Briggs Insurance Agency, was the Smith's Store, the small general store that also served groceries. He climbed out of the car.

The car that was following him parked a few spaces down. He stepped quickly, trying to give the impression he was in a hurry.

"Mr. Wayne!"

He ignored the woman's voice. She had a British accent.

"Mr. Wayne!"

The sound of footsteps and high heels followed him on the sidewalk. The person was running at him as the press does. He stopped. He'd have to be nice. No telling what the press would say, but he hoped she got the hint that he'd not have much time. Maybe he'd give a short quote or something.

"Mr. Wayne!" the woman closed in on him. He recognized the voice. Liz Stevens. The woman columnist with the London magazine was pretty high on herself for once getting an interview with the Duke and Duchess of Cambridge.

Tom put on his fake grin.

"There you are," Liz said.

Tom lifted his eyebrows.

"I've been trying to find you."

"Well, I've been around."

Liz wore her business attire, with black pants, high heels, and a black blouse with a yellow coat. She was an attractive woman, but she knew it and she tried to use it. "How do you feel about Sean getting out of the hospital."

"Is this an interview?"

Liz's lips pursed. "Oh, Tom. We've talked before. You know I'm not like that."

"I'm sorry. I'm in a hurry, that's all. Can we do this some other time?"

"Do what?"

"You're the one who's been following me. I'm sure it's not just to ask how I feel about Sean's coming home."

"I understand. I'm trying to finish my column, and I want to make sure I get the last pieces right. Since Sean's coming home, I remember you mentioning he was inventing again."

"Did I say that?"

"Yes."

Tom shook his head. The past few weeks had been so chaotic, he couldn't remember what he said to whom, only that he wanted to believe he had said enough. "I suppose I did."

Liz stepped closer. "I think you're good people, the three of you. I know things have not been easy, but I believe your story."

"You believe the story will sell magazines."

Liz paused. "Okay, yes, I do. Is that so bad?"

"Great. An honest reporter."

"That's right," Liz said. "And one who believes you. You've been honest, too, haven't you?"

Tom didn't answer. What was she going after?

"Let me be straight with you. I know you're in a hurry. Can I get an appointment with you, though? One more interview. It'll help me get the story right. Maybe I can help Sean gain some exposure for his inventions. You know, help kick-start his business?"

"I don't know…"

"I promise it will be the last interview," Liz said. "After that, I'll go on my way, and you can go on yours, and we'll call it a day."

Tom rubbed the back of his neck. He had met with Liz before, and though her attractive features were easy on the eyes, her questions had worn on him within minutes. How she got a meeting with royalty was obvious - it wasn't with her words. He wondered what the Dutchess had to say about that. But, she did have a highly read column in a popular London magazine. He hadn't yet had the time to read her other works, however, so his judgment came from his personal experience.

Maybe he'd take a chance. If it helped Sean's business and helped Marella, maybe it was worth a shot. "Okay. Tomorrow?"

"That would be great. Shall I meet you at Annabel's?" Liz smiled as she said it.

Tom shuddered.

She knew where he slept. Marella wouldn't like that.

He had to think of a place, someplace where no one would care. He shook his head. "No," he said.

"Then how about Guthrie's?" Liz said.

Guthrie's Pub would have too many people there, people with eyes and ears. If they saw him there with another woman, they'd talk. Even if it was innocent, Marella wouldn't like the gossip. "No. Not there either."

"Well, where?"

There were many places around town. While some places might be okay for a social setting, he wanted a safe place, a place where he was on his home turf. Yet, he was an alien from another country. He had no home turf.

Except maybe one. He had been going to the eight-thirty Mass at Saint Michael's Catholic Church every morning since Caleb's funeral. Father Gibson was there; the secret was there. He'd be safe there. "Okay. Saint Michael's."

"The church?" Liz shifted, frowning. Tom suspected the idea made her uncomfortable, and that made him like the idea even more.

"Yes. Saint Michael's. Mass will be ending at nine. I'll see you in the rear pews once Mass is over."

Liz fidgeted with her coat before she grinned big and said, "Okay. It's a date." She stuck out her hand.

"No, it's an interview."

"Yes, an interview."

Tom waited a second.

Liz kept her hand out.

He reached down and shook her hand.

She released her grip, her eyes sparkled, and she walked away.

Tom remained where he was. What had he agreed to?

Liz's head whipped around. She grinned like she had won a hand of blackjack. Then she went to her car, climbed in, waved, and drove her car on the cobblestones and out of the Thurwick square.

"Unbelievable," Tom said. He was not sure he liked doing another interview, especially now. He wanted to be done with the past, to let it disappear into history. He wanted to focus on Marella. While Sean's losing his leg was horrible, both he and Tom survived the curse of the Loch Ness monster, and they wanted to move on - Sean with his invention business, and Tom with Marella.

Marella wouldn't like to hear from anyone else that Tom had granted an interview with an attractive London magazine reporter. "Ugh. Why did I do that?" He said. He committed right then to telling Marella and Sean about the interview as soon as he returned with the steaks. If Marella didn't like it, he'd find a way to cancel.

Or maybe he would skip the interview.

He saw someone out of the corner of his eye. A figure leaned against the wall. The woman was small, wearing a long brown coat that went past the feet. A brown hood covered her head. White hair fell upon her chest, blowing in the breeze. A pale finger held the hood over her face.

The woman's eyes bored into him. He turned his head toward the wall.

There was no one there. No figure. No woman. No hooded coat?

"Strange," he said.

He stepped closer to the wall. His eyes must have played tricks on him. What he thought was a person was an odd shape in the stone walls near a crack in the building. A sudden chill came upon him. Tom shuddered while he tried to understand why his imagination played tricks on him.

Why did he feel edgy? Jumpy?

A cool breeze blew at him from behind, causing him a deep chill. A black feather rolled on the ground next to the wall. There were no birds around. "Strange place for a feather," he mumbled.

He shrugged. A few steps away was the Smith's Store where he would get tonight's steaks for grilling and Sean's Old Mortality. Maybe he'd get one for Marella, and himself - a sort of celebration.

He walked along the sidewalk, past the strange crack and feather, chuckling about Sean. Despite the loss of his leg, the man was happy to get on with his life.

As was Tom.

Maybe tomorrow's interview would be the last. Then he'd reclaim his life with the woman he loves.

He thought of Marella, and how she had warmed his heart. How he longed to laugh with her. He wanted to take her on adventures. He even eyed rings inside Smith's Store. What kind of engagement ring might he get for her? Yes, he had already thought of that.

But then a thought slipped inside his mind. He shuddered before entering the store. He sensed someone behind him, watching him. He tried to picture the figure in the brown hooded coat along the wall, but no one was there.

The black feather blew in the breeze against the wall.

Tom studied the scene one more time before he opened the door to Smith's Store and went inside.

CHAPTER 12

Emily pulled past Thurwick square. As she rounded a corner, her eyes caught him.

Tom Wayne.

He had opened the door to Smith's Store, the small general store that all the locals went to. Except Tom wasn't a local. He was a stranger. Since he showed up, there had been nothing but trouble.

And now James, her husband, was missing.

She glared at Tom.

He didn't notice her, and he went inside the store.

She needed to go to the dock, to find James, but she had a good mind to chew Tom out.

What would James think of that? Would he be proud of her? Would he expect that of her?

What about Fleming? Would it somehow hurt the investigation, and hinder bringing Tom Wayne to justice? He had to have done something to her husband. She knew it. It was him.

Without thinking, she pulled the car in front of Smith's Store and waited.

Could she confront her husband's killer? Was it true Tom Wayne had killed James?

Fleming had given the impression he didn't think so. But his logic had holes in it. Tom could have said he was at Saint Michael's - a likely lie to pretend he was a Christian (and she was sure he was anything but) - when in reality he had ambushed her husband on the dock and ended his life. She had confidence in her story. It would come out. It had to. She had to help it along, to bring her husband justice. The justice system would find out. James had always appreciated the justice system.

Except now. If Tom had been tried and found guilty of those other deaths, perhaps James would still be alive. Perhaps he would have come home last night.

Perhaps she wouldn't have had to spend last night alone.

Emily wanted to go inside the store, to study Tom, learn more about him, find his weakness, and make a plan. The system had failed James. It had left him vulnerable to the killer inside, and now he walked, and her husband was missing, and probably dead. She was sure James was dead. That was the only reason he wouldn't have come home last night, the first time in thirty years.

And Tom did it.

She opened the car door, her face scowling.

But then she heard it – singing, the same singing at her house. It was faint, but it was there. It was mournful and beautiful. It spoke to her, agreeing with her thoughts of loss and sadness and anger and justice.

She shut the car door, the lock clicking as it connected to the frame. Tom was inside Smith's Store behind the glass, but the music continued, beautiful, uninterrupted, resonating with the feeling deep within her heart.

"Where is tha' music comin' from?" she said. Other pedestrians walked the square. Not one of them sang. Not one of them pretended to notice the singing.

Who was singing? Where did it come from?

Tom could wait.

She had to find that music.

It came from the North, past Guthrie's Pub toward the loch. Was it at the dock, where James was last seen?

No, it came from a place farther northeast. The dock would be more west. She opened her car door again and climbed inside.

The music disappeared inside the cab.

She rolled down her window, letting in the cool spring air. The music returned, whispering to her to listen, to hear it, to find it, to be entranced by it. Follow the music, it said.

She drove her car out of the parking space. She took one last look at the Smith's Store. She would get Tom Wayne later, but now she had to know what happened to James.

And the music wanted to tell her, to show her. It knew where James was. That's what her heart was saying.

She pulled forward and exited the square. The car bounced on the cobblestone road, a road that went out of the Thurwick square, past Guthrie's Pub and northwest, before becoming a dirt road alongside the Loch Ness shore north of Thurwick.

As she went, the music increased through the window, becoming friendly to her ears, becoming more persuasive. She bounced along, her eyes searching under her knitted cap and graying hair. The blue water of Loch Ness was magnificent this time of year, and behind it so were the green hills of the Scottish Highlands.

The road came to a green field. There were no buildings around, just an old brick wall, about three feet high, that went alongside the shore of the water. It had been built centuries before but had been long since abandoned. Old stones stacked upon each other, except for the few that fell after the mud dried and the force of gravity caused them to fall and roll onto the grass.

Emily Anderson parked her car. She climbed out and buttoned her coat.

There was no one near her, not within any hearing distance. Thurwick stood a full kilometer behind her, the roofs of its buildings visible over the green highland hills.

The music came from the right, several hundred meters off the road behind an embankment near the water.

A gust of wind hit her face, causing her to shiver, whipping her heavy clothes around her body. She stepped onto the grass, off the cobblestones and dirt, and trudged through the high green blades toward the music, stumbling at first, but gaining confidence as she stepped with her boots onto the tufts of green Scottish grass.

She had to find where the music came from. She wanted to feel it.

It hypnotized her. It knew the rhythm of her heartbeat. It knew James; it knew where he was.

It would take her to him.

Her lips smiled like a shy schoolgirl's. How she wanted to see James again!

If she kept going, she'd find him. She couldn't say how she knew it, but she did. Perhaps James was on the other side of the knoll.

Her boots kicked grass, slowly at first, but more forcefully as she learned to balance over the terrain. She moved forward on a mission. James would be proud. She was no longer at home, waiting on bad news. She was there, outside, working, searching for the man who came home to her every night. Searching for the man she loved.

She was a few meters from the embankment. The singing was louder. It was the voice of a woman, a beautiful mournful woman who knew her pain and how she longed for her husband who didn't come home last night.

She was close enough to hear the words, and she paused to listen.

> *Th' heart longs fur love*
> *All th' nigh' through.*
> *But when he turns away*
> *Th' livin' are few.*

Emily's heart longed for love. She ached for James, and the woman singing the song somehow knew that. She had to find this woman. She had to find James.

Emily stepped up over the embankment.

A rush of wings flapped, like a flock of pigeons leaving the square's cobblestones and flying together toward a roof. But there were no birds.

The music stopped.

James was nowhere in sight.

On the ground were several black feathers. The feathers rested a meter from the water.

Strange, she thought. "Where are th' birds? Where's th' music?"

She studied the ground. She searched for boot prints, James's boot prints. Maybe he had been here. The music suggested he had been. But there was no sign any person was there in the recent past: not James, not a singing woman, nobody.

Nobody except her.

The wind blew, and the music was gone. The hope the music brought Emily went away. The attachment to it left her.

Emily stood alone, the green grass blowing with the wind.

Something didn't sit right.

She faced north, along the shore of the loch. The water stirred from the wind, and larger-than-normal sized waves crashed into the shore, the water running up the elevated land, spraying drops of water that were caught by the wind and fell upon the grass.

A splash sounded behind her, like when she pulled a wet rag from the sink and the water dripped into the tub. "Wha' was tha'?" she said.

She spun.

Three large serpentine heads lunged at her, each bearing hundreds of sharp white teeth. One head bit into her shoulder, another clamped upon her thigh, and the third covered her head. Teeth penetrated her knitted cap, crushing her head.

Pain and pressure attacked her skull; her eyes went blind.

She thought of James, and that she would see him soon.

CHAPTER 13

Tom left the Thurwick square and neared Annabel's Bed and Breakfast, across the street from Saint Michael's Catholic Church. The bag of groceries rested in the passenger seat, the steaks wrapped in cellophane along with three Old Mortalities and a bottle of red wine. He didn't know if Marella would want an Old Mortality, but since Sean was having one the three of them could toast to his being alive. He imagined Marella's features: her flowing red hair, her bright green eyes, her lovely smile.

Yes, the future looked bright. It deserved a toast.

And if Marella didn't want the Old Mortality, the red wine would play as a substitute.

As he approached Annabel's, the unique two-story stone house with its many shrubs and trees and flowers, he thought he might pull in for a moment. He had been going all day since this morning, and he wanted to appear fresh. The barbeque wasn't a date, but he wanted it to be special. He thought he should check his clothes, maybe put on something less worn, brush his teeth, comb his hair, and rub any dirt off his shoes. He told himself he was being too cautious, but he didn't want to take any chances. Marella was the girl for him.

He would take a minute. He parked the car out front, leaving the steaks in the passenger seat with the window down so the cold highland air kept them cool. A flock of birds flew away around the corner of the house near the tree that stood outside his window, but he was too focused on entering the front door to care to watch where they went.

He opened the front door. A cool breeze blew at him. The kitchen window was open behind a vase of yellow spring flowers, causing a draft. Annabel sat in her den chair in her green blouse and brown trousers, a pen in her hand, and the Thurwick newspaper in her lap. She held the paper down as the draft fluttered the edges of the paper. She was doing a crossword puzzle. "Oh, ye back so soon? I didn' expect ye 'til tonigh'."

Tom smiled. "Just want to freshen up." He ran upstairs before Annabel responded. He opened the door to his room and ran inside. He checked his clothes in the mirror by the closet. His shirt was okay, but he decided he'd put on a new one anyway. He changed his coat, too, putting on a green waxed coat with a brown collar, something warmer for outside, just in case. He faced the mirror and flashed his teeth. "Needs cleaning," he said. He brushed his teeth and combed his hair. He didn't have any cologne. Should he shave? He decided to keep his five o'clock shadow. He splashed aftershave onto his cheeks, patted his neck, and applied his deodorant. He checked his shoes and brushed off the mud that O'Malley's car had splattered on them.

That reminded him of the morning's meeting. "I hope that's all over with," he said.

He shut his bedroom door behind him and ran back downstairs, skipping the final step when he reached the hardwoods on the first floor.

Annabel said, "In a hurry, are ye?"

"I'm sorry," Tom said.

She had put the crossword puzzle on the small table in front of her. "Ye know, if ye keep this up, ye'll be payin' fur me retirement."

"What do you mean?" Tom said. He stopped by the door.

"I mean yer no' workin', yet yer still payin' fur room an' board."

Tom said, "I have funds back home still. We talked about this."

Annabel stood up. "Tom, lad. Yer a good man. Bu' yer still learnin'." She stood from her chair and came over to him. "I'm na' worried abou me money. I know ye'll pay me wha' ye owe."

"What are you saying?"

Annabel smiled. "Now, I know I'm no' yer mother, bu ye've been here lon' enough tha' I wan' tae see ye successful. All I'm sayin' is tae save some o' yer money fur a ring."

Tom blushed. "Is it that obvious."

Annabel grinned. "Aye. 'Tis."

Tom lowered his eyes. "I don't know what I'm doing," he said. "But I'm crazy about her."

"I see tha'. In fact, I think th' whole town sees tha'."

"Do you think she does?"

"Aye. I do."

"I don't want to mess this up."

"Relax, and be yerself," Annabel said. "And jus' do me one favor."

"What's that," Tom said.

"I wan' front row seats tae yer weddin'."

Tom laughed.

Annabel leaned in and hugged him, and Tom hugged Annabel back.

A sudden gust of wind blew in from the open kitchen window, knocking the vase of yellow flowers off the window sill and into the sink. A soft scream carried through the air. Then the wind died down, and there was quiet.

"What was that?" Tom said.

"Just a draft," Annabel said. She left Tom at the table and went to the kitchen. "Highland weather. 'Tis so unpredictable."

The wind unnerved Tom. Was there another open door that created the draft? He wanted to check it out, but Annabel had it under control. He said, "Can I help?"

"No. Ye have things tae do. I can ta'e care o' this." She bent down and soaked up spilled water with a paper towel.

"Okay," Tom said. I've got to be running. Wish me luck."

Annabel picked up the vase of flowers and set them on the sill. "Good luck tae ye, lad. Remember wha' I said. Be yerself, and ye'll be alright."

"Thanks, Annabel."

Tom opened the front door. He went to the car door. The steaks, Old Mortalities, and bottle of red wine still sat in the seat where he left them.

Tom backed the car out of the parking space and pulled forward. Saint Michael's Church was on his right, its stone steeple rising high into the air. He'd be there tomorrow, maybe. He wanted to avoid telling Marella about Liz Stevens.

He drove forward. He thought of Marella. Should he take Annabel's advice? Maybe he should forget everything. The past was in the past. Forget the interviews and the detectives and the chaos that came at him the past few weeks. Today was a new day. Sean was home. Marella was healing.

And so was he. As he drove toward Mackay Rd., the dirt road that led to Sean Paterson's house, Tom's next chapter was about to begin.

CHAPTER 14

"Not again," Tom said. The car bounced on the dirt road. Sean Paterson's windmills spun from the Highland wind and shimmered in the sunlight. As he approached the small cottage in the country, he noticed another car.

O'Malley's car.

It sat off the road in front of Sean's house. "What does he want?" Tom said.

He pulled into the parking space, grabbed the bag of groceries, and went in through the side door.

The door closed behind him.

"Whatever yer askin', I wan' na part o' it," Sean said. His voice came from the den on the other side of the wall.

"Mr. Paterson, I understand." It was O'Malley.

"I don' think ye do." It was Marella's voice. "This mornin' ye dragged Tom and me tae yer station, and accused us o' homicide."

"We did na such thing." O'Malley's voice raised, getting defensive.

"Aye, ye did." Marella was growing irritated.

Tom carried the bag of groceries through the kitchen, holding them as he came into their view from behind the wall.

In the den, Sean sat in his wheelchair, his cane in his hand, Marella on the old worn-out sofa, and Detective O'Malley on the wooden chair in the corner, his fedora in his lap. Marella had put a cardigan sweater over her shoulders. Had she changed for the occasion, as he had? Her dress and her posture exuded beauty, both inside and out. Her eyes, though, carried a hint of worry, her lips pursed. She managed to flash a smile when Tom appeared in the room.

Tom blushed.

"Aye, Tom," Sean said. "Did ye brin' me my Old Mortality?"

Tom lifted the grocery bag. "Right here."

"Great. I'm goin' tae be needin' it sooner thanks tae Detective O'Malley."

Logan O'Malley stood up. "Mr. Wayne," he said. "Could I have a word wit' ye?"

"And I hope ye bought one fur yerself," Sean said. "Ye migh' be needin' it."

"Don' agree tae anythin'," Marella said.

O'Malley held his fedora in his hand and walked past Tom. "Outside, if ye don' mind."

Tom shrugged, raising his eyebrows at Sean and Marella. Then he put the grocery bag on the kitchen table next to the binder with the newspaper clippings and followed O'Malley out the side door.

O'Malley walked a short distance into the sunlight. He put his cap on over his gray hair. He flipped open a lighter and stuck a cigarette into his mouth. He offered a cigarette to Tom.

"No. I don't smoke."

"Me either," O'Malley said, the cigarettes moving in his mouth as he lit it.

"Well, what do you call this?"

"Stress relief." O'Malley blew smoke into the air. The nicotine smell mixed in the spring Highland air.

"What do you want?" Tom said.

"There's a problem," O'Malley said.

"So? What's that got to do with me?"

"We found more evidence about Anderson."

Tom put his hands on his hips. "I told you, I don't know anything about his whereabouts."

O'Malley took the cigarette from his mouth and kicked a stone. "Unfortunately, ye might."

"I told you, I was with Marella at Guthrie's last night. Then we went for a walk along the loch next to –"

"I don' mean tae interrupt ye, Tom. I belie'e ye. Bu' wha' we found isn't good. No' fur Captain Anderson, anyway."

"What'd you find?"

"Fleming and I wen' tae th' dock again, ye know, lookin' fur anythin'. Well, we foun' somethin'."

"What?"

"His police cap."

"Okay. So?"

"I found it in the wa'er, floatin' next tae th' dock. When I picked it up, I knew somethin' had happene' tae him."

"What do you mean?"

"It was bitten in half," O'Malley said.

"Bitten?"

"Aye."

"How are you sure?"

"We have it at th' station if ye'd like tae see it. One look and ye'll know."

Tom's mind flashed back to his fight on Coffee's yacht, and the last image he had of Alex Vaas before the plesiosaurs lunged at him like cobras striking their prey. It was an image Tom tried to forget. "What's this got to do with me?"

O'Malley put the cigarette back to his lips and sucked in the nicotine, and blew the smoke from his lungs one more time. "We nee' yer help, lad."

"I told you all I know," Tom said, though in his interviews he had been very vague in describing the details of the Loch Ness monsters. He didn't mention the creatures ate Vaas. He wanted them to believe Vaas had died in the boat crash and subsequent explosions. If the authorities decided the monster hunted people, then they'd search for it. Tom had said he believed the monster existed, even that he had seen signs of it, but he decided not to tell them that there were three of them. He had a good view of one in the clear sunlight as it thrashed to get out of Coffee's net. The creature was both powerful and beautiful. Tom sensed something majestic about it then, and he knew it was best to keep it hidden.

"I don' thin' ye have, lad." O'Malley threw the cigarette on the ground and stepped on it with his shoe, twisting his foot and pressing it into the ground. "I think ye've seen more than yer lettin' on."

Tom pressed his lips together, not sure how to answer. Was O'Malley suspicious? Did he give something away?

"So, lad. Will ye help us?" O'Malley said.

The side door on the house opened. Marella stepped down the small steps and walked in their direction. In a moment, O'Malley would be outnumbered.

"I've told you what I know," Tom said. "I can't help you." He watched Marella approach. Her hair shone red as it bounced in the sunlight, her cardigan sweater swaying with her movements as she walked.

"Suit yerself," O'Malley said. "Bu' if yer curious, th' hat is at th' station. We plan tae send it tae th' lab tae be analyzed. We'll have it on th' premises until tomorrow afternoon."

"Not interested," Tom said.

"Okay," O'Malley said. He put his hands in his pockets.

Marella stood next to Tom. Tom said, "If you'll excuse me, I've got to get going."

O'Malley tipped his fedora to Marella. "M' lady."

Marella put her arm around Tom's. "Come on," she said. She pulled Tom, and the two of them walked together to the house.

O'Malley paced a few steps toward his car before he stopped. "Oh, one more thin'."

Tom and Marella stopped.

"If yer goin' tae walk alon' th' shores o' th' loch again, ye migh' wan' tae learn tae have eyes in th' back o' yer heads. Ye ne'er know if th' monster will get ye." O'Malley opened his car door and climbed inside.

"Wha' did he wan' from ye?" Marella said.

Tom shook his head. "Forget it. He's crazy."

"Don' ye mean doolally?"

"Yeah. That, too."

"Remember, yer in Scotland still."

He squeezed her arm. "And still glad I am."

He led Marella into the house and he shut the door behind them.

CHAPTER 15

Assistant Police Captain Ian Fleming lumbered onto the wooden porch and knocked on Emily Anderson's door. Her car was gone, and he doubted she'd be home. But he'd follow protocol, and if asked he'd say he knocked.

That's when he noticed a folded clean white sheet of paper behind a yellow potted flower. She had left a note. She had tried to leave it in the door hinge but didn't do a very good job, and it fell onto the front porch.

He read the note. Then he folded it up and put it in his pocket. Emily had left to find her husband, James. Fleming wasn't surprised. If he had gone missing, he'd suspect his own wife, Sharon, would do the same.

A cat meowed on the other side of the door, Emily's orange and white tabby. Emily was gone. The cat wouldn't meow if she was home.

What were Fleming's options?

Emily wrote she'd be back by sundown. It would be best for her if she did get out and look. That way she'd feel she was contributing.

Except for the bad news. How would she handle seeing her husband's hat ripped apart with razor teeth marks? Probably not well.

God help her if she comes across a piece o' him.

Regardless, he would have to tell her. Would she believe him? Doubtful. She convinced herself the American had done it. She had hinted at that. When traumatized, people believed what they wanted.

He faced away from the house. Thick clouds hovered in the distance, a typical pre-afternoon occurrence. Soon, the mist and the rain would come, blocking out the sun. Spring Highland weather was nothing if not unpredictable. It was best to enjoy the sun when it came because it didn't stay around for long.

Fleming took a step away from the house and off the wooden porch. He walked down the small pathway between the small green shrubs that James and Emily had planted.

He took another step. His large boot crunched gravel.

A sound came from the distance.

Singing?

Fleming wasn't a sympathetic man by any stretch, a personality trait that made him a good police officer. This music, however, had something unusual about it. What was it about it that caught his attention?

Who was the one singing it? It sounded beautiful. He had never heard anything like it before.

He shuddered. No, he thought. He had to find Emily. She needed to know about her husband's cap. His job as an officer was to protect and inform. The hard part was informing someone of bad news. It was why he was paid.

He took pride in his job. He delivered the tough news when necessary. The good officers did it and did it well. Those were the ones who received promotions, made more money, and who found leadership positions. It was why he had advanced so quickly in his career.

The singing continued. He paused as the mournful notes drew him toward it.

Fleming went to his car, climbed in, and shut the door, his broad shoulders tight against the small space. The singing stopped, unable to penetrate the metal and the glass of the cab. He needed to think. He put his hands on the steering wheel and tapped his fingers on the leather.

Emily had left. She probably went to the dock. That was the last place James had been seen. He debated whether he should find Emily first, or if he should return to the station.

O'Malley had gone to find Tom Wayne. They had agreed they'd need his help at some point. O'Malley and he had separated at the dock, O'Malley searching for Tom, and Fleming going to give the bad news to Emily.

But there was something else they had to do. There was a possible danger in the waters of Loch Ness. O'Malley suspected Tom knew something about that. They had to warn the politicians.

But did the Loch Ness monster kill Captain James Anderson? Would they accept that?

Fleming clenched his jaw. The press would have a field day if that got out. What if a mythological creature killed Anderson? If it happened a second time, and Fleming and O'Malley did not report it, his job would be on the line.

Sharon wouldn't like that, he thought.

He made up his mind. If Emily was at the dock, she had to be warned. She shouldn't cross the crime scene tape anyway. But if she did, Fleming would be wise to return her home, and she'd be wise to come with him to the station to see her husband's hat.

Then, he'd be sure he and O'Malley warned the Council. Privately, of course. He'd let them figure out how best to warn the public.

He pulled forward. He remembered the singing, and how it soothed him. Whose voice was that? His wife would appreciate the voice, too. Sharon liked music. Maybe they'd meet this skilled singer one day. Whoever she was, she had talent. Maybe she'd enter and win one of those reality music contests on television. He tried to imagine the singer, what she was like. Was she skinny? Fat? Tall? Short? Blonde? Brunette? Old? Young? No telling.

These thoughts stayed with him as he drove away from the Anderson residence, down the small road toward Thurwick on his way to pick up Emily Anderson from the boat dock. He preferred thinking about the singing instead of Anderson's half-eaten police cap.

CHAPTER 16

After turning on the propane gas tank, Tom Wayne tossed three large red steaks onto Sean Paterson's grill behind the house. He pressed them into the flames with the metal tongs. The fire danced around the red meat, and the flesh sizzled. The heat warmed him, a welcome relief as a cold front had moved in from the west. Rain threatened. His green waxed coat helped him keep warm.

The last time he saw a steak he was on the water of Loch Ness, on a small rowboat with Sean hunting for the Loch Ness monster. That trip had not gone well. Tom had hooked Sean's face to the fishing line, and they had to abandon their hunt before they intended.

His train of thought drifted to the monster. As the grill flames grew, he had a flashback of Coffee's burning yacht, of Caleb's death, of his fight with Vaas, and of the memory of the Loch Ness monster trying to free itself from the giant net before it and Tom went down with the boat. He remembered how powerful it was, how majestic, how mysterious. Two other plesiosaurs joined the one in the net, swimming around him, black as night, quick and agile like a dolphin in the water–.

"Wha' are ye thinkin?" Marella said. She appeared behind him, holding a glass of her red wine. Hanging from her ears were the four-leaf clover earrings. They glinted like emeralds in the sunlight.

"Hey, they look good on you," he said.

"Thanks. I think I'll keep them."

Tom blinked, his mind struggling to the present.

"Are ye alright?" She put her hand on his shoulder and squeezed. The touch of her hand made him feel good.

"Yeah. You like your steak medium?" He tapped a steak with the tongs.

Her green eyes connected with his. They didn't want to make small talk.

"I'm sorry. I guess I'm a little unnerved, still," he said.

"Ye haven' had much time tae reflect since th' rescue, had ye?"

"No. I guess not." He pointed his tongs at her glass of wine. "No Old Mortality?"

"Oh, I don' mind them. 'Tis jus' tha' my da' decided he wanted two. He may have lost his leg, bu' he still considers it a happy occasion."

Tom chuckled, and Marella smiled.

"Ye think we'll e'er have a normal life?" Marella said.

Tom thought before he spoke. He remembered his scheduled meeting with Liz Stevens, and what O'Malley shared also didn't sit too well with him.

And something else was bothering him, but it was something he couldn't put his finger on.

"Tom?"

"Just thinking."

"Ye've been different since ye came back from town. Wha' did Detective O'Malley say tae ye?"

Tom held his breath.

"Well?" Marella said.

He bowed his head. "It's Anderson."

"Did they find him?"

"No. They found his police hat."

"At th' dock?"

"Yeah."

"Good. Maybe they're close tae findin' him."

"It doesn't sound like it."

Marella frowned. "How come?"

"O'Malley says the hat's been bitten in half."

Marella opened her mouth and covered it with her hand. "Naw."

"He asked for my help."

Marella's face grew cautious. "Help how?"

"He said they're suspicious I hadn't told them everything."

Marella put her wine on the grill table and folded her arms. "And so wha' if ye didn't. 'Tis na' yer responsibility."

"I did say no to him."

"Well, tha's o'er. Na need tae dwell on it."

Tom pressed the tongs into the cooking steaks. Their juices fell into the flames, causing them to dance higher, close to his fingers. The smoke lifted the aroma into the air. "There's more."

"Wha' do ye mean?"

"A reporter came at me outside Smith's Store wanting another interview."

"Which one?"

Tom gritted his teeth. "Stevens with The London Adventure magazine."

"Tha' harlot!"

Tom flinched.

"Ye told her no I hope."

Tom shook his head. "I wish I had."

Marella uncrossed her arms. The sparkles in her green eyes went away, replaced by a flash of anger.

"Marella—"

Marella stepped back.

Tom's shoulders tensed. "Look, it's no big deal. You can trust me."

"Apparently na!" she countered.

"Come on–."

Marella gestured toward her father. "*We're* movin' on. If *ye* want tae save th' world and meet with yer little girlfriend, go righ' ahead."

"It's not like that."

Marella took off the earrings and slammed them on the grill table next to her glass of wine. "Ye can have these back!"

"Marella–."

"I don' wan' them. In fact, ye need tae go tae Annabel's. I'm sure ye can prep fur yer interview there." She marched away.

"Wait!"

Marella went inside the house and slammed the door.

"You forgot your wine!" Tom shouted, still holding the tongs.

She didn't come back out.

The steaks sizzled on the grill, and smoke drifted into the air, past her glass of wine and the four-leaf clover earrings he had given her. Storm clouds had formed above him, and it would rain soon. Should he ignore her words, go inside, and eat with them? What was he supposed to do? Stop cooking and leave? They hadn't had their toast for Sean yet.

Perhaps Marella was emotional. He understood why, with her father coming home today in a wheelchair and minus a leg. He decided to remain calm, to not overreact. He'll finish the steaks–.

The door opened. "Are ye still here?" Marella said.

Tom stood, holding the tongs in his hand.

Behind her, Sean's voice from inside said, "Don' be so hard on th' lad."

Marella ignored her father and glared at Tom. "I told ye tae go!"

That was Tom's cue. He set the tongs down next to the wine glass. He reached down to extinguish the grill.

"Go!" Marella pointed.

Tom lifted his hands like a man surrendering. He stepped away from the grill.

"Go!" she repeated.

He backed away, leaving the grill burning. The rain was coming. If he was going to get to Annabel's before the weather hit, he had to move. "Okay. If that's what you want."

"I do." Marella waited. She crossed her arms again, wrapping her cardigan sweater around her.

Tom took the hint.

Marella scowled.

Tom left the grill, went around the outside of the house, and walked onto the dirt of Mackay Rd. Thunder rumbled overhead, and the first drops of rain hit his head. He jogged in his green waxed coat, trying to get to Annabel's before the rain drenched him.

CHAPTER 17

The rain fell hard upon Tom as he sprinted down the main road. Annabel's was a hundred yards ahead. He hurried, his clean shoes splattering mud in the puddles. Water fell off his hair, down his forehead, and onto his neck. His green waxed coat dripped with rain, but it didn't matter. Water fell everywhere.

He reached the corner of Annabel's, leaped up to the top of the steps, and opened the door. His eyes were closed as he wiped the water away from his face. He couldn't believe Marella had told him to go like that, and in the rain, too. He never had the chance to explain that the interview might help Sean kickstart his business. Maybe he'll try again tomorrow.

When he lowered his hands, his mouth opened and his eyes widened.

Annabel's sofa, where she sat each morning to do her crossword puzzles, was over. The small table was on its side. The kitchen sink was running, and water was splattering onto the tiles. The vase on the windowsill was knocked over again, the flowers on the floor several feet from the vase. Water dripped from the ceiling and splattered onto the kitchen floor.

Tom stepped into the room. His wet shoes squeaked on the wooden floor.

"Annabel?" he said. The place was a wreck. *What happened to Annabel?*

There was a soft rumble of thunder outside the walls. The rain echoed through the open window in the kitchen. The constant dripping of water, the splattering into puddles, and the noise of rain and of wind through the window downed out all other potential sounds. An attacker could be in the house, and he'd never hear him.

Tom stepped forward again. Pictures had been ripped off the walls and thrown down.

He bent down and picked up one picture of a flower and vase. The picture had a gash in its corner. A tear ripped across the vase. The frame crumpled when he picked it up. It cracked along its edge. He examined the wall where it fell from, and he noticed four long claw marks, white against the wood.

He was getting nervous. "Annabel?" he said again, hoping he'd hear something. The beating inside his chest competed against the noise from all the water. He could not hear anything else.

He followed the damage. It was everywhere. Each wall had pictures ripped from their hooks. More claw marks scratched the walls in several places. He went to the steps. Water was dripping down them in small waterfalls, and running off the side where the railing was. A puddle was forming next to the stairs. The stair railing was pushed from its base, ripping the screws from the wood underneath it.

Whoever did this was strong.

The room past the steps was also in disarray. The curtains were torn down and lay upon a ripped sofa, its pillows slashed. More pictures were tossed and damaged throughout the room.

Tom peered up the stairs. His eyes widened.

Blood.

It was on the fourth step going up. It wasn't much, but it was there. "Annabel?" he said a third time, observing the steps at the top, hoping to hear a response. He stepped up, putting his hand on the broken railing. When it fell, Tom's foot slipped on the water. He lost his balance and his knee hit the stairs. He put his hand on the fourth step, missing the blood.

He regained his footing, and went up the steps, his shoes splashing in the falling water.

A small section of glass hung where the mirror used to be. The rest was on the floor, its glass shattered on the tile. Water ran into the tub. It spilled out over the side and splattered on the glass and tile. He went closer. The towels had been ripped from the bar. They lay on the tiles, soaking up the spilled water. The sink, too, was also running, except the water here was going down the drain.

He stepped inside his room. He had closed his door when he last left, but the door was smashed through. Pieces of it hung from its hinges, while the rest of it was in the room leaning on the wall.

His bedsheets were torn, their pieces scattered. His bed sat twisted and moved to the other side of the room, its headboard smashed into the closet, breaking the door. A large gash went across the mattress.

The window had been smashed. Glass pieces lay on the wood floor. The light glinted off their shards. A piece of delicate green cloth moved from the draft near the window. Tom moved closer, taking cautious steps, his knees bent in case he had to move. As he approached, the green cloth hung from the windowpane. It blew in the wind from the broken window. The leaves from the tree outside rustled with the breeze.

He came to the cloth and picked it up. It was a part of Annabel's shirt, the one she wore this morning. There was a spot of red on a frayed corner.

Tom leaned out the window, careful of the glass. The tree seemed okay. A couple of black feathers hung in the leaves. He looked down.

Annabel lay motionless on the ground, her head twisted backward, her gray hair wild, her legs broken and cut, her green blouse ripped off her back which was red with giant claw marks running down her skin, leaving long giant gashes.

A crack of lightning lit up the sky, while loud thunder boomed across the Highlands.

Unprepared for the scene, Tom brought his head back inside and heaved. He suddenly felt dizzy. He put his hands on his knees. He waited to catch his breath.

What had happened? Annabel was attacked, but by whom, or what? He didn't know. Could it still be in the house?

Tom righted himself and backed out of the room. Then he hurried past the bathroom and down the steps, slipping on the water and landing on his backside. He bounced to the floor. He got up and sprinted out the front door.

As the rain fell outside, fear rose inside him. For the first time in a long time, he was alone.

Across the street, Saint Michael's Catholic Church stood, its large wooden doors closed.

Tom had to check the doors. He sprinted across the street, his coat getting soaked, the rain running down his hair and down his neck and shirt. His socks and feet were wet from the water.

He reached the doors and pulled.

The door didn't budge.

"Oh, not today!" Tom said. He tried the other door, and it, too, was locked. "Dammit!" Tom banged on the door with his fist. "Father Gibson!" He slammed his fists into the door. "Father Gibson!"

The rain continued to fall. The door to Annabel's hung ajar. Inside was chaos. Annabel was dead.

Tom pounded on the church doors with his fists until they hurt.

Tom put his hands on his head. Where should he go for help?

CHAPTER 18

Tom leaned against the solid wood church doors. Annabel's Bed and Breakfast was across the street. He tried to calm down, but the image of Annabel's lifeless body - crumpled and torn upon the ground - stayed fresh in his mind. What should he do?

Seeing Annabel's body like that made Tom want to sit in Church. A holy place didn't seem like a bad idea.

But the doors were locked. The Church was out for now.

Should he go back to Marella and Sean? No. The last thing he wanted to do was bring more trouble upon them.

And what was this trouble? Who killed Annabel? Who cut her and destroyed her place? Was it one person? Was it more than one? Did Annabel have enemies? Sweet old Annabel? No. He doubted that.

But, did that mean the killer wasn't after Annabel? Maybe he was after him. Maybe the killer had broken in wanting to kill him, but then finding he wasn't there went into a fit of rage, destroyed the house, tore her up, and threw her out his bedroom window?

As the rain fell, he remembered he didn't have a cell phone. But he needed to call for help.

Who best to call? He shuddered, for he knew the answer.

O'Malley.

Great, Tom thought. He had rejected O'Malley's request for help. Now the shoe was on the other foot. What if O'Malley turned on him? What if O'Malley considered him a suspect and hauled him in for questioning as he did this morning?

He was Annabel's only tenant. The police would consider him a suspect. So would the town residents. Or perhaps even Sean, and Marella. He didn't want that.

Should he run? No. Running wouldn't work. They'd find him and they would suspect him all the more.

Tom brushed the rain from his eyes. What were his options? He'd have to call O'Malley, and he'd have to do it right away.

He remembered the card O'Malley gave him earlier. It was still in his wallet.

He needed a phone. With the church doors closed, the closest phone was across the street, inside the bed and breakfast.

Tom did not want to return to Annabel's, but it was either that or he would have to leave the scene, and running from the scene would increase the authority's suspicions against him.

The rain fell outside Annabel's open door. No cars drove past. Tom trudged back over, his shoes soaked by the rainwater collecting on the road. He reached the door and put his hand on the wall, preferring the cold rain outside to the uncertainty inside. He studied the scene again. This time he noticed more claw marks on the walls. They were everywhere. And white. All white.

He stepped inside. The dripping water splattered in puddles on the kitchen tile and the wood floors.

On the floor, to his left, the phone was lying on its side. Tom picked up the receiver. The line was dead. He picked up the phone base and pressed the switch. He listened to the receiver again.

There was a dial tone.

Tom pulled out O'Malley's card. He dialed the number.

A woman answered.

"Uh, yeah. This is Tom Wayne....yes that Tom.... I'm sorry. I can't talk.... I'm at Annabel's....yes....How's she doing? Well....she's dead....Yeah. I came here a few minutes ago and the place was trashed. I found her outside. It's bad....Yes. I'm here....Yes. I'll wait, but across the street at the church. I can't wait here....okay....no....I won't wait here. This place gives me the creeps....no I won't....Tell O'Malley I'll be across the street outside the Church....yes, I promise....send Detective O'Malley right away....I'll be waiting." Tom pressed the switch and put the phone on the floor. The woman said the police would be there soon.

He backed toward the door. A black feather leaned against the drawing-room wall. It had the same resemblance to the feather he saw outside the Smith's Store.

Something about the feather unnerved him. He had to leave, and now. The house haunted him. He sprinted across the street, the rain falling on his head and his shoes splattering rainwater, but he did not care. He reached the doors to the church and spun around. The open door at Annabel's revealed the overturned furniture inside the shadows.

Tom leaned back against the doors to Saint Michael's Catholic Church, feeling the hardwood of the solid doors against his back. The church gave him comfort as his eyes fixed on the memory of death across the street. He said a quiet prayer as he waited for O'Malley.

CHAPTER 19

Two police cars arrived, their checkered design unmistakable against the backdrop of Annabel's house. Two police officers exited the cars, both men. They looked about his age. Tom hadn't seen them before. He worried their youth would drive them to recklessness instead of caution. Tom walked across the street, making sure they knew he was not trying to run.

Another car arrived. It was O'Malley's. He climbed out, his face concerned as his fedora blocked the rain.

"It's as I found it," Tom said. "Except for the phone. I used the phone inside."

O'Malley paused a moment, then he went into the house.

Not ready to go back inside, Tom stood in the rain. The cold water dripped down his jacket and soaked his jeans and shoes. His body shivered. He wanted to leave, to run, but he knew it would be best to keep his feet planted right where they were.

One of the officers came outside. His hair was red under his black police hat. His face had a reddish tint from his many freckles. His eyes, though, were bright blue, and they contained suspicious thoughts. "Yer Tom?" he said.

"Yeah."

"Ye called this in?"

"Annabel's behind the house."

"I'll stay here with ye." He stood close to Tom as if he expected him to run at any moment and would have to give chase.

Tom said, "I'm not going anywhere."

The officer didn't respond. They stood outside, the rain falling on them both.

O'Malley stepped through the doors. The rain splattered on his hat. He rubbed his gray beard. "Officer Burns, O'Reilly's goin' tae need help."

"Ye wan' me tae take him in?" Burns said.

Tom didn't flinch. He expected the police to rush him, handcuff him, and accuse him.

"Na'," O'Malley said. "I'll take him. Ye call Fleming. Tell him tae brin' e'eryone."

"Aye," Burns said. He left the two of them standing there as he went into his police car and picked up his radio.

"I didn't' do it," Tom said.

O'Malley put his hands in his pockets, the rain dripping from his fedora. "Ye know I'll need' tae take ye in fur questionin'."

"I figured that."

"Two times in one day. Wha' do ye think is goin' on?"

"I don't know." Tom brushed the rain from his face. "Annabel didn't deserve this."

"Na', she didn'."

"Can I ask you something?" Tom said.

"Aye."

"Do you think someone is after me?"

A sunbeam broke through the clouds and highlighted a green hill in the distance. "Don' know, lad."

"I'm worried about Marella," Tom said. "What if they go after her next?"

O'Malley blinked, his face remaining expressionless.

"What if she's in danger?" Tom said.

"She may be."

The way he said it made Tom lift his eyes "Oh, come on. You don't think I did this, do you?"

O'Malley didn't respond. The sunbeam shone in the distance.

"I had nothing to do with this," Tom said.

O'Malley stepped toward the police car. "Officer Burns," he said.

Burns exited the car. "Aye,"

"Are they comin'?"

"On their way."

"Alright. Go tae Sean Paterson's house. Tell him and Marella wha' we discovered here. Le' them know we're takin' Tom tae th' station, but tha' they need tae be on th' lookout fur anythin' suspicious."

"Now?"

"Aye," O'Malley said.

Burns gave Tom a condescending frown, then he saluted O'Malley like he was still in training.

O'Malley fanned his fingers at him. "Go."

Burns climbed in the car, and Tom watched as it rolled toward Mackay Rd.

"While O'Reilly's in the house, tell me. Have ye given any more thought tae my offer?"

Tom rubbed the back of his neck, wiping the rain from his hair. "Yeah."

"Ye have? Tell me. Wha' do ye think?"

"Something else is going on."

"I would agree with tha'."

Officer O'Reilly appeared in the doorway. The man was not so young, in his mid-thirties, not too old to be a senior officer, but also past the years of inexperience. "Detective," he said. "Ye need tae see this."

"What?"

O'Reilly said, "Come with me."

He disappeared behind the wall. O'Malley shrugged and followed O'Reilly inside the open door. As the cold rain fell upon Tom's head, he decided he should go inside, though his nerves jumped at the idea of reentering the house. He stepped through the door. The overturned furniture, the white claw marks, the torn paintings and curtains, and the overflowing water sent a chill down his spine.

O'Reilly climbed the stairs, balancing without the railing. O'Malley followed, his hand on the wall for support, his eyes watching the steps.

Tom studied the steps again before climbing them. The whole house was a disaster area. What happened in here, he thought?

O'Malley gave no indication that Tom shouldn't go with them, so Tom navigated the steps behind them, putting his hand on the wall for support, and making sure not to step on the blood, now mixed in with running water, on the fourth step.

O'Reilly ignored the rooms on the left, instead focusing on the room on the right.

Tom had forgotten to go into the far room after the shock of witnessing Annabel's crumpled body on the ground outside the window. He had rushed down the stairs with the sole purpose of escape.

O'Reilly pointed, and then took off his hat and rubbed his brow with his sleeve.

"Creike," O'Malley said as he peered into the open door.

O'Reilly stepped back. O'Malley walked into the room.

Tom followed and stood in the doorway. "What happened in here?"

Inside, the bed had been lifted and thrust against the far wall. A hole had been punched through the wall revealing two-by-fours. The chairs had been knocked over, and long gashes exposed the inner springs and stuffing that poured from their outer plaid cloth and onto the carpet.

Covering the floor and the overturned furniture were hundreds of black feathers. The far window had been shattered, and the draft moved the feathers into circling clumps on the floor and furniture.

"Here, too," O'Reilly said. The same white claw marks as downstairs were on the walls. Most of the marks were in long gashes that stretched several feet down and across.

Tom noticed the difference, though, on the far wall. Centered within the white claw marks was a word. It was made with a single claw, its white gash written like an angry toddler.

The word was four letters - MINE.

"Wha' does tha' mean?" O'Malley said.

Tom shuddered. A strange chill came over his entire body. "I think we should leave," Tom said.

"Mr. Wayne," O'Malley said. "Ye have any idea wha' tha' is?"

"None," Tom said. "But let's leave and regroup before something else happens."

"Tha' means ye'll help?"

Tom thought of Marella. He had to protect her from whatever *this* was. "Yes," he said. "I'll help."

CHAPTER 20

Inside the police station, Tom sat at the table in the small room, the door open, and towels draped over his shoulders and under his rear. He was glad to be drying off. Across the table from him lay a yellow notepad and a pen.

O'Malley entered the room with two green ceramic cups of coffee in his hands. Steam hovered above the cups and lifted into the air.

He set a cup in front of Tom. Tom picked it up, took a sip, and appreciated the warmth in his hands.

O'Malley shut the door. He sat behind the notepad. "I'm gla' ye decided tae help. Tha' will make my questions easier."

"I'm worried about Marella," Tom said.

"Understood." O'Malley sipped his own coffee, then picked up his pen. "Foremost, tell me wha' happened."

"When I arrived–."

"Na'. Why'd ye leave Paterson's place?"

Tom replayed the conversation in his mind. He fidgeted in his seat. "Marella and I had an argument."

"Abou' what?"

"I told her you asked for my help."

O'Malley tapped his pen on the table. "She go' mad?"

Tom paused. "It wasn't that. I have an interview scheduled for tomorrow."

"With who?"

"Liz Stevens. She is a reporter for a magazine."

"And Marella didn' like it?"

"She wants life to get back to normal."

"Are ye sure she wasn' jealous?"

Tom shrugged. "No reason to be."

"Maybe na' fur ye." O'Malley's eyes resembled that of a sports coach after his player made a bonehead play on the field.

Tom lowered his eyes. He didn't answer.

"So ye left because she was mad?" O'Malley said.

"No. I left because she told me to."

O'Malley wrote on the pad. He tapped his pen some more. "Then wha'?"

"I ran in the rain trying to beat the storm. When I got to Annabel's, I found it as you did."

"Did ye touch anythin'?"

"I climbed up the stairs and slipped. When I saw blood on the steps, I sort of freaked out. The railing gave way, and I knocked that over. And when I went into my room, I touched a green piece of cloth that was hooked on the glass in my window. I think it was a part of Annabel's shirt. That's when I looked out the window and saw her lying there."

"Where's tha' cloth now?"

"Don't know," Tom said. "I must have dropped it in the room. When I saw Annabel, I was so shocked I booked it out of the house and ran across the street. I tried going in the church to get help, but the doors were locked. So, I went back to the house and used Annabel's phone to call you. That's the only thing I touched when I went back inside."

O'Malley took notes with his pen. "Did ye go into th' room with th' feathers?"

"No," Tom said. "I wanted out.

O'Malley wrote on his pad.

Tom squeezed his coffee mug. "I have to tell you, I've never seen anything like what we found in that room."

O'Malley lifted his eyes.

"I mean, have you seen anything like that before?"

O'Malley said, "Can't say tha' I have."

Tom sat back. "Nothing phases you, does it."

O'Malley smiled. "Just Digger."

"Who's that?"

"My dog."

Tom sipped his coffee.

"Wait here," O'Malley said. "I need tae show ye somethin'." He climbed from his seat and went into the main room.

Tom waited, sipping his coffee and holding back the random chills that entered his body. O'Malley's upside-down handwriting on his notepad resembled chicken scratch. He couldn't read it.

O'Malley returned to the small room. He set a clear plastic bag on the table. Inside it was a dark blue material. O'Malley slid it over to Tom. "Don' take it ou' o' the bag, but examine it."

"Is that…?" Tom said.

"Aye." O'Malley said. His eyes focused on Tom, watching his reaction.

Tom held the bag in his hand. Inside it was what was left of a police cap. The front of it had the unmistakable shield and checkered front. The back, however, was a different story, for it was not there. Down the middle, from left to right, the material was shredded, ripped apart by what was like jagged teeth. The cloth was sliced in many places. Where it wasn't sliced, the material was frayed. Threads had been pulled from the main material where they snapped, leaving strings that spread in all directions. "This was Anderson's?" Tom said.

"What do ye suppose did tha', Mr. Wayne?" O'Malley said.

Tom closed his eyes, remembering the image of the Loch Ness monster closing its jaws upon Alex Vaas's head as the man flailed in the water. The teeth of the creature, in his mind, bore a strong resemblance to the bite mark on Anderson's hat. He shuddered. If the creature had done this, then Anderson suffered the same fate as Vaas.

"Well?"

Tom held his mouth shut. Should he tell O'Malley what happened? If he did, no telling what that would conjure up. If he didn't then that could prompt the police to accuse him of the crime at Annabel's. He set the coffee cup down and pursed his lips. He had to say it. "It's the monster," Tom said.

"The monster?"

"Yeah."

"The Loch Ness monster?"

"Yes. Nessie. Whatever you want to call him."

"How do ye know?"

106

"Because I saw it," Tom said.

O'Malley tapped his yellow notepad with the back of his pen. "Yer statements before said ye didn' see it clearly."

"I lied," Tom said. "Yes, I saw it clearly. I saw it clear enough to watch it eat Alex Vaas."

O'Malley's eyebrows raised. "Say tha' again?"

"You heard me," Tom said. "And there wasn't just one. There were three of them."

"Three?"

"Yes. Three. They lunged at Vaas and tore him apart." Tom waited as O'Malley watched him. O'Malley tapped his pen on the table again, but this time a little faster. The rapping of the pen continued until Tom said, "That's why you didn't find him. And I imagine Coffee, too. Consider them both lunch."

"Why didn't ye say this in yer statements?"

"Because I didn't know how to explain it. Briggs was trying to get the monster for his own power. If I proved the monster lived, then the whole world would be here trying to find it."

"Ye didn' want tae find it yerself?"

"I did, but it was wrong."

"Why?"

"It's hard to explain. Something came over me, like an obsession. Once we rescued the monster, though, the obsession left. Any desire to find it went away."

"But ye could have been famous. Rich, e'en."

"Look at Sean. He lost his leg. I almost got killed. You think we wanted more of that?"

O'Malley said nothing. He tapped his pen on the table.

Tom said, "All we wanted was for things to go back to normal." He shook his head. "Marella didn't want this."

O'Malley kept his eyes on Tom, tapping his pen. "And ye ne'er considere' th' monster might pose a danger tae th' residents o' Thurwick?"

Tom lifted his head. "No." O'Malley's question posed a new danger. Tom had said nothing. Now a man was dead - the beloved police captain, no less.

Would the town suggest Anderson's death was his fault?

If the town ran with the story in that way, no telling how the authorities would act. He admitted he had lied in his statement. And with Anderson and Annabel both dead, Tom knew he would need help. Tom rubbed the back of his neck, piecing his options in his mind.

O'Malley's eyes grew sad. He wrote something on his notepad and shook his head. Then he reached for the clear plastic pouch. "Wai' here." He stood up with the pouch in his hand and left the room.

Tom leaned back in his chair. He wasn't so sure waiting was the best idea.

CHAPTER 21

Tom stood up. He went to the open door. The two women faced their computers, their eyes focused on the monitors. Tom supposed they typed something about him, but he was too cautious to ask. Perhaps he could walk past, pretend his meeting was over, and disappear through the entrance. The front door was several steps away. If he ran, he'd escape....

"Let's go back inside." O'Malley appeared behind a corner.

Tom jumped. *How does he do that?*

O'Malley held a small card, and there was handwriting on it. When they reentered the small back room, O'Malley shut the door. He peered out the window to make sure the women weren't trying to listen in.

"I think I need to leave," Tom said. "I don't have a place to stay tonight." It was a good excuse, he thought. Maybe O'Malley would buy it.

"I think ye'll need this." O'Malley handed Tom the card.

"What is it?"

"Jacob Stewart. He's an attorney in town. His number's written here. Best ye call him soon."

Stewart's name and phone number were written in blue ink.

"And one more thing."

"What's that?" Tom said.

"Ye didn' get tha' from me."

Tom took the card, folded it, and stuffed it inside his wet coat pocket.

"Ye best be goin'." O'Malley said.

"Thank you." Tom said.

O'Malley opened the door. As Tom left, O'Malley said aloud, intending the women to hear, "And if ye find anythin' suspicious, anythin' at all, ye be sure tae call me. Okay?"

The women raised their eyes from their computers.

Tom said, "Yes, sir," appreciating the public hint that he was not a suspect. He shook O'Malley's hand. Tom went through the station to the front door.

O'Malley stayed behind.

The women watched Tom.

He smiled at them. This time, they did not smile back.

When Tom opened the front door, the damp evening air filled his lungs. He was glad the rain was gone, but the mist cloaked everything. He stood upon the sidewalk and studied the middle of Thurwick. The sun was setting and shadows stretched over the road. What should he do first: run back to Sean and Marella, or find a place to stay? He didn't think Marella would let him stay with them after how she forced him to leave.

Across the cobblestones stood Guthrie's Pub. Tom was hungry. He never had the chance to get his steak. He had to think.

While food sounded good, what he needed was help, a friend.

He knew of one place to go.

Saint Michael's. Father Gibson had been there each day since they met. Why was he not there today, and today of all days?

It didn't matter. He had to try.

He stepped onto the cobblestones of downtown Thurwick, his shoes squishing the cold water with each step.

He needed to find a bed, and get changed into warm clothes.

Clothes. All his clothes were at Annabel's. If he mustered the courage to go back inside, would the police even let him?

He had to go. He welcomed the chance to get moving again, and he jogged through Thurwick toward Saint Michaels.

After several minutes, the sun had set behind the green mountains and left a cold breeze that whispered through the budded leaves. He arrived at the Church. It was made of solid stone, put together centuries ago as Catholicism made its way to the British Isles. Deep shadows stretched between the stones. The tower stood dark against the pink and orange clouds.

Behind him was Annabel's. Several checkered police cars were out front, their lights flashing, illuminating the coming night. A muffled voice came over a distant radio. The door to the house was still open. While his dry clothes remained upstairs, he decided he'd rather find Father Gibson. Something strange was happening. Father Gibson had known the secret to the Loch Ness monster. Maybe he knew what was going on now.

He ran up the steps to the old wooden doors. He pulled the large sturdy handles.

The doors did not open.

Tom backed up. There had to be something going on, he thought. Father Gibson wouldn't leave the Church empty.

With the sun down, he scanned the windows to the Church and to the rectory. He searched for a light. Anything that showed a hint of occupation.

The rectory was attached to the church, extending outward along the shores to the loch. The structure stood three stories high, though where he stood the first level was below ground, the foundation taking advantage of the landscape as it sloped toward the shores of Loch Ness.

At one time, the rectory housed several men in the seminary, studying to become priests. These days, however, the rooms were empty, except for Father Gibson, and perhaps a visiting priest or two.

The police lights flashed behind him, and the investigators were too occupied to notice him. He jogged down the length of the rectory, studying the windows. All of them were dark. He traveled past the dark windows, with room after room showing empty darkness. He rounded the corner. More windows faced the fading light of the setting sun. They, too, were dark.

He rounded the final corner. The waters of Loch Ness rippled behind him as he jogged on the grass next to the rectory. These windows were also dark. He kept going. What was happening? He slowed his pace. The structure on this side was three stories, and he wanted to give more focus so as to not miss a lighted window.

But none of the windows had any light. All of them were dark.

He neared one window and put his hands up to view the inside. Through the black window, he peered around dark curtains that blocked most of his view. He made out the shape of a cot, a small desk, and a chair, and that was it. The walls were bare, except for a cross above the door on the opposite end. It was a small room, no doubt fitting for one choosing a life of poverty.

Tom proceeded to the next window, and the next. All the rooms were the same.

He reached the end of the rectory, and he was at the rear of the church. The breeze from the loch blew his hair. The water rippled with the breeze. The moonlight sparkled in the ripples. Out there, a few weeks earlier, he almost died. Yet he had survived, and he found the creature so many had tried to find.

The secret to finding the monster remained hidden. Only he, Sean, Marella, and Father Gibson knew the secret.

What should he do? They suspected him of knowing about the disappearance of the local police captain, they coerced him into another interview with the press, the love of his life pushed him away, and he found Annabel dead. Would the town blame him for lying in his initial reports about the Loch Ness monster?

Where the hell is Father Gibson?!

A chill came over Tom. He folded his arms. While he shivered, plotting his next move, a squeak came from the church.

A rear door to the church was ajar, cracked only an inch but it was open.

Tom approached the door. He propped it open and peeked behind it. There was no light in the room. He saw only shadows.

"Hello?" he said. His voice echoed. There was no answer. "Father Gibson?"

When no response came, Tom pushed open the door. The hinges squeaked as he stepped inside the dark church, and the shadows surrounded him.

CHAPTER 22

Fleming did not find Emily Anderson at the dock. When he arrived mid-afternoon, he expected her car to be there. But the parking lot remained empty. Rather than go searching for her, he figured he'd wait. She would come to the dock eventually. After all, it was the last place her husband, James Anderson, was seen. If she did not show up for investigative purposes, she'd at least show up for emotional ones.

Yet, she did not arrive.

Then the police call came about Annabel. The call unnerved him. Captain James Anderson had handled the chaos on the loch several weeks ago. But now, with him gone and another person dead he, as the acting police captain, had his work cut out for him.

He had left the dock and drove the short way to Annabel's Bed and Breakfast. Officer O'Reilly was taking pictures of the scene and directing the EMTs who were wrapping Annabel's lifeless body in the bag before carrying her to the morgue. There were many things to take pictures of: the running water, the torn overturned furniture, the broken glass. But the claw marks, the feathers, and the word MINE on the upstairs wall gave him chills.

The easy thing to do was arrest her only customer, the American, Tom Wayne.

But Tom visited Sean and Marella Paterson, and he had left their home a short while before he called in the emergency. By their statement, it would have been hard for Wayne to inflict the amount of damage upon the house in that short amount of time, let alone get away with murdering Annabel. It didn't make sense.

Detective O'Malley had taken Tom Wayne in for questioning.

But as the team gathered samples of feathers, collected splinters from the claw marks, took pictures of the chaos, and carried Annabel's body away, a chill came upon Fleming.

He stepped outside. The air was cold. The sun had set. The flashing lights blinded his vision. He was becoming more concerned about Emily. She had said she'd be home by sunset. Her not showing up at the dock surprised him.

He put his hand on his car. *Was that singing?* It was very faint, but it carried in the mist from somewhere far away, somewhere past Thurwick.

O'Reilly stepped outside. "Sir, we have abou' all we can get."

Fleming blinked.

"Sir?"

"Uh, sorry. Good," Fleming said.

"Are ye alrigh'?"

"O' course I'm alrigh'. Now ge' on wit' yer checklist." Fleming did not expect to speak so forcefully. As soon as the words left his mouth, he regretted them.

O'Reilly went to his car. Fleming bowed his head. If he was going to get promoted to Captain by an official vote of the Council, he'd have to keep his wits.

Still, the singing continued.

"O'Reilly," Fleming shouted.

O'Reilly stood up from his car. "Aye, sir."

"Do ye hear tha'?"

O'Reilly paused. "Hear wha', sir?"

"Singing. Do ye hear any singin'?"

O'Reilly stood tall. He searched the sky. "Na. Can't say tha' I do."

"Thanks," Fleming said.

O'Reilly stood, concern showing on his face.

"I'm alrigh', lad," Fleming said.

O'Reilly's face remained blank like he didn't believe him. Then he went to his police car and shut the door. In a minute, he pulled away and drove his car back to Thurwick.

Great, Fleming thought. If word gets out that I'm losing it, Sharon won't be happy.

The singing continued, its melody touching the feelings in his chest. It made him think of Emily.

That was it. He had to check on her.

Fleming climbed into his police car. He started the engine. The music stopped inside the car, but the memory of it stayed with him, like a song on the radio that keeps replaying in your head over and over again.

In a few moments, he was at downtown Thurwick. He pulled into the boat dock parking lot. The lot was empty, with three glowing lamposts casting an orange glow upon the gray pavement under the cloudy misty night.

Fleming opened the car door.

The music drifted through the night. It was coming from the dock. Fleming studied the scene, but the boats were in the way. Interestin', he thought. He had been at the dock earlier, and there was no music then. Perhaps Emily arrived while he was at Annabel's.

Was it Emily? Was she singing? If she was, she sounded mournful, like a woman who had lost her husband. The grief in the music was sad, yet beautiful. Who else but Emily to sing a song like that, and at this hour of the day, right after she lost her husband?

It had to be her.

Fleming lumbered toward the orange crime scene tape that stretched between the two round wooden posts, his heavy feet crunching gravel and rock. He lifted his leg and hurdled the tape. His boot thumped upon the wooden dock.

The boats creaked as they rocked back and forth by the ripples of the water. The music traveled from the back of the dock, at the farthest point away from the land.

He stepped again. Then he stopped. "Emily?" he said.

The singing continued.

"Emily!"

The singing stopped.

There was silence except for the creaking boats.

"Is tha' ye?"

There was no answer.

Fleming rubbed the back of his neck. What should he do? The music had been beautiful, and he wanted to hear it again.

When it stopped, though, a chill came upon him. It was the same chill that came to him at Annabel's.

Regardless, the dock was closed. It was a crime scene. He took another step.

"Fleming!"

He stopped.

Behind him, Logan O'Malley pulled up, his nondescript car flashing his headlights at him from the parking lot.

Fleming lifted his hands over his eyes, blocking out the lights.

"I thouht tha' was ye." O'Malley walked toward him and hurdled the crime scene tape. "Are ye done at Annabel's?"

"I have a bad feelin' about Emily. Somethin' tells me she's here."

"Here?"

"Aye."

"Why?"

"I heard singin'," Fleming said.

"Singin'?"

Fleming pointed. "Back there."

"Well, let's have a look then, shall we?" O'Malley gestured for Fleming to move.

As they went, the singing did not continue. They searched between all the boats at the wooden docks, each space empty save for the coiled ropes. They examined the dock until they arrived at the end. To their right was the place they found Anderson's police hat, half chewed off by something with large sharp teeth.

The night sky left the area in darkness. "Did ye brin' yer flashlight?"

"Na. 'Tis in th' car," O'Malley said.

He studied the water. Its ripples moved like black oil under the dark clouds. Everything was black except for the white paint on the boat hulls reflecting the Thurwick light. He lumbered along the dock, watching the water. Whoever had been singing wasn't there, unless she was hiding in one of the boats. Still, that wouldn't explain how music carried all the way to Annabel's.

"Wha's this?" O'Malley bent down.

"What'd ye find?"

O'Malley raised up and held something dark between his thumb and forefinger. It fluttered in the night breeze.

"Is tha' wha' I think 'tis?"

"Aye," O'Malley said. "We're seein' a lot o' these lately."

Fleming raised his hand and lifted his palm.

O'Malley put the object in his hand. "Wha' do ye think it means?"

Fleming studied the black feather in his hand. "Don' know," he said. "But I think we nee' tae check if it matches th' ones we found at Annabel's."

"My thoughts exactly," O'Malley said.

"I need tae check on Emily," Fleming said. "Take tha' tae th' station, and let's compare samples in th' mornin'."

"Aye." O'Malley said. He walked upon the wooden dock, but he stopped when he noticed Fleming standing still. "Are ye comin'?"

Fleming said, "Strange. I know someone was here."

"How?"

"I heard singin'."

"Maybe t'was a ghost." O'Malley said.

The idea sent a chill down Fleming's spine. "Maybe."

With the singing gone, Fleming and O'Malley left the dock and returned to the parking lot.

CHAPTER 23

Tom pressed his hand against the wall, trying to feel his way through the back of the church. He had never been in this part of the building, so he moved slowly, his hand touching the rough surfaces of the stones and the cracks between them. He kicked something large, wooden, and heavy.

He stubbed his toe. "Ow!" he said, more from surprise than from pain. The sound echoed within the room. He fell silent. Had anyone heard him? After a few moments, he stepped forward.

He imagined he was working his way out from behind the altar, but the church was a floor above him. There was no altar where he stood. He was somewhere else. A basement, perhaps.

But then it dawned on him.

Was this a crypt?

He never imagined there'd be a second church below the main one. But it made sense. At one time, as mass was integral in the lives of the Thurwick citizens, there'd be a Mass above in the main chapel, with spillover down below in the crypt.

But the idea of being in a crypt gave him an eerie feeling, for crypts often had tombs in them.

His hand moved, and he touched a piece of wood and a small switch. He flipped the switch.

The room lit. Old electric light bulbs buzzed above his head. Fifty dark wooden pews stood in rows under black iron chandeliers. The walls were dark gray with stones that had not been cleaned in some time. At the far end stood a small altar, and behind it was a wooden crucifix that hung against the wall. Dust covered the pews. Spider webs hung everywhere.

"Why was this door open?" Tom said. He moved down one of the pews to the center aisle. When he reached the aisle, he noticed a large square flat stone on the floor. Etched into it with deep smooth grooves was a cross. Tom stepped around the stone, afraid to incur the wrath of God upon him for stepping on a cross, or a dead saint, or both.

He moved to the altar and noticed the dust upon it. He blew the dust off. The altar was made of marble and shined once the dust was removed.

That's when he noticed a cleft in the left wall. He went to it. A set of stairs circled up into a black corridor. Along the walls were iron handles where torches had been placed in the past. Leaving the lights on, he climbed the steps into the darkness. He circled and circled until he came to a place where the stairs continued up, but there was a platform and a door to his right.

The stairway continued higher. "Where do these go?" he said. He tried to remember the construction of the church. Then it came to him. "The bell tower. So that's where they ring the bell!" he said.

He had no time to climb and see what was above. He had to get to Father Gibson.

He went to the door. The door was wood, old, and heavy. He grabbed the handle and pushed the door, but it did not budge. He pulled and it opened, creaking and groaning with each torque of the hinges.

He stepped through the doorway, leaving the stairs behind. The coolness of open air pressed against his face. Though the lights were off, he knew that he was in the main chapel. The heavy door he had opened had blended in with the chapel walls, a secret door to the crypt below. All the times he had been to Mass in this room, he had not suspected the door. The empty space held cool air, the dim lights from Thurwick casting hints of light in the room.

Tom, knowing where he was, decided to work his way to Father Gibson's office. It was the one place he thought to go. He went between a set of pews to the center aisle. He stopped, bowed to the crucifix hanging behind the altar, and moved to his left, feeling his way between the pews through the darkness.

He reached the side door. It opened. He thought about turning on the lights, but he decided not to. It was best not to attract attention with the police across the street, and him being the main suspect.

He stepped cautiously down the hallway, running his fingers along the wall. If he remembered correctly, Father Gibson's office door was on the right, a few doors down.

He counted the doors as he passed them.

When he reached the office door, he knocked. Was it a sin to break into a priest's office? Would that be breaking and entering?

He didn't know.

He found the door handle. He twisted the knob.

The knob rotated. The latch clicked. The door opened.

He pushed the door inside. He went in.

He needed light. Should he flip the switch? Since Father Gibson's office window looked out over the loch and away from Thurwick, he decided to chance it.

He flipped the switch.

The room was as he had last seen it in his meetings with the priest. His globe stood on the desk. The many theological and philosophical books were arranged on the bookshelf. The small cd player that played "Veni Veni Emmanuel" was still resting in its place.

Tom moved toward the desk, and he found a single white envelope. He noticed handwriting on it. It said one word.

TOM

Father Gibson had left him a letter?

Tom opened it.

In hurried handwriting, the note said:

Tom,

You, Sean, and Marella are in severe danger. Come and find me in London. I fear for your lives if you don't. Close the crypt door on your way out. It will lock. Call me when you arrive.

Father Gibson

Then he wrote a phone number.

Severe danger? Tom thought. Yes, strange things were happening. Why had Father Gibson left town and not told him before doing so? That was why the church bells didn't wake him this morning. The priest had already left.

The office couch was against the back wall. Tom didn't know how much time he had. Should he run to Sean and Marella and show them Father Gibson's note?

Or should he sleep on the couch and wait until morning?

His adrenaline pressed him on.

If Marella was in danger, he had to let her know.

Father Gibson's phone sat on his office desk. Tom picked it up and dialed Marella's number.

The phone rang.

He waited.

"Aye?" It was Marella.

"Marella, it's Tom—"

There was a click and a tone. "She hung up on me," Tom said aloud.

He dialed again.

The phone rang again, and he waited. Sean's voice came over an answering machine. "Marella, Sean. I got a note from Father Gibson. First, I'm sorry about our argument earlier today, but he says we're in extreme danger, and we need to leave and go to London to meet him. I don't know what it's about—"

There was a beep and a click. "Did she turn off the answering machine?" He held the phone away from his head. "Boy, when she's mad . . ."

126

Tom put the phone down.

He studied the note in his hand. He dialed Father Gibson's phone number and listened.

The phone rang. He expected a quick answer, but after twenty rings he gave up. There was no one on the other line. He put the phone down.

There was a flash of light outside, the sign of another oncoming storm. Raindrops splattered on the window gently at first, but then hard and loud. Another flash came through the window, followed by a crack of thunder that rumbled inside the stone office walls.

Tom put the note into his pocket, went to the couch, and sat down. What should he do? If he was in danger, and Marella and Sean were, too, he had to warn them. Her telling him to go, though, unnerved him. At some point, she would have to trust him. What would it take for her to trust him?

He closed his eyes. Weariness was overcoming him. He forced his eyelids open, trying to think.

He had a sudden chill. Outside the window, the shape of a woman appeared. Her hair was white, and her eyes were beautiful. Her image was blurred by the rain. The image lasted for an instant, and then it was gone.

He rubbed his eyelids. "I'm losing my mind," he said. He leaned over onto the couch. He shut his eyes, and he fell asleep.

CHAPTER 24

The rain fell upon Fleming's car windshield as he pulled into Emily Anderson's parking space. No lights came through the windows.

"Where is she?" he said before he opened the car door. His cell phone rested on the passenger seat. There had been no calls. He left it there as he climbed from the car. Rain fell onto his face and shoulders. He lumbered toward the front door, his large boots splashing in the puddles.

He reached the door and knocked. There was no answer. After a second, Shamus meowed from behind the door. The rain that fell and hit the roof of Anderson's house echoed with the soft patter of drops on wood and shingles. He waited, listening.

Shamus meowed over the rain, the sign of a cat that was alone and hadn't been fed.

He knocked on the door. "Emily?" he said.

Meow!

He held his ear to the door.

Meow!

There was no sign of anyone coming to the front door.

Then he heard it again–singing.

It was faint and distant, but it was the same voice as before. It was like the music was following him, calling to him, beckoning to him.

Meow!

Fleming scratched his head. Things were getting strange. She said she'd be home by sunset, but that had not happened. Her car was not at home. Her cat had not been fed.

And, with James missing, his hat chewed in half by something large, and Annabel now dead by some feathery monster, Fleming worried that something sinister was afoot.

As acting police captain, he knew he needed information. O'Malley had been working on extracting what he could from the American, Tom Wayne.

They could not wait. It was time to get some answers.

The singing grew more intense. It was not louder, though it penetrated his head and his heart in a way he hadn't experienced since he was a teenager when he was more susceptible to the sounds and the lyrics that related to him.

He was scared. Sad and scared. He had lost a friend. Perhaps two. And a third was dead.

That's it, he thought. He had to find whoever was singing that music.

He hurried through the rain to his car. He stepped into a puddle that covered his ankle. His shoulders and head took the brunt of the heavy raindrops. He reached his car and threw the door open. His cell phone remained in the passenger seat. He listened before climbing inside. The music came from the north, near the loch. It was not near the dock this time. Had she moved?

He was going to find her. He lowered himself into the car and shut the door. The singing did not reach his ears, but the memory of the song remained, pulling his imagination to the spot where the singer would be. He suspected if he drove his car in that direction, he'd find her.

And, something told him he'd find Emily Anderson.

He backed his car from the parking space, his headlights reflecting in the drops of rain that fell hard from the sky.

A light appeared in the passenger seat next to him. It was his cell phone. He stopped his car and held the phone in his hand.

In glowing white letters was the name: Councilman Mark Bain.

Fleming answered the call.

"Fleming," Bain said.

"Aye, Councilman."

"I've heard wha' happened tae Annabel," Bain said. "And I've heard tha' Emily Anderson is missing."

O'Malley must have said something, Fleming thought. He had to. With things getting strange, it was better to get to the Council first before word spread on the street. "Aye," Fleming said. "I'm at the Anderson house now. She left me a note tha' she'd be home by now, bu' she's na' here."

"Word is Annabel's place was torn up."

"Aye. Pretty bad, tae."

"Was it th' American?"

"Wayne?"

"Aye."

Fleming had to measure his words. "Na' sure," he said. "If he had done it, it would have been a tremendous feat. There was a lot o' damage. I'm na' sure how one man did it, if ye ask me."

"Ye think there was more than one," Bain asked.

"Maybe," Fleming said. "That's my guess."

Bain paused, his breathing coming through the phone speaker. "Do ye think Wayne knows something?"

"Aye, I do," Fleming said.

"What do ye think he knows?"

"O'Malley could answer tha' better than me," Fleming said.

"Alright. I nee' ye tae meet me at th' station. Word's spreadin' about somethin' strange goin' on, and th' Council is wantin' answers."

Fleming thought of the singing, how it wanted him to find the voice. "I may have a lead on Emily," he said, though he couldn't believe his words. The singing was a lead? Would it help him find Emily Anderson? It made no rational sense at all, and yet he believed it. "If I could investigate one thin', I could meet ye after."

"Na. It has tae be now," Bain said.

"I'm worried about Emily," Fleming said. "She said she'd be home by now, but 'tis obvious she hadn' been. Her cat hadn' e'en been fed."

"As actin' police captain, ye should know a person isn' missin' unless they've been gone fur twenty-four hours. If ye saw her this mornin', then ye can search fur her in th' mornin'. Fur now, the Council needs tae ge' a handle on this....situation."

Fleming lowered his head. The music demanded his attention.

He wanted the police captain job. If he blew this chance, and the pay raise that came with it, Sharon would not be happy, and he'd hear about it at home. She complained about not having enough expensive vacations and undone home projects. No, he had to forget the music. The career mattered more, and that meant listening to the Council.

"Alrigh'," Fleming said, his tone agreeable. "I'll meet ye there in fifteen minutes."

"Thanks," Bain said, then the line went dead.

The singing pulled at his imagination, pleading for him to find it. It knew the turmoil inside him, the pull to advance his career, to make his wife happy and earn more money, that if he went to it he'd find what he needed, and the person singing it would have all the answers. If he could find her, he'd know everything, and it would all be alright.

His windshield wipers brushed the rain off the glass. He watched the sparkles of light as his headlights reflected off the rain.

The singing called to him. But Bain did, too.

Sharon would be very upset if she found out he ignored Bain to find a mysterious singer of songs.

By a sheer act of his will, he pressed the gas and turned his steering wheel toward Thurwick. What was Bain going to ask him?

CHAPTER 25

L ogan O'Malley sat in the chair in the small police station room. Councilman Tim MacGillivray, Councilwoman Loretta Morehead, and Councilman Mark Bain sat across from him. Their faces were stern. O'Malley picked up his coffee mug and took a sip, not allowing himself to be pushed around by the political class. He was a detective, and his work was about finding facts, not catering to the whims of the masses.

He offered them a cup of coffee, but none of them would take it. They sat like vultures, waiting to pounce on the roadkill as soon as it became available.

Fleming walked into the room. O'Malley's shoulders dropped, glad he was no longer alone with the three politicians.

"Shut the door," Bain said.

Na' even a hello, O'Malley thought.

Fleming did as he was told and pulled up a chair next to the table in the small room.

O'Malley sipped his coffee cup, thinking. With Chairman Gordan Briggs now in the Inverness penitentiary, how had Bain become the defacto person in charge?

His detective skills ran through his mind. He pieced together the facts of Bain's recent history.

Though young, Bain had managed a placement on several committees thanks to then Councilwoman Joan Martelle. Martelle had seen the potential in Bain; his rising maturity, his good looks, his effort to understand. All Bain needed, according to Martelle, was some direction and some experience, and one day he'd be a fine Mayor of Thurwick. Martelle had suggested to several committee chairs that Bain join their committees, and the endorsement worked.

Bain had not only found himself on the Thurwick Festival Committee but soon had joined the esteemed Planning Commission. His rise continued, and with the change in the Planning Commission leadership, the committee had voted to elect Bain, the youngest member of the Board, as the Chair.

Rumors circulated, however, that Mark Bain and Thurwick Chairman Gordon Briggs had developed a relationship about the same time that Briggs and Councilwoman Martelle had voiced some differences of opinion. Briggs and Bain had been seen at events together and had even arrived at those events from the same vehicle. Bain's loyalty had shifted toward Briggs's power, rather than Martelle's kindness. With Martelle's reelection nearing, some had suggested to Martelle to watch out for Bain. His relationship with Briggs had grown. Martelle, though, had remained firm in her loyalty to Bain. "He would never stab me in th' back," she had said.

Yet, when it came time to qualify for reelection, Bain had scheduled a meeting with Martelle. Word was that Bain had told her he was going to run against her, that he had raised tens of thousands of euros to campaign against her from his father's business, and then he had announced that he was doing her a favor. "You should drop out," he said. "Your time has past."

Martelle had left the meeting. Observers had said her face was ashen. Bain *had* stabbed her in the back, even after all the support, kindness, and opportunities she had given him.

The shock of Bain's betrayal had been too much for Martelle. She had decided not to defend her seat. Briggs's and Bain's plan had worked. Bain had been unopposed for the seat. Without spending a dollar, Bain's disloyalty had propelled him into one of the most influential positions on the Thurwick Council.

Politics, O'Malley thought.

Today, Councilman Mark Bain sat on the Thurwick Local Council, saying little, voting, and waiting. When Briggs was arrested, Bain said nothing. Some accused him of knowing about Briggs's plot, but because of his quick rise in local power, those voices quieted within a few days. Yet, there remained a vacuum of leadership in the Council. Who would fill the leadership void?

His answer arrived soon enough. Within a few days, Councilman Mark Bain became a front person in the media, appearing in the papers and giving speeches.

It was obvious Briggs was hoping to make Bain his successor. But now that Briggs was gone, Bain had to learn to work if he was to advance. Perhaps Bain's aggressiveness came from his needing to compensate for his youth.

Why did the other Council members - with more experience, no less - let Bain take the front position? Did they not want it? Were they playing the waiting game, expecting Bain to fail and then jumping in to save the day?

The Council members sat across from Fleming and O'Malley, their faces stern.

"Gentlemen," Bain said. "We nee' tae know what is happenin'."

Fleming said, "So de we."

"Tha's na' wha' we need tae hear," MacGillivray said. The dark circles under his eyes told O'Malley that the man was tired. "Patti Johansen is wearin' me out about people disappearin' and she's cousin' a stir among th' ladies."

"That's na' our business," O'Malley said. "That's yers."

"I'd advise ye tae watch yer words," Bain said.

"Tis true," O'Malley said. "Our job is tae find th' facts."

"Th' fact is I went tae Sally's Coffee Shop this afternoon, and I heard two women discussin' Anderson. Ye wan' tae know wha' they think?" MacGillivray said.

"I'm sure ye'll tell us," O'Malley said.

"They think Nessie ate Anderson."

Fleming and O'Malley shifted their eyes to each other. Neither spoke.

MacGillivray rapped his fingers on the table. "Did ye hear me?"

"Aye," Fleming said.

"Well…"

"We don' know tha'," O'Malley said.

"Very well, then," said Councilwoman Morehead. She put her hands on the table in an aggressive posture. "Wha' do ye know?"

Fleming pursed his lips like he had information he was afraid to share with them. O'Malley decided to play along and take the reigns. "Very well. Police Captain James Anderson is missin'."

"We know tha'," Councilwoman Morehead said.

"If ye'll be so kind as tae le' me finish," O'Malley said. He lifted his coffee cup and took a sip, intending to give them the impression he'll take all the time he wanted.

Morehead took her hands off the table and put them in her lap.

"Fleming, why don' ye get th' hat."

Fleming stood and left the room.

"Wha' hat?" MacGillivray asked.

"Ye'll see." O'Malley took another sip from his coffee, maintaining his poise. He was not about to lose control. He waited, sipping his coffee. He watched their aggravated eyes grow more frustrated. His lips curved upward, a soft change from his normal poker face. He enjoyed poking at the politicians.

Fleming returned with the bag. He removed the hat. There, with the checkered pattern on the dark blue material, the back side was missing, leaving shredded and torn cloth where it had been cut in half.

Morehead gasped and put her hands on her heart. "My god!"

Bain and MacGillivray's faces went white. MacGillivray's jaw dropped.

Bain pursed his lips. "Is this all ye found?" Bain said.

Fleming shook his head. "Na'. We're findin' a lot o' feathers."

"Feathers?" Morehead said, her hand still on her chest.

"Aye."

"Wha' do feathers have tae do with Nessie?" MacGillivray said, picking up the hat and examining it in his hand.

"We don' know," Fleming said.

O'Malley watched Fleming as he said his words. The more he watched him, he suspected the assistant police captain was holding something back. He'd have to ask him, later.

"It's the American," Morehead said. "He's behind this!"

O'Malley grimaced. As he was about to speak, Bain said, "I agree. We nee' tae question him."

"I've already done tha'," O'Malley said.

"Wha' did he say?" Bain said.

"I brought him here today. He did admit somethin'."

"Wha'?"

O'Malley measured his words. "He said he saw Nessie. Tha' he lied on his original statement, and tha' he saw th' creature." O'Malley expected a snide comment from one of the Council members, but as MacGillivray twisted Anderson's half-chewed hat in his hand not one of them went that route.

"Is tha' all?" Bain said.

"Na'. He said tha' he saw th' creature eat Alex Vaas."

MacGillivray pulled his eyes from the hat. Bain sat, unmoving. Morehead placed her hands back on the table, resuming her aggressive posture. "It ate him?"

"Tha's wha' he told me," O'Malley said.

"He saw it happen? He told ye this?"

"Aye," O'Malley said.

"But, he reported Vaas as drowned. Dead from th' fire."

"He did."

"So tha' wasn't true?"

"It wasn'."

Fleming appeared startled. This was news to the assistant police captain, but the way his eyes shifted told O'Malley that Fleming was trying to piece the information with what he was hiding.

Bain leaned back. "So, why didn' Mr. Wayne attempt tae warn us?"

"He had been through a lot," O'Malley said. "Remember, Sean Paterson left th' hospital today in a wheelchair, minus a leg, mind ye, and don' forge' tha' Briggs is in jail. Na only could he na' trust ye, he figured ye'd jus' call him doolally, anyway."

"But a man is dead," Morehead said, her posture coming forward, "and he jus' happens tae be our beloved police captain!"

"And a woman," Fleming said. "Though, I think 'tis safe tae say tha' Nessie didn' get Annabel."

"Tom Wayne was her only customer," MacGillivray said.

"Aye," Fleming said. "But I don' think th' lad could have done it."

"I think th' lad is cursed," Morehead said.

There was a pregnant pause.

"Where is he, anyway?" Bain said.

O'Malley sipped his coffee. "Don' know," O'Malley said.

"Wha' do ye mean ye don' know."

"Wha' I said. He was here, and he left."

"Ye jus' let him leave? Why didn' ye keep him here?"

"He's na' a suspect." O'Malley took the hat from MacGillivray and pointed to the missing half. "I donna' believe he did this. And wha' we saw at Annabel's was far more than anythin' one man could do."

O'Malley observed the eyes and the facial expressions of the Council members. He guessed they had met earlier, plotting ahead how they would handle their decision.

Bain said, "Very well. We'll issue a subpoena. Find Mr. Wayne. We nee' tae brin' him before Council. Th' people nee' tae know wha' danger they are in."

Fleming said, "We'll ge' right on it."

Logan O'Malley sipped the last of his coffee and swallowed. He set the cup down. "Wha' about Tom's danger? And th' Paterson's?"

"Wha' do ye mean?" Bain said.

"Who's goin' tae protect them?"

The Council members frowned. It was obvious they did not care about Tom's, Marella's, and Sean's safety.

"I mean, th' Thurwick Local Council didn' do a grea' job o' lettin' Mr. Paterson keep his leg, did it?"

"Detective O'Malley—" MacGillivray said, the circles under his eyes growing darker.

O'Malley raised his eyebrows.

"Very well," MacGillivray continued. "Fleming, assign one o' yer men tae keep watch o'er them."

"Will do, sir."

"In the meantime, go find Mr. Wayne. We will have some questions tae ask him."

"Send me th' subpoena foremost, then I'll brin' him tae ye."

The Council members flashed their eyes, not happy with O'Malley's response.

"We do have tae follow th' law," Fleming added.

O'Malley was pleased Fleming came to his aid.

Bain stood. "Very well. Ye'll have it on th' morrow."

O'Malley stood and offered his hand. "Happy tae oblige ye, Mr. Councilman."

MacGillivray and Morehead stood as well, and they left the room.

O'Malley sat back down. "Shu' th' door, will ye?"

Fleming stood up. "I have tae go."

"I have some questions fur ye."

"I canno' do it now," Fleming said.

"Where are ye goin'?"

"I have tae find Emily Anderson. She's missin'." Fleming's large frame left the room, and he shut the door behind him. The blinds shook against the glass window.

Logan O'Malley remained sitting. He raised his coffee cup an inch off the table, and then set it down hard. "Damn," he said.

CHAPTER 26

Fleming drove his car down the dark cobblestone streets of Thurwick, making a left past the coffee shop and through the streets until they came to the residential homes that housed many of Thurwick's middle class. The rain fell through the headlights, making the shadows dance between the houses.

He held his cell phone to his ear, listening as it rang. His wife's voice answered. "Where are ye?"

"I'm sorry, Sharon. I have some emergencies today."

"Did ye find Anderson?"

"Na'," he said. "And Emily is missin', tae."

"Oh?"

"Aye."

He pulled up the stone driveway that led to Emily Anderson's house. With the rain falling upon the roof, the house was dark. There was no car in the driveway.

"Did she go tae find him?" Sharon said.

"I think so, bu' she said she'd be home a' sunset and she hadn' come back."

"I don' like th' sound o' this."

"It gets worse," Fleming said. "Annabel's dead."

"Th' sweet ol' lady a' th' bed and breakfast?"

"Aye," Fleming said.

"Wha's goin' on," Sharon said.

"I don' know. . . Somethin' strange."

"Maybe ye shouldn' look fur her alone."

Fleming pressed his lips together. "I have a strange question. Have ye heard music lately?"

"Music?"

"Well, singing. Have ye heard a woman sing in th' distance?"

"Na. Have ye?"

"Aye." Fleming rubbed his hair with his large hand.

"Ian," Sharon said. "Are ye alright?"

Fleming paused.

"Ian?"

"Aye. I'm okay."

"Maybe ye should come home?"

"I canno'. I'm sorry. I have tae go."

"Ian, get help. Don' do it alone."

"I'll be alright."

"Ian–."

"I'll call ye later." Fleming hung up. He had to find Emily. He climbed out of his car, leaving the motor running and the windshield wipers swaying back and forth. The rain reflected the headlights as it fell to the ground in front of the vehicle, and their drops were cold as they landed upon his hair and his shoulders. The singing echoed between the splattering of rain drops.

Shamus's meowing had grown louder behind the Anderson front door. "Poor cat," he said. "I'd feed him myself if I could ge' in."

The singing traveled through the rain. The rain fell upon his head and dripped down his wet hair, but he paid it no mind. Away from the house, to the north, somewhere, someone was singing. It was a woman's voice, beautiful and enchanting. He had to find her, and if he did he'd know what happened to Emily. Maybe even James Anderson, perchance.

He climbed back in his car, his large frame twisting to get comfortable in the driver seat. He shut the door. The singing did not travel through the cab, but Fleming focused his eyes where he imagined its origin. He pressed the gas pedal. The car pulled forward.

He drove along the narrow backroads around Thurwick's outskirts, passing the small homes and doorways of its local residents. The lights in the homes were out, save for two homes whose residents stayed up late. The time was almost midnight. Weariness wanted to overcome him, but his adrenaline kicked in as he pressed forward. He'd find the singer, and he'd find Emily Anderson. And when he did, he'd answer many of the Council's questions.

Wouldn't Sharon be happy when, after all this, he became the hero. He imagined a scene where he'd be called up by the Thurwick Council, and awarded a ceremony for acting heroically during a time of the town's distress. He pictured the Council giving him a pin in front of the residents with Sharon next to him, smiling.

He passed Thurwick, then he stopped. He opened the car door and stood outside, leaving the engine running. The rain was now a heavy mist, and it moistened the skin on his face. The singing traveled from beyond the headlights, somewhere in the misty darkness beyond the city and near the loch. Fleming returned to his car, shut the door, and drove forward. His car bounced upon the cobblestones until the road was dirt and mud. He drove slowly, his headlights reflecting the mist and the windshield wipers moving left and right in their rhythmic fashion, leaving streaks upon the glass that hindered Fleming's vision.

He drove until he was near the water. The mist covered the loch like a dark soup, the water reflecting no light like a black blanket laying over the landscape. He could not make out the green hills on the other side of the water. Everything was dark, like he had reached the River Styx at the entrance to Hades.

He stopped the car and climbed out.

A mysterious chill ran through him. The thick air filled his lungs.

The singing came from his right. He squinted through the headlights. Beyond their beams, in the shadows, he noticed a hint of light, a reflection that bounced off something metal. He reached into his car and turned off the engine, leaving the headlights on. He walked forward, his heavy shoes squishing in the mud.

What was the reflection? As he drew closer, its shape became more clear: a car. His steps quickened.

Was it...?

Yes, it was Emily's car. And beyond it, the singing grew louder.

He ran to the vehicle.

The car door was shut. He looked in the windows.

Emily was not her car. "Where's Emily?" he said.

Her car faced the loch, toward the singing.

Fleming turned on on his flashlight. He shined the light in front of him. He swung the beams left to right. The tall grass was wet with rain. Most of it was bent over from the weather, but there was a line of grass that was darker than the rest. It lay flat like someone trampled it underfoot.

It was a path. These had to be Emily's footsteps.

Fleming pointed the flashlight in the direction of the path. The footsteps went down a slope toward the loch and around a knoll.

The singing came from the same direction. The singing pulled at him, calling his heart to come to it.

Should he call for help? The path did not go far. It was a short way to the knoll, to the singing, and he'd find the answers.

He stepped forward, his large feet pressing down on the wet bent-over grass, leaving the cars behind. His flashlight swung left and right as he moved, searching for any more clues.

The singing grew more intense. Whoever had the voice was a few meters from where he stood. He stepped faster, taking longer strides, his boots sloshing through the wet grass. He reached the knoll. The singing was clear.

The woman had to be there. He went around the knoll.

There, sitting cross-legged on the grass, her back to him, was a pale woman, her long hair bleached white and draped down to the small of her back and over her shoulders. She was naked, her body leaning forward and her arms crossed in front of her. Her singing, though, was beautiful.

Vows are made
Inside th' church.
If one escapes
Th' other will search.

Th' pain caused by one
Means chaos will spread.
'Tis sacrifice atones
'Til many are dead.

"Emily?" Fleming said, doubting it was her but not trusting his sleep-deprived eyes and the effects of the weather.

Mourn all the souls
Every one shall drown.
When the moon is full
Ne'er more the town.

Fleming blinked.

The woman stopped singing. Her eyes were red with sadness.

Her eyes captivated him. They exuded anger and lust, torment and sadness.

He had never witnessed such emotion in a person's eyes.

Suddenly, she burst into a pile of feathers.

Fleming's mouth opened, and his hand trembled. The flashlight bounced as his nerves unsteadied his arm.

The feathers were black. First, they took the shape of the woman, but then they floated to the ground until a strange wind circled the area. The wet grass bounced and the feathers blew in a whirlwind in the misty air and scattered in all directions.

Then the wind stopped. The feathers floated to the ground.

There was an eerie silence. The mist clung to his face and his clothes.

A chill enveloped him. It penetrated his bones.

Fear spread throughout his body.

There was a splash behind him—something large.

He spun around. His flashlight reflected off a large black muscular mass. It was the last thing he saw before rows of teeth clamped down on his head, tore into his ribs, and latched onto his femur. He knew what happened to James and Emily before his body was ripped apart.

CHAPTER 27

L ogan O'Malley rolled onto his back. His cairn terrier, Digger, snored on the bed next to him. O'Malley rolled onto his side, his eyes were wide awake. He tried to sleep, but the previous day's events kept him awake.

What was going on in Thurwick? A few weeks ago, everyone was excited about all that had happened on the loch. Briggs's arrest, the yacht explosions, the funerals, Vaas's and Coffee's disappearances, and Sean Paterson's missing leg all contributed to the gossip.

Something further was happening. There were missing and dead people in town. And torn clothing, damaged homes, and God knows what else.

And what was with all the black feathers showing up at crime scenes? He didn't know. Thinking about them sent shivers down his body, yet he couldn't explain why.

His alarm clock glowed behind him, but he didn't want to roll over and check the time. In a few hours, he'd receive a subpoena for the Council to bring Tom Wayne to the chambers for questioning in a public forum. O'Malley didn't like that for the lad, but what could he do? He had stalled as best he could. Tom seemed like a decent fellow. And Marella was a good lass. Feisty at times, but that was because of her father's history, an understandable behavior considering his decades-long obsession with the Loch Ness monster.

Digger whined. He shook, rattling his collar.

"It's okay, lad," O'Malley said.

Digger circled three times before lying down again on the mattress. The dog huffed as boredom overtook him.

O'Malley rubbed Digger behind his ears, hoping it would help both him and the dog relax. He needed sleep. He closed his eyes, and tried counting sheep....

The phone rang.

Digger jumped to his feet. His ears pointed upward at the sound and the chance at adventure.

"A' this 'our?" O'Malley said. He sat on his bed.

The phone rang again.

Digger pawed at O'Malley on the mattress and wagged his tail.

O'Malley patted Digger's head. He stood and picked up the phone. "Hello?"

"Logan. It's Sharon."

O'Malley blinked. The alarm clock read 4:00 a.m. "Are ye alright?"

"I'm worried," she said. "Ian hasn' been home."

"He hasn'?"

"He called around midnight. Said he was lookin' fur Emily."

"Aye, he was doin' tha' when I last saw him."

"But there's somethin' else," she said. "He asked if I heard music."

"Music?"

"Aye. Do ye know wha' he was talkin' about?"

O'Malley didn't know. Was that the thing Fleming had in his thoughts while they met with the Council members? "Na', I don't."

"Logan, I'm scared. Somethin's happene' tae him."

"Na', Sharon. He's probably just ou' searchin' fur her. Tell ye what. I'm na' sleepin' anyway. I'll go find him."

"Will ye, please?"

"Aye," he said.

"Thank ye."

"I'm sure he's okay," O'Malley said. "I'll call ye once I find him."

Sharon thanked him again as he hung up the phone. Fleming was a big man, and he had done well in his training. O'Malley was ninety percent sure that Fleming was alright. It would take a monster to do him in, which he still hoped was a myth despite what Tom had said.

Digger jumped off the bed and stood in front of him, his one paw up, his tail wagging. The dog opened his mouth in a toothy grin.

O'Malley shook his head. "Alright, boy. Ye can come."

Digger barked, and he ran to the side door where he pranced and wagged his tail.

"Just a moment, lad," O'Malley said as he dressed, stepped into his shoes, and put his fedora upon his head. "Let me find th' keys."

O'Malley rotated the steering wheel. Digger panted and wagged his tail in the passenger seat as the car bounced upon the dirt road. "Where is he?" O'Malley said. He had driven to the boat dock parking lot, and he had sat there for a few minutes even though his vehicle was the only car in the parking lot. There were no signs of Fleming's or Emily Anderson's vehicles. Not to be discouraged, he turned the car around and drove east, following the shore road, if you could call it that, between Thurwick proper and Loch Ness. He navigated the cobblestones and fishing platforms in the dark, his headlights burning through the rising mist left over from the overnight rain.

Digger barked.

"Wha' do ye see, lad? Anythin'?" O'Malley squinted through the windshield, the wiper-blade streaks hampering his vision. There was nothing out of the ordinary.

Digger's tongue hung from his mouth. He panted next to him.

O'Malley said, "Yer goin' tae have tae help me, ye know."

Digger smiled and wagged his tail some more.

After the car passed over the Thurwick cobblestones, it wheeled onto mud and dirt. The town lights drew farther away in the rearview mirror. The grass was long, except that the rain and dew weighed down the blades. He went around a bend. His headlight caught sight of a faraway vehicle.

"Tha's strange," O'Malley said. He pulled forward.

Digger put his paws on the dashboard, his furry face glued to the windshield, his twenty-pound body stretched high over the floorboard as his hind paws pressed into the passenger seat. His tail wagged harder, his tongue panting with anticipation. His nose left little smear marks on the window.

The chequers of the paint on Fleming's car glistened under the moonlight. "It's him, alrigh'." O'Malley parked his car behind the vehicle. He grasped his flashlight and said to Digger, "Ye wait here."

Digger barked.

"Na', ye canno' come."

Digger stood on the passenger seat. The dog's eyes fell with disappointment at not being allowed to join him.

"I won' be long," O'Malley said, and he shut the door.

Digger jumped to the driver's side door and put his paws on the window, begging to join him. He barked, and the sound came muffled through the window.

"Hold tight," O'Malley said. He stepped toward the car. "Should've given him a pill before comin'." O'Malley went to Fleming's vehicle. As he approached, he noticed a reflection in the distance from his flashlight. Was it a second car?

With a quick scan of the flashlight beam, he confirmed Fleming's vehicle sat empty. He thought of shouting for him, but being a detective he liked to sneak around unannounced. It was always better to examine the environment before those in it were aware of his presence. That way he'd investigate what was happening.

He moved past the police car to the reflection. His light shined in the shadows as the first hint of morning transformed the eastern horizon. The reflection had come from a bumper. It was another car. Was it Emily Anderson's?

He moved through the grass, his feet pressing into the mud. He was alone out here, or was he? He couldn't say for sure.

He shined his light in the grass. Several blades had been pressed into the mud ahead of him. No doubt they had to be Fleming's tracks. O'Malley would know those large feet anywhere. The tracks advanced to the other car.

O'Malley followed. When he reached the other car, he pressed his thumb onto the rear side of the trunk, a trick he learned to leave his thumbprint in case something happened to him and detectives needed to find fingerprints. He shined his light in the car. It was empty, like Fleming's.

He scanned the ground. Fleming's tracks went off ahead. They appeared to be following another set of tracks. The pressed blades were not as wide and not as crushed into the ground. He deduced they were either made by a child - or a woman.

His gut told him they were Emily's tracks.

O'Malley waited. The distant horizon stretched in a line of orange. A chill blew at him from the water, and he shivered. He scanned the area again. He admitted he didn't like being alone out here. He wasn't happy being near water, and searching for two missing people added to his rapidly beating heart. He forced his legs to inch forward, each step like his feet had filled with lead. He followed the flashlight beam as it lighted the tracks ahead.

He came to a knoll, a small hill near the Loch Ness water's edge. Both sets of tracks rounded the narrow bend three meters from the loch's shore and went behind the knoll. O'Malley squatted lower and studied the tracks. From where he was, both sets of tracks left prints with longer strides, a sign that whoever made them hurried their pace from this point. What made them hurry? It had to be one of two things; either they were chased here or they found something and ran to it.

O'Malley shined his light around and behind him. There was no sign of a third set of tracks in the grass. Being chased was out of the question.

There was a splash.

O'Malley lifted his eyes to the loch. The dark water made him nervous. Was something in there? Did something come from the water, and that made them hurry their steps?

O'Malley studied the tracks. Though the paces were more distant here than at the cars, they weren't far enough apart to indicate a threat that made them run. No, there was an urgency that implied discovery, not panic. They found something on the other side of the knoll.

O'Malley imagined Digger waiting for him in the car. He had to keep going. He faced the knoll and studied the tracks that went around the bend. The waves from the loch splashed against the rocks of the shore. He'd have to move past the water to view what was behind the knoll. "Okay, Fleming," he said. "What'd ye find?"

He stepped between the water and the knoll. His eyes grew wide.

The scene had changed before him. Trampled grass blades twisted in haphazard directions. The grass was covered in a bright red coating that spread across the mud and the grass.

It was a kill site. O'Malley covered his mouth, waiting for the shock of the scene to dissipate. After a few moments, he lifted his head and shined the light.

Fleming and Emily were nowhere to be found.

A black feather rested upon a grass blade. Once his eye caught the first one, he noticed another...and another...and another. Black feathers were everywhere.

The chill returned. Something splashed in the loch, this one bigger than before.

Digger's bark came from his parked car at the top of the hill. It was muffled under the sound of waves on the shore.

O'Malley pointed his flashlight at the dark water of Loch Ness. Something large and black breached the water, but it was gone in an instant. He tried to tell himself his imagination was playing tricks on him, but then he remembered James Anderson's half-eaten police cap. He pictured something coming at him from the water. His knees trembled.

Digger barked again.

O'Malley didn't wait. He ran over the wet grass as best as his old legs carried him. The beam of his flashlight jumped in all directions.

Another large splash echoed behind him. Was it a fish, or something worse? He didn't want to wait to find out. The thought of whatever happened to Ian Fleming and Emily Anderson and James Anderson and Annabel ran through his head. He hurried up the hill.

He passed Emily's car, then Fleming's police cruiser. His vehicle was a few steps away. Digger was barking over and over. O'Malley tried to control his breathing so he could hear if a threat came at him from behind, but the barking only made things worse.

He grabbed the door handle to his car.

Digger barked again.

When O'Malley opened the door, Digger tried to run past him to get outside, but O'Malley blocked his way and he forced the dog back inside. Then O'Malley threw himself down into the driver's seat.

Before he jerked the door, a strange sound hit his ears. It sounded like a woman. She was singing.

He didn't wait to hear more. He yanked the handle and slammed the door. "We're goin' back, lad!" O'Malley shouted. He fumbled the keys.

Digger barked at the windshield.

O'Malley found the key and forced it into the ignition. He turned the key.

Digger barked two times, no longer excited but defensive.

O'Malley put the car in reverse and stepped on the gas. The car retreated several meters until he spun the steering wheel and he whipped the vehicle around. Then he threw the gearshift in drive and he sped back to the town of Thurwick as Digger barked.

CHAPTER 28

Tom Wayne's eyes opened. The morning light came through the window. He rubbed his eyes, trying to remember what he had dreamed. Had a woman peered at him from outside the window? Her face was pale, her hair was white, and her eyes were red from tears.

Tom stood and went to the window.

There was no woman.

Through the glass, the loch reflected the light from the morning sun. The green hills of the Scottish Highlands rose above the far side of the loch. Out there, in the water, the monsters swam. Out there, he had been on Coffee's yacht, and out there he had survived Chairman Brigg's and Alex Vaas's scheme to eliminate him and keep the monster for themselves.

A gray mist hung over the cool water. The room Tom was in was two stories above the ground. There was no way a woman would be able to peer inside the window without a tall ladder. It had to have been a strange dream, his subconscious trying to work things out in his head after the day he had had.

Tom studied the office. There was the small refrigerator where Father Gibson kept his wine. A bible was open on the ledge of the bookshelf. The globe that sat on the desk was still where the priest had left it. And a Far Side cartoon was taped on the opposite side of the desk, no doubt Father Gibson's attempt to remain humorous despite the difficulties of the priestly vocation.

He pulled Father Gibson's note from his pocket and read it a second time. The note said that he, Marella, and Sean were in great danger and should leave Thurwick and go to London.

London? Why London?

Tom had to know more. He went to the desk and picked up the phone. Holding Father Gibson's note in his hand, he dialed the number.

The phone rang. Tom leaned against the desk, waiting for someone to pick up on the other end of the line. He watched through the window as the morning light grew stronger.

While he held the phone, his eyes moved to the wall on the other side of the room. There was a large bookshelf. Tom had never observed the other side of the office as he had never been on this side of the desk. The bookshelf contained hundreds of books, each of them containing titles regarding religion, philosophy, psychology, politics, and family dynamics. A thin crucifix hung beside the bookshelf above a picture of Mary surrounded by angels. To the left of the bookshelf was an image of Jesus walking along a path with two men.

There was a picture above that, though, that seemed out of place. It was a painting that Tom hadn't noticed before.

The phone continued to ring, but the painting drew his attention. He lowered the phone, studying the picture. It was a painting of a man, middle-aged, perhaps. He had a gray beard and heavy clothes. His eyes were deep blue, and around his weathered neck hung a brown rope and a wooden cross.

The eyes in the portrait appeared as blue and as mysterious as the waters of Loch Ness. Who was he?

He rubbed his eyes and shook his head.

A faint voice came from the desk. Tom jumped.

"Hello?" said the voice.

It was the phone. Tom picked it up. "Hello, Father Gibson?"

"Just a moment," said the voice.

Tom studied the man's eyes in the painting. He didn't know who the man was, probably someone from the past, some religious figure in the Highland past.

"Aye, Tom?"

"Father Gibson," Tom said. "Am I glad to hear your voice. I've got to tell you—."

"Have ye made it tae London?"

"No," Tom said. "I found your note last night."

"Wha' are ye still doin' there?" the priest interrupted. "Didn' ye read my note? Ye've go' tae leave Thurwick right away. Get as far away as ye can. Take Sean and Marella wi' ye. Come tae London. Ye'll be safe here."

"Annabel's dead," Tom said.

There was silence on the other end.

"Did you hear me, Father?"

"Aye," Father Gibson said. "How?"

"I don't know. The place was trashed, and there were claw marks all over the walls. She was thrown from the upstairs window. I won't tell you what condition she was in."

160

"So, 'tis begun."

"What's begun?" Tom said.

"Lad. There's na time. Ye've go' tae get out of there. Get away from th' loch."

Tom ran his fingers through his hair. "Why? What's happening?"

"There's a curse upon th' town."

Tom studied the portrait of the bearded man on the back wall. "What kind of curse?"

"A bad one," Father Gibson said.

Through the door, a commanding voice came from the rectory hallway. "He's in one of these rooms. Check in there!" There was a crash.

Tom shuddered.

"Empty!" said another voice.

"Someone's in the rectory," Tom said, his voice hushed.

"Ye've go' tae escape. They won' be able tae protect ye."

Another crash echoed in the hallway. It was louder, closer. It sounded like a door being kicked open. "Empty!"

"He's in one o' these rooms. Keep lookin'!"

"They're coming," Tom whispered. He lowered himself behind the desk.

"Hide!" Father Gibson said.

"I'll call back." Tom hung the phone up. He held the note in his hand. Should he keep it? He needed Father Gibson's number, but what if they caught him, and found the number? Or threw the note away? He had to think. He ducked his head behind the desk.

The sound of a boot breaking wood opened the door one room away. "Empty!" shouted a voice. They were right there.

Sweat beaded upon his brow. He searched his pockets in his coat, anything that might be a weapon. In a second, they'd be upon him. He slid the note under the bookshelf near the window wall, under the small statue of Saint Michael. "I could use your help right about now," Tom whispered. He lifted his head. He grabbed the paperweight. Maybe he'd catch them by surprise and escape. What were his options? If they captured him, he'd have to let Marella know to get Father Gibson's phone number from under the bookshelf. That is if she'd even talk with him.

Then the door to the office burst open, and shards of wood flung across the room and landed near the far wall.

"It's the office!" said a loud voice.

Tom flinched, his back pressed against the desk. He squeezed his grip on the paperweight. He wished he had a better place to hide.

"Check inside!" said another voice. The footsteps were upon him, and a policeman carrying a black baton stood next to him, blocking his view of the portrait of the man on the back wall.

"Found him!" said the officer.

Two policemen rushed through the office and surrounded him. The first officer, a freckled red-haired man in his twenties, grabbed Tom by his coat and jerked him to his feet. Tom swung the paperweight at the officer and smacked him across the jaw.

The officer fell backward.

Tom leaned back to swing again, but the freckled officer grabbed his arm. Then the officer slammed Tom's torso upon Father Gibson's desk, knocking over the small globe and the phone receiver. He cuffed Tom's hands behind his back.

"The bloody lad knocked a tooth loose!" said the freckled officer. He swung his baton and smacked Tom in the hamstring.

Tom yelled and fell to his knees, his jaw knocking upon the edge of Father Gibson's desk.

"Ye've caused enough trouble around here," the officer said.

Tom raised his eyes. He had not seen the freckled red-haired officer before, but the other he had. It was O'Reilly, the police officer who was with Tom and Detective O'Malley when they were in Annabel's house. "What'd I do?"

"Ye'll tell us a' th' station!" The freckled officer said, "It's time we take care o' this troublemaker."

"Na' until th' Council has had their say," O'Reilly said.

They grabbed Tom by his coat collar. Tom glanced one more time at the man in the portrait, his blue eyes unmoving as the freckled red-haired officer jerked Tom away from the desk and across the room.

"Come on," O'Reilly said. He marched out the broken doorway and went down the hall.

The freckled officer shoved Tom. "Follow him."

They passed the broken door and went into the hallway, the officer pressing Tom by several shattered doors until they came to the side door of the main church. The pews and the walls of the church were undamaged in the shadows of the morning light, but Tom was pushed to the rear. The solid wood doors had been broken down with an axe. Shards of wood from the ancient doors spread across the floor. Father Gibson wouldn't like that, he thought. They forced him down the steps where he stumbled but the freckled officer jerked him back to his feet.

Several police cars surrounded him, their lights flashing. Two news trucks were parked behind them. Reporters and cameramen watched as the police forced him to one of their cruisers.

Across the road, Annabel's was also a hub of activity, with multiple cars and flashing lights disturbing the morning.

"I didn't do anything," Tom said.

"Enough!" said his handler, who shoved his head down into the rear of the police cruiser. Tom pulled his feet inside before the officer slammed the door. He laughed as the door shut. Through the window, O'Reilly gave the freckled red-haired officer commands.

With his hands cuffed, Tom straightened himself and watched the commotion. Everyone was staring at him.

The freckled red-haired officer climbed into the front driver seat. "Ye'll have some explainin' tae do," he said, his eyes boring into Tom.

"Tell me what I did!" Tom said.

"Ye know what ye did."

Officer O'Reilly climbed into the passenger seat. His head was down as he wrote on a form, documenting the arrest. "Alrigh', Burns. Let's go," he said.

"Aye," Officer Burns said. He turned the ignition and the car engine rumbled.

Tom shook his head. He remembered what Father Gibson had said, that the police would not be able to protect him, yet Tom doubted that they'd even want to.

The car pulled forward. The heads outside watched him as the police car drove him away from the church into downtown Thurwick.

164

CHAPTER 29

"Put him in cell number two!" O'Reilly said.

Officer Burns shoved Tom through the office.

Felicia and Sandra looked up from their computers. Neither smiled.

Burns pushed Tom into the cell. The faces of the wanted posters on the walls appeared to jeer at him. The lips of the Loch Ness monster on the painting on the far wall smacked in anticipation of the creature making him into a meal. Tom was still handcuffed as Burns slammed the cell door. He glared at Tom while rubbing his jaw.

"Don't I get a phone call?" Tom said.

"Ye'll get somethin, alright!" Burns said. He rapped his baton against his open palm.

O'Reilly said, "He stays there 'til th' meetin'. Bain told me they're goin' tae move it up after th' news about Fleming."

What happened to Fleming? Tom flexed his wrists, hoping to free his arms. The cuffs wouldn't budge.

Burns leaned close to Tom's cell. He lifted his baton and slammed it against the iron bars. The impact reverberated a metallic clang that echoed inside the police station. "Ye have it in fur us, don' ye? Well, I'll make sure ye don' get another one!"

Tom stepped back. "I don't know what you're talking about."

"Burns!" O'Reilly said. He stood at the door to the small office. "There'll be time fur tha' later. Come in here."

Burns snarled at Tom. He pointed to his swollen jaw. "I'll remember this. Better hope I don' find ye alone."

Tom blinked.

Burns stiffened his jaw and he went into the small office and shut the door.

Felicia Morgan raised her eyes from her computer and frowned at Tom. She shook her head, then she resumed typing.

"What's all this about?" Tom said.

Felicia and Sandra continued typing, pretending not to hear him.

Shouting came from inside the office. O'Reilly and Burns were yelling, but Tom wasn't sure if it was at each other or out of frustration. Through the shades, it appeared that Burns raised his arms above his head. Tom tried to make out the conversation, but their voices were muffled. Fleming's name was mentioned, and something about the loch.

The two women typed. Neither appeared happy. Quite the opposite. Both seemed nervous.

Tom pulled his wrists again, but they were held together by the cuffs. There was no way he'd get free of them without assistance. The cell door was locked. No keys were lying near.

Across the room, the image of the Loch Ness monster mocked him from the far wall.

He had to get help, to warn Sean and Marella. Something had changed since last night. But what? Was it Annabel? Was it that he had found her first and they suspected him of foul play? Was it that he had lied about how he had seen the Loch Ness monster and he had failed to warn them? Did the Council decide they wanted revenge for Anderson's disappearance? Should he have alerted the town? But why? Briggs, Thurwick's Chair of the town Council, had tried to kill him. Tom didn't owe anything to Thurwick's Council.

The front door opened. The outside morning sunlight cast a silhouette of a man in a suit as he stepped through the station door. As the man stepped further into the room, Tom recognized him.

It was Councilman Mark Bain.

Bain glared at Tom, then marched past Felicia and Sandra. He said hello to them, then he went into the small office with Officers O'Reilly and Burns. So, the Council was behind his arrest. "Figures," Tom said.

Another man entered the station. Logan O'Malley. He took his fedora off his gray hair and held it to his chest. His eyes were red.

Tom rushed to the cell door and pressed his face to the iron bars. "Logan. You've got to get me out of here!"

O'Malley stepped toward Tom's cell. "Can't help ye, lad. Na th' now, anyway."

"Why am I here?"

"Best we not talk." O'Malley motioned toward the small conference room.

"Wait. Can't you at least take these off?" Tom circled and pointed at the cuffs with his index finger.

"I'm tryin', lad," O'Malley said. He lowered his eyes and walked to the small conference room, where he opened the door, went inside, and shut the door.

"Won't anybody tell me what's going on here?"

Felicia raised her eyes. She said, "Be glad yer still alive. I thought they'd 've killed ye when they found ye. Lucky ye were in th' church. Tha's why they didn', if ye ask me." She huffed, and then went back to her typing.

"I don't understand."

The women ignored him.

"Don't I get a phone call, or a lawyer, or something?"

Felicia and Sandra continued typing.

"Unbelievable," Tom said. He stepped to the rear stone wall and sat on the small cot. His wrists ached behind his back.

The Loch Ness monster image loomed on the wall. There was danger growing, and he had to get out to protect Marella, but he was locked in the police station and he didn't know why.

He told himself to think of a plan, some way to escape. Father Gibson's advice seemed better with each passing moment. He should find Sean and Marella, and the three of them should go to London where they could get away for a while. They'd be ignored, lost in the big city, where the self-absorbed would pay them no attention.

The station door opened, and an attractive female figure blocked the sunlight. Tom stood. "Marella!" he said.

The door shut, and the artificial light revealed the woman.

Tom sat back down.

It wasn't Marella. It was Liz Stevens.

She walked past Felicia and Sandra toward Tom.

"Forget it," Tom said.

"You're trying to avoid our appointment," Liz said in her British accent.

She wore a white blouse, skirt, and high heels. A red coat was draped over her shoulders. Her lipstick was red. Her hair was loose and waved over her shoulders.

"It's your fault I'm in here," Tom said.

"Mine? Oh, Tom. I didn't know the police would want you first."

Tom looked away.

"Imagine my surprise when I got up early to visit Saint Michaels and prepare some paragraphs for my article, only to see the police break down the front doors and haul you out in handcuffs."

"Yeah, I bet your editor is going to love that," he said.

Liz shrugged. She grabbed a chair and slid it outside the cell door. She pulled out a notepad and pen. "Okay. Can you tell me why you're here?"

Tom leaned forward. The old cot bent under his shifting weight. "That's just it. I don't know."

"You don't"

"No. No one will tell me."

The voices raised inside the small conference room.

"Miss," Felicia said. "Please step away from th' cell."

Stevens stood. "Okay." She approached Felicia. "Do you think he did it?"

"Did what?" Tom said.

Felicia stopped typing. "And who are ye?"

"Liz Stevens. The London Adventure magazine." She stuck out her hand.

Felicia did not reciprocate. "Best ye go tae Dorlan Hall," the woman said. "The Council be meetin' there in half an hour. Ye'll get yer questions answered then."

Stevens put her hand back in her coat pocket. "Town meeting?"

"Aye."

"It's public?"

"Aye. 'Tis."

"Will someone tell me what the hell is going on!" Tom shouted. His shoulders ached from the handcuffs.

Stevens approached Tom. "You don't have many friends here. You might want to be nice to me. I may be the only friend you have."

The conference room door swung open. "The handcuffs stay!" Councilman Bain said.

"'Tis wrong," O'Malley said.

"Ye heard him," O'Reilly said.

Burns left the room, grinning at the decision.

Liz Stevens winked at Tom and smiled. "See you soon." She marched away from his cell and exited the door.

Burns approached Tom. He flexed his jaw. Then he rapped his baton against the iron. "I'm jus' countin' th' minutes," he said.

"Burns," O'Reilly said. "Keep him in one piece. Grab th' prisoner. We're takin' him now."

Burns grinned. He glared at Tom and rubbed his jaw, then he unlocked the iron cell door and swung it open. He slapped his baton against his open hand. "I should finish this."

Tom stepped back and braced for Burns to swing the baton at him.

"Burns. Now!" said O'Reilly. "No injuries yet. We don' want th' Council tae ask us questions."

Burns grimaced. "Alrigh'." He grabbed Tom's coat collar and jerked him forward.

"Where are we going?" Tom said.

"Dorlan Hall. There's a mob there tha' wants ye."

Burns shoved Tom past Felicia, through the station, and out the police station's open door.

Across the cobblestone square, several dozen people had gathered, shouting and waving their fists. A woman yelled, "There he is!". They pointed at Tom and rushed in his direction.

Burns laughed. "Should I feed ye tae th' sharks, laddie?"

The crowd marched at Tom. Officer O'Reilly stepped forward and held his baton in front of his body - a small effort at crowd control.

Burns jerked Tom forward. "Na goin' back now. Time fur ye tae do some explainin'" Burns tugged Tom forward toward the oncoming angry mob.

Tom pulled on his handcuffs, not knowing how he was going to get through this day in one piece.

CHAPTER 30

"He's cursed!" a woman shouted.

Burns yanked Tom through the crowd.

A red-faced man leaped forward, his fists in the air. O'Reilly shoved him. "Move aside!"

"Stone him!" said a woman.

Another man rushed past O'Reilly and Burns and punched Tom in the ribs. Tom's legs buckled as he lost his breath. O'Reilly lifted his baton, swinging as the man retreated into the crowd. "There'll be none o' tha'!"

Burns pulled Tom back up. "Ye stay here, and they'll finish ye off. I want tae have my turn foremost!"

Tom gathered his legs as a woman spat at him. "He's nothin' bu' trouble!"

"How many have tae die because o' him!"

"Move back!" O'Reilly said. He held out his baton, and the crowd backed up, leaving some space between Tom and the mob. Tom wobbled forward on the cobblestones. Dorlan Hall stood a few paces away.

Burns jerked Tom's coat. Tom gathered his legs and stumbled forward over the steps, ducking as a rock flew past his head.

O'Reilly threw the Dorlan Hall doors open. Burns pulled Tom inside. Tom tripped on the uneven floor.

The crowd swarmed toward the entrance, but O'Reilly pulled the doors closed and locked them. The mob's angry voices were muffled through the solid oak. Fists pounded on the doors, and their beating echoed inside the hallway.

As he worked to catch his breath and recover from his bruised ribs, Tom recognized his surroundings. Small statues of dignitaries and portraits of former politicians adorned the old stone walls. The familiar dusty odor filled the air. A suit of armor stood like a knight against the wall near the chamber entrance.

"Alrigh'. In ye' go!" Burns pulled Tom into the chamber. The rows of benches sat on either side of a stone aisle that led to a podium and a dais where the local Council held its meetings. Gray stone walls surrounded them, a constant reminder of the centuries of history in the town of Thurwick.

Tom's shoulders and wrists ached from the cuffs that locked his arms behind his back. "Can you take these off?" he said.

"'Yer keeping them on," O'Reilly said. "'Tis been decided."

"Wha' do we do about th' crowd?" said Burns.

"Tis a public meetin'," O'Reilly said. "They'll have tae come in." He checked the other doors. They were locked except for the side door where the Council members would enter.

"Where's O'Malley? Where's Fleming?" Tom said.

"Don' play games wi' me," Burns said, his freckled face shading redder with anger. He grabbed Tom's coat collar and pulled him down. Tom sat hard on the front wooden bench. "Stay there!"

"I don't understand!" Tom said. "Will somebody please tell me what is going on?"

O'Reilly shouted from the back of the room. "Stand with th' prisoner. I'll let them in."

Burns grinned from ear to ear. "Yer like a minnow in a shark tank. Who'll get ye foremost? Them.... o' me?"

The back door opened and loud murmurs and heavy feet entered as the citizens of Thurwick poured into the room. The crowd swarmed in and filed among the pews, taking their seats. Some stood along the stone walls, gathering in small groups where they discussed the events in raised voices, their conversations interrupted by the occasional emotional outburst.

"He's a curse!" shouted a woman. "Burn him!"

O'Reilly stood at the front of the aisle facing the crowd. He pulled out his baton. "We'll have order here durin' this meetin'. After, we'll do wi' th' prisoner whate'er th' Council decides."

The crowd lowered their voices. Their angry murmurs echoed in the chamber.

The side door opened. Councilman Bain entered the chamber. He strode to his seat and sat in the dais chair, the chair that Briggs once occupied. He relished his sudden rise to power.

Councilwomen Harris and Morehead sat in the seats surrounding Bain. MacGillivray and McCollough entered the side door.

Another man and woman walked behind the dais and sat down. They were members of the Council that Tom had forgotten from last time. The man sat down. The nameplate before him said,

"Thomson". Where the woman sat had a nameplate that said, "Brown".

One seat remained empty, a symbol of Chairman Brigg's departure after his arrest. The seven-member Council shifted in their seats as they readied themselves for the meeting.

Tom bent forward on the bench, trying to free his wrists. The metal cuffs dug into his skin.

The crowd's voices filled the air.

Bain banged the gavel. "I call this meetin' tae order."

A hush fell upon the room. Many people found seats. Others leaned against the cold walls and folded their arms. As Tom shifted, their eyes told him none would be satisfied unless he was sentenced and punished for the deaths of their neighbors. Tom didn't have a friend in the room.

Bain continued, "On th' agenda is th' questionin' o' th' American, Tom Wayne, regardin' his statements tae th' police."

Tom noticed Bain was not reading from any paper but was speaking off the cuff. This meeting was far less formal than the one Tom attended several weeks ago.

"If th' officer would please brin' Mr. Wayne forward."

Burns rose and grabbed Tom's collar, but Tom shifted his shoulders and pulled his coat collar from Burns's grip. "I can stand on my own," Tom said.

Burns clenched his jaw.

Tom stepped past him to the podium. His hands remained behind his back. His coat was wrinkled. His hair was uncombed. His stubble of beard darkened his face. He hadn't showered. He knew he looked a sight. Bain must have planned it this way so he'd appear less human, making a harsher sentence an easier vote among the Council.

He scanned the faces in the crowd. Marella and Sean were absent. To his right, Liz Stevens sat on the front bench in her white dress and red lipstick. Her press badge hung from a lanyard around her neck. A notepad was in her lap and she held onto a pen. Her eyes, with her dark lashes, blinked with lust for getting her story.

Or was it something else?

Tom shook his head, and his shoulders dropped.

Then the back door opened. The crowd muttered as people spoke in surprised voices. Sean entered the doorway in a wheelchair, and Marella pushed him forward. Sean swung his cane back and forth. "Begone from m' way," Sean said. Marella grimaced as she pushed her father through the people. The crowd backed away from them as they found a spot along the side wall.

Tom grinned. He took one step up the aisle toward them.

Burns grabbed Tom with a fistful of his coat. "Na ye don'," and forced Tom back to the podium.

Sean rested his cane on his lap.

Marella shook her head, despair growing upon her face.

It made Tom's heart sink. The last thing he wanted was for her to worry. Yet, here he was, handcuffed and brought before an anxious mob. If he made it out of here, he would grab her and they'd get out of Thurwick as soon as he put the keys in the ignition. If only he could find a way to get free.

CHAPTER 31

"Mr. Wayne," Bain said. "We have some questions fur ye."

"Burn him!" shouted the same gray-haired woman near the front row. Several individuals shouted "Aye!" and clapped at her suggestion.

One man said, "I have an old wagon aroun' th' bend. Load it up wi' hay, and we can have ourselves a bonfire!"

Tom shuddered at the thought of being tied, quartered, thrust upon a haystack, his arms roped to a post, and him standing helpless as flames and smoke burned his flesh from his bones. No, he didn't like the idea. He had to escape.

Bain hammered his gavel. "Enough!" "We will have order durin' this meetin'. I know wha' yer lookin' fur, but we have a process, and we will follow it." He pointed at O'Reilly. "Any more outbursts and ye can throw them out' o' here."

O'Reilly stepped from his place and positioned himself near Tom, trying to appear imposing.

Burns huffed, irritated that the Council would delay the inevitable.

Tom's knees wobbled at the uneasiness in the room. The crowd's vengeance toward him was rising and the Thurwick authorities gave little indication they wouldn't satisfy it. Tom tried to think. He was an outsider, which made him an easy scapegoat for any ills the community experienced.

"Now. Mr. Wayne," Bain said. He leaned forward in his chair, and his eyes narrowed. "Can ye tell us why people are disappearin'?"

Tom searched his thoughts for the right words. He wasn't sure what to say. He hadn't been read his rights. He was being accused of something he didn't do, and he was forced to testify about something he didn't understand. He was tired, and his body ached. The pressure of the room closed in on him.

The rear doors swung open, and a sobbing woman entered with the help of two men.

Hearing the people murmur and shift in their seats, Tom ignored Bain's question. The woman, in her mid-forties, wore her brown curly hair down. She lowered her handkerchief and pointed at Tom. "There he is. He's th' one tha' killed my husband!"

Marella's eyes widened and her jaw dropped.

"I didn't do it," he mouthed.

Marella shook her head before she buried her face in her palms.

Tom leaned to the microphone, his wrists still cuffed behind his back. "I didn't kill anyone."

"Liar!" said one of the men who helped the sobbing woman into the room.

Bain leaned into his microphone. "Now, Sharon. I promise we'll ge' tae th' bottom o' this."

Sharon took comfort in an outcome that was already decided. They just had to go through the formalities. She blotted her eyes with the handkerchief and she sat in the far pew. She sobbed again.

The eyes in the room bore into Tom. "I didn't kill anyone," he said again.

"Mr. Wayne," Bain said. "We have testimony tha' ye lied under oath on yer statement tae th' authorities."

Tom remembered O'Malley's yellow notepad. The detective must have told them. Whatever influence O'Malley had in the police department appeared to have waned.

"There's concern among th' public tha' th' people are in danger, and tha' ye have somethin' tae do with it," Bain said. He leaned forward. His brow furrowed. "We want tae know wha' ye know abou' the disappearances of Police Captain James Anderson, his wife Emily Anderson, Assistant Police Captain Ian Fleming, and th' death of Annabel Donner."

Fleming is gone, too? Tom thought. And Anderson's wife? Four people either dead or missing in the last two days? Tom bit his lip. The people were mad. They were scared. And they wanted to take it out on him.

Bain continued, "We also have reason tae believe ye had somethin' tae do with th' deaths of Ewan Coffee and Alex Vaas."

"What!" Tom said, shocked at the implication. "*They* tried to kill *me*!"

The crowd's voices rose in the room. Bain hammered the gavel, trying to restore order, but the crowd ignored him.

Tom remembered Father Gibson's warning - leave Thurwick right away. He wished he hadn't fallen asleep in the rectory office. If he had left the church, warned Sean and Marella, and driven with them out of Thurwick–.

The rear door burst open. All the room's eyes shifted to the man who had entered with such force. A tall skinny man in a silver suit marched into the room, his black hair puffed out, his face unshaven. Tom had never seen the man before.

Detective Logan O'Malley followed the man through the rear door. He tipped his fedora at Tom, then he went to the side of the room and stood behind Marella and Sean.

The man in the suit walked down the aisle, his face like a boxer about to step into a ring. He raised his hand. "Stop this meetin'!" the man said, his voice confident and insistent.

"Ye canno' interrupt this meetin'," Bain said. "Officers, please remove Mr. Stewart."

Tom paused, trying to place the name. Where had he heard the name "Stewart"?

O'Reilly and Burns stood and approached the man.

"I am Mr. Wayne's attorney. Jacob Stewart. Ye have arrested this man, Tom Wayne, a visitor from America, without jus' cause o' due process."

Tom remembered the note in his coat pocket. That was it. The attorney! O'Malley had referred Tom to Stewart.

"Has Mr. Wayne signed an agreement with ye, Mr. Stewart?"

Stewart strode up to the podium next to Tom and leaned into the microphone. "Ye didn' give Mr. Wayne th' chance, Councilman Bain."

"He's na a British citizen," Bain said.

"He refused th' right tae an attorney," Burns said. The policeman glared at Stewart, angry that his revenge was threatened.

"Did he now?" Stewart said. "Why don' we ask Mr. Wayne if that's true?"

Burns pursed his lips. O'Reilly stood ready, waiting for orders from the Council.

Stewart lifted a paper in his hand. "I also have sworn testimony from a witness that Mr. Wayne ne'er was given th' chance tae make a phone call."

Bain leaned his head back. He glanced at the other Council members. Who was the witness? If it wasn't O'Malley himself, it had to have been Felicia or Sandra, one of the two women typists in the police station.

"We have na time fur this," Councilman Bain said. "Officers, please show Mr. Stewart tae th' door."

O'Reilly went to Stewart to remove him, but Stewart lifted his arms. "I'll have ye know tha' th' Highland Council, th' American Embassy, and th' British parliament have all been made aware o' yer handlin' o' Mr. Wayne. Each entity is very concerned about yer procedures fur havin' this meetin'."

The Council members raised their eyebrows and glanced at one another.

"He's killin' people," said the gray-haired woman in the front row.

"My husband is dead!" Sharon sobbed. She blotted her eyes with her handkerchief. The man sitting next to her put his arms over her shoulder to comfort her. Tom suspected the man was her son or younger brother by their resemblance.

Tom shrugged at Marella. Doubts rose inside him that he may not escape the situation. If only he could get to Marella, tell her to find Father Gibson's note under the priest's bookshelf, call the priest to find out where he was, and escape with her father to London.

Liz Stevens sat with the notepad in her lap. She didn't take any notes. She blinked at Tom, pursing her red lips.

"Aye, and ye all are here wit' yer pitchforks and torches tae burn th' evil monster," Stewart said. "Look a' him. Why, even his handcuffs are withou' cause."

Burns glared at Stewart and lowered his police cap. "He punched me in th' jaw," he said.

Bain hammered the gavel again. "Order!"

"Oh. Now ye wan' order," Stewart said. He slammed his hand down on the podium next to Tom. "So long as it serves yer purposes." He spun around and directed his comments to the people. "This meetin' is an abuse o' power. This is a government travesty. Tis na' a meetin'. Tis a precursor tae a crucifixion!"

Tom shuddered, not liking the sound of that. Somehow being burned at the stake sounded better.

"I'll tell ye wha'," Stewart said. "Show me a warrant signed by a judge, and maybe th' Highland Council, British Parliament, and American Embassy won't demand yer resignations fur violatin' yer oaths o' office."

"Now see here–," Bain said.

Stewart pointed to Liz Stevens, her press badge hanging around her laniard. She picked up her pen, pretending to be ready to write. "'Tis a good thin' th' press is here. I canno' wait tae see how they report on the' international incident ye are making."

Bain opened his mouth and lifted his finger, but he was unable to speak before another voice interrupted him.

"Perhaps Mr. Stewart has a point," Councilman McCulloch said. The man, with his glasses and gray hair, wore a suit and tie. His kind face had reddened since he first sat on the dais. "I have concerns about this meetin'. Serious concerns."

A person in the audience booed.

Councilman MacGillivray leaned forward next to McCulloch. Tom thought he would say something, but he did not. Instead, he rested his chin upon his palm as he considered what McCulloch said.

"Councilman McCulloch," Bain said. "We are experiencin' a growin' threat, and this man is a part o' it."

Councilwoman Harris's eyes widened.

"People are dyin'," Councilwoman Morehead said. "There's na time fur formalities."

"I agree!" Councman Thomson said.

"Aye!" shouted a man in the crowd.

The sunlight flickered through the small high windows. The wind whistled as the tree leaves swayed, casting strange shadows upon the angry faces in the room. Tom hoped he would escape Dorlan Hall and get as far away as he could.

"Formalities exist precisely because o' our threats," McCulloch said. "O' else our government dissolves intae mob rule and anarchy."

A sudden crack of thunder came from outside, and the rumbles echoed within the stone chamber walls. The lights inside the chamber flickered. People ducked and exclaimed in surprise, then the room fell into a nervous silence.

Marella's face grew paler. Sean, too, expressed concern. From his wheelchair, he gripped his cane and scanned the room. His fists flexed over the cane as though he'd whack the first person that came near his daughter.

Tom had to get Marella out of town. The crowd's threat grew, and he imagined whatever danger he faced would spill over to her and Sean if they didn't escape Thurwick.

"Councilman Mark Bain," Stewart said. He gripped the podium with both hands, standing tall and confident with his speech. "Since ye didn't follow procedures, may I suggest we remove Mr. Wayne's handcuffs."

Bain's mouth opened. "Absolutely na!"

Tom studied the attorney next to him. Though Stewart's suit and his hair appeared like he had rushed out of bed, the man had determination in his eyes. Tom was grateful he had come.

"I want tae make a motion tha' we vote on it," McCulloch said.

Councilwoman Brown nodded in agreement.

Several gasps arose from the crowd.

Bain leaned forward and glared at McCulloch.

Tom's muscles tensed. He might have a chance.

After a slight pause, Councilwoman Harris said, "Second."

"No!" shouted someone from the crowd.

O'Reilly pointed at the noise maker, restoring order.

Councilwoman Morehead's jaw dropped. She glared at Harris. An alliance had been severed, Tom thought.

Bain stiffened in his chair. His face contorted, anguishing over having to say the words. The other Council members watched him. Bain's face grew red. McCulloch had challenged Bain's power, and Bain didn't like it. After several tense seconds, Bain said, "We have a motion and a second...." He paused several moments before he finished, "... tae vote tae remove th' prisoner's handcuffs."

Tom counted the votes on the Council. Bain and Morehead would vote 'No'. McCulloch and Harris would vote 'Yes'. Brown and Thomson seemed split.

The question was what Councilman MacGillivray would do. The man had voted against Sean in the first meeting, as had they all. Yet he had come to his own reasoning for his decision. Would he break from the others, and thereby challenge Bain's assumed power?

The crowd was hushed. The strong wind and heavy rain fell upon Dorlan Hall's roof, drawing out the silence. Another rumble of thunder rolled from outside and echoed between Dorlan Hall's stone walls.

Bain put his hands on the table in front of him. "Alrigh'. All in favor of the motion, please say 'Aye'."

McCulloch, Harris, and Brown raised their hands and said, "Aye."

Tom lowered his head. Only three votes. It wasn't enough.

Stewart anticipated his next words for rebuttal.

Bain smiled. "Alrigh'. All against?"

Bain raised his hand in sync with Councilwoman Morehead and Councilman Thomson. "Nay," they said. Bain continued, "Alright, th' motion is defeated–,"

"Uh, Councilman Bain?" Harris said. "It's three tae three. We're missin' a vote."

Every eye in the room focused on Councilman MacGillivray. The crotchety old man sat stern-faced in his chair, his eyes staring into the back of the room.

Tom shifted his wrists, pleading in his heart that he might have a chance to get the cuffs off and be free.

MacGillivray leaned forward. "Mr. Wayne, I do wan' ye tae answer some questions, but 'tis na righ' fur ye tae have been brough' here this way. As a member o' this body, I wan' tae apologize fur any inconvenience tae ye." MacGillivray glared at Bain. "Mr. Bain, I vote 'Aye' tae th' motion. Free th' man."

The audience gasped. A woman shouted, "He's a curse!" Another man stood and paced in the back of the room.

Bain's eyes flashed with anger. Then he composed himself. "Alrigh'. Th' motion passes. Officer O'Reilly, remove th' prisoner's handcuffs.

Officer Burns's freckled cheeks grew red.

Tom breathed a sigh of relief.

A member of the audience booed. Bain hammered his gavel.

Marella didn't smile. Her face grew paler.

Liz Stevens batted her eyes at Tom, her hand taking notes, but her face watching him.

O'Reilly held a small key and unlocked Tom's handcuffs. Relief flowed through Tom's muscles as he swung his arms. He rubbed his wrists and shoulders, straightened his coat, and rubbed his fingers through his hair.

Stewart leaned forward into the microphone. "Thank ye, Council. May I suggest we cancel this meetin', let Mr. Wayne recover from his treatment, and reschedule fur sometime this afternoon?"

"He's a killer!" someone shouted. The crowd's voices grew agitated. Their eyes focused on Tom like a pack of wolves rushing in for the kill. The policeman that might help him was O'Reilly. Burns, he thought, would join the wolves.

Bain hammered his gavel.

O'Reilly stuck his chest out, trying to appear in control.

Burns was conflicted, wanting not to retain order but to unleash the crowd upon Tom.

O'Reilly motioned with his hand for Burns to do his job and establish order in the room. Burns obliged, angry at the events but careful to bide his time.

"Also, may I suggest ye offer Mr. Wayne police protection while he's under subpoena?" Stewart said.

Burns grimaced.

Councilman Bain clenched his fist.

"I think tha's a good idea," Councilman McCulloch said.

Councilwomen Brown and Harris nodded at the idea.

Tom rubbed his shoulders. He mouthed to Marella in the back of the room, "Go outside."

Marella shook her head.

Tom nodded.

Bain said, "Should we vote–."

"I don' think a vote is required tae keep people safe," McCulloch said.

"What about us!" shouted a lady in the crowd.

Several people shouted, "Aye!" and booed.

"Someone's goin' tae be next, and 'tis all because o' him!"

Tom mouthed again at Marella, "Go!"

Marella took Sean and wheeled him out. Sean said, "Where are we goin'? We've go' tae help th' lad!" Marella pushed and they went out the doors.

Tom exhaled, glad Marella left the room and avoided danger.

Stewart stood close to him, waiting.

Bain shook his head. "Alrigh'. O'Reilly, please escort Mr. Wayne tae th' police station."

Stewart said, "Is he under arrest?"

Bain rapped his fingers on the table.

"Ye can subpoena him fur a meetin'. I suggest ye schedule tha' meetin', but unless ye have a warrant, ye canno' arrest Mr. Wayne."

Tom rubbed his fingers behind his neck, hoping upon hope that he'd get away.

"Mr. Stewart is right," McCulloch said. "Let's schedule th' meetin' fur this afternoon. If he doesn' show up, then we have cause tae arrest him."

The thunder rumbled outside, and the lights flickered again. The wind whistled around the contours of Dorlan Hall. Tom hoped Marella and Sean were safe.

Bain rubbed his forehead with his fingers. His eyes remained fixed on Tom. "Okay. I'd like tae hear a motion tae have another meetin' at four o'clock this afternoon." Bain grinned. "Tha' should give Mr. Wayne time tae prepare himself."

Stewart put his arm around Tom, a welcome shield against the crowd's rising anger. O'Reilly faced the people. Burns watched Tom, his eyes flashing with rage under his police hat.

McCulloch made the motion, and the Council members all voted "Aye," though some said it more enthusiastically than others.

"He's goin' tae kill someone before tha' meetin'. Jus' ye wait!" shouted the old gray-haired lady.

"I wan' justice fur Ian!" Sharon said. The younger man put his arms around her and glared at Tom.

Tom made a move to the back of the room, but a hand grabbed his coat.

"Na' tha' way," Stewart said. He pulled Tom toward the side door. "Quick, before anyone says anythin'.

With O'Reilly and Burns attending to the crowd, Tom followed Stewart, his sore legs and aching shoulders moving like he finished halftime of a rugby game, and he had another half to go. "I don't know who you are, but thank you."

Stewart smiled. "'Tis alrigh', lad." They exited the side door before the crowd and the Council knew where they went.

"How do I repay you."

Logan O'Malley snuck in behind them. Stewart said, "'Tis yer lucky day. Ye don' owe me anythin'. Fact is, I owed Detective O'Malley a favor."

O'Malley shut the door. He tipped his fedora again at Tom. "Quick. Best we ge' ye tae yer friends and away from here."

Tom was thankful he wasn't being tied to a stake on a burning haystack.

CHAPTER 32

O'Malley and Stewart led Tom around the side of Dorlan Hall. The clouds had grown dark and lightning flashed across the skies while the wind blew the leaves on the courtyard's trees. "Wait behind th' corner," O'Malley said, holding onto his fedora.

Tom peered around the corner as Marella and Sean climbed into their small sedan. She helped him in first and then loaded the wheelchair into the trunk.

"Stay here." O'Malley said. He disappeared past the old brick walls.

Tom leaned against the building, the stone pressing against his coat, his sore muscles welcoming the stone's gentle massage. He leaned his unkempt hair against the wall. "That was a great show you performed in there."

Stewart said, "Gla' tae help, lad. Best though ye' don' dilly dally. Ge' yer friends and ge' ou' o' town."

"But the subpoena?"

"Subpoena o' na', they aim tae hang ye."

O'Malley appeared from behind the corner. "Yer friends will be here wi' the' car. They're pulling around th' buildin'.

"I'm advising th' lad tae ge' goin'," Stewart said.

O'Malley said, 'Aye. And he best hurry."

Members of the crowd exited the Dorlan Hall entrance. Some went to their cars. Many headed straight to Guthrie's Pub, raising their fists into the air and speaking with their hands. No doubt they marched there to drink their anger away.

A lightning bolt streaked across the square, and many people ducked. A gust of wind blew past them A woman wailed in the wind. The sound chilled him.

"What is up with this place?" Tom said. "Did you hear that?"

"Wha'? The thunder?" Stewart said.

"No. In the wind."

Stewart and O'Malley shrugged.

"Never mind," Tom said.

The small blue sedan rolled to Tom. Marella was driving. Her angry eyes did not prevent Tom from melting at the sight of her curly red hair as it floated down her shoulders.

Sean was in the back seat, with the window down. He waved with his outstretched arm. "Ge' in, lad!"

Tom held out his hand. "Thanks!" he said.

"There's na time fur tha'. Now!" O'Malley said, and he went around the car and pulled the door open.

The cold wind blew Tom's hair. He climbed into the car.

O'Malley, his hand holding his fedora on his head, shut the door behind Tom and shouted, "Move!"

Inside the car, Tom leaned over to Marella and smiled. "You look great."

"Shut it!" she said.

Tom flinched.

She put her foot on the gas and the small sedan pulled forward. The car tires bumped up and down on the cobblestones.

The wind blew a newspaper across the street. A man on the street pointed to Tom in the car and ran at him. Soon, others noticed them and gave chase.

Sean shifted in his seat, watching the oncoming crowd. He leaned forward, his eyebrows raised in alarm. "Marella, gun it!"

She slammed her foot on the gas pedal, and the small sedan bounced over the cobblestones, past the old buildings of downtown Thurwick and through the exit toward St. Michael's Catholic Church, leaving the shouting people behind.

"At four o'clock, ye'd better be back there," Marella said.

"No. Stewart and O'Malley said we need to get out of town," Tom said. He reached up and grabbed the handle above his head, trying to support himself as the car rumbled upon the ancient road.

"Bu' they'll arrest ye if yer na there," Sean said.

"They'll do worse than that," Tom said. "And not just to me. The three of us need to leave town."

"Together? I don' think so," Marella said, her feminine frame moving up and down as she drove the car over the stones.

"Didn't you hear my voice message?"

"Nothin' ye say's worth hearin'."

"Marella. Le' him speak," Sean said.

She huffed.

"Go on?" Sean said, his voice rattled by the bouncing car.

"Father Gibson said the same thing," Tom said. "We need to go to London."

"Why?"

"He said the town is cursed."

"Wouldn' surprise me," Marella said.

"Why London?" Sean said. "It's a ways away."

"I don't know," Tom said. "He didn't say. He said he's there, though, and he said we'd be safe there."

The blue car pulled up to St. Michael's Church. The dark clouds swirled overhead and the wind blew the trees so that their branches whipped back and forth like they were being shaken from below. Behind the church, the waves of Loch Ness rolled and splashed against the rocks, spraying water high into the air before it landed on the shoreline.

Across the street, Annabel's Bed and Breakfast door stood open with crime scene tape stretched across the entrance. A lone police car was parked outside, its lights flashing.

Marella pressed the brakes.

Tom put his hand out front, surprised they were stopping. "What are you doing?" Tom said.

"Leavin' ye off."

"But we need to get out of here."

"Maybe so." Marella's eyes flashed at Tom. "But na wi' ye."

Tom leaned back. A rush of emotion filled his heart. He didn't know what it was, except that it hurt.

"Get ou'," Marella said. "And good luck tae ye."

"Please don't feel that way."

"Don' tell me how tae feel."

"Marella. What happened?"

"I saw tha' reporter eyein' ye."

Tom remembered Liz Stevens sitting on the front row of Dorlan Hall. "There's nothing there!"

"Ye may be tae much a coward tae tell her yes, bu' yer na' man enough tae tell her no."

Tom sank into his chair. He turned to Sean, hoping for help.

Sean raised his eyebrows and shrugged.

"Now!" Marella said.

Tom bowed his head. "Alright. If that's how you want it."

"I do."

Tom pressed his lips together. He wanted to tell Marella so many things, but he didn't know what to do. Her red hair curled over her sweater, and her green eyes flashed wild emotions. He wanted nothing other than to comfort her, to tell her everything would be alright. But they had to get out of Thurwick.

He squeezed the door handle, and the door clicked open. He stepped outside the car.

Before shutting the door, he leaned back inside. "Promise me you'll leave town."

"Off we' ye," Marella said.

"I'll call you soon."

"Don' bother!" Marella drove forward, and the door swung closed as she and Sean pulled away, leaving Tom in the road.

Sean watched Tom through the rear window as the car bounced upon the dirt road and disappeared behind a dust cloud in the distance.

The wind whistled through the trees and around the church walls. "How can a woman kick a guy in the stomach without actually doing it?" he said.

Then voices echoed from town. They were loud, and coming in his direction.

Locals. And they were coming for him!

Tom had to think of a plan. It wasn't over. Whatever Marella was thinking, he'd show her. He'd find a way to protect her. First, get Father Gibson's note, the one he left under the desk in the priest's office.

Then, he had to convince Marella and Sean to leave town.

And keep them safe until they did.

He checked the solid church doors and pulled. They opened this time, still unlocked after the police had arrested him and led him out the front doors. The church was dark and musty. The large crucifix clung to the rear wall.

A chill hung in the air.

He sprinted through the main church, and into the side door. The hallway was dark except for the light that leaked through broken doors on either side. He ran down the hall to Father Gibson's office.

A strange howl came from outside the church, a howl that sounded like it came from another world. The sound chilled him. "What in the world? Maybe this town is cursed," Tom said. He went to the desk and reached under it. He found the note.

He put it in his pocket. He had Father Gibson's phone number. He wanted to call it to get more information, but there was no time. The locals would be in the church any moment.

What next? He knew leaving town was urgent. He had been told he should leave by not one but three people he trusted. He did not doubt the townspeople wanted to burn him at the stake. They'd do the deed themselves if they found him.

He didn't like thinking that.

He had to hide.

He left Father Gibson's office and ran back to the main church. He sprinted past the pews toward the front door, but as he arrived, a man's voice said, "He has tae be in here!"

Tom stopped. He swore under his breath. He had to find a place to hide. Somewhere they'd not suspect.

Footsteps neared the front doors.

A boom of thunder echoed throughout the church's stone walls.

"Quick. Think!"

The solid pews stood in their rows. Stained glass windows adorned the heights of the church. Then on the side of the church was the hidden door, the way he came in from the crypt. That was it! He never knew it was there when he attended Mass. They might not, either!

The voices and footsteps grew louder. He ran toward the crypt doorway. He reached the hidden entrance when the front doors pulled open. A soft light filled the main aisle of the church, lighting the front altar.

"He's go' tae be here!" said a man.

"Search the place!"

Tom squeezed inside the cavity, hidden by the shadows. He slipped past the door and pressed it shut behind him.

"Wha' was tha'?" said the man.

Tom held his breath.

"It came from th' right."

Tom squinted and leaned on the door. They couldn't find it.

The footsteps grew louder. "O'er here!"

The door was shut against the frame. Tom held the handle and pushed, leaning his shoulder into the door. Behind the door, fingers pressed upon the wall. If they pressed hard, they might discover the hidden door and find him.

Tom held his breath.

"I don' understand. I heard somethin' right here!" said the voice.

"It's just a stone wall," said another voice. "A rat o' somethin'."

"Bu'—"

"If he's anywhere, he'd be in th' rectory."

The fingers stopped pressing on the door.

"Come on,"

"Aye!"

The footstep and voice echoes lessened as the men ran to the far side of the church.

Tom pressed the door handle, keeping his exit shut. He waited in the darkness, the spiral stairways leading up into the bell tower, and down into the crypt. When the sounds outside disappeared, Tom relaxed his shoulders and let go. He lowered himself down the stairway into the blackness below.

CHAPTER 33

Tom leaned against the wall, the cold stones chafing his coat. He moved down the black stairway, leaning against the outside wall and hoping not to step on a mouse or a rat or something worse.

The wind whipped past the church contours. It howled through the thickness of St. Michael's stone walls.

Claps of thunder rumbled. Their sound echoed inside the church's chambers.

Tom shook his head. How strong was the storm outside?

He proceeded with caution down each lower step. Soon a light illuminated the stone walls of the spiral staircase. He remembered he had left the lights on when he exited the crypt the day before. As he stepped off the stairs and into the room, his eyes went toward the crucifix behind the altar. He focused on the head of Jesus leaning forward, his eyes lowered and a crown of thorns adorning his skull.

"You should turn the lights off when you leave," said a woman's British voice.

Tom jumped.

In the pew on his right sat Liz Stevens. She was still dressed in her business attire, except she had taken her press badge off. She looked good. Too good. She had sex appeal and she knew it.

"What are you doing here?" Tom said, bewildered.

"You left the light on, and the door was cracked. Honestly, Tom, if you're trying to hide you ought to be more careful." Liz leaned back and smiled.

Tom backed against the wall. He'd have to get past her to exit the crypt. Worse, now she knew his secret entrance.

She raised her slender arms and placed her hands on the pew in front of her. "We never had our interview."

"Something's come up." It was all he thought to say.

"I'm not here to hurt you," Liz said, her English accent sounding sensitive but playful. She pursed her red lips together and brushed her hair over her ear. She stood up and exited the pew, her business skirt and blouse wrapped tight against her body. She walked toward Tom confident of her physique. "I am here to help."

Tom remembered Marella's words, and he mouthed, "Come on, Tom. Be man enough to tell her no." As Liz approached him, he slinked against the stones behind him. He was trapped.

Liz smiled, her high cheeks blushing. "I'm glad they didn't tar and feather you."

Tom leaned back, thinking of Marella. "Me too."

"You don't say much."

"Kind of had a rough day."

"I see," she said. She brought her finger up to brush Tom's unkempt dark hair.

Tom moved his head to the side.

Liz brought her hand down. "Are you going back?"

"What?" Tom asked, hoping not to be put on the spot.

"The Council. Are you going back at four?"

Tom pressed his lips together. "Yeah," he lied. "I have to."

Liz watched him, her lips slanting. Her head nodded like a mom agreeing with but not believing her child. "I see," she said again.

"Look, I have to run," Tom said. He slid along the wall, trying to get past her while averting his eyes from her natural features.

"I don't think you're going back," she said.

Tom stopped, caught.

"All I want is an interview."

Tom didn't think that was all she wanted.

"It'll be twenty minutes."

Tom rubbed his fingers through his hair. "And if I don't?"

Liz shrugged. "I don't know." She gestured toward the rear door. "Are you sure it's safe out there?"

"It's just a storm. You'll be alright."

"I mean you."

There was a bang on the rear door.

Tom shuddered. Voices entered the chamber as the door was pushed and pulled against its frame. Tom put his hands against the wall, ready to bolt.

"Don't worry," Liz said. "I locked it."

The voices shouted outside, and the door banged against its frame some more as the locals outside tried to pry it open.

Tom tried to think. Could there be another way out?

Liz said, "I think they have you surrounded."

Tom left her and searched the crypt. He pressed his hands on the stone walls hoping to find another secret exit.

"They'll get in here eventually," she said.

"I know!" He searched the cracks and crevices of the crypt but found nothing that indicated another exit.

"If you want to escape, I can help."

Tom stopped. Marella would not like him talking with Liz, but here he was. If he went out the back, they'd find him. If he went upstairs, they'd find him.

Liz sighed and returned to the pew where she had sat. Reaching down, she pulled up her laniard and hung her press badge around her neck. She picked up her notepad. Her slender legs showed under her skirt.

The voices outside grew louder. A man shouted, "There's lights in there!"

Tom stopped. He didn't want to speak with her, but the walls closed in on him. If he ran, he might be able to sprint past them. But with so many people after him, they'd catch him. His shoulders slumped forward. "Okay," he said. "What's your idea?"

"Do we have an interview?"

"You're blackmailing me."

Liz held her notebook to her bosom. "Tom," she said, acting surprised.

Tom thought of Marella's words "man enough to tell her no." Now, the situation was unavoidable. He had tried to do the right thing earlier, and now Marella had kicked him out of her sight. But she was in danger. He had to escape, and Liz had the only plan. Could he avoid talking with her? Did he have a choice? Could he fight a mob and get through to Marella, sprinting across the countryside to Sean's house and escaping all the way to London? The odds were against him, and he knew it. "Okay," he said.

Liz raised her eyebrows. "Okay, yes?"

Tom rolled his eyes. "Yes!"

"Very well," Liz said. "Follow me." She poised herself and stuck out her chest. Then she marched to the rear door, unlocked it, and pulled it open.

"What are you doing?" Tom said.

There were male voices outside.

Liz waved for Tom to follow.

He stood still, waiting.

"Boys!" Liz said. She showed her legs as her skirt blew in the wind. "Gentlemen!"

Tom waited by the stairway, his hand on the wall, expecting to hide and run.

Liz stood by the crypt door. Rain blew past her in the wind. Soon, a man, his shoulders wet with rain on his brown coat, stood in the doorway with her. He pointed at Tom. "There he is!"

Tom waited, but his muscles tensed, ready to disappear. Could he trust her?

"Sir," Liz said. She gripped her notebook hard with one hand, while she held her press badge toward the man's face with the other. "Mr. Wayne and I have an interview scheduled, and we can't do it when you're making all that fuss."

"He's tryin' tae run!" the man said.

"He's not," Liz said. "We had an interview scheduled and you and your brutes won't leave us alone."

Another man showed up. He pointed at Tom and tried to move past Liz. But the first man stuck his arm out and held him back.

"If you want to have at him, you can," Liz said. Then she held up her press badge. "I'll write about it. I'll make you famous, but not in a good way."

The men eyed each other and then Liz. As the wind blew past them, Liz put the press badge down across her breasts. The men followed her badge with their eyes. The lead man said, "Sorry, ma'am." Then he walked away, and the second man followed.

"Tell th' others we don't want any interruptions!" Liz said. Then she waited.

Tom remained next to the crypt's hidden exit, his hand still on the wall, ready to launch himself up the stairway.

Liz motioned for Tom to approach her. She held the door open as the wind blew her silky hair over her shoulders.

Tom approached her near the crypt's rear door. A bolt of lightning flashed. Its light reflected and bounced off the churning waters of Loch Ness. As the wind and rain blew past them, the woman in the wind wailed, except this time she was angrier.

Liz leaned close to Tom. "Twenty minutes."

"Okay."

"You promise?"

"Twenty. That's the deal."

Liz motioned for Tom to leave the crypt. "Come." She went forward into the wind and rain.

Tom stepped outside in the wind as small raindrops landed on his face.

"You owe me more," Liz said.

Tom pressed his lips together, not sure what to make of that.

CHAPTER 34

L ogan O'Malley climbed in his car, his aging joints aching in his knees. There was a lot going on, he thought. The weather threatened to storm, the government was on the brink of collapse, and the townspeople were itching to make a sacrifice to halt another death without knowing if it would stop the disappearances. What had happened to those who disappeared: Captain James Anderson, Annabel, Emily Anderson, and Assistant Captain Ian Fleming? Two men, and two women.

Three of them had disappeared near the loch. That would imply the Loch Ness monster had something to do with that.

What troubled him was Annabel. She had been nowhere near the loch. Her distorted corpse had remained, and her building torn to shreds.

And what about that word written in claw marks on the wall? MINE. What did that mean? And who did that? Surely not the Loch Ness Monster. A creature that size, if it existed, couldn't fit inside the house, let alone write.

As he twisted the key in his ignition, someone rapped his window. Councilman Bain held a black umbrella with a tight fist. O'Malley rolled down his window. The wind and rain blew past the young Councilman who was now intent on fighting for power.

"Detective," Bain said. "I wan' ye tae follow Tom Wayne."

"Why?" O'Malley said.

"He'll run."

"Wha' makes ye say tha'?"

"Intuition."

O'Malley kept his face still. He had learned to keep a poker face for interrogations during his early years of training. He was not about to reveal to Bain that he advised the American to get out of town.

"Who's runnin' th' station?"

"We're makin' O'Reilly in charge," Bain said. "Fur now."

O'Malley feigned compliance. He would have to sit down with O'Reilly at some point and discover where his loyalties lie. Would the police officer lean toward power for the sake of advancement, or would he lean toward the rule of law? Whatever monster was killing people in Thurwick, another monster appeared to be growing among the people. "Wha' are yer plans fur th' lad?"

Bain's lips curled, a tell used often during interrogations. "Ye le' me deal with tha'," Bain said.

"Aye," O'Malley said, tipping his fedora.

"Go find Mr. Wayne. I wan' him back here a' four."

"Shall I bring th' tar and feathers, tae?"

Bain's curled lips changed into a frown.

"I mean, if we're goin' tae have a sacrifice, we migh' as well be ready."

"Don' toy wi' me, Detective."

O'Malley said, "Yer th' Chairman, Councilman Bain."

Bain stood straight. The rain fell upon his umbrella, but it also blew in from the side and hit the man's black coat. Bain appeared focused on his mission and was unbothered by the weather.

O'Malley gave an empty salute and he rolled up his window and drove away. His tires bounced upon the old cobblestones, and he rotated his wheel toward the street that led to St. Michael's.

The wind splattered the rain upon his windshield. His wipers went back and forth in rhythm.

He thought again of the disappearances. Three missing persons. One dead body. One potential kill site. One half-eaten police cap. And one American everyone wanted to scapegoat.

Not to mention the previous Chairman in jail for murder.

And a claim about the Loch Ness monster having killed two additional Thurwick residents.

Logan's car rolled forward. If he found Tom Wayne and Sean and Marella Paterson, he'd load them all in his car and drive them out of Thurwick himself.

CHAPTER 35

The wind blew gusts at Tom, and the spring leaves on the trees whipped from side to side. Rain splattered near him in random and unexpected patterns, sometimes on the grass, sometimes on the muddy parking lot, and sometimes hitting Tom's disheveled hair and face. The wind whistled past the church's structure, and again heard the wailing woman of the wind. There was a strange feeling about it. Something ominous was in the wind.

"Get in," Liz said. Her car was parked on the lot.

"Where are we going?" Tom's nerves were on edge. The last thing he wanted was for someone to tell Marella he was climbing into Liz Stevens's car. Yet the local men - Tom counted eight of them - stood outside the church watching him and Liz get into her car. Any one of them could spread the word that would get back to Marella.

He climbed into Liz's car and shut the door. He tried not to make eye contact.

Liz said, "Are you ready?" like a teenager anticipating a ride on a roller coaster.

Tom kept his eyes on his car door window.

"Let's go." She pressed the gas and the car rolled forward.

"Where?"

"Not here." The men gathered into a cluster and watched Tom and Liz pull away.

"This counts as our twenty minutes," Tom said.

"Does it?" Liz said. She headed the car back to Thurwick. "I think you'll want more than twenty."

Tom raised his eyebrows. "Why are we going back to town?"

"Relax. You're in a different car. The locals won't recognize you." She reached into the back seat and grabbed a notebook. "Here, pretend you're reading and keep your head down."

Tom took the notebook. He ducked his head and slunk down in his seat as another car drove past them in the other direction.

"And don't look out the window."

Tom did as Liz suggested. They returned to the Thurwick square and drove past Dorlan Hall. The angry people had dispersed, and with the weather most of the people who remained were ducking their heads or hiding under umbrellas, holding tight to keep them from blowing away. Tom focused on the notebook, pretending to read.

Liz drove through the square and drove past the small museum. Tom remembered the hanging plesiosaur in the museum. The replica didn't do the real Loch Ness monster justice. The creatures in the water were far bigger, faster, and more powerful than any artist's depiction.

But what had happened to Annabel? The police captain had disappeared near the boat dock. The Loch Ness monsters' necks could have stretched out from the water and attacked the man. But that didn't explain Annabel's death. She was such a nice lady, Tom thought. She had not participated in the town's judgment against him, and she wanted what was best for him. She was several hundred yards from the water, and on the other side of the church. Her death had been caused by something non-aquatic, something that was on land.

Something that could enter a house.

The car pulled up to a large building off Thurwick square. Its roof was on top of two stories, an old brick building with new Scottish green awnings and shutters. "What's this?" Tom said.

"My hotel," Liz said.

The wind blew and the car rocked. Tom said, "I can't."

"Twenty minutes," Liz said, smiling.

Tom shook his head. "Okay."

Liz climbed out of the car, and though her hair blew in the wind she paid the weather no mind and she marched to the front door.

Tom scanned the area with his eyes. No one was around to watch him follow her. "Twenty minutes." He exited the car and went to the door of the hotel. Inside, there were several pictures of the Scottish Highlands and the cool blue waters of Loch Ness. None of the pictures contained any image of the Loch Ness monster. An older man wearing glasses and a vest stood behind a wood counter. He was reading a newspaper.

Liz said, "Upstairs."

"Can't we do it in the lobby?"

The clerk noticed Tom and raised his eyebrows.

Liz stopped halfway up the stairs. "We won't be bothered up here."

Tom smiled at the clerk. "It's not what you think."

The man frowned and adjusted his glasses.

Tom followed Liz up the stairs. Her firm legs and features moved like an athlete under her tight business attire. He moved his eyes to the stairs below his feet, trying not to notice.

Liz opened a door down the hall and walked into the hotel room. The bed was in the middle of the room, and over the headboard hung a painting of a castle. Across the room, two chairs adjoined a small table with a lamp. Outside the rain-streaked window, the countryside was gray and damp. "Put your coat over there," she said, pointing at the bed.

Tom put his hands in his coat pockets. "I'm okay."

Liz sat on the bed and took off her boots and socks, revealing slender calves, white feet, and red toenails. "Get comfortable," Liz said.

There was a tap on the window, and the wind howled again from outside. Tom's eyes went to the window. "What was that?"

"Don't be so jumpy," Liz said. "It's the weather. There's a tree outside. A branch tapping the building."

Tom stood still, watching the window. "I'm not seeing a tree."

"What's the matter? Do storms make you nervous?" Liz said.

Tom rubbed his fingers through his disheveled hair. "Can we start?"

Liz leaned back on the bed, crossing her legs and sticking out her chest. She rubbed her hand through her hair over her ear and said, "I think storms are exciting."

Tom didn't answer.

"Okay." Liz stood and picked up her notebook and pen, then she sat at the table with the small chair. She pointed to the other chair. "Sit down."

Tom obliged. There was a clock on the table next to the headboard. 1:23, it said. Time was ticking. Twenty minutes for Liz, and less than three hours to get out of town. He worried about Marella. Something was going on, and he sensed danger. He had to get her out of town.

The tapping hit the window again.

"Okay," Liz said. "Tell me what you know about the Loch Ness monster."

"That's not a question," Tom said.

Liz smiled and leaned forward. She put her pen to her mouth. She observed him for a few moments. Her eyes flashed. She said, "You know, I always get what I want."

"I bet."

"You might as well play along."

"Nineteen minutes."

Liz bit her lip. She put the pen to her notebook. "Alright then. Is it real?"

Tom had already confessed the existence of the monster to O'Malley, and the Council stated as such in the morning's meeting. There'd be no point in hiding it. "Yes," he said.

The tapping on the window increased, both in frequency and in intensity.

212

Liz leaned forward, her cleavage showing under her suit. "What'd it look like?"

Tom kept his eyes on the window. "Well, kind of like the pictures, only bigger."

Liz grinned. "Bigger?"

"Yeah."

"What impression did it give you?"

"Strong," Tom said. As the tapping increased, he watched the window. "Powerful."

"I like big, strong, and powerful."

Tom frowned.

Liz huffed, annoyed. "Remember, you owe me."

Tom wanted to answer, but the tapping distracted him. He remained sitting, watching the window. Was there music outside the wall?

Something banged outside the window, and the glass vibrated with the howling wind. Was it a woman? Did she wail? Was he hearing singing? His nerves tingled and the hairs on his neck stiffened.

Liz lost her patience. She shoved her pen and notebook down on the armrest and stood up. She unlocked the window and opened it. The curtains blew as the wind rushed inside the room. Her hair blew back over her tight suit. "It's just the weather."

"What's doing the banging? Is there a branch?" Tom said.

"I don't see anyth—."

A terrible howl came through the open window. The window shattered. Glass flew into the room. Tom jumped from his chair and retreated near the bed.

Liz let out a panicked scream.

Two long black arms with branch-like fingers wrapped around both sides of Liz. At the end of the arms were long slender fingers, each of them ending in pointed black nails that curved at their tips. The arms closed in upon Liz's back, the claws digging into her business suit and penetrating her skin. The room filled with howling and wailing, the sounds hurting Tom's ears as they echoed off the hotel room walls. The castle painting fell off the wall and crashed onto the headboard, falling face-first onto the bed.

Tom fell over upon the bed and broke the picture. His face was white as fear gripped him.

Liz's scream filled the room, but soon the wind and the wailing overcame her. Then another sound, a woman's voice, filled the room. It was angry and possessive. It said, "Mine!"

Liz's scream ended as her lungs ran out of air. The green curtains whipped on either side of her. The black arms and claws clutched her and squeezed.

There was a tremendous howl, and the arms jerked Liz Stevens through the window, her hair, kicking legs, and white feet pulling out after her tight suit. She disappeared from view. The wind blew, and the curtains flapped and flew.

A presence entered the room. The wind's howl filled his ears. A woman's voice said, "Tom!"

Tom's eyes widened with panic. He rolled over the bed, and his elbow broke through the picture. Tom landed on his feet on the other side of the bed. He rushed to the door and opened it.

An invisible force slammed the door in his hand, shutting him in.

"Oh, no way!" Tom said. He backed up.

"Tom!"

He sprinted at the door and lowered his shoulder. He crashed through the door, splintering it into hundreds of pieces. He rolled over the hotel carpet in the hallway. He stood up and sprinted down the stairs.

The clerk had left his position behind the desk and was on his way to the stairway. "What's goin' on up there?" he said.

Tom didn't answer. He ran past the man through the lobby and thrust open the front door. He sprinted out of the hotel and down the sidewalk into the alleys of Thurwick.

CHAPTER 36

"Is this rain e'er goin' tae stop?" O'Malley said. He squinted through the streaked windshield as he drove his car to find Tom. Another car passed him before he reached the church and Annabel's. Was the driver that reporter that was hanging around town? He thought another passenger was in the car with her but, through the rain and the wind, he couldn't be sure. No matter. He had to get to Tom. He'd be with Sean and Marella at their home. He had to warn them it might be best to leave town.

Of course, if Tom didn't show up for the subpoena after Bain had told O'Malley to find him and make sure the American showed up, O'Malley would have some explaining to do.

Detectives didn't make much money working for small Highland towns like Thurwick. But he had lived modestly, his expenses being his house, his car which was now paid for, and Digger, splurging on dog treats for his furry companion once a week. Digger was his only vice. His frugal living allowed him to save more. He remembered his last bank statement. Could he retire on what he had saved and what he'd get from his small pension?

He drove past St. Michael's Catholic Church and Annabel's Bed and Breakfast. Officer Jordan's car was parked outside the bed and breakfast, still investigating the premises after Annabel's death.

The wind blew the countryside's spring leaves, whipping and flattening them under the pressure of its gusts. The dark clouds moved low and quickly over the green hills around Loch Ness. He had lived in Thurwick for ten years. O'Malley had begun his career in Edinburgh and had enjoyed the experience. But it was never home in the emotional sense.

When he had been offered the detective job he decided the slower pace would be good for him. Sort of a semi-retirement. He adopted Digger from the local pound seven years ago. He had planned in another year or two he'd leave the force and collect his pension. Maybe he'd do some security work at the museum to stay active.

But with the way the Council was changing, maybe he'd do best to leave Thurwick and go somewhere else.

A gust of wind broadsided his car, and he adjusted the steering wheel. The clouds overhead hurried over the hills, leaving a gray fog over their ridges. The weather in Scotland's Highlands was often worse than this. This storm was different, though. He couldn't put his finger on it as to why.

He pulled up to Sean and Marella Paterson's house. Sean's blue sedan sat in the parking lot. He climbed from his car and, holding his fedora, he walked past the several spinning pinwheels to the front door and knocked.

The door opened. Marella said, "Wha' do ye wan'?"

"May I come in?"

Marella said, "Are ye goin' tae arrest me again?"

"Was jus' doin' my job, m' lady," O'Malley said. "I mus' speak wi' Tom."

"He's na here."

O'Malley blinked. "I thought he was wi' ye."

"He's not."

Then he remembered the car he passed, the one with the reporter and the passenger with her. Was that Tom? Should he mention that to Marella? He said, "I was told tae watch Tom tae make sure he shows up at four."

"I said he's na here," Marella said. She leaned back to shut the door.

O'Malley stopped the door from shutting with his hand. "I'm na wi' th' Council, though."

"You work fur them."

"Aye," O'Malley said. "But I serve th' law foremost. Bain's gone doolally. He's na following th' law. He aims tae convict Tom in a sham trial. I came here tae tell him and ye, and yer father, tae ge' ou' o' town."

Sean's voice came from down the hallway. "Marella, who is it?"

"No one," Marella said.

"I hear a man's voice." Sean stepped forward, his crutch keeping him standing in place of his missing leg. "Oh, Mr. O'Malley."

O'Malley tipped his fedora. "Aye. Ye need tae ge' ou' o' Thurwick."

"Tom said th' same thin'."

218

"Tis best. I think th' Council will convict him, and if the town isn't satisfied, they'll come after ye next."

Marella said, "Aye, so let's ge' ou' o' town as fast as we can. Da', ye and I should leave."

Sean said, "Wha' about Tom?"

Marella said, "Le' him dig his own grave."

Sean shook his head. "Th' lad was jus' tryin' tae help."

Marella huffed and walked past Sean into the kitchen.

Sean moved his crutch and leaned toward O'Malley. "Do ye know where th' lad is?"

"Na at th' moment." O'Malley scratched his forehead. "But I think he's wi' tha' London reporter."

Sean frowned. "Oh. My daughter's na' goin' tae like tha'."

"I passed a car on th' way here. She was drivin'. I saw a passenger but I couldn' make him ou' in the rain."

"Do ye think he's in trouble?"

"Aye," O'Malley said. "Ye and yer daughter should leave now. Go tae Edinburgh o' Inverness, somewhere populated where people will se ye."

Sean shook his head. "Wha' about Tom?"

"I'll find him. That's wha' Bain told me tae do."

"What happens if ye find him?"

"I don't know. Maybe we'll all leave town."

The countryside flashed white as a streak of lightning stretched across the clouds over Loch Ness. In a second, a crack of thunder echoed over the valley. O'Malley and Sean flinched in surprise. "Storm's getting intense," Sean said.

"Aye," said O'Malley. "Take Marella, and get away."

Sean thudded his crutch on the floor. "Can't."

O'Malley raised his eyebrows. "Why na?"

"Th' lad saved my life," Sean said. "If na fur him, I'd have lost more than my leg."

O'Malley said, "Wha' de ye wan' tae do?"

Sean walked with his crutch and his one leg to the coat hanger. He grabbed his brown coat and slipped it on while moving his crutch out of the way and leaning on the wall. When it was on, he put his crutch back in position under his arm. "Come on," Sean said. "I don' know why, bu' I have a feelin' th' lad's in trouble."

"Wha' about Marella?" O'Malley said.

"Las!" Sean yelled.

Marella said, "Wha' is it?"

"The Detective and I are goin' tae find Tom."

Marella put her hands on her hips. "Yer not!"

"Aye," Sean said. "The lad's in trouble. He saved my life. I owe him."

Marella stormed into the kitchen. "I don' belie'e this," she said. "Don't count on me tae be here when ye get back. He can have fun wi' tha' other girl, bu' he won' have me!"

Another flash of lightning streaked over the dark sky, spreading over Thurwick's central square in the distance.

"Ye can solve yer romance later," Sean said. He said to O'Malley. "Let's go."

O'Malley stepped out the front door, followed by Sean with his one leg and his crutch. "Do ye need yer wheelchair?"

"Na fur a rescue mission," Sean said, and he walked with his crutch on the path toward O'Malley's car.

CHAPTER 37

Tom sprinted through a Thurwick back alley, not sure where he was. The wind whipped through the stone walls, blowing leaves and paper. He rounded a corner and ran into several black feathers. He jumped and sprinted the other way. He imagined the voice of the woman. "Tom!"

He tried to get the image of Liz being pulled through the window out of his head, her being bent over backward, her hair, legs, and her white bare feet the last things he saw of her.

He ran, his hair blowing in the wind, his lungs burning with exhaustion, his muscles aching from his earlier treatment by the police and his ramming through the door. He rounded another corner, not sure where he was. He approached a young woman in a long dark coat, her head bent low under a hood. Her face was unrecognizable save for several long strands of white hair that extended from her hood. The thought occurred to him that he should remain calm, to not try to attract attention in case the locals should want to find him.

The woman's head remained down.

Tom stopped running, put his hands in his coat pocket, and pretended to be another local, hoping she wouldn't alert anyone to his location.

The woman's feet were bare.

Tom paused. Why was a woman not wearing shoes in downtown Thurwick in the wind and the storm?

Then he heard it – singing.

The voice of the woman whispered through the alley.

> *When ye found th' one ye love*
> *And th' heart becomes entwined*
> *Ye'll ne'er have another*
> *No matter whom ye find.*

The woman walked in his direction. When she was a few feet away, she lifted her head. A beautiful sad face was under the hood, and the hood fell back revealing her full head of white hair and dark blue eyes. She loosened her robe around her shoulders, and it hung down her arms, revealing the top of her chest. Her eyes flashed at him. Then her lips moved. "Tom."

Tom leaned back.

"Come back to me," she said.

Tom stepped backward and took his hands from his pocket. "Who are you?"

"Return to me," she said again.

A pull tugged at Tom's chest; a strange desire swelled inside him.

Under her coat fell several black feathers.

Tom backed away.

"Come to me," she whispered again.

Tom shut his eyes.

The woman said "Tom," and she sang once more:

My hope is ye and I
Remain as one and true.
Together we shall try
Tae avoid becomin' blue.

"I don't even know what that means!" Tom said. He sprinted in the other direction.

The wind picked up and whirled around him. There was the sound of flapping like a flock of pigeons taking flight.

Tom pumped his legs, swinging his arms, trying to get distance between himself and the woman.

Behind him, the wind wailed. The wailing, without a doubt in his mind, came from the woman in the hooded coat.

And the wailing woman was not happy with him.

CHAPTER 38

Tom sprinted, pumping his arms and legs to get away from the woman. Who was she, or rather what was she? The sight of the feathers and the sound of the wailing chilled him. This woman was somehow connected to whatever pulled Liz from the window. Was she the same creature? If so, why did she pull Liz from the room?

And what did she do with her?

Tom had to find safety, and fast. Somewhere public. Somewhere that had a phone so he could call Father Gibson and find out what he was dealing with.

In the corner of his eye, he found an alley where the end of it was someplace familiar - downtown Thurwick. He ran, trying to get to the public square before she, whatever she was, caught up with him. After what had happened to Liz, he thought it better to take his chances with the locals. He reached the end of the alley and burst out into the open, not caring who noticed him.

When he entered the square, two onlookers noticed him, but most of the others were too busy shielding their faces from the swirling wind and the sideways rain. Those closest to the stores stood inside their doorways or under their awnings, hoping the weather would soon subside.

The museum, the police station, and Smith's store were on his right. Across the way was Dorlan Hall. Several small stores and the hospital were on his left. But past the museum was Guthrie's Pub. Guthrie's would have men there. They may want to beat Tom to a pulp, but perhaps there was a chance that he'd be safe inside.

The wind whipped past him, and a strange sensation pressed upon him. A lightning bolt flashed in the dark overhead clouds. A loud thunderclap boomed over Tom's head, causing him and the Thurwick residents in the square to duck and flinch.

Tom ran over the cobblestones while praying another bolt wouldn't strike him where he was. He reached the pub. He opened the door and shut it behind him. A strong gust of wind pushed against the door, but Tom leaned back to keep it shut. After a few moments, the wind stopped.

His eyes adjusted to the darkness. The snugs inside Guthrie's Pub had small lanterns over each table. The bartender was cleaning a glass. When the bartender recognized Tom, he took a double take.

Tom remained pressed against the door. Behind him, the wind howled and wailed.

"Yer a brave man tae come in here," the bartender said.

A few of the snugs were occupied, fewer than he had anticipated. He figured the men he had to worry about were the ones he had left at the church. The men at the snugs sat at their tables like wolves shocked that a deer had walked into their den.

Tom adjusted his coat and brushed his disheveled hair, pretending to be confident and hoping the men were too interested in their beers to get up from their snugs and give him trouble.

The men eyed him, watching.

Tom went to the bartender. He leaned over the counter. "Can I use your phone?"

The bartender grimaced. "Payin' customers only."

Tom reached for his wallet. It was not in his back pocket. "Damn. It's at the police station."

"Then best ye go get it."

The bartender returned to cleaning his glass.

The other men in the snugs watched him. One or two continued their conversations, but the rest waited for Tom's next move.

The door to the pub remained shut. The howling and the wailing went away, and the wind no longer pressed against the doors.

Tom could try to go outside again, but no telling what would happen if he did. Could he make it to the station? Was O'Malley there? Did he have friends anywhere in town? He'd have to find his wallet anyway if he was going to escape Thurwick with Marella.

Tom would have to rush through those doors and run for the station.

"Yer na' goin' tae win," came a voice in the back.

In a far snug sat an old man with a beard. A brown hat covered his gray hair. His cheeks were flushed, and his hands that wrapped around his beer were spotted and rough like they had been worn from years of outdoor use.

The other men in the snugs paid no attention to the voice but, losing interest in Tom, they returned to their beers and their storytelling.

The bartender cleaned his glasses, not paying Tom or the man in the back any attention.

The old man in the far snug held a glass of beer and waited, eyeing Tom with his intense blue eyes.

With no other options, Tom went through the pub past the darkly lit snugs and sat down.

The man's skin appeared rough, like an old farmhand whose skin had been weathered by years of tilling under the sun, or an out-of-work seaman whose hands leathered from tying too many ropes. Hanging around his neck was a brown string. At the end of it hung a hand-carved wooden cross.

He swore he had seen him before. But where? "What do you know?" Tom said.

The old man hunched over his beer. Bits of foam had collected on his gray mustache. "Plenty," he said.

"Enlighten me," Tom said.

"You don' know wha' yer dealin' wi', lad."

"You're right."

The old man leaned back. He took another swig of his beer, then set it down on the wood table. He brushed the foam off his face with his sleeve. His deep blue eyes watched Tom like a rancher watching his livestock. "Are ye leaving town?" the old man said.

"I've been told I should."

"So why are you still here?"

"I'm trying to protect someone."

The man squeezed his glass, and his white knuckles showed. His eyes flashed like they held a memory of some event from long ago. A slight curl formed on the edges of his lips. "Ye've go' hero's blood in ye, lad."

Tom studied the man. Where had he seen him before? He tried to jog his memory, but the events of the past few days occupied his mind. The old man's skin had been roughened more than any of the other locals in Thurwick.

Tom relaxed his jaw, letting show a hint of a smile. "Been a while since I heard a compliment from a stranger."

"Don' le' it go tae yer head." The old man took another swig and wiped his face with his sleeve.

Tom was growing impatient. He didn't know what the old man was going to say, but Marella was out there, and that thing pulled Liz out the window. He remembered the hotel clerk. No doubt the man would find the damaged room and call the police. He'd be easy to find in Guthrie's Pub. The four o'clock subpoena was approaching, yet he'd been advised to leave town and not show up, or else his life was at stake.

"Look," Tom said. "I'm kind of in a hurry. Why'd you call me over here?"

"Yer dealing wi' powers ye don' understand," the old man said.

"You already said that."

"Trus' me."

"Sir, with all due respect, I don't have time for riddles."

"Ye better make time, lad."

Tom shifted in his seat, edging to the end of the table. "Thanks. I have to get going."

228

The old man eyed his beer. Tom slid on the wooden bench to leave.

"Yer ha'ing women troubles, aren't ye, lad?"

Tom stopped in his seat. He studied the man, pausing.

"I though' so," the old man said. "Had a few disappear on ye, hadn' ye?"

"You could say that."

"What ye need is in the barn. Find it."

"You know about the barn?"

"Aye," the old man said.

Tom squinted as chills ran down his body. The last time Tom had crossed the loch, he had lost control of his senses, ever since he went inside the old barn on the other side of Loch Ness. Sean Paterson had warned Tom not to go there, but something had pulled him toward it. While the townspeople searched for the Loch Ness monster during Thurwick Local Council Chairman Briggs's Nessie Day, Tom leaped from Sean's boat and swam to the opposite shore. Nothing could stop him. Upon his landing, he climbed up the muddy slope and entered an old barn under a tree. The old barn contained hanging rusty tools and a sandy floor under a disintegrating roof.

Nothing else.

It was upon his leaving the barn that things changed. People claimed he had disappeared for several days, but his memory told him no time had passed at all. When he had learned he missed his flight, things got strained with Marella. Worse, after the barn, Tom had acquired what Father Gibson said was an obsession curse. The curse urged him to find the Loch Ness monster. It was the same curse that Sean had had for thirty years.

Once the monster was found and rescued, however, the obsession curse left Tom and Sean. Both of them had been freed from the curse. Tom was going to live happily ever after with Marella. "What is that place?" Tom said.

"Tis na th' place tha' matters, lad. Tis wha's inside it."

"There's nothing in there but a bunch of old rusty tools."

The old man shook his head. He shifted like he was getting up to leave. "Maybe yer na th' hero I though' ye were. Since ye already know everythin'—."

Tom put out his hand. "Wait. Okay. That place gives me the chills. But I have to help someone. I'm afraid a friend of mine's in danger. If it means going back in there will protect her, I'll do it."

The old man returned to his seat. He put his hands around his mug of beer. His eyes sparkled like he remembered a flashback of a time long ago. "Alrigh'. Wha' ye need is buried underneath th' barn."

"In the ground?"

"Aye."

"What is it?"

"The amulet."

"What amulet?"

"The one that'll answer yer questions"

"Which questions? I have so many."

"There's many secrets about th' loch," the old man said. "Some ye don' wan' tae know."

"I saw something I never want to see again," Tom said.

"Ye'll see worse," the old man said, "if ye don' recover th' amulet. Some are sayin' fur ye tae leave, but wha's ou' there will follow ye where'er ye run."

The doors to the pub burst open. Officers O'Reilly and Burns stood in the doorway, letting in the gray sunlight. The wind blew past them, blowing Tom's hair.

Tom's muscles tensed. He swore. "I gotta run!"

The bench across the table was empty.

"What the—?" Tom said.

There was no beer. No man. No weathered hands. No hanging cross.

"Where'd he go?" Tom's face grew pale. He grabbed the table, searching under and around the snug.

The old man had disappeared.

"He's over there, talkin' tae himself." The bartender pointed at Tom.

O'Reilly and Burns ran up to Tom, cornering him. Burns grabbed Tom by the arm around his coat sleeve.

"You again," Tom said. "Didn't the Council tell you to leave me alone until four?"

"Trouble follows ye wherever ye go, doesn' it?" Burns said. His freckled face grew red as he lifted Tom from his seat.

"Back tae th' station wi' ye," O'Reilly said. Burns and O'Reilly pulled Tom from the snug and led him past the bartender.

The police officers gripped his arms and they forced him out of the pub amidst the delighted eyes of the beer-drinking locals. While Tom was being moved through the door, questions ran through his mind.

Who was the old man?

How did he disappear?

And where had he seen him before?

CHAPTER 39

"Where do ye think he is?" Sean said.

Detective O'Malley's car entered the square. The detective steered as they entered the familiar bumpy cobblestone streets. Sean sat in the passenger seat. He squinted as he studied the scene through his rain-streaked windshield.

"Na far," O'Malley said. He pointed out the window. "There."

Sean scanned the scene through the rain. In the middle of it, O'Reilly and Burns pulled Tom across the windy square toward the police station. "Oh no," Sean said.

"Aye. They've go' him."

"Will they hurt him?"

"Na tellin'."

Sean scratched his temple. "Wha'd th' lad do now?"

"I'm sure they thought o' somethin', whether he did it o' not," O'Malley said. "We've go' tae get him free."

"Wha' do we do?"

"We wait," O'Malley said.

"Wait? Fur wha'?"

"Hold on." O'Malley pulled to the side of the road. O'Reilly and Burns had their focus on Tom, pulling him via his arms across the awkward cobblestones and through the rain and wind toward the police station. As the three of them approached the building, a sharp white blast of lightning struck a nearby tree, releasing an instant thunderous clap.

"Woa!" Sean said. "That'll keep ye on yer toes!"

A strong gust of wind blew three large shingles off the coffee shop's roof. They fell with a thud and twisted and rolled with the wind past the men until they settled near the sidewalk.

"Nature isn't tae happy today," O'Malley said. "Digger'll be hidin' under th' bed."

The officers and Tom reached the station where they went inside the door. Sheets of rain splattered upon O'Malley's windshield.

Sean leaned forward, trying to clear his vision through the rain. He was ready to run inside and help break the lad out, but then he remembered he no longer had his leg. It was something he had to remind himself: where before he could just get up and walk, he had to get used to the fact that his mobility had changed - permanently. "Wha' do we do now?"

"Let's go," O'Malley said. He put the car in drive and it rolled to the station. He parked it right out front, a prime place in case they needed to escape. O'Malley opened his door, and the rain outside echoed as it hit the stones on the road. "Need me tae help?"

Sean shook his head. "Na." He reached for his crutch, opened the door, and pulled himself out into the rain, balancing on his one good leg and holding the car roof to steady himself until he propped the crutch under his arm. "Come on," Sean said. "Let's go in for a rescue!"

CHAPTER 40

Marella held the four-leaf clover earrings in her hand. She had brought them inside after they were on the grill, still not sure what she should do with them. She placed them on the dresser. One of them glinted green from the overhead light.

She threw her dress, some blouses, a pair of pants, and her hair dryer in her suitcase. The small house was quiet in the countryside with her father gone. The pouring rain and the wind made Sean's small home all the more isolated. It was a good house - quirky in places where Sean left the remains of his failed experiments - but it was home.

On the wall next to her was a framed photo. The picture held an image of her, her father, and her mother when she was a small girl. Marella stopped her packing for a moment and gazed upon the photo.

She remembered the day from her childhood. Marella had awakened and entered the kitchen. While her father was in the garage, making all kinds of noise removing his scientific gadgets from the car to make room for her and her mother, her mother was cooking eggs in the frying pan. Her mother mentioned how she had seen bird feathers near the mailbox.

Marella asked her if she was cooking the eggs left by the birds. Her mother had laughed and pointed to the refrigerator.

The eggs were good, and her mother asked Marella if she was excited about going fishing. Marella, a certified tomboy, couldn't wait to go. She loved the loch, splashing in the water, watching for fish, and feeling the cool highland wind upon her cheeks.

Half an hour later, Marella was on the boat dock, racing to the edge of the pier. Her parents followed with their fishing gear, and Sean soon set up her fishing pole.

It wasn't long before Marella had caught a fish and it hung at the end of her pole. Her face beamed like she had just won a major award.

Her mother had brought a camera. A nearby boater offered to snap the image of them, Sean and her mother standing behind Marella's proud moment, and a fish hanging by a line and flapping its tail in the air.

"Tha' was a fun day," Marella said aloud.

She studied the image of her mother. Marella admired her mother's curly red hair, her high cheekbones, and her athletic build. Marella had grown slightly taller than her mother. In her heart, she wanted nothing other than to look up to her.

She closed her eyes and breathed through her nose, imagining her mother's scent when her mother tucked her into bed. She would read her bedtime stories of knights in shining armor who fought giant fire-breathing dragons and rescued princesses trapped inside high towers.

Th' real world isn' anything like tha'.

A few days after the picture was taken, things changed.

Sean had another one of his hunts to find the monster, except he didn't come home. Her mother was worried sick. So was she. For two days, her mother had paced. She went to the police and asked neighbors if they'd seen Sean. Marella remembered how she prayed for her father to come home.

Then, two days later, Sean appeared at the front door like nothing had happened.

Marella's mother was furious. She yelled at Sean for hours, but he insisted that he had come straight home. It wasn't until he saw the paper the next day that he understood he had been missing.

Things calmed down for a few days, slowly returning to normal. Then, less than a week later, Marella had run into the kitchen, ready to sit down and eat her mother's cooked eggs.

The kitchen was empty. No eggs were cooking in the frying pan. There was none of her mother's scent. There were no words spoken about the birds. It was quiet, and her mother was gone.

Sean had searched the cottage and the surrounding countryside, but she was gone. There was no goodbye letter. No clothes had been packed. She had just up and left.

Marella went into the countryside, too, sometimes with her father, and other times on her own. She returned each evening with tears streaming down her face.

The crying continued for weeks. Then it was replaced with bouts of anger and disappointment. She refused to play with her friends. Instead, she went to the loch alone, waiting on the shore, calling for her mother to come back. She'd call for hours until the sun had set. Sean had to come to retrieve her and bring her home.

The weeks advanced into months. Marella refused to blame her father then, as even in her youth she believed Sean was confused to learn he had disappeared for two whole days.

She also believed Sean when he said he had discovered the Loch Ness monster. For a young girl who dreamed about knights in shining armor who fought dragons, the idea of her father finding a creature such as Nessie in Loch Ness excited her. Some nights, instead of missing her mother, she went to sleep imagining that she was riding the creature over the waves of the loch between the green Highland countryside. She often dreamed the creature would carry her to find her mother in some magical city deep below the water's surface.

A tapping rapped on a window in another room. Probably a bird, she thought. She picked up her blue jeans, folded them, and placed them in the suitcase.

She wore jeans when she accompanied Sean on his hunts for the creature. While her father hoped to capture an image or some other evidence to prove the monster's existence, Marella used the trips to search for her mother and fuel more hopeful dreams of finding her.

Her father, though, happened to be a clutz. On one excursion, he dropped an expensive device into the water where it sank to the bottom. On another, he stood and slipped, falling backward into the loch. Marella had to reach down and help him into the boat.

The worst trip, though, happened when Sean thought he might lure the creature with a bright light. He brought a flare gun, which he intended to shoot high into the sky. Not knowing how it worked, he accidentally shot it in the middle of their boat, causing a leak under the flames and rising smoke.

The boat sank, and Sean and Marella held onto it, kicking it to shore.

Sean never brought home the proof of the monster, the evidence he needed to restore his reputation and restore his ability to get scientific research grants. Instead, he brought more stress upon the house. When the bills came, he would spend the evening wondering how he would pay them.

Marella, though, continued to join Sean on the loch, hoping upon hope that the monster would bring her mother home.

Marella held onto that hope all her young childhood.

Then she became a teenager. Though Sean refused to abandon his search, Marella's doubts grew. Why had her father spent more energy searching for the Loch Ness monster rather than searching for her mother? She wanted to ask him that question, but she held her tongue.

Until one day she couldn't hold it anymore.

It was August 8th; her mother's birthday. Marella was nineteen. On that day, Sean finished loading another camera machine into the trunk of his rusty car. He was making final preparations, writing figures in his notebook, before driving to the boat dock and hunting for the creature.

Marella had said, "Shouldn' we do somethin' tae celebrate mom's birthday? Ye know, in honor o' her?"

Sean raised his eyebrows. "Well, I guess we could. How about when I ge' back?"

A flash of anger ran through Marella. It was the nonchalant way he said it, as though it was a chore to add to the list rather than an acknowledgment of special memories she had from her childhood.

His words hurt her, and that night, as the sun retreated behind the green hills and Sean was late coming home from his excursion, she had had enough.

The next day Marella had written a note for her father and set it on her bed and closed the door. Then she left the house, went to Thurwick, took a bus to Inverness, and bought a plane ticket to America. No matter the difficulty, she promised herself to find out what else was out there.

She first arrived in New York, but the busyness of the city, though at first exciting, was too much. She discovered she did miss the countryside of the Scottish Highlands, so she researched other cities where the pace was less intense.

She moved to Atlanta, landing an apartment through a connection she met at a church, and then getting a job as a waitress in a Buckhead restaurant.

That was where she met Tom Wayne. She had figured he had a crush on her, but when he asked her out after coming to her aid, she accepted his invitation for a date.

The day of their date happened to be the same day her father phoned her and said he needed her help. Date or not, Sean was the only family she had, and despite her hurt, she left Atlanta and returned to Thurwick.

A few days after Marella had arrived back home, Tom had appeared on Sean's doorstep. When she no-showed on their date, she told herself somehow she'd make it up to him. A short while later, however, he stood on her father's front steps, his handsome face shining in the sun with the Highland countryside behind him. She flushed with joy.

Unfortunately, her family's history was not one for the record books. She was convinced once Tom learned of her father's belief about the Loch Ness monster he would abandon her.

But Tom didn't. Despite her disbelief, Tom helped her father prove the monster existed, and the obsession curse that haunted her father all those years went away.

Today, her father was a different man. Though he only had one leg, Sean's mind and his thoughts were no longer held captive to the creature in the loch. Instead, Sean focused on his engineering experiments. Sean had changed, and Marella was happy that things were getting back to normal.

And Marella owed it all to Tom. He had fought the local conspiracy, saved the Loch Ness monster from their evil plans, and reunited her father with her, giving her the only family she had.

Marella stopped packing. She went to the earrings. She admired them, not wanting to throw them away. She remembered the past several weeks.

While Sean recovered in the hospital, Tom and Marella spent time together. She had let her guard down, getting to know him as he, too, recovered from his injuries. How had he survived? Imagine the violence he, an ordinary man in his early twenties, had witnessed when he didn't ask for it!

Yet he took his recovery in stride, focusing on her and helping Sean with his therapy after the loss of his leg. Tom was attentive to Marella, and he helped with all the things she needed. Things were improving for her. She imagined a family might be possible.

And she was falling for Tom.

Something, though, bothered her. This weather, for one. It made her nervous like it was threatening her. But there was something else she couldn't quite put her finger on. Tom was in danger.

But from what? She couldn't say. A strange, ominous force grew around Tom. Something inside her said the strange weather was a part of it.

She also didn't like that the reporter, the girl from the London magazine, was trying to get an interview. It wasn't the interview that bothered her, though. Any interview that helped bring attention to her father's work would help fix their financial situation. Sean might even get grants from universities, and they'd recover his losses.

Of course, the tale of the Loch Ness monster - and what a tale it was - was the primary interest among salacious periodicals written in travel and cryptozoological magazines. They paid handsomely for Tom's and Sean's story. Still, she didn't like the attention.

What she wanted was a normal life.

Except the Loch Ness monster was anything but normal. For some reason - whether by fate or pure coincidence - her father and Tom had found it. Now, if only the world would leave them alone so they could go on with their lives.

Marella hummed a song. The earrings sparkled. "Ah, hell," she said. She picked up the earrings and hooked them into her lobes. They glinted green as they adorned her ears. She smiled, thinking of Tom.

She folded another blouse and put it in the suitcase. As she hummed, she imagined Tom coming back, and the two of them leaving Thurwick. She imagined a new life with Tom somewhere where there were no monsters, no conniving politicians, and no reporters.

As she paused her humming, the faint sound of music drifted through the air. It came from off in the distance. She shook her head.

Why were the hairs stiffening on her arms?

CHAPTER 41

The gate slammed behind Tom after Burns threw him into the cell. Tom grunted when his shoulder slammed into the far brick wall. He righted himself and brushed the dirt from his coat.

Burns stood outside the cell bars, his shoulders tense from pulling Tom across the Thurwick square.

Rain echoed through the ceiling, falling hard upon the station roof. O'Reilly stood next to Felicia, handing her his form of Tom's arrest. Her eyes shifted between O'Reilly and Tom, unable to hide her disappointment.

Sandra typed, paying no mind to the others in the room.

Was Felicia the one who had helped him earlier? Sandra, on the other hand, acted like she was only interested in work.

Officer Burns's face remained red from pulling on Tom. He watched him from the other side of the cell bars, his chest rising and falling with each breath.

"While I'm here," Tom said, "Can you give me back my wallet?"

Burns shook his head. "Ye should have thought about tha' before ye blew up th' hotel."

Tom pressed his lips together, remembering the last scream of Liz Stevens as those strange arms yanked her through the window. He shuddered. Rather than say the wrong thing, he decided to remain quiet. He sat on the floor with his back against the wall.

"Wha'? Nothin' tae say?" Burns said, focusing his eyes on Tom with laser-like precision.

The front door opened, and two familiar shapes entered the doorway while the wind and the rain blew in from the outside. Tom recognized them, and he stood. "Am I glad to see you!"

Detective Logan O'Malley and Sean Paterson came inside. Several papers blew off the interior desks as the wind entered the open door. Felicia put her hand on O'Reilly's form to keep the wind from blowing it. Even Sandra stopped typing for a moment to straighten her hair. Her eyes held a hint of worry. A faint wailing whistled through the wind.

Sean shut the door and walked straight to Tom, limping with his crutch and his one leg. "Ye alrigh', lad?"

Burns held his ground, putting his arm out to block Sean's path. "Na talkin' tae th' prisoner."

"What's th' charges?" O'Malley said. He stood next to Felicia, picking up O'Reilly's form from her desk and scanning it with his eyes.

"Destruction o' property," O'Reilly said. The officer approached the cell. "And suspicion o' murder."

Tom shook his head. "That's not what happened."

"Hadn' we been through this already?" O'Malley said.

"New event," Burns said. "Got a call from th' Sterling Hotel's clerk. Mobley."

"I know him," O'Malley said. "Quiet type."

"Aye," O'Reilly said. "But na' today. He was all a mess when we responded tae th' call, and it checked ou'. Same as Annabel's."

O'Malley raised his eyebrows. "What do you mean?"

Sean stood still, watching the conversation. His eyes studied the cell lock like he imagined a key that he could fashion and break Tom free.

O'Reilly said, "It was th' same. Claw marks and black feathers scattered across a room. Furniture ripped tae shreds. Except 'tis time th' window was shattered. The lady who rented th' room, Liz Stevens, went upstairs wi' him," pointing at Tom, "but she didn' come down wi' him. Being th' detective, ye'll wan' tae see this one, tae."

O'Malley said, "Stevens, th' reporter?"

"Aye."

"Did ye find her?"

"Na," O'Reilly said. "Bu' I bet Mr. Wayne knows where she is."

Tom kept his mouth shut, listening. So Liz was missing. They didn't find her body, unlike how he had found Annabel crumpled next to the exterior wall of her bed and breakfast. Should he tell them? They'd never believe him.

O'Malley frowned. "Does th' Council know about this?"

"Na," O'Reilly said. "But ye know how word spreads. I bet it won' take long before they do."

The wind slammed against the outer walls of the station, and a sudden flash of lightning lit up the windows. The interior lights flickered before a thunderous boom covered the town of Thurwick. The shudders shook from the sound waves.

Sean reached out and grabbed the cell bars. "Tha' was tae close," he said. "I'm gettin' a feelin' we're na safe in here."

There was a loud crash outside, and with the sound, the interior lights went out and the station went dark.

"Dammit," O'Reilly said.

"Tree?" said Burns. The weather was enough to pull his focus away from Tom.

"Somethin' must have taken out a power line."

Sandra had stopped typing. She picked up her phone. "Line's dead, tae." She grabbed her desk.

Felicia stood up. "Wha' should we do?"

Another clap of thunder rolled over the town, and the men and women in the station ducked. Even Burns crouched at the lightning's loud thunder.

Tom watched their puzzled faces. He had to tell them. They'd never believe him, but he had to try. "There's something else going on," he said.

They all stared at Tom, but what the hell? The far wall contained the image of the Loch Ness monster. Hidden by the shadows, the image had transformed into something black and ominous. Less than a month ago, he believed the Loch Ness monster was a myth. Once he had seen it for himself, in all its speed and muscle and power, everything changed. There was more to the world than he imagined.

And that included strange poltergeists dressed in hoods that spread black feathers and yanked unsuspecting women from their bedrooms. He opened his mouth. He had to give it a try, to warn them, to let them know.

Felicia and Sandra left their desks and approached Tom. Everyone huddled close, like a herd protecting itself from the storm. The wind and the rain pounded the station.

"Well?" O'Reilly said. "We're waitin'."

Everyone's attention was on Tom.

"I was in Liz Stevens's room. She was going to interview me."

Sean's face grew stern. Tom got the impression that the man, protective of his daughter, was questioning if he should believe him. Did he suspect Tom was seeing another woman behind his daughter's back?

Tom knew he was innocent. He also knew what had happened. No matter what Marella had accused him of, he knew he was in love with her. He had been since he first saw her in the Atlanta restaurant. It would work out. It had to. Stick with the truth, he thought. I can't control it if they don't believe me.

Tom said, "What happened next is hard to explain. There was a noise at the window, like a tapping. It wouldn't stop. Liz put her notebook and pen down and got up to check on it. Then the glass shattered, the wind blew in the room, and . . ." Tom swallowed hard. ". . . two arms stretched through the window."

"Arms?" O'Malley said.

"Yeah. And not human, either. The hands had long dark claws. They grabbed Liz, wrapping around her." He paused, trying to say the words but not focusing on the horror he witnessed.

"Arms." Burns repeated. "From th' second story window."

The others waited, their eyes and ears listening to hear under the noise of the rain and wind that hammered the police station.

"That's right." Tom said, "The arms yanked her from the window. I turned tail and ran. The door wouldn't open, like some force tried to keep it closed, so I lowered my shoulder and broke through it. Once I was through, I high tailed it down the stairs and out the front door."

"I don' believe this," Burns said.

Detective O'Malley, Officer O'Reilly, and Felicia looked at Tom like he had lost his mind. Sean nodded at least, willing to believe as he, too, had seen the Loch Ness monster.

Burns put his hands on his hips and stepped away from the group.

Sandra put her hand over her open mouth. Her eyes widened with terror. Behind her hand, she exclaimed, "Caoineags!"

"Don' be ridiculous," Burns said.

The thunder cracked again, lighting the room.

"I'm not lying," Tom said.

"You think we're goin' tae belie'e tha'?" Burns said. He pulled his nightstick with his right hand and thumped the end of it into his left palm.

Sean leaned against his crutch and said, "Put tha' away."

Burns's eyes flashed at the one-legged man.

"I'm telling you I was freaked out!" Tom said.

Through the walls was another crash, like the combination of wood and metal colliding. Excited voices echoed in the Thurwick square amidst the wind and the rain.

Sandra bumped into a desk. She gathered herself and went to the coat hangar where she grabbed her coat. She threw it over her shoulder like she was going to miss her bus.

"Where are ye goin'?" Felicia said.

"Far away from him!" Sandra said. She hurried out the door. "If I were ye, I'd do th' same!" The wind hit her broadside and she stumbled through the rain as the door closed behind her.

"What's a caoineag?" Tom said.

More excited voices came from outside, including a woman's scream.

Then the door was thrown open, and a man ran inside the doorway. He slammed the door and put his back on it. He saw O'Reilly and Burns in uniform and ran up to them. "We're all goin' tae die!"

Through the windows, men and women ran past the station, all hurrying in the same direction with desperation on their faces.

What are they running from?

Tom was afraid it had to do with him.

CHAPTER 42

The music stopped. The lonely sound of wind and raindrops echoed from outside.

"I'm imaginin' things," she said aloud.

There was a noise on the window in the spare bedroom across the hall. It sounded like a branch blown by the wind and tapping the glass.

Marella paid it no mind. She took the picture off the wall. "Wherever we go, mum, yer comin' with us." She laid it in her suitcase. She hummed her song again, picking up where she left off.

The tapping touched the window again.

Rat, tat. Rat, tat.

"Tha's funny," she said. "I don' remember a tree by tha' window." She left the picture and the suitcase on the bed and went into the other room. The blinds were down, and the lights were off, making the spare bedroom dark.

Outside, the wind howled, and sheets of rain hit the window.

She flipped on the lights.

Rat, tat.

It came from the other side of the blind.

She went to the window. She listened, her ear near the blind.

There was singing. But where was it coming from? It was so faint she almost didn't hear it over the sound of her heartbeat.

Rat, tat.

Marella jumped and put her hand over her heart. Gathering herself, she opened the blind.

There was nothing there.

No tree branch hit the window. No bush blew in the wind. The rain splattered on the grassy fields in the distance, leaving muddy puddles throughout the landscape. The rainwater was running past the foundation. A single black feather floated next to the mud. The grill to her left remained uncovered. She had forgotten to cover it after she had demanded that Tom leave. She regretted making him go. She had hoped he wouldn't and instead remain with her and forget the interview.

He didn't disobey her.

She wished he had.

She wished he was with her right now.

The soft melody of sad singing touched her ears. She shivered as a chill went down her body.

She looked around the window again. Nothing was there to make that sou—.

Rat, tat.

Marella put her hand over her heart.

The sound came from a different window. This time it was outside her bedroom, the one where she left her suitcase. Marella's held her breath. The tapping had moved. The singing, too. Its whisper bypassed Marella's ears and entered her head. It had to come from somewhere.

There was only one conclusion; someone was at the house.

Marella left the blind open, and she walked to the hallway. The music stopped again, retreating under the noise of wind and rain.

Rat, tat. Rat, tat.

She inched into the room where she was packing. Her mother's face watched her from the picture laying in the suitcase. Her expression had changed. She was worried.

"Be brave," Marella said, but she was afraid. It was the same fear she had regarding Tom and the woman reporter. Something was wrong with the whole situation.

And now that situation had found her.

She wished that Tom was with her right now. He'd know what to do. If only she hadn't run him off.

Rat, tat.

This blind was closed. She tried to remember what was on the other side of the window. She hoped there was some tree that Sean had planted, and because she was too worried these past few weeks she never took the time to notice it. With the wind blowing, it had to be a branch—.

Rat, tat.

She jumped. She stepped past the bed. This time, she didn't open the blind. Instead, she lifted the edge of the blind and tried to see through the crack. The rain was hitting the window. In the front yard, Sean's pinwheels spun as the wind blew across the landscape. Like the backyard, mud puddles had formed everywhere. Three black feathers floated in a puddle a few meters from the house.

Rat, tat.

It came from the front door.

Marella let out a small scream before she put her hand on her chest.

Rat, tat.

She froze in place, listening. The hairs on her neck and arms stood at complete attention.

Rat, tat.

Sweat formed on Marella's brow. What was out there? Should she run? In the rain? By herself? If she ran into the country, they'd never find her.

Rat, tat.

Marella thought of hiding, waiting it out. The closet was near. But she was alone, and the house was small. Whoever it was would find her in a few moments. Hiding was not an option.

Rat, tat.

The sound had moved to the kitchen door - where the knives and pans were. She crouched and slid along the wall, leaving the bedroom, the family picture, and the suitcase behind her.

Rat, tat. Rat, tat.

Marella reached the edge of the hallway where it intersected with the kitchen. The light in the kitchen was poor without the sun, the light dim under the cover of the storm. A knife block sat across the tile floor, the knife handles sticking out of the block's many notches.

Rat, tat.

Marella tip-toed toward the knives.

A shadow moved outside the window.

Marella jumped back behind the wall, hiding in the hallway.

Her heart raced, and she lost control of her breath as she tried to stop from hyperventilating.

Rat, tat. Rat, tat.

She crouched low, frightened.

A woman's beautiful voice sang a sad song. Something about the song chilled Marella.

She regretted that she was alone. She had done this to herself.

She held back thoughts asking why she ran Tom off. She prayed he would rescue her at any moment.

CHAPTER 43

Tom clasped the cell bars with his hands, watching as O'Malley, O'Reilly, Burns, and Sean ran toward the front door of the police station. Outside, men and women scrambled across the cobblestones. O'Reilly, Burns, and O'Malley sprinted into the chaos and were soon out of sight of the doorway amidst the shouts and yells.

Sean held the door frame with his good arm. He leaned on his crutch, bracing his unstable leg from the oncoming wind.

The scared man, the witness who alerted the police to the trouble outside, remained in the center of the room, ready to duck under Sandra's desk at the first sign of trouble.

Felicia leaned against Tom's cell, afraid of what was happening outside. Her back pressed against the bars.

"Felicia, help me," Tom said.

Felicia didn't answer. She was transfixed on the commotion outside.

"Can you get me out of here?"

Felicia said, "Wha's happenin'?"

"Get me out of here," Tom said, his hands grappling the cell bars and tugging. "Help me!"

She rubbed her hands, anxious about what to do. "I don' know tha' I should."

The wind wailed again from outside. Felicia's shoulders trembled as the wailing circled the building. The ruckus in the street grew louder. Sean braced himself inside the door frame while behind him, people either ran past him or stood and pointed. What were they pointing at? The wind blew debris that rolled on the streets, and the rain splashed hard upon the cobblestones.

Tom shouted over Felicia's shoulder, "Sean. What is it? What's outside?"

"'Tis th' loch," he said, steadying himself from the wind. "Three water spouts. I've ne'er seen anythin' like it!"

Suddenly, there was a loud thud on the brick walls to Tom's left. The illustration of the Loch Ness monster silhouetted the far wall. The wall was dark, the windows being too far away to let in light. A second thud. Something outside the police station was banging on the bricks. There was a third thud. The sound of breaking bricks cracked at the far wall.

The male witness whimpered and ducked his body and head under the desk. "Oh God!" he said. He grabbed the rolling chair and pulled it in front of him, hiding in the cavity.

Behind Sean and through the front door came the sound of a whistle, shouting, and swearing. Tom knew he had to get out of the jail cell. Society was losing its grip to some mysterious force, a force that was killing people.

A fourth thud hit the wall, this time much more intense. A brick cracked and fell to the floor. The sound of breaking bricks made Tom's heart race. He remembered Liz Stevens's scream as she was pulled through the wall. Was that the fate that awaited him?

Not if I get out of here!

The wind wailed again. A woman's voice was in the sound of the wind as it circled the police station, then flew past the length of the roof before it centered its power on the far dark wall, her voice entering through the small holes that remained above the broken bricks on the floor.

Felicia pressed her back against the cell, the steel bars indenting her blouse. She stared at the wall. Her breathing went up and down as panic built up in her core. Tom needed her help, but fright had overcome her. "Felicia," Tom said. "It'll be alright. Help me, and I'll get you out of here."

Several more thuds hit the bricks.

Felicia froze; her knees trembled. Her face went white with fear.

"Oh God!" the man under the desk said. "It's coming inside!" He pulled the chair closer. He tried to make himself smaller as his body contorted around the chair and he hid under the desk.

Tom leaned his mouth to the cell close to Felicia's ear. "Felicia. Give me the keys to the cell. I can't help you from in here."

The wall was hit with a great thud, and several bricks broke inward. Dust and wind and rain blew into the large hole. The dust billowed into the air. The outside light was blocked by a dark shadow that moved with the swaying of a hungry predator.

More thuds hit the bricks. The wailing grew into a piercing scream.

Felicia threw her hands up and covered her ears.

"Felicia!" Tom reached through the bars and grabbed her shoulder.

She was frozen, panicked. She shut her eyes. Her hands and fingers grew white as she pressed them against the sides of her skull.

"Felicia, give me the keys!"

She blinked. She took two steps to the nearest desk. She opened a drawer and pulled out a keyring carrying several keys. The keys jingled in her trembling hands.

"Here!" Tom said, his hand outstretched between the bars.

Still in the doorframe, the wind hit Sean, knocking him off balance. He fell to the floor inside the police station, losing his crutch.

The scream pierced the air, and there was a crunching sound as several bricks in the far wall flew from their place and rolled upon the floor. Inside the broken image of the Loch Ness monster, a gray hand with dark claws reached inside the hole, its outstretched claws swinging wildly, first toward Tom, then at the bricks, scraping and twisting to make the hole bigger.

The arm frightened Felicia. She ran from the desk back to Tom. She pressed her body against the cell bars like a rabbit about to be pulled from its den. "Don' le' it take me!"

Tom tried not to look. The cracked walls fall apart.

"Mine!" came a voice through the walls.

Felicia shivered.

Tom reached through the cell bars and took the keys out of Felicia's hands. While she hyperventilated in front of him, he worked the keys, frantically trying one after another to open the lock.

The wall tore apart, and bricks collapsed. The image of the Loch Ness monster disappeared in a pile of dust. The far roof fell, and the wailing voice screamed in anger.

The man under the desk yelled. "Oh God. It's inside!" An invisible force grasped the man's leg, and he let out a panicked scream as it dragged him toward the dust and the bricks and the arm and the falling roof. He yelled, begging for help. His leg was lifted into the dust, and the man let out a terrifying scream that lasted a moment in the darkness and then was no more.

"Mine!" the voice yelled again from the dust covering the broken wall.

Tom's hands shook, trying more of the keys. Felicia slinked her body along the bars, but inches at a time as her legs were paralyzed with fear.

Tom tried the last key, and it opened the cell. "Got it!"

Felicia's blouse ripped forward from her body. An invisible force pulled her with a violent tug. She yelled in terror as her torso lifted and her feet dangled in the air. Her arms flailed at her sides. She kicked her legs, but she was helpless.

Tom leaped for Felicia. He grabbed for her leg against her panicked kicks, but his hand fell off her calf, taking her shoe with him. He fell to the floor and watched as the force pulled Felicia away from him.

"Help!" Her face went white with terror.

She flew across the room toward the wall, through the air into the dust and the darkness. The clawed arm outstretched its hand, its palm and its claws open wide, waiting for her to arrive into its clutches.

Felicia screamed.

Tom arose from his belly on the floor, Felicia's shoe in his hand. He took a step after her, but it was too late.

Felicia disappeared into dust and shadows. She let out a scream that ended, replaced by the sound of whirling wind and outside thunder.

Tom backed away. The piercing cry of the wailing spirit echoed inside the room.

"Tom!" Sean yelled. "Ge' away from there!"

A lightning bolt struck outside. The air in the room swirled around Tom.

The arm reappeared through the dust. "Tom!" came the voice.

Tom threw Felicia's shoe at the arm, where it disappeared into the hole in the wall.

"Tom!" the voice said again. It cackled like a witch stirring her brew.

Papers lifted off their desks and flew through the swirling air, orchestrating a circle around him.

Tom spun, checking his surroundings. The noise outside remained in chaos, but the darkness of a powerful spirit spread through the room.

"Return." the voice said. "Return to me!"

The papers spun closer to him. The air was closing in on him.

"You are mine!"

"The hell I am!" Tom said. He ducked his head and, lowering his shoulder, jumped through the papers.

A powerful force swung him over Felicia's desk. Several invisible hands grabbed his arms and legs. The hands had power and strength, holding Tom down like a lion that captured a gazelle.

He twisted and punched at the air, knowing something was there but he was unable to see it. The invisible force clasped upon his legs. It pulled him hard, hurting his hip and his knee.

"Let go of me!" Tom shouted, kicking through the invisible hands that pressed upon his calves, shins, and thighs. He twisted and grabbed for whatever he could reach, something strong enough to counter the strength of the force that pulled him. He extended his hand and grasped something metal.

Sean's crutch!

"Hang on!" Sean said. He was holding one of the cell bars with one hand, while his grip held the crutch with the other. Papers, staplers, paperclips, and post-it notes flew past his head. They spun in a whirlwind around and over the two men, increasing their speed with each rotation of the wind.

Tom was lifted into the air as the force jerked his leg.

"Tom!" wailed the cackling voice. The sound of the wind grew and rumbled inside Tom's ears like a train was next to him, rumbling upon its tracks. The floor vibrated.

Tom flexed his muscles, straining with all he had to hold on. He kicked, but the forces that held him were too strong.

Black feathers appeared in the circling whirlwind, blocking out the light. The sight of them confused Tom, and he yelled like a warrior fighting a lion, knowing his days were numbered but he was not going to go down without a fight.

Tom's grip slipped. He strained to hold tight, his hand slid down the shaft of Sean's crutch.

Sean's face grimaced, his arm straining like a man preparing to lose another limb but had predetermined not to let go no matter the cost.

The feathers swarmed all around the men, spinning, circling, closing in.

A deep chill penetrated Tom. It pressed inside him.

His grip grew weaker.

He wouldn't be able to hold on much longer.

CHAPTER 44

Marella pressed her back against the wall. The heaviness in the air came down upon her. Somewhere a woman sang.

My love has gone and run
Tae another, tha' they say,
It is ye who offer fun
Bu' na longer in th' way.

Marella held her breath, trying to understand the words.

A force grabbed her ankles. It felt like hands. She couldn't see them, but they were there, pressing around her legs and pulling.

She didn't have time to brace. The force dragged her down the hallway, then pulled her into the kitchen.

Marella reached for the wall but was unable to hold it. Her torso swung around as the force lifted her legs. She grabbed the kitchen table leg. The table slid across the floor, then broke and collapsed. She kicked. Her legs freed. She climbed to her feet and reached for the block of table knives.

The block flew from its position and hit her in the chest, then fell to the floor. Marella fell backward, her spine landing against the counter. The knives slid from their places while the block crashed to the floor. Black feathers floated in the room.

Marella held onto the counter, but her legs lifted into the air. She fell to the floor, her arms and elbows bracing her face from hitting the floor.

The force dragged her, breaking the door open. The door flew wide and hit the outer wall.

It pulled her outside the door and over the grass.

Feathers hovered in the wind and fell upon the ground.

The house slipped away from her behind the grass and the dirt. She clawed at everything, pulling up weeds and feathers and soil, but nothing stopped the force that dragged her into the country.

She went over a hill. There was the wailing of a woman, the song of music, the whirlwind of air, the spinning of black feathers, the feeling of mist, the glow of light, and the hint of darkness. She let out a final scream, and then she lost consciousness.

The invisible force let go of Tom's legs. The feathers fell for a second and then they regrouped. Tom used the half-second to strengthen his grip on Sean's crutch. A raging wail echoed inside the room as the invisible force grabbed Tom's leg again and pulled him. The grips clawed and dug through his jeans and into his skin.

Sean wrapped his hands on the other end of the crutch. "Hang on!" he yelled. "Don't let go!"

Tom yelled a final time, expecting to lose his grip.

Then the wind stopped, the invisible grip let go, and the feathers and papers and office equipment fell to the ground.

Tom lay on the floor, his lungs energized, his grip still holding Sean's crutch in case the force came back.

Sean remained on the ground. After several seconds, he twisted and sat up with his back against the cell bars, his one leg straight ahead. He let go of the crutch. He gasped, adrenaline flowing through his aging body. "I'm na' made fur this," he said.

"What happened?" Tom said. "Why'd it let go?"

Outside, the wind and the rain lessened. Small rays of sunlight streaked through the clouds. The shouting and the chaos subsided. The running Thurwick inhabitants slowed their pace. Many covered their eyes at the surprising sunbeams that fell upon the Thurwick courtyard.

A whistle blew. O'Reilly issued commands, telling people to get back inside until they learned what had happened.

Tom's chest rose and fell. His hand remained clasped to Sean's crutch. Across the room, the dust settled. The end of the police station looked like a wrecking ball had pulverized it. The collapsed roof covered the broken wall where the painting of the Loch Ness monster had been. All that remained was the floating dust and the outside air. More sunlight revealed the exterior setting: a side road and a fallen tree in front of the wall to a nearby pharmacy. There was broken stone, shattered glass, broken limbs, torn leaves, crumpled paper, and debris.

There was no sign of the clawed arm. Or the whimpering man. Or Felicia.

Sean picked up one of the hundreds of black feathers that covered the floor. He held it in front of his eyes, studying it. "Wha' are these?"

"I don't know," Tom said.

Sean examined the feather, closing one eye while keeping the other open. "They didn' jus' show up ou' o' nowhere. I wan' tae examine them."

Tom rose to his feet. He picked up Sean's crutch, then lifted Sean to his feet as well. The two men leaned on each other until Sean balanced with his crutch under his arm.

"Wha' is goin' on here?" Sean said.

Tom shook his head. "Something very strange." He studied the room. He kicked the feathers at his feet. Several desks had been overturned. Dust, paper, and black feathers covered the floor. "Man, a tornado's been in here."

Tom reached down and rubbed his legs. They hurt like they had been scratched with cat claws.

"Ye alrigh', lad?" Sean said.

"I'll be okay," Tom said.

"I hate tae tell ye this, bu' trouble is followin' ye."

Tom remembered, "Felicia!"

He ran to the hole in the wall, jumping on top of the collapsed roof. A small portion of the wall still stood, holding up the rest. The head of the Loch Ness monster remained on the bricks. It grinned mischievously at Tom.

Tom jumped into the opening, keeping his balance upon the fallen beams and shingles. The fallen tree rested outside. The windblown papers had blown through the hole. But Felicia and the man were gone. There were no creepy arms, no claws.

An outstretched hand stuck out from under a piece of the roof. Tom paused, holding his stomach, not sure if he should check. Was it Felicia's? He leaned forward and stretched out his arm, lifting the roof with a finger.

The hand was a man's. There was the muscle of a forearm, but that's where it ended. The arm was detached at the shoulder.

Sean limped to Tom, his crutch under his arm. "Where'd she go?"

Tom leaned over and heaved.

"Wha'?"

Tom pointed.

"Oh," Sean said. "Wha' about th' lady?"

"I don't see her." Tom was bent over, his hands on his knees. He spat the bile from his mouth.

Sean limped left, then right, examining the area, unaffected by the arm lying in the debris.

"Doesn't that make you sick?" Tom asked.

Sean patted the stump where his leg had been with his free arm. "I know wha' tis like tae lose a limb, lad."

Tom wiped his mouth with his coat sleeve.

"She's na here," Sean said.

O'Reilly's whistle blew again. Burns shouted orders.

Detective O'Malley came through the far door. He took his hat off his head and rubbed his hair. "I've ne'er seen anythin' like tha'." Then his eyes widened when he noticed Tom and Sean at the far end of the room, standing on the collapsed roof. "Creyke. Wha' happened in here?"

"Escaped wi' our lives," Sean said.

"Where's Felicia?"

"It took her," Tom said.

O'Malley frowned. "Wha' took her?"

Tom focused his eyes through the hole toward the ground. In the mud next to the wall there was a strange track. It was shaped like a clawed foot. It resembled a crow's foot, its length eight inches from heel to toe, far larger than any crow's foot Tom had seen. Amidst the shadows, the felled tree, the soil, and the severed arm several black feathers were scattered.

He pointed at the strange track. "Whatever left that."

CHAPTER 45

Tom balanced himself and searched the area while he stood upon the collapsed roof, searching for Felicia and the man, though he doubted he'd find either and, if he did, he doubted they'd be alive. He remembered the noises of the screams, the flesh and the bones being destroyed. The power of the invisible force that had held him had been tremendous. No way either would be alive. He would not either if it hadn't been for Sean.

As he searched the ground, he thought that there should be blood. Tom studied the ground he was on. The broken bricks were scattered all over. Black feathers blew in the breeze. The clouds overhead broke in places, and the sun's rays hit Tom's face.

O'Malley said, "Council is goin' tae want tae talk wi' ye."

"Still?" Sean said. "Ye think these events would distract them."

"Quite th' opposite. After what jus' happened, they'll want tae ge' rid o' him more than e'er."

Tom said, "I don't know what's happening. But I think I know who does."

"Who?" Sean said.

"Father Gibson." Tom reached into his pocket and pulled out the paper and the phone number. "I need a phone!" He jumped back into the damaged police station. He shoved a desk out of his way and ran to Felicia's desk. Her phone had fallen on the ground. He picked up the phone and set it on the desk, placing the receiver into its holster. He lifted the receiver to his ear. "Damn. No dial tone."

O'Malley lifted his cell phone. He pressed a button, then put it down. "I'm na gettin' a reception," he said.

Sean pointed. "Power's out everywhere."

Tom scanned the scene outside. Local Thurwick residents were leaving their businesses. The attorney, Jacob Stewart, talked with a lady who waived her arms. There was the bartender at Guthrie's pub, wiping his hands with a towel. And O'Reilly blowing his whistle and ordering people to stay inside.

Officer Burns pointed at people. Self-proclaimed Chairman Bain hurried across the square, talking with O'Reilly and giving orders.

Tom stepped off the rubble and went to the corner of the square. He wanted to see the buildings for himself. The building windows were dark. Where before they displayed the warm glow of activity, now everything was off.

Bain shouted to O'Reilly, "Where's th' American?"

O'Reilly and Burns walked toward the police station. The three of them, as if remembering Tom, suddenly hurried in his direction.

"I need to go," Tom said.

"Aye. Run!" said O'Malley.

Tom gave a soft salute, then leaped over some debris.

"Wait!"

Tom stopped.

Sean said, "Where are ye goin'?"

"I have an idea," Tom said.

"One thing."

O'Reilly and Burns were almost at the door.

"Hurry!" Tom said.

"Stay away from me daughter."

Tom flinched, hurt by the words. After all he had done for Marella. After all he had done to help her. And help Sean. He had been loyal. It wasn't his fault.

"Ye might put her in danger. Promise me ye'll keep yer distance, at least until ye figure out wha's happenin'."

Burns was at the door. Tom ducked behind the wall. As much as it hurt him, Sean had a point. He wanted Marella's safety, but something was happening to people around him. First Annabel. Then Liz Stevens. Then Felicia and the man who hid under the desk. He had to find out what was happening, and the only one who sounded like he had any real idea was Father Gibson, the priest hiding out in London. There was also the old man, the one he had met an hour ago at Guthrie's Pub. Except that man had disappeared.

Tom didn't know what to think. He knew he needed answers. He sprinted past the felled tree, and ran through the corridors, avoiding the locals and leaving Sean and O'Malley to stall the police and Councilman Bain.

Tom knew as he ran through the town that it wouldn't be easy to be unseen, but it didn't matter. Somewhere there was a phone. He had to find it.

And he had to call Marella.

CHAPTER 46

Tom sprinted between the two stone buildings, his feet running upon the cobblestone streets. The sunlight shone through the clouds, a welcome relief from the calming storm. The air was still cool, and he sweated under his green coat. But there was no time to take it off. He had to find out what was happening.

He stepped in a puddle as he rounded a corner, soaking his shoe and the bottom of his jeans.

He gathered himself, running, searching.

The building windows were dark. There were no lights.

He passed a window where two children, a girl and a boy, stared at him through the glass. He passed another, and a woman watched him run. Terror covered her face. The power was off inside all the buildings, giving Thurwick the eerie presence of a ghost town. There had to be a phone nearby, something that worked, something that would let him call the priest.

He had to find out what was going on. Father Gibson had said the whole town was cursed. What did that mean? Annabel was dead, and her Bed and Breakfast was trashed. There was a strange woman in a hood. Three locals, two of them police officers, were missing. He shuddered at the memory of the arms that grabbed Liz Stevens and Felicia, and the invisible hands and nails that clawed at his legs.

And the feathers. Those black feathers appeared whenever there was an incident.

What was going on? And was Marella in danger? He had a sinking feeling that she was, though he couldn't explain why. Was it the women around him? The old man in the bar, the strange one that disappeared without a trace, had mentioned Tom was having "women problems," as if he understood. Would that mean that Marella was a target?

He had to find out, but that posed two questions. First, would Marella even be receptive to him? If he called her, would she listen? She was pretty mad when he mentioned the interview with Liz Stevens. Marella had told him to leave. He had agreed. Maybe he shouldn't have. Maybe he should have stayed and argued with her. He should have convinced her he should stay. He should have told her he wanted to protect her whether she liked it or not.

Yes. That's what he should have done.

Sean told Tom to stay away from Marella. Was Sean right? Was Tom the reason for the deaths of Annabel, Stevens, and Felicia? No, Tom thought. He did not cause their death. He was not some carrier of some evil spirit, some curse. He refused to believe that.

If Marella was in trouble, despite her demanding his separation, despite her father's concern, Tom knew the danger was real. Those claws wrapped their clutches around Stevens. The invisible force yanked Felicia through the air toward those same outstretched arms. No way was he going to let that happen to Marella.

No way!

He decided he was going to go back to Marella. He would find her. He hoped that she hadn't given up and left without him. She had too much pride. It would be the thing she'd do. But, if that's what she did, he would track her down and find her, make sure she was safe. Make sure she was alright. With each motion of his arms and legs, concern swelled inside him. As he ran around each corner, his body now sweating under his green coat, trying to find a phone, his worry increased. Should he forget Thurwick and sprint to Sean's country house?

Then Tom had a thought. Maybe the storm hadn't affected Sean's electricity. Maybe, because they were outside the city limits, Sean's phone still worked. If so, he'd solve two problems at once: make sure Marella was safe, call Father Gibson, and get his questions answered.

There were so many questions. Who was that old man in Guthrie's Pub? He knew he had seen him before. But where? It had to be in a different setting, like when you know a person at work, but when you run into them at a grocery store you forget his name.

Was the old man another patron at Smith's Store? Was he a one-time patient at the hospital and had overheard Sean talk about the Loch Ness monster? Was he another priest down the hall from Father Gibson?

And how did the man disappear?

Tom stopped and put his hands on his knees, sucking in air, his eyes up and studying his surroundings. He had exited the business district and was now in a residential section of Thurwick. Townhomes stood in rows on either side of the street. On the windowsills, spring flower arrangements were damaged from the day's storm. Again, all the windows were dark. The more he thought about it, he decided he had to go to Sean's house, find Marella, and call Father Gibson. No matter what she said, no matter how Sean told him to stay away, he was going to fight for her, even if he had to fight her fears and those of her father.

But he had to get to her. He had no car. It would be a twenty-minute run, and his body was bruised, scratched, and tired from all he'd already endured. His lungs ached. Still, he had to keep going.

The townhomes extended down rows alongside the street. He noticed a bicycle lying in a garden bed next to a set of stairs. He ran up to the bicycle. Its tires were thick, equipped to handle the changing terrain of Thurwick. Someone had left it. He listened. Inside the door at the top of the stairs, someone yelled. A man and a woman were arguing; a lover's quarrel. The lights were off as the couple argued in the shadows, a common fight amid stress.

He was about to be in an argument himself. Never mind it, he thought. He had had to get to Marella.

He picked up the bicycle, righted the handlebars, ran several steps, and jumped on, pressing his feet against the pedals. He hadn't been on a bike in ages, not since he was a kid. He wobbled at first, but he rotated the tires. In a few strokes of his feet, he was moving, passing the front stairs and damaged flower beds of the local townhomes. He prayed the arguing couple hadn't noticed.

A door slammed behind him, and a young man yelled in his direction. "Hey. Tha's my bike!"

"Sorry!" Tom shouted. "I'll bring it back!"

"Police!" the man yelled. "Police!"

Tom rode the bike through the Thurwick square, over the cobblestones, and toward the road to meet Marella. He expected Officers O'Reilly and Burns to give chase. Not seeing either, he focused his eyes to the west, squeezed the handlebars, and strained his legs on the pedals to ride faster and faster out of downtown Thurwick.

CHAPTER 47

The wind hit Tom's face with each rotation of the pedals. He wiped the sweat from his brow, but too late. A bead of sweat burned his eye. He squinted.

He did not see the curb.

The bike's tire slammed into it, knocking him off balance. He overcorrected and rolled into a trash can. The can fell, and he lost his balance, the bike falling upon its side. He skidded upon the ground, tearing his green coat and bruising his elbow as he flailed over the stones. He rolled upon his torso, then he hurried back to his feet, rubbed his elbow, grabbed the handlebars, and jumped on the bike again, hoping the noise and commotion attracted little attention.

The people in the square hardly noticed him. Most held bewilderment upon their faces. They discussed the water spouts. A crowd congregated outside the police station, studying the collapsed rear roof. Several pointed at the tornado damage that thrashed the inside.

If only they knew what had happened, they'd run the other way, Tom thought.

Tom pedaled, hoping to exit the square before anyone pointed at him. No one did. Perhaps it was because they didn't expect him on a bike. Perhaps it was because they were too frightened by the damage to the town, and to the police station. Whatever it was, he rolled the bike past the square and toward Saint Michael's Church. He had to get to Marella. He had lost track of time. The four o'clock deadline had to be approaching. It didn't matter; the police already wanted him arrested, and the Council would want answers right away.

Tom knew he had to find the answers before they found him!

As he neared the church, there was Annabel's Bed and Breakfast. A police car remained out front, its lights still flashing from its roof. No doubt a detective was inside analyzing evidence.

With the church nearing Tom's right, he slammed on his brakes. "That's where I saw him!"

He remembered the man in Guthrie's Pub, and then the picture in Father Gibson's office, the man with the crucifix around his neck.

They were the same person!

Tom was sure of it. The man in the bar, the one that had disappeared, was the man in the painting.

Should he run up to Father Gibson's office, just to make sure? No, he thought. Marella could very well be in danger. Tom had to take care of her, first. Next, he'd call Father Gibson and ask him about the man in the painting.

And, what was it the old man had said? Find an amulet. In the barn. Tom shuddered about returning to the barn. The memory of that experience had messed with his head. He told himself to focus, to make a plan. First, find Marella. Second, call Father Gibson. Third, find out why Thurwick was cursed. Maybe get to the barn. Find the amulet. Get Marella and Sean and go meet Father Gibson in London.

No. Forget the barn. Grab Marella and get the hell out of town!

Tom pedaled fast along the pavement, then rode upon Mackay Rd and pedaled hard upon the mud and dirt. Sean Paterson's house was a mile away, but the wet terrain made the ride more difficult. Hints of clouds remained above the small cottage house in the country. Behind him, the clouds over Thurwick had all but vanished. Here, the clouds remained dark. There was a steady wind, not threatening, but not pleasant, either.

He approached the house. The garden propellers spun with the wind. Sean's blue car was still in the parking space. Tom parked the bike and threw it down, jumping forward past the car. If the car was there, that meant Marella was still there. The lights inside the house were out, like those in town. He hoped the power and the phone still worked. He ran up to the front door, then stopped.

Feathers. Black feathers by the door.

Tom scanned left and right. Black feathers lay around the house, congregating in clumps near the windows. The windows were dark. There was no light inside.

"Oh no!" Tom said. He grabbed the door handle and pushed, praying the door wasn't locked.

He opened the door. Its hinges squeaked as the door swung inside.

There was a draft. More feathers covered the sofa and the carpet flooring. "Marella!" he yelled. He ran inside the house.

There was the sound of the wind as the draft moved through the rooms.

Feathers covered everything, bringing a blackness into an already unlit house. There were scratch marks on the walls, the same as in Annabel's.

Tom burst into the den, his hands formed into fists, ready to beat senseless whatever spirit took his girl.

He entered the center of the room. The draft swirled clumps of feathers on the carpet. The sofa had been gashed, its white stuffing sticking out of the torn upholstery.

Tom's adrenaline rushed through his body. "Marella!" he shouted. The quiet breeze blew through the house. Drapes blew and knocked against the wall.

Marella did not answer.

Tom tip-toed to the kitchen, listening for the first sign of noise.

The kitchen window had shattered. Knives lay scattered on the floor. The block that held them lay on its side near the refrigerator. The table had been overturned. His shoes crunched upon broken glass.

There had been a struggle.

"Marella!" Tom yelled, hoping for an answer.

Glass hung from the broken window. He was careful not to touch the shards.

"God, no!" he said.

He scanned outside, praying he would not find the lifeless body of the woman he loved the same way he found Annabel.

The uncovered grill lay on its back. Propane hung in the air.

Tom searched for footprints. Trampled grass pointed in many directions. The grass left a trail like someone was dragged into the field.

Mixed within the blades of grass were hundreds of black feathers. They covered everything, the grass, the puddles, the rocks, the grill.

"Marella!"

He remembered how Marella told him to leave. He wished he had disobeyed her. Now she was gone. It was his fault. "Where is she!" he said.

He took a step, crunching more broken glass. He picked up the largest of the knives on the kitchen floor. It lay atop several black feathers. He held its point in front of him. If he stabbed the creature, exactly what would he stab? Those grotesque arms? Those black feathers? There was also the claw print and the invisible hands that had grabbed at him. What was it? Would it bleed? Could he kill it?

He opened the back door and went into the yard. He smelled the propane, mixed with the constant ozone the wind blew in from the storm.

"Marella!"

There was no answer.

"Dammit!"

He followed the path of trampled grass and black feathers. It zig-zagged first left then right as a fight had ensued. He went over a hill.

There was a glint. It sparkled green. Something dainty. Tom reached down to pick it up.

"Oh, no!" Tom fell to his knees. One of Marella's earrings, with the four-leaf clover, lay on the ground. It sparkled at the end of its silver metal hook. Marella had been wearing it.

Tom's heart sank.

Marella wouldn't have worn that earring if she was still mad at him. But this was confirmation that something had grabbed her.

She strugged against those arms, tearing at her body and ripping her clothes. Tom scanned the grass. He tried to find where the fight ended, but he was standing in the middle of it. The rest of the field was normal, its blades blowing in the wind. There were no more tracks; no more signs of struggle.

There was no blood.

Had the other earring fallen? He scoured the area on his knees and hands, but there was no sign of it in the circle of trampled grass. He backtracked amidst the boot tracks and broken grass, trying to figure out what had happened. There was a track in the mud. It had three toes, like a crow, except it was larger than his hand.

Tom lifted his head and yelled. "Marella!"

The wind blew from the west. A single bird flew overhead. The clouds rolled, dark and threatening.

"Marella!"

There was no answer.

CHAPTER 48

Tom ran back inside Sean Paterson's house. His boot crunched more glass. He still held the knife, gripping it like he was going to kill the first living thing he came across. He pushed the overturned table out of his way and went into the living room. The gashed furniture and the white claw marks on the walls were the same as at Annabel's. O'Reilly also said something similar happened inside Liz Stevens's hotel room.

"Marella!"

The wind blew through the house.

Tom stepped down the hall. He paused. More white gashes ripped through the halls. He opened the first door on his right - Marella's room. A suitcase on the bed was packed and open. Marella had been packing. Black feathers rested on the bedspread, on the dresser, and on the carpet.

He opened the closet door. Hanging clothes were in front of him, and he brushed them aside, but Marella wasn't there.

Tom went across the hall and into the guest bedroom. Black feathers covered the bed and the carpet.

A word was etched on the far wall.

MINE.

"What the hell does that mean?!" he said aloud. He gripped the knife, expecting an adversary to attack him at any moment.

There was none.

Tom went back into the hallway and into the master bedroom. Sean's bed was covered with black feathers.

Tom tried the light switch.

The lights did not come on.

"Dammit!"

Sean's phone sat on the bedside table. Tom went to it. He pulled out the piece of paper that was in his coat pocket. He lifted the receiver.

There was a dial tone!

Tom called Father Gibson's phone number.

"Pick up. Pick up. Pick up!" Tom said. His eyes moved from left to right, expecting an attack from whatever had grabbed Marella.

"Hello?" came a voice from the receiver.

"Father Father Gibson!" Tom said.

"Aye, lad. Are ye in London yet?"

"No. I need help!"

"Yer na here?"

"No. I'm still in Thurwick. Something took Marella!"

There was silence on the other end.

"Did you hear me!" Tom said. His grip on the knife handle tightened.

"Aye," Father Gibson said, his voice melancholy.

"I need your help. I've got to find her. What am I dealing with?"

"When'd ye see her last?"

"Earlier today. We had a fight. But I'm at Sean Paterson's house in the country. She was here, but this place has been thrashed. There's clawmarks and feathers everywhere. And something wrote 'MINE' on the walls."

"Okay, lad. Le' me think a moment."

"And, I met a strange man in Guthrie's Pub. He said something about the barn across the loch. I can't say for sure, but he resembled the guy in the painting."

"Wha' paintin'?" Father Gibson asked.

"In your office. The one across the room, next to the shelf."

"Saint Columba?"

"Who?"

"Saint Columba. He first found th' Loch Ness monster."

"Well, where do I find him?" Tom wiped the sweat from his brow.

"Ye canno' find him," Father Gibson said. "He's a saint."

"So what does that mean? He's a priest somewhere? Is he in a church?"

"Lad, he's a saint. Tha' means he's dead."

Tom paused. "What do you mean he's dead?"

"He lived in th' sixth century. He hasn' been alive fur fourteen hundre' years."

"Then what's he doing in Guthrie's Pub?!"

"I don' know, lad. Are ye sure it was him?"

"Father, I've been tried, arrested, attacked, beaten, and I saw three people grabbed by some poltergeist. Now Marella's missing. I need some answers, quick, before the police come and have me burned at the stake. I need to find her and get us the hell out of here."

"I see," Father Gibson said.

"You said earlier the town was cursed. What did you mean by that?"

"Ah, yes. I did. There was an old curse placed upon th' town a long time ago. We didn' know it until recently."

"What are you saying?" Tom said.

"Th' obsession curse had more tae it."

"What does 'more' mean?"

"When ye went intae th' barn, and ye disappeared fur those two days, something happened."

Tom shuddered thinking about the barn across the loch. He had been lured there by some strange pull, to the chagrin of Sean, of course. Tom had acted like he had been entranced. He had leaped from their small rowboat into the water and swam to the barn.

When Tom reached it, there was nothing unusual about it; sand floor, rusty tools hanging from rotting wooden planks. But when he left the barn, disorientation hit him. The world had changed. People had disappeared. Even the weather outside was different.

When he first made contact with another person, he acted like Tom had lost his mind. Tom was convinced he was only in the barn for a few minutes, but the police said two days had advanced.

288

Tom refused to believe everyone until he confirmed he had missed his flight back to America.

"I know something happened," Tom said. "That's why I lost two days of my life and became obsessed with finding the Loch Ness monster."

"Aye, lad. But th' ladies in th' barn though' different."

Tom studied the receiver in his hand. "What ladies?"

"Caoineags."

"What the hell's a Caoineag?"

Father Gibson paused. "Years ago, I had heard a story about tha' barn. There was a man in th' mid-500s tha' was wealthy fur his day, and th' men who worked fur him built his estate. A part o' tha' estate was across th' loch from Thurwick."

"Let me guess. He built the barn."

"His slaves did, aye. But there's more. There was no Christianity in Scotland those days, and when th' religion is empty, there's a vaccuum. Th' man wasn't an atheist. He was led intae rites by a dark spirit."

"What kind of rites?"

"Bad ones. Rites of power. Though he was wealthy, it wasn' enough. He wanted tae build a navy and conquer th' isles."

"Like the vikings?"

"Aye. Except he had a secret weapon."

"What's that?"

"Th' spirit taught him how tae reincarnate creatures from th' past."

"What?"

"That's th' legend."

"So that's where the Loch Ness monster came from?"

"We think so. Aye."

"If I hadn't seen it for myself, I'd say you're nuts."

"I'm na doolally, lad."

"I don't think you are," Tom said.

"I tried doin' more research," Father Gibson continued, "but I found tha' many records o' those events were sealed tight. They were written in scrolls, and those scrolls were brought tae th' London Archdiocese and put under lock and key. By God's grace they remained here and weren't taken tae the Vatican archives."

"What did they say?"

"Th' wealthy man was married tae a woman. By all accounts she was beautiful. All she wanted was a family, bu' her husband's lust fur power drove her mad. While he was practicing his rites, she snuck in and spied on him. Tha's where she learned o' th' same dark spirit."

"Okay."

"She found ou' how tae perform her own rites. Once, in th' middle o' th' night, she went tae th' barn."

"The same barn?"

"Aye, lad. While she was there, she performed th' rite. But somethin' went wrong. Rather than gain power o'er her husband, she opened a portal intae th' spirit world, and she was pulled in."

"What's that got to do with my finding Marella."

"'Tis na' jus' her, lad. It's ye."

"Me?"

"I'm sorry, lad. Since tha' night, she's been cursed tae marry th' next man who enters tha' barn."

"Wait, what!"

"Well, 'tis na' a valid marriage, o' course. Bu' she thinks it was."

"What do you mean 'she thinks it was'."

"Jus' wha' I said, lad. While ye were cursed, she was married tae ye."

"Are you telling me some poltergeist woman thinks she's married to me?"

"Well, since ye broke th' curse, she wants ye back. What's more, she's insanely jealous. That's why she's goin' after th' women around ye."

"What's she doing with them?"

"The legend says her torment consumes her. So much so tha' she is considered a harbinger o' death. She comes with a song before someone passes. Bu' they don' always die. Sometimes, they go with her intae th' spirit realm."

"What do you mean 'they go with her'?"

"They become one o' her. They become a caoineag."

Tom jumped up. "What!"

"Sorry, lad."

Several yards outside was the place where he found Marella's four-leaf clover earring. "Father, Marella was here. But I don't see her anywhere. There was a struggle outside, and I found her earring surrounded by a bunch of black feathers. I found Annabel dead. But Marella isn't as far as I can tell."

"Maybe there's a chance, lad."

An engine rumbled outside. He noticed the clock on the bedside table. It flashed 3:46. "They're here. I gotta run!"

"Wait," Father Gibson said. "There's more."

"I'll get back to you," Tom said, and he slammed the receiver down.

Footsteps and voices approached the house. They came to the front door. A muffled voice said, "There's the bike."

That was Tom's cue. He put the kitchen knife in his mouth to free his hands, and he unlatched the bedroom window, slid it open, and popped the screen. He lowered the blinds.

The front door squeaked open. "Damn. Wha' happened in here?" said a man's voice.

"He's go' tae be in here!"

"Look down th' hall!"

Tom slid out the window and steadied the blinds in place. He had no time to shut the window, and he feared doing so might alert them to his whereabouts. He put the kitchen knife back in his hand. He crouched under the window next to the cottage's exterior wall and he crawled around the corner.

"Na' in th' bedroom," said the voice.

Tom studied the landscape. Ahead of him, through the high grass, was a small knoll. He had to make a break for it. He ran to the knoll. He leaped over it and slid over grass and mud before the rear door opened.

"Grill's knocked o'er," said the voice. "Tracks went this way, tae."

They were going past the grill to where Tom had found Marella's earring. They hadn't seen him.

Tom's muscles ached.

His coat was torn. His jeans were covered in mud.

He gripped the kitchen knife; it was all he had to protect himself. He studied it in the dim afternoon sunlight. Could he cut a person to escape if he had to? Marella was in trouble. Yes, he'd do what he had to. He had to escape. Get across Loch Ness, and get to the barn. Find the amulet–.

A black club swung down above his head. It came from a shadow that stood atop the knoll. When it knocked into his skull, Burns said, "Council will be glad tae ge' rid o' him."

Tom dropped the knife. Then the cloud-covered sky turned black, and Tom lost all memory of what happened next.

CHAPTER 49

The call came on Detective Logan O'Malley's police scanner. Though the power was out in all of Thurwick, he happened to be in his car, going back to check on Digger while he tried to piece together what was happening.

The water spouts over Loch Ness had frightened the townspeople. The arm under the crumpled building belonged to the frightened man that alerted them to the chaos outside.

But O'Malley had not known what had caused the man's death, Felicia's disappearance, or the collapsed wall and roof of the police station.

After he wrote a quick description of the deceased, he handed the case to another officer and left to try to comprehend what was happening.

His mind could not put it together. All he came up with were questions, each leading to something illogical, insane, or mysterious.

On the scanner, the announcement came through that Burns and O'Reilly had caught up with Tom Wayne. The lad had stolen a bicycle and rode to Sean Paterson's cottage to find Marella, except Marella wasn't there. The place was torn apart. In a small field not far from the cottage, they found evidence of a struggle.

And they also found Tom hiding over a hill on the other side of the house.

O'Malley left the car door open, listening for the radio as he walked into his house. Digger ran up to him, wagging his tail and smiling the way cairn terriers do. All the power was out, and the room was full of shadows. He tried the light switch, but his lamp remained dark.

"Hey, lad," O'Malley said, rubbing Digger's head. He put a leash on Digger and took him outside to do his business. The wind was still blowing, and O'Malley held his fedora. He added the strange intense weather to his mental list of mysterious circumstances plaguing Thurwick the past twenty-four hours.

In all his years of detective work, he had never had a time like the one he was experiencing. While Digger sniffed a nearby stone wall and hiked his leg, O'Malley asked the hard questions. What if Tom Wayne was right? What if the Loch Ness monster did exist?

What created those feathers?

What power caused the water spouts?

What destroyed the building?

Was Tom Wayne cursed, or was something else causing it? How come they found some people dead, and others were missing?

"We're takin' him tae Dorlan Hall," Officer O'Reilly had said on the scanner.

Bain's voice came on the other end. "Is he alive?"

O'Malley paused. Was Bain trying to have Tom killed?

"Aye. But he's unconscious."

Bain paused. "Very well. Bring him. I'll call a meetin' right away."

O'Malley clenched his jaw. He needed answers. For whatever reason, Tom Wayne went to Paterson's cottage. Maybe there was a clue there.

Digger's ears went up, and he buried his face in a small hole, raising his rear and tail which wagged in excitement.

O'Malley tugged on Digger's leash. "Okay, lad. We nee' tae go."

Digger paid no attention, but his front paws flung dirt behind him onto O'Malley's pant legs.

"Alrigh'. That'll do." He pulled Digger's leash. Digger resisted, his happy face covered in mud and dirt.

"I'll have tae clean ye when I get home." O'Malley said. He pulled Digger inside his dark house, shut the door, and locked it. Digger barked from the other side of the door.

O'Malley returned to his car. From the radio, Bain said, "Do ye suspect Wayne killed her?"

Over the static, O'Reilly replied, "At this point, who else is there?"

CHAPTER 50

The first thing Tom noticed was the noise, a sort of muffled sound of someone speaking in the far-off distance. His eyes were shut, but a sudden throbbing pain in his head made him open his eyes. His vision was blurry. He was sitting upright. Someone next to him was holding him up. His arms were locked behind his back by something metal around his wrists.

In front of him stood a wooden dais. Seven people sat upon it. Tom blinked, and his blurry vision cleared.

"Fur Pete's sake, ye didn' need tae bludgeon him wi' a nightstick!"

Tom raised his head. The voice was familiar.

"And another thing. Wha' gave ye th' right tae trespass on my property!"

Tom recognized him. It was Sean. The man was sitting, but pointing his crutch at the dais.

"This whole thin' is a waste o' time. We shoul' be organizin' a search party tae look for my daughter!"

The man sitting in the middle of the dais, who Tom now recognized as Councilman Bain, slammed his gavel. "There'll be none o' that, Mr. Paterson. We make th' rules up here, na' ye."

Voices mumbled behind Tom. Jacob Stewart, the attorney, was sitting on his left, his hair still a mess though he wore his sports coat. Stewart was the one holding Tom up. Behind them were the residents of Thurwick, squeezed into the pews and standing shoulder to shoulder along the back and side walls.

Their scowling faces told Tom they were not happy with him.

On the other side of Stewart, and across the aisle, sat Officers O'Reilly and Burns. O'Reilly sat tall, his nightstick in his lap. Burns leaned forward, his foot tapping upon the floor.

The officers wore holsters, and the butts of their pistols pointed forward.

"If I may," said Councilman MacGillivray. He rubbed his unshaven chin with his thumb and forefinger. "We don' know wha' is goin' on here. I fur one want tae hear from Mr. Wayne. Find out wha' he knows."

"He's a killer!" shouted a woman in the crowd.

"Aye. He'll kill us all!" said another.

The crowd's grumbling grew. Bain hammered his gavel several times until the room went quiet.

Bain said, "Wi' all due respect, Councilman MacGillivray, bu' we have ourselves a crisis here. At least four buildings have been damaged, but worse people keep disappearin' or windin' up dead. And th' loch is actin' like it wants tae swallow Thurwick."

The other Council members agreed.

Councilwoman Harris said, "I've ne'er seen anythin' like wha' I saw a an hour ago. Since when did we have water spouts o'er th' loch?"

"None since *he* showed up!" Councilman Thomson said, his eyes glaring at Tom.

"I agree," said Councilwoman Morehead. Her face was cold stone white. Her eyes were angry, like a mother ready to hit her child's bully over the head with a hammer. "Th' people o' Thurwick are in danger. There are now eight poor residents who are gone from this earth, and it all began wi' him!" She lifted her long fingers and pointed at Tom. "He's th' one who brought this upon us. He needs tae go!"

"Aye. Aye!" shouted several in the crowd. The grumbling elevated.

Sean Paterson lifted himself from his seat and stood on his one leg, leaning upon his crutch but shaking his fist at Morehead with the other. "I should remind ye 'twas yer Council who tried tae murder Mr. Wayne a few weeks ago!"

"Sit down!"

"End them both!"

Bain hammered the gavel hard against the rising calls for Sean's silence.

Morehead pointed at Tom, "Make him pay!" She rose her voice. "Make them both pay!"

"We're losin' control here," Councilwoman Brown said.

"Everyone. Silence!" Bain said.

Officer O'Reilly stood and blew a whistle. Bain hammered his gavel on the table.

Under the cover of the noise, the attorney Jacob Stewart leaned into Tom's ear. "I'm goin' tae do th' best I can fur ye, lad. But th' people in here are scared."

Tom said, "Can you get my hands uncuffed?"

"I'll try."

"Thanks." Tom fidgeted with his wrists, trying to guess how tight the cuffs were. The metal dug into his skin, his thumb joint unable to squeeze through the metal.

Stewart leaned back to Tom. "But na promises, though."

Tom understood.

Sean pointed at each member of the Council. "I'll have ye know if ye hurt my daughter, I'll be comin' after each one o' ye!"

"It's ye and yer daughter's fault this man is among us. She go' wha' she deserved!" Morehead said.

"Why I. . . ," Sean shouted. His face had flushed red.

Tom tugged on his coat.

Sean pressed his lips together and sat down. His chest heaved as a man fuming from a fight. He stood his crutch in front of him and rested his hands on top of it.

"Where's O'Malley?" Tom said.

Sean tore his red glare from Morehead. "Who th' hell voted fur these people!"

Tom touched Sean's arm.

"I sure as hell didn'!"

Tom said, "Sean! O'Malley? Where is he?"

Sean shrugged. Beads of sweat clung to his forehead.

"Silence. Please. Everyone!" Bain's voice echoed inside Dorlan Hall. He hammered his gavel. "Please, so th' meetin' can begin."

The crowd's grumbling quieted.

"Tha's better," Bain said. "Now, there's a lot o' questions. Tis obvious we have a problem. Wha' we don' have are answers."

"But we do. Ge' rid o' him, and th' curse goes with him!" said a woman in the crowd.

Tom flinched at the woman's anger. He twisted to see the woman despite his wrists cuffed behind his back.

Officer Burns went to the woman. He placed his hand near one of his pistols. He motioned with his finger for her to stand and follow him.

"I have e'ery right tae see I'm protected!" she said.

He put his hand on his pistol.

She stood and left the pew. He escorted her to the back of Dorlan Hall. "He brought a curse upon us!" she shouted. The heavy doors closed behind her. "He should burn at th' stake!" she said again. Then the doors shut, and the room was quiet for a moment until some in the crowd mumbled.

Tom shuddered at the thought of being tied and burned alive like some medieval witch.

"Does anybody else wan' tae interrupt?" Bain said.

The crowd went quiet again.

Stewart raised his hand. "Councilman Bain, may I speak?"

Bain glanced at the other Council members.

Harris, Brown, and McCulloch shrugged. Morehead, Thomson, and MacGillivray shook their heads.

Bain said, "Tis th' Council's desire tae hear from Mr. Wayne himself."

Stewart stood at the podium, his hands clasping it on each side.

Tom flexed his legs and stood, his hands still cuffed behind his back. Stewart sat down while Tom approached the podium. Tom leaned into the microphone, but as he did so he realized how dark Dorlan Hall was. None of the interior lights were on. The only light in the room came from the small overhead windows. Outside, clouds covered the sun, and the wind blew nearby trees. The power was still out. Then, through his pounding headache, he remembered.

Tom lifted his head. "Marella!"

"She's missin'," Sean said.

"I know. I went to look for her."

"We didn' find her," Sean said.

"I have a clue."

Bain leaned forward. "Wha' kind o' clue?"

"Will you take these cuffs off, first? I'll show you."

Bain and the other Council members waited. Officer Burns walked down the aisle and took his seat next to O'Reilly.

"Where is it?" Bain said.

"It's in my pocket," Tom said. He remembered Father Gibson's phone number. "I can't get to it with my hands cuffed together.

O'Reilly approached Tom and searched his pockets. "There's nothin' there."

Tom remembered he was on the phone with Father Gibson as the police showed up. "Dammit. I left it on the table next to the phone."

"Wha' did ye leave?" Bain asked.

"Father Gibson. He knows what's going on. He's doing research on this thing from London."

"He's stallin'," Councilwoman Morehead said. "We don' have time fur this."

Bain said, "Wha' did he say?"

"This thing comes from across Loch Ness. Something to do with the old barn across the water."

Sean bowed his head between his arms. The crowd grumbled, their irritation growing.

Tom shouted over their voices. "Whatever's attacking us, it comes from there, from the old barn across the loch."

"Tis a distraction," Morehead said. "He's tryin' tae save his own skin."

Bain lifted his hand up, quieting her. Morehead folded her arms across her chest and raised her haughty nose.

Bain shook his head. "Mr. Wayne. How do ye know?"

"Because all my problems began there."

The crowd's mumbling grew louder, but Bain ignored them. "Tha's na enough."

Tom persisted. He pointed at Sean. "And all his problems began there, too."

Sean raised his head. His red face was white.

"And, I talked with Father Gibson. He's doing research on the place. He says the whole thing began at the barn."

Under the rising grumbling, Bain hammered his gavel several times, demanding silence. O'Reilly stood again and put his whistle to his mouth, but the crowd quieted before he blew it.

Bain said, "How do we know yer tellin' us th' truth?"

"You can't," Tom said. "Not until we go there and dig up what's inside."

"And wha' exactly will we dig up?"

Sean's eyes were worried. Tom didn't want to go back to the barn, and he knew Sean didn't either. But, with Marella missing (and hoping to God she wasn't dead), what other options did they have?

To Tom's surprise, Sean mouthed, "Aye."

That confirmed it. They had to go back.

Tom said, "What will we dig up? Answers!"

CHAPTER 51

Detective O'Malley opened the door to Sean Paterson's cottage. An uncomfortable silence had spread over the area, a strange sensation that accompanied him when he arrived at a murder scene. As the door opened, his eyes caught the white claw marks etched on the walls. He took a mental note - same as at Annabel's.

Hundreds of black feathers lay scattered on the furniture and floor.

Again, same.

He stood still, listening. The wind was blowing outside. There were no strange noises except for a small clattering down the hall.

He stepped forward. The kitchen was a mess. Glass shards covered the floor. The table was overturned. Knives scattered across the tile. Window broken. Back door open.

He tip-toed to the window. The wind pushed air through the opening and it cooled his face. He was careful not to touch anything so as to leave no fingerprints or, for that matter, cut himself on the broken glass. Outside, the grill had been knocked over. He smelled propane among the ozone. In the distance, there was a trail of broken grass blades and moved dirt. Something pulled someone out of the house and over the hill. Whoever pulled her had a struggle. Marella was dragged by her hair from the house and into the field, kicking and swinging the whole way.

Clanking sounded again down the hall. He would go outside and check the trail in a moment, but after he examined the house. He left the window and the kitchen, and he tip-toed down the hall.

The walls were etched in claw marks and black feathers. The clanking sound came from a room on the left.

O'Malley leaned his head around the doorway.

It was a bedroom. It was untouched with no feathers on the ground or markings on the walls.

The window was open. The wind from outside was causing the blind to lift off the wall and bounce against it.

Someone opened the window, O'Malley thought. He stepped across the floor around the bed to the window. Next to the window stood the bedside table, and on the table sat an old phone. It was connected to a landline. O'Malley pulled out a handkerchief and with his thumb and forefinger behind it he picked up the receiver. There was a dial tone.

O'Malley raised an eyebrow. The cell towers and the power station in Thurwick were not working, but here, Sean Paterson's landline worked. Did Tom make a phone call?

O'Malley set the receiver down. He studied the room. All the evidence of excitement was in the other rooms, but O'Malley wanted to check one more thing. He bent down and raised the bed skirt. A white piece of paper lay on the carpet. He picked up the paper and opened it.

In messy handwriting, it said:

Tom,

You, Sean, and Marella are in severe danger. Come and find me in London. I fear for your lives if you don't. Close the crypt door on your way out. It will lock. Call me when you arrive.

Father Gibson

Father Gibson's phone number was written below his name.

O'Malley examined the number, and he studied the phone on the table. He shrugged. Using the handkerchief as before, he lifted the receiver and held it up. With his fingernail, he dialed the number on the paper.

The phone rang three times before there was a voice. "Tom?"

"Hello. This is Detective O'Malley with th' Thurwick police force. Who is this?"

The voice paused a moment, then said, "I'm Father Gibson. I'm th' pastor at Saint Michael's Catholic Church in Thurwick."

"Are ye at th' church now?"

"No. I'm in London. Is Tom there?"

What should O'Malley say? He needed answers, and he didn't want the priest to hang up. "Na, bu' he's in trouble. I'm tryin' tae help."

"I was on th' phone with him abou' an hour ago, bu' he hung up. Said he had tae go."

"He's in Dorlan Hall. Th' Council wants him fur murder."

"Oh my!" Father Gibson said.

"I don' have much time," O'Malley said. "There's people missin', and people dyin'. I need tae know wha's happenin' quick o' th' townspeople will burn Tom alive."

"And, Marella?"

"Missin'.'

"Oh." Father Gibson paused.

O'Malley waited.

Father Gibson said, "Tis na Tom's fault. There is a curse, but tis on th' town. 'Tis always been there, only now 'tis angry."

"Go on."

"Do you know about caoineags, Detective?"

O'Malley hesitated. He hadn't been to church in decades, but when he last went no one mentioned ghosts. Especially not a man of the cloth. "Aye," he said.

"This may sound hard tae hear, but there's some strange fiction tha's now coming true in th' town o' Thurwick. Foremost, th' Loch Ness monster is real."

O'Malley pictured the remains of Captain Anderson's police cap. Without hesitating, he said, "I'm open tae tha'."

"Okay. Second, Nessie's a creature tied tae th' caoineags. According tae my research, th' caoineags want a livin' spouse. When they have one, th' town is okay and th' monster is free, though th' one who plays th' spouse carries a curse. Howe'er, when th' spouse breaks th' curse, th' caoineags get jealous, and they want th' spouse back."

O'Malley tried to picture a caoineag. In his childhood, there were stories of women spirits who showed up in mysterious places, shedding sad tears and singing sad songs. Sometimes, the legends said, the caoineags wailed. One's appearance signified someone's oncoming death, and that was supposed to be the reason for the spirit's wailing. "Father, I've heard th' legends, bu' I've heard they wail because someone's abou' tae die. I've ne'er heard they ge' jealous."

"They're a tortured spirit," Father Gibson said. "Th' first caoineag was th' wife o' a landowner across th' loch. Apparently, he was not a good man as he wanted power and delved intae divination books tae gain more o' it. His wife found his books and tried tae gain some power fur herself. Unfortunately fur her, th' spell went sour and turned her intae a caoineag."

O'Malley shook his head. "If na' fur th' clawmarks and th' feathers, I don' know tha' I'd believe ye."

"Feathers?"

"Aye. There's hundreds o' them."

"Interesting," Father Gibson said.

"Why?"

"Well, th' legends say tha' when a caoineag appears, she's often accompanied by feathers."

"Do we know why?"

"I canno' say. Perhaps 'twas somethin' tae do with th' spell."

"So, are ye sayin' there's na hope fur th' missin'?"

"There may be. I was tellin' Tom about it righ' before he had tae run."

"Explain," O'Malley said.

"In my research, there's some strange writings, some in English, others in Gaelic. I'm havin' tae go slow, but I found one passage tha' caught my eye."

O'Malley pulled his small notebook from his coat pocket. He set it on the bed and leaned down to write. "Wha' did it say?"

"Here, let me dig fur it. Hold on." Father Gibson flipped through books and pages. "Oh, Lord, where is it? Ah, here 'tis!"

"Well?"

"It says, 'Help must come before 'tis night, fur th' doorway shuts at th' end o' light'."

O'Malley barely read his own handwriting. "Wha' doorway? Wha' light?"

"I'm na sure. But there's another passage further up tha' might be a clue."

"What's it say?"

"Let me look. Okay, here. 'When ye dig th' earth and find th' one, raise it up tae th' settin' sun'."

"Wha' one?"

"Buried beneath th' church ye'll find th' key tha' opens th' door in kind."

O'Malley tried to process what Father Gibson was telling him. "So, there's a key buried under a church. When tis held up tae th' sunset, a door opens, and tha's how we can help th' missin', such as Marella Paterson?"

"I'm new tae this, tae, Detective. All I can do is tell ye wha' I've found in my research. There's much more . . ."

"We don' have time. "Tis four-thirty already. Th' sun will be settin' at six-thirty this time o' year. Accordin' tae ye we've go' two hours!"

"Yer right. Wha' are ye goin' tae do?"

"I have tae hurry and get tae Tom. Foremost, we need tae find tha' key!"

"Detective, wait. Before ye run, there's one more passage ye need tae hear."

"Wha's tha'?"

Father Gibson flipped some more pages. "Oh, where is it?" More pages flipped.

"Th' clock is tickin'."

"I know. I know!." More pages flipped, then Father Gibson said, "Found it!"

"What's it say?"

"Okay. Right here it says, 'Th' monster swims beneath th' waves. She feeds it everythin' it craves. If yer ears detect her sorrowful song, 'tis ye who'll feed her pet before long."

O'Malley found Fleming's and Emily Anderson's cars near the Loch Ness shoreline. Captain Anderson's half-eaten police cap was also in Loch Ness.

Was that what happened to them? They were lured to the water, and then. . . ?

A chill ran through his body. He was afraid of the water. He didn't need to add the idea of a man-eating creature to his fear.

"Detective?" Father Gibson said.

"Aye. Thanks fur th' information. I better get goin'."

"One more thing."

"Hurry."

"Aye. It says here, "When women mourn, worry, o' tear, they receive exactly wha' they fear. Reject th' choice tae keep yer breath and th' caoineag comes tae give ye death."

"Wha' does tha' mean?"

"I don' know. I just thought it may be important."

"Is tha' all?"

Father Gibson paused. Over the receiver, he said, "I suppose so. Is there anythin' else I can do?"

O'Malley closed his notebook and rubbed the back of his neck, thinking. "Just pray, Father. Pray much."

CHAPTER 52

Tom, Sean, Stewart, O'Reilly, and Burns stood at the entrance to the wooden boat dock. The sun was lowering in the sky, and in a few hours, darkness would spread over Thurwick.

Councilwoman Morehead's skirt blew in the wind as clouds swirled overhead. "We shoul' throw him in th' loch. Let his monster have him."

Morehead shook her fists at Tom. His hands still cuffed behind him left him unprotected. Burns and O'Reilly held their hats to keep the wind from blowing them off their heads. They didn't act concerned about his safety.

Councilman Bain stepped in front of the group of people congregating at the dock entrance. The orange crime scene tape that hung between the two wood posts whipped in the wind. Bain pointed at the tape, then waved his hand signifying he wanted it gone. O'Reilly pulled out a pocket knife and cut the tape. Bain said to Morehead, "Maybe on th' way back, Councilwoman. Foremost, let's see what's in th' barn."

The way he said it gave Tom pause, for Bain's eyes flashed with a hunger for power. The last time Tom noticed that look was in the eyes of Bain's predecessor, Chairman Briggs. And, it happened to be on this same dock, right before Tom had been forced to climb aboard millionaire Ewan Coffee's oversized yacht.

Burns gave Tom a shove. Tom stepped forward and kept his balance.

Sean Paterson and Jacob Stewart followed.

The dock bounced with the weight of several people marching across the planks over the water, their footsteps thudding with each step.

The wind blew the odor of the loch into Tom's nostrils. Across the loch, the first shadows appeared on the edges of the rolling green mountains as the sun continued its descent. The wind blew into Tom's ears, and he shrugged to keep his exposed neck warm.

"As Mr. Wayne's attorney, I respectfully request a life jacket fur him," Stewart said.

Burns's freckled face grew red under his cap. The white Sillitoe tartan checkers on his police cap reflected the light from the sun.

Bain walked along the dock. He pointed at Tom's wrists. "Go ahead, Officer."

"Sir, I don' think tha's a good idea," Burns said.

Tom lifted his head, surprised at Bain's comment. "I'll be good," Tom said.

Burns's eyes flashed at Tom.

"I promise," Tom added, smiling.

Burns's ears were covered in red as his blood boiled.

"If there's somethin' in th' barn, he'll have tae dig fur it. Whatever it is might be useful," Bain said. He stood next to a sleek black cruiser yacht, with a black roof over several leather seats and two engines in the rear.

"This is yers?" Sean said.

Bain untied the ropes attaching the boat to the dock. "Aye. Just bough' it, tae."

"Yer councilin' must be makin' someone happy tae get a nice new boat like this," Sean said.

Bain ignored the comment. Stewart chuckled. Sean's crutch thudded on the wooden planks as he approached the boat. "Where will we all sit?"

Bain said, "Yer na' goin'. Na with us, anyhow." Bain said to O'Reilly. "Go ahead. Uncuff him. Then ye two will accompany Mr. Wayne and me."

Officer O'Reilly did as Bain told him. Relief entered Tom's shoulders as the cuffs came off and his arms swung free. Everything in his body ached. He rubbed his arms and shoulders, working to get the blood flowing again.

Sean said, "Wha' about us?"

"Na my problem," Bain said. "Officer Burns, please escort the two gentlemen off th' dock and come back."

Stewart said, "Maybe we can hitch a ride."

Bain said, "Very well. I canno' keep ye from joinin' th' others."

Behind Sean Paterson and Jacob Stewart, the other Thurwick boaters were loading their boats. Councilman MacGillivray and Councilman McCulloch were loading a small fishing boat near Bain's yacht.

Across the dock, a red-headed father and a son were also loading their boat.

Tom said to Sean, "You don't have to come. I can do this, but this may be how we rescue Marella."

Sean said, "She's my daughter, lad. I'm goin' tae come."

Stewart left them and went across the dock. He struck up a conversation with the father and son who were untying their fishing boat.

Tom said, "She's in this position because of me. If I hadn't left when she told me to, if I had stayed away from the reporter, none of this would have happened."

"Ye don' know tha', lad."

Bain sat upon the driver's seat and put his hands on the wheel. "Touching conversation, bu' tis time tae get goin'. Officers, if ye'll escort Mr. Wayne ontae th' boat wi' me?"

O'Neil and Burns surrounded Tom. Tom got the hint and climbed aboard the yacht, stepping onto the floor and balancing himself with the swaying rhythm of the loch's waves. O'Neil and Burns stepped aboard, also. Bain motioned for Tom to take a seat. Tom sat down, keeping his hands in front of him. O'Reilly and Burns also sat down, taking positions on either side of Tom so as to keep him corralled.

Tom shouted at Sean over the engine and the wind, "Whatever happens, we'll get Marella."

The boat's engined roared, and the boat pushed away from the dock, leaving a trail of bubbles and stirred water in its wake.

Burns glared his eyes at Tom.

O'Neil didn't watch Tom but watched the nose of the boat and the direction they were going. He kept his hand on his hat to prevent the wind from blowing it off.

"Well, boys. Are we having fun yet?" Tom said.

Bain leaned back, keeping one hand on the steering wheel. "Tis always fun, Mr. Wayne. But it'll be more fun when we get control o'er th' source o' all tha' power."

Tom pressed his lips together.

Just another politician.

Sean leaned against his crutch, balancing with his one good leg. He watched Bain's black boat pull forward and veer out onto the dark Loch Ness waters. McCulloch revved his engine and pulled forward. MacGillivray saluted Sean.

There was a tap on Sean's shoulder. Stewart said, "We have a ride."

"Who?" Sean said.

Stewart walked across the dock and Sean followed. The red-haired father and son finished untying their ropes and approached them. "Mr. Paterson," the father said, extending his hand. "I'm Keith Wallace. 'Tis is my lad, Cameron."

"Yer willin' tae give us a ride?"

Keith grimaced a moment. He lowered his eyes, then raised them. "We saw Anderson on this dock th' night he died. Cameron and I were goin' tae find th' monster, but Anderson caught us before we set off. Na one was here with us tha' night. When we heard o' his death, it shook us. We haven' been right since. We want tae know wha' happened, since we were th' last ones tae see him. We ought tae help if we wan' tae know th' truth."

"Yer both good men," Sean said.

"I'll have ye know, though, tha' we aren' like th' rest o' th' town. Neither o' ye were with us tha' night, and we have na reason tae suspect either ye o' Mr. Wayne had anythin' tae do wi' wha' happened tae Captain Anderson."

Sean's shoulders dropped. He didn't realize how tense he was until Keith's kind words. "Thank ye," he said.

"Da," Cameron said. He was aboard the boat. Other boat engines whirred as their captains loaded their passengers and pulled their boats out upon the water. A group of boats congregated and moved over Loch Ness, each of them going north over the water to the enclave. "We better get goin'. We're burning daylight."

Sean shuddered. At least twenty boats hurried to the spot where Chairman Briggs last held his "Nessie Day," the spot right next to the barn, the mysterious building that had changed Sean's life several decades earlier.

Keith gestured to Sean and Stewart, raising his palm to the boat. "Shall we?"

Stewart climbed aboard the boat.

Sean stepped forward with his crutch and his one leg. He watched the boats speed away, their wakes causing ripples in the dark waters of Loch Ness. "Aye. We don' want tae miss th' party!"

CHAPTER 53

O' Malley's car pulled up into the parking lot. Several people stood watching the boats leave the docks. The boat engines motored across the blue waters of Loch Ness, and soon their bows veered north to the opposite shore.

He climbed out of his car and jogged through the crowd, hurrying to find Tom Wayne, hoping to catch him before he left upon the water. He ran around several people, his face red as his legs were not used to running. The wind blew his fedora off his head, blowing his gray hair. He returned to get his hat, then carried it as he rushed to the dock entrance.

The orange crime scene tape had been cut. Most of the boats had pushed off from the dock, and their passengers were focused on the far shore. One boat remained, a mid-sized fishing boat that was down the pier up on the right. The captain was at the controls, scanning his surroundings for a safe departure.

O'Malley hurried forward, his boots thudding upon the wooden planks, his eyes watching the water. He hesitated. His fear of water swelled in his chest, and his legs wanted to slow down, to make sure he stayed in the center of the dock. But he had to press on. He tried to not imagine a prehistoric head lunging out of the water and into his rib cage. Press on, he thought. He had to get to the boat.

He reached the boat as it was six meters from the dock, the waters bubbling under the surface. The captain, a red-haired man, and his son had sat down. Two others faced north. He couldn't recognize them by the backs of their heads.

O'Malley waived. "Wait. Can ye take one more?"

One head spun around.

Logan O'Malley paused. The face was familiar. *Sean Paterson!*

"O'Malley. Tis O'Malley!" Sean said. He tapped Keith Wallace on the shoulder and pointed. "We want him tae come with us!"

The boat was now twenty meters from the dock, but Keith reversed the motor and he brought the boat back to the dock's edge. Stewart reached over and helped O'Malley. O'Malley's hair stood up on his arms as he leaped over the water and onto the boat. He sat down on one of the seats, catching his breath.

"Let's go!" Sean said, waiving his crutch and pointing it across Loch Ness like he was a sea captain directing his vessel out into the open water.

Jacob Stewart asked, "Ye alrigh'?"

"Aye," O'Malley said. He put his fedora back upon his head. The wind pressed against his gray beard. "I have tae tell ye what I know," he said, speaking loud over the noise of the engine.

"What's tha'?" Sean said.

"I talked with Father Gibson. He said there's a key."

320

"A key?" Sean said, raising his eyebrows. "Tae what?"

"I don' know. Some kind of door."

"Where is it?" Stewart asked.

"Tis under a church."

"Saint Michael's?" Sean asked.

"Maybe. Father Gibson didn' say, but that's th' most obvious choice."

Stewart rubbed his messy hair. "Then why are we goin' across th' loch?"

"I'm afraid Tom's goin' tae th' wrong place. Whate'er this key is, Tom has tae find it and raise it tae the sun before it sets if we're goin' tae have any chance tae rescue yer daughter."

"Raise it tae th' sun?"

"Don' shoot th' messenger," O'Malley said. "Tha's wha' Father Gibson said."

Sean shook his head. "These days, I'll belie'e anythin'." The western horizon glowed with the orange sunset. The shadows in the countryside were lengthening as the sun lowered behind Atlantic clouds. "We don't have much time, then. Perhaps ninety minutes o' so?"

Stewart leaned toward Keith and Cameron. "Ye lads better step on it!"

"Where's Tom?" O'Malley said.

Sean pointed across the water. A white fog was forming over the surface of the water, but the boats were still visible through the mist. "Bain has him. They're in tha' black boat."

Up ahead, amidst several boats speeding across the loch, one black yacht led the others. Above them, the clouds spun in a wide circle, their circumference winding in gray and black spiral arms.

Lightning flashed within its spirals, streaking between the overhead shadows across the sky.

Keith Wallace's fishing boat bounced over the many wakes that trailed the preceding boats. He pressed the gas, revving the engine in an effort to catch them.

Stewart's hair blew in the wind.

Keith's teeth gritted as he steered the boat over the bumpy water.

Cameron's jaw clenched in the passenger seat.

Sean's crutch fell to the boat floor and slid below his feet. He gripped the railing, trying to maintain his balance upon his seat with his single leg and praying a wake didn't launch him out of his seat and into the loch.

"O'Reilly and Burns are guardin' Tom?" O'Malley asked.

"Aye," Stewart said, sitting back down and holding onto the side railing for his own support. "Armed wit' guns, tae."

O'Malley tried to think of a plan, anything that might help them pull Tom from Bain's boat and then bring him back to Saint Michael's.

The light fog grew thicker. It covered the boats in front of them with an eerie gray haze. A thunderous crack echoed as a bolt of lightning flashed and struck the distant green hillside somewhere behind the fog. The men all ducked their heads. "We shouldn' be out here in a lightnin' storm," Keith shouted.

"This fog is na' good, either!" Cameron said as the mist surrounded them, casting a hazy white glow where the sun used to be.

"Aye, but we go' tae get Tom, o' we may all be lost," Sean said.

Another flash of lightning streaked across the sky and shot toward the ground. Sparks flew beyond the fog on the far hillside within an elongated shadow.

"Wha's th' plan?" O'Malley said. He covered his eyes as the fog cast the sun's glare in sporadic directions, and he worked to maintain his vision.

Sean shrugged. "Improvise. Wha' else?"

Bain's boat sped through the water into the eerie white fog, which cut Tom's visibility in half. Drops of water misted upon his face and his green waxed coat, scuffed and torn from the events of the past two days. He squinted, trying to see through the fog and the sporadic western sunlight. Where was the barn? How far away was the shore? He couldn't tell. The white fog closed in around them, as did the dark water at the edge of the boat.

"Damn fog," Bain said. He slowed the boat's motor, and their speed lessened. The motor's engine hummed, its noise echoing within the wall of fog that surrounded them.

The quiet made Tom nervous. "I'm not liking this," he muttered.

Through the fog, the other boats remained in formation. Their captains slowed their motors, lessening the noise upon the water. Some shone bright bow lights that reflected over the water's surface. Their lights glared from their source, but their beams faded by the cover of the slow drifting fog.

The fog reflected the lights from the boats and the setting sun in unpredictable directions. Though the fog cast a shadow, the glare made Tom squint.

Bain kept the boat moving through the water. "Shouldn' be far now," he said.

"Careful, sir," O'Reilly said. "Tis hard tae see the shore."

Bain kept his eyes facing forward, watching the water and looking for the shoreline. He showed no fear, determined to press on.

Tom couldn't say the same for O'Reilly. The officer observed the spinning clouds, then the fog, and then the dark waters of Loch Ness. Even Burns's features no longer showed anger. Instead, his eyes widened as he squinted upward through the white fog and he watched the spiraling clouds. Then he, too, peered over the side and studied the water. He kept his hand on the butt of his pistol, ready to pull it out, shoot first, and ask questions later.

A few meters behind them, Councilmen McCulloch and MacGillivray's boat followed. They had drifted forward, their motor continuing to run. Tom estimated they were about thirty yards from Bain's port side. The rest of the boats followed in a 'V' formation, like a flock of geese flying north. Their lights beamed into the fog, but the farther ones appeared as a distant candle as the fog grew thicker.

As far as Tom could tell, no one in the other boats would be friendly to him.

"Fog's gettin' dark," Burns said. He kept his hand on his pistol.

Behind them, some boat engines grew louder. The headlights of two boats veered left and then disappeared. The boat sterns formed gray silhouettes, and then they were gone.

"Where are they goin'?" Burns said.

"Must have had second thoughts," O'Reilly said. The rest of the captains motored forward, following Bain's lead.

Tom tried to think of his next move. Both police officers carried guns. If he tried to grab one, the other would shoot him before he pulled the trigger. He studied the scene from the aft of the boat: McCulloch and MacGillivray still in their post, other boats following them, the headlights of other boats pointing forward, the sunlight of the sun casting glaring rays through the fog.

He hoped he had a friend on the water - Sean, maybe, or O'Malley, or even Stewart. But there was no indication they had followed Bain's boat into the fog. And if they had he wouldn't be able to see them.

He watched the others on the boat, thinking. Whatever was to happen, he was on his own.

CHAPTER 54

The still dark waters rippled small waves away from the boat, which disappeared under the white fog's glare. Tom rubbed his hands together to keep them warm, but also to limber his fingers. He'd use his hands soon. He wasn't sure how. Maybe he'd go for O'Reilly's or Burns's guns in their holsters, or maybe he'd make his hands into fists and uppercut Burns. The thought of that made Tom's lips curl into a smile.

He needed a plan, a way to escape. The fog thickened around them, blanketing them so they could not see the hills or the heights of Thurwick. How far was the shore? Could he swim to land? He didn't know. He rubbed his hands some more, thinking.

"Tell me about th' monster," Bain said. His hair was wet, his countenance unfazed by the thick fog and glaring light.

How should Tom answer? Bain already knew the monster was real, but the creature's power and muscle were far more intense than he imagined. Perhaps that was the answer - build up the monster so that his imagination played with his head. Who knew? Maybe Bain would make a mistake by not thinking. "It's real," Tom said. "Big. . . and fast."

Burns gripped his pistol tighter and pointed it at the water, which rippled in thousands of dark triangles until they disappeared into the fog.

Bain's eyes flashed with curiosity and an intense desire for having it satisfied. "Wha' color is it?"

O'Reilly and Burns were now staring at Tom.

"Same as the water. That's why it's so hard to find."

"Do ye think it go' Anderson?"

Tom shuddered, remembering how he had witnessed the three monsters strike down upon Alex Vaas, Chairman Briggs's henchman. Vaas had yelled his last before the creatures lunged and devoured him beneath the water. The sound of his cry still haunted him. After a deep pause, Tom said, "For his sake, I hope not."

"Why do ye say tha'?"

Tom said, "It's not a good way to die."

Bain chuckled.

O'Reilly and Burns sat unmoving on the yacht seats.

Bain said, "Which o' ye two wan' tae be th' next police captain? Th' last two go' eaten by a monster!" Bain laughed, showing his perfect teeth, his expression like a man unable to resist the lure of power. "Maybe third time's a charm?" He laughed again.

Bain's laughter echoed within the fog. The air closed in around the men on the boat. The dampness of the fog filled Tom's breath.

O'Reilly and Burns appeared confused about whether they should laugh with Bain or not.

Did they sense Bain's unpredictability? Could he convince one or both of them to revolt against Bain?

Tom had to think. Marella needed him. God only knew what had happened to her, but something inside him said she was still alive. He told himself to hope, that he would do whatever it took to find her and get her back.

Even if that meant he had to fight a Scottish poltergeist.

He forced his thoughts to remember Father Gibson's words and the words of the strange old man in Guthrie's Pub. The old man had said there was an amulet buried beneath the barn. And now a convoy had come with him to verify the claims. Was the old man a Saint, as Father Gibson suggested? Was someone from Heaven watching over him?

Tom raised his eyes, hoping a bright ray of holy light would shine down on him through the clouds. The strange gray and black spirals spun overhead, with the occasional flash of silent white lightning. Tom hoped for a sign, but there was only danger.

"Wha' are we goin' tae dig up?" Bain said.

Tom raised his eyes. Bain was becoming intoxicated with the thought of power. Intoxicated people often made mistakes. Tom decided it would be best to play along and fuel Bain's imagination. Then, when the unexpected happened, Tom might use the moment of confusion as a chance to escape. He imagined an amulet. All he could think of was an old corroded coin he once saw in a museum

"Old, like a large metal circle," Tom said.

Officer Burns raised his head. "Who told ye tha'?"

Tom swallowed. He dared not say some dead saint from the sixth century. "Father Gibson," he lied.

Burns pressed his lips together.

"Is it gold?" Bain said.

"No. More like rust-colored."

"How wide is it?" Burns said, still pointing his pistol at the water.

O'Reilly watched the conversation, his eyes shifting between them and awaiting any sudden noise that arose within the fog.

Tom lifted his hands, imagining a make-believe amulet in his hands. "Four or five inches."

Burns said, "He's lyin', Chairman. I can see it in his face."

Bain grinned. "Doesn' matter. If he's lyin', we'll burn him in th' barn, satisfy th' people, and go on wi' our lives. If he isn', we'll get our hands on somethin' mysterious tha' can change th' world."

Burns watched Bain while keeping his pistol pointed at the dark waters.

Something moved under the surface. The hairs on his neck stiffened.

Bain laughed again, showing his white teeth.

O'Reilly blinked and shifted in his seat.

Tom straightened his back; his eyes scanned the water. He tried to tell himself it was a fish, but his imagination ran with pictures of giant fins, long necks, and hundreds of white teeth.

McCulloch and MacGillivray were talking in their boat, their voices traveling through the fog. The fog covered the other boats. Their headlights shone through the fog like eerie specters floating above the water. Above him, the spiraling clouds swirled, forming a moving ceiling over Loch Ness. Silent lightning flashed.

Tom thought of getting to shore, to get out of the boat. But if he jumped in the water, he'd never make it.

Burns and O'Reilly sat on either side of him. O'Reilly had his hands on the railing. Burns still had his pistol pointed at the water.

What if Tom punched Burns, knocking him into the water?

Their guard was down. He may not have much time. If he swung at one, he might–.

Bain crinkled his nose. "Ugh! Wha' is tha' god-awful smell?"

O'Reilly and Burns made a face. A dank odor of rotting fish filled Tom's nostrils.

Bain stopped the boat's engine. The boat drifted forward into the fog.

The smell permeated the air.

Tom covered his nose.

He knew what it was. He shifted, watching the water.

The other boats approached through the fog, their engine noises getting louder.

There was a splash.

"Somethin' bumped th' boat!" MacGillivray shouted, his voice traveling from their boat and through the fog.

"Are ye sure?" said McCulloch.

"Aye. Canno' ye feel tha' rockin'?"

"I thought tha' was ye!"

Bain leaned from his seat. "Will ye two shut it o'er there. We're tryin' tae listen."

"Somethin' hit us!"

Bain stood up and waved to the following boats. He slashed his finger over his neck, telling their captains to cut their engines.

One by one the engines went quiet, and an eerie silence spread amidst the fog.

"Wha' do ye hear?" came a distant voice.

"Shut it!" Bain shouted over the water.

The boat rocked back and forth. The lights from the boats stretched through the fog, while the sunlight waned.

Several moments of tense silence filled the air. Burns pointed his gun at the water. O'Reilly had his hand on the handle of his pistol, ready to pull it out, but not wanting to. The smell was still there. Tom waited, watching.

A splash came from the other side of the boat.

O'Reilly and Burns jumped from their seat. Burns leaned over the rail, pointing his pistol.

There was a bump under the boat. The force rocked the bow left and right.

Tom's legs tensed. He grasped the boat rail, hanging on.

O'Reilly's gripped the boat and crouched next to his seat. "Wha' was tha'?"

Tom gulped. As his heart pounded in his chest.

He knew what it was.

He knew it was the Loch Ness monster.

CHAPTER 55

Burns swung his pistol back and forth at the water, ready to shoot at the first thing that moved.

"I heard it again!" McCulloch shouted from his nearby boat. His voice drifted through the fog in an eerie vibration.

Burns stood straight, watching the boats behind them. He pointed his gun at the fog, first port side, then starboard.

"Be sure tae shoot th' water. I don' need ye tae hit one o' my constituents," Bain said.

Voices came from the other boats in the fog. As Tom listened, the voices became anxious. The tension grew among their passengers as people spoke in hushed tones about strange splashes and fast movements under the water.

Tom's breathing increased; he tried to hold it back to hear what was happening. One man through the fog yelled in surprise. Another laughed. The fog masked his vision, but he could tell that the boats were spread wide in their "V" formation because of the passenger voices and the soft glow of their lights.

If there was a Loch Ness monster under the boats, there would be one or two voices exclaiming surprise.

There were more than two voices. They were spread across the water.

That meant more than one monster - many more!

Bain grasped the yacht's wheel and returned to his seat. His leg tapped the floorboard. His face grew stern, trying to appear in control. He examined the water. He reached into his glove box and pulled out a black pistol.

Burns and O'Reilly said nothing. They didn't even raise an eyebrow. Laws have a way of disappearing on the water, Tom thought.

A cold chill ran through Tom's body, an unnatural wind that blew right through him. There was a strange sensation, a pull inside him.

Tom closed his eyes; he knew what it meant. They were close to the barn.

It was calling to him.

The barn was hidden by the fog. He imagined it was there, coated in ivy. He remembered it was small. Old. Ordinary, except for the fact it had somehow remained standing for hundreds of years. Its walls were made of stone, and its roof was covered with wood that had rotted and fragmented over the centuries.

The tug inside Tom grew more intense. A whisper entered his ear, like a woman mouthing her seductive lips next to his earlobe.

"Tom."

Tom shook his head. He imagined Marella, the woman he came to Scotland for, the woman he wanted to spend his life with, the woman who misjudged him, but she'd learn. He would fight for her. He had to find her. He had to rescue her if it was the last thing he did.

"Tom," came the seductive whisper again. A mysterious melody drifted through the fog.

He put his hands over his ears and he shut his eyes. "No!" He was more afraid of the whisper and the barn and the creature in the water than he was of Bain or the two armed police officers.

The boat still rocked from the unnatural bump that came below the water.

Tom raised his head. "We need to get out of here!"

"I'm fur tha'," O'Reilly said.

Bain ignored their statements. He leaned forward, the gun in his hand, and he watched the water.

The boat drifted forward, rocking back and forth.

The other boats floated in their places. A flash of quiet lightning lit up the overhead clouds.

Bain said, "Do I hear humming?"

Burns lowered his pistol, confusion upon his face.

Tom opened his eyes. Bain was standing. So was Burns. Their eyes focused forward over the yacht's stern. O'Reilly crouched in the deck, nervous.

A woman's voice drifted through the fog. Her beautiful song arose from a soft melody to a strong serenade.

> *She hoped fur eternal love*
> *Ne'er shall they part.*
> *His betrayal leaves a gaping hole*
> *Inside her wounded heart.*

Bain pointed ahead. His mouth dropped, stunned.

Tom lifted his eyes forward.

> *Alas, he's come back tae me.*
> *Will his love endure?*
> *The prison of Oblivion*
> *Is th' only cure.*

"Will ye loo' at tha'," Burns said. His pistol was lowered, defenseless.

The fog separated over the water. The shore was twenty yards from them. Beyond the shore, the old barn stood, covered in ivy and shadows from the lowering sunlight. Upon the shore, a woman wearing a reddish-brown hooded robe walked barefoot over the grass. Her movement was graceful, elegant, and seductive. Her white legs drifted out of the coat that draped over her hips. She stopped. She lifted her head under the hood. Her face was white. Her eyes were red with tears. Strands of her long white hair fell out from the hood and down her coat.

"Wha' is goin' on?" Bain said, his mouth open.

Her lips moved as she sang her slow, sad song.

> *We shall be joined again*
> *Once the vows are said.*
> *Then love will grow when*
> *We lay upon our bed.*

She lowered herself, sitting upon the shore. Her white legs appeared out from under her robe. Her arms wrapped around her knees. Her toes tipped the edge of the water. Her eyes were sorrowful as tears dripped past her cheeks and onto the grassy shore at her feet.

Tom stood. "We need to get out of here. Now!"

Bain raised his hand. "Na so fast," he said, keeping his eyes on the woman. He was entranced by her song, wanting to hear more.

Her song drifted over the water. It traveled through the air like it was a part of it. Bain, O'Reilly, and Burns tilted their heads, listening.

> *The waters drift under yer bow,*
> *seeming still and black.*
> *While ye lust fur th' maiden's glow,*
> *Ye should rather watch yer back.*

"She's beautiful," Bain said.

"Aye," Burns said in a long whisper.

O'Reilly said nothing.

Tom watched. The chill grabbed hold of his chest.

The woman opened her red eyes. Her pupils bore into Tom's soul. Tears streamed down her perfect cheeks.

> *I wish upon my bosom*
> *yer heart remained with me,*
> *Bu' I see ye wan' tae wander*
> *So they'll block ye as ye flee.*

She closed her eyes tight, and she opened her mouth. A loud wail pierced the silence. Tom, Bain, O'Reilly, and Burns put their hands up over their ears.

"Wha's tha' scream?"

The woman's wail vibrated through the air. The wail entered through Tom's ears and his skull rang within. Bain, Burns, and O'Reilly covered their ears and twisted, trying to stop the pain. Tom shut his eyes, waiting for the sound to end.

The woman's voice stopped, and she closed her mouth. Relieved, the men uncovered their ears and stood in disbelief.

Then the woman lifted her hood off her head and she sang her sad melancholy tune in minor notes.

> *When th' monsters come tae greet ye*
> *Yer breath won' last tae long.*
> *But yer kin will tell th' story*
> *How yer end came with this song.*

The men paused, not sure what they should do next. There was no other noise for a few moments other than the sound of the small Loch Ness waves tapping their hull.

"I think we should leave," Tom said.

Bain said, "I think yer right." He sat in the driver's seat.

From another boat, there was a yell and a splash. Tom jumped in surprise.

A man shouted, "Wha' was tha'?"

"I don' know!"

Another yell and a scream. Then a splash.

Then a third.

"Jes–!"

Splash!

"What is tha–!" Scream. Splash.

The boat headlights in the distant fog rocked back and forth in erratic motions. Some spun from right to left, or left to right, as their boats shifted.

Bain's yacht rocked back and forth from the strong ripples that emanated through the fog. He stood, his pistol at his side. "Wha' should we do?"

Large waves hit the hull, rocking the boat and keeping Tom off balance. If anything was below him, he couldn't see it. The water was too dark. The fog was too thick.

A gunshot rang through the fog. A man screamed, then yelled, "Shoot it! Shoot it–," but the voice trailed off into a dying whimper.

"Wha's happenin'?" Burns said. He straightened his arm and pointed his pistol at the fog and the spinning headlights.

Tom said to O'Reilly. "We've got to get out of here!"

O'Reilly widened his eyes. He gripped the edge of the boat with white knuckles.

Bang! Bang! Bang!

The gunshots echoed over the water from one of the distant boats. More men shouted. "Tis go- me. Help! Hel–"

Splash!

Bang! Bang!

In the boat next to them, Councilman MacGillivray. "What's gettin' them!"

McCulloch reached for his engine.

"Get out o' here!"

A motor's engine revved in the fog.

More men shouted.

A flare gun went off and streaked across the water, then landed against the hull of McCulloch and MacGillivray's boat before it fell, its red flame burning on the water. Then, the side of the boat caught fire.

"We nee' tae leave!" MacGillivray said.

"If we catch fire we'll ne'er make it!"

More men shouted behind them.

A long black neck breached the water next to McCulloch's boat. It stuck out from the dark water - the red light of the flare gun shimmering off its smooth neck - then it was gone.

Bain said, "Well?"

Burns got the hint. He pointed his gun into the fog. He shot several shots.

Bang! Bang!

"Wha' are ye shootin' at?" O'Reilly said.

"Whatever's gettin' them!"

"But ye canno' see anythin'!"

A man screamed from a nearby boat. The fog hid him from view.

There was the sound of water separating behind them. Tom spotted a large black fin exiting and reentering the water.

"Shoot it!" Bain said. He pointed his gun and shot three times into the water.

Burns lifted his gun and pulled the trigger four times.

Bullets disappeared into the loch.

"Where'd it go?" Burns shouted.

The fog dissipated the sounds of men's screams and shouts.

Through the fog, someone yelled, "They're e'erywhere!"

The smell of rotting fish grew putrid. A sound of dripping water emerged behind Tom.

O'Reilly let out a yell. He was lifted out of the yacht and pulled into the water, his surprised voice disappearing as his head and legs went into blackness.

Bain pointed. "Shoot it!"

Burns didn't hesitate. He pointed his gun and fired off several rounds.

There was no confirmation that he hit his target.

Bain was frantic. He searched for the boat ignition. He dropped his gun. It fell at his feet and slid on the floor. He reached down for it, but a presence caught his attention. A long slender black neck hovered before him. At the end was a large head with two dark eyes.

Bain lost his voice, but stood and pointed, shocked at the sight of the living creature whose eyes bored into him. "Shoot!. . . Shoot!"

Burns fell backward. He failed to point the gun in time.

The creature moved like a cobra, launching its jaws into Bain's shoulder. Bain yelled in surprise. The creature lifted him from the yacht and yanked him head-first into the water. His legs disappeared with a flip and a splash.

Burns regained his balance and pulled the trigger, shooting at the water, but the bullets missed their target and disappeared into the deep waters of Loch Ness.

The woman remained on the shore and sang her sad song, her sad eyes tearful, oblivious to the chaos on the water.

> *Yer friends, they canno' help ye*
> *Nor will they survive.*
> *Th' only comfort fur thee*
> *Is tae take my hand and dive.*

Tom tapped Burns's shoulder and pointed at the woman.

Burns lifted his gun and fired multiple rounds at her. The ground behind her splattered.

The woman did not flinch. Her sad eyes watered red as she moved her mouth.

> *Yer violence agains' me*
> *Will only do ye harm.*
> *My love will overcome thee*
> *Ye can' resist my charm.*

"I hit her!" Burns said.

Tom shook his head. She's still there.

An explosion over Tom's shoulder caused them to duck.

The fire grew on the side of McCulloch's boat. MacGillivray held a fire extinguisher, and he sprayed it at the growing flames. It made a whooshing sound as he leaned over the boat. The two men shouted orders at each other as they scrambled to keep from sinking and burning alive. MacGillivray ran back and forth on the deck. He went to the driver's seat. The boat's motor whirred and grew louder, and the boat pressed forward into the fog.

A long serpentine neck lifted from the water and lunged at MacGillivray. He let out a scream, which McCulloch didn't hear because of the fire extinguisher.

The creature lifted MacGillivray into the air. His foot caught the steering wheel, and the boat veered sharply.

McCulloch dropped the fire extinguisher as the creature pulled MacGillivray over the side and into the water. McCulloch lunged, but missed MacGillivray, and fell over the boat's railing and into the loch. He splashed and yelled for help before his voice let out a panicked scream and cut into silence.

McCulloch's unmanned boat spun in a semi-circle, the fire from its hull growing and catching the deck. The flames rose higher into the foggy air; their glow reflected off the waves of Loch Ness.

Tom and Burns watched the boat. It bounced over the water as it circled. The bow of the boat adjusted, pointing at them.

"It's coming here!" Tom shouted. "Move the boat!"

Burns stood still, shocked.

"Get out of my way!" Tom said. He pushed past Burns and sat in Bain's seat. He found the ignition and started the engine.

Burns pointed his gun at the boat and fired until he was out of bullets. The boat did not stop. "Tis goin' tae hit us!" He backed up near Tom.

The boat burned like a harbinger of death.

Tom revved the engine. The black yacht jerked.

A loud crash came from behind that sounded like shattering wood and crunching metal. The stern flew into the air. Tom's neck whiplashed with the impact. His rear flew from his seat. Heat and smoke filled Tom's lungs.

Burns fell forward onto the stern. He held onto a rope, his body pressed against the wood, his legs hanging over the edge.

There was crunching metal and breaking wood.

Tom found himself off the seat and onto the floor. The burning boat slid off the back of the crushed yacht and sped forward toward the woman on the shore.

Burns climbed back up off the stern and fell onto the deck. "We're on fire and sinkin'!"

Tom shifted to a crouch and saw what Burns was yelling at: the stern of the yacht was crushed, the engine on fire, the water pouring onto the floorboard. No telling what damage was done to the hull beneath the water. In a few seconds, they'd be sunk and falling to the depths.

McCulloch's burning boat sped past Tom and Burns and aimed at the woman and the barn. Its flames spread on either side like a floating missile. The woman did not move. The boat soon covered her, crashing into the shore. It bounced once upon the land, then launched into the old barn. The old stones, rotting wood, and ivy broke apart and scattered as the boat exploded.

Shrapnel flew through the air and the fog. Tom and Burns both ducked and covered their heads.

Several streaks of white lightning spread through the spiral clouds.

Tom lifted his head. Where the barn used to be was now a burning inferno of McCulloch's boat and heated stones. Thick smoke rose up and twisted into the clouds.

The woman was no longer there. Tom thought perhaps the boat had killed her, but then her wail vibrated over the air. It was the sound of pain. Anger. Vengeance. Sadness.

"We're goin' down!" Burns said. Water now poured the edge of the boat and covered his ankles as he continued to point his pistol at the water. "Th' creatures 'll ge' us!"

Tom watched the flames. Somewhere underneath the heat and the stones was the amulet he was supposed to find. The glow of the fire reflected off his eyes. How was he going to save Marella?

CHAPTER 56

The shore was twenty yards away, but the water underneath Tom was deep. The edges of the loch steeped down into depths of over 750 feet, the second deepest loch in Scotland. With the creatures under the water, Tom would have to swim. He hoped the burning fire and explosion scared them away. Tom stood and went to the edge of Bain's yacht. He balanced his legs on the sloping deck. He removed his green coat, now wet and scraped and torn, and threw it in the water.

Bain's legs wobbled as he tried to balance. Water covered his legs up to his knees. He held his pistol, pointing it at the water. "Wha' are ye doin?"

"Stay here if you want, but I'm going to shore."

"They'll ge' ye."

"Since when did you care?"

Burns stood still, his freckled face white with fear, the boat angling downward and water rising up to his knees.

Tom said, "Hope you know how to swim." He dove headfirst into the water.

The icy water hit his skin, and he rose, sucking in air to recover from the shock. He kicked his legs and his shoes fell from his feet. Water pulled at his socks. Would Burns shoot at him and try to make him stay? There were no gunshots.

There was a splash. Tom imagined the head of a plesiosaur. He opened his eyes.

Burns, in his black police suit, swam next to him. He kicked and stroked, his red hair dark from the water.

"Come on!" Tom said. He walked toward the fire upon the shore, hoping it would warm him when he reached land.

The two of them swam through the water, splashing, kicking, spitting out ice water, and inhaling against the pressure of the cold upon their torsos. Tom tried not to think of the monsters, how they could pull him under the surface in an instant. He moved his arms and kicked his legs. Then, upon one last stroke, his finger hit a rock. They had reached the shore.

He and Burns dragged themselves from the water. In front of them the fires burned, and a tower of black smoke twisted up into spiraling clouds. The heat of the burning boat warmed Tom's face and arms as water dripped off his shirt, pants, and skin. He stood on his soggy socks. His feet were wet and cold. He wrapped his arms around his chest to keep from shivering.

Burns stood, his legs wobbly. His police uniform was drenched as the water dripped off him. He had lost his police cap somewhere in all the chaos, and his short red hair lay flat upon his scalp. His boots were tied above the ankles. He made it to shore with them still on his feet. Water squished inside his boots with every step. "Th' other boats. They're na movin'." Tom ignored him and focused on the burning boat, the barn, and the fire that consumed it. While the flames rose, he studied the situation. There was no sign of the woman. Had she been crushed by the boat? Was her wailing her final cry of death?

Also, the barn wasn't completely destroyed. The boat was burning, but it was on one side of the barn. The north end of the barn was still intact. He ran to the far edge. It was the section of the barn he had entered several weeks earlier, and he had lost all concept of time. He stood at the doorway. Fifty percent of the ground was exposed. Brown soil glowed burnt orange from the rising flames. The boat burned behind it. Smoke drifted in the barn ruins. Tom lifted his hand, a poor attempt to try to keep from inhaling it.

Burns followed and stood next to Tom. He breathed hard, his adrenaline still rushing through his red freckled face. He coughed, his lungs filling with smoke.

Tom said, "I'm going in. Stay here. If I disappear, tell the others."

"Disappear?"

"Just do it."

Burns shrugged. "Okay."

Tom closed his eyes. He coughed but regained his composure. "For Marella," he said. He held his breath, then he extended his dripping sock and foot, and he stepped through the door. His wet socks soaked up dirt. The fire crackled before him. Had he been transported again to some point in the future?

Tom opened his eyes.

Burns stood in the doorway.

"Do you see me?" Tom said.

"Aye."

"Alright." Tom exhaled and fell to his hands and feet. He dug through the dirt while covering his mouth with his wet shirt.

Burns watched, also covering his face. "Wha' was tha' all abou'?"

Tom said, "Are you going to help me or what?"

Burns said, "Yer serious, aren' ye?"

"There's something in here," Tom said. He pressed his fingers and hands into the dirt, throwing it at the fire, trying to dampen it.

Burns joined him on his hands and knees, covering his mouth and throwing dirt.

"Check the edges," Tom said. "I'll take the center."

Burns stood and went to the side of the stones, then went back to his knees digging and throwing dirt.

Over the crackling fire, a voice shouted, "Hello! Are ye in there?"

The smoke made Tom's eyes water. In the doorway was Logan O'Malley. Next to him was Jacob Stewart. "Detective." Tom said. "Where's Sean?"

"Still in th' boat. Where'd everybody go? All th' boats are empty. And whose boat is burnin'? Where's Bain?"

"No time to explain. Get down here and help us dig!"

Stewart shrugged and went inside. He covered his mouth and shoveled dirt with his hands. "I've seen tae much already tae waste time askin' questions."

"Yer diggin' in th' wrong place," O'Malley said to Tom. "Father Gibson said wha' ye need is in th' church."

"The old man said it was in here."

"Wha' old man?"

"Never mind. Get in here and dig."

O'Malley rubbed the back of his neck, then touched his gray beard. "Okay," he said. He covered his mouth and he fell to his hands and feet and threw dirt, digging beneath the soil. "Ye better be right, lad. Father Gibson said ye need tae hold it up tae th' sun before it sets, o' else yer friend Marella is lost."

"The sun?"

"Aye."

"Did he say why?"

"It'll open a door."

"Door to what?"

"He didn' say."

The roof was destroyed under the spiraling clouds. The sunlight was waning in the west underneath the clouds. Tom shook his head and dug. "What do we have left? Forty-five minutes?"

"I'd say half an hour, lad." O'Malley coughed.

Tom swore. He worked harder, trying to keep from coughing and slowing down, knowing Marella needed him.

Burns sifted sand around the edges. "This whole thing is doolally. If I hadn' seen th' creature fur myself, I'd brin' ye in."

Tom had convinced himself the creatures were animals that happened to survive a mass extinction. But now, with the caoineag, the disappearing old man, and the strange clouds, was it possible he was dealing with something worse, something beyond the realm of evolution?

He dug hard, holding his breath, getting into a rhythm. His wet clothes caught the soil, his cold toes like ice inside his socks.

"I found somethin'," Stewart said.

The others stopped digging. "What'd ye find?" O'Malley asked, coughing.

Stewart reached down. He yelped and pulled his hand back, shaking it. "Tis sharp, whate'er it is."

Tom got up and ran to Stewart. Without asking questions, he threw his hands in the dirt and dug.

"Careful lad," Stewart said.

Tom flew dirt beside him. Something white and brittle appeared as he brushed the sand away.

"Wha' is it?" O'Malley said.

Burns got up, and stood over Tom, watching.

Tom kept brushing dirt aside, now flattening his fingers and trying to uncover the edges like a paleontologist. "It's a bone," Tom said.

"Bone? Of what?"

"I don't know." He brushed aside more dirt, and a small round skull appeared with a long beak.

"Is that a bird?" O'Malley said.

Tom paused.

"Are there feathers?" added O'Malley.

Tom said, "I don't see any." He kept going, revealing the skeleton of a large bird. "What kind is it?"

"Crow?" Stewart said.

"Raven," Burns said, coughing.

The others raised their eyes.

"My mother watched birds," he said.

"Is tha' wha' yer lookin' fur?" O'Malley said.

"I don't think so." Tom lifted the skeleton of the bird and set the pieces aside. "Keep it there in case it is." He coughed several times and he returned to digging. "Help me."

The others got down and dug, their fingers pulling at the dirt and throwing it while the burning boat crackled several feet from them.

O'Malley said, "I feel something." He brushed dirt aside, and the corner of rust showed through the soil.

The others jumped at it, revealing the item. It was a small wooden chest, its lock held together by rusted iron. Tom bent down, put his hands around it, and pulled it from the soil, his eyes and nose burning from the smoke. He set it next to the skeleton and tried to open it. "It's locked."

"Here," Burns said. He took out a flashlight from his belt and hammered at the chest lock with its back end. After four strong knocks, the rusted lock broke apart, splintering some of the wood. Burns backed up and Tom bent down. Tom opened the lock and pulled out an old iron crucifix that had been hammered together with nails. Its length and width were made of iron, similar to what the Romans had used to hammer people to crosses.

"Wha' is it?" Stewart said.

"I don't know," Tom said. He lifted it up.

"Tis a cross," O'Malley said.

Tom remembered the crucifix that hung from the old man's neck in Guthrie's Pub. "Yeah," he said.

"Tha's na amulet," Burns said.

Tom said, "You see another one?"

Burns shook his head, his mouth covered.

"Quick, th' sun," O'Malley said, pointing out the door.

"Right!" Tom stood and ran outside, away from the broken barn and the burning boat. The sun was setting behind the darkening highland hills. The coolness of the shade made the wind that much colder. His skin shivered with the loss of his coat and his soaking wet clothes. If he didn't get warm soon, hypothermia would set in. But he had to remain focused. He kept his thoughts on Marella, her long red hair, her green eyes, and her warm face. She'd trust him. He'd find a way to rescue her. He was almost there.

O'Malley, Stewart, and Burns followed Tom outside. With them watching, he held the cross up high in the air, the wind blowing around his wet torso, his arms shivering with cold. The shadow of the hills kept the cross dark against the spiraling clouds.

Nothing happened.

Tom stood on his toes, trying to reach the sun rays above the shade, but he was not tall enough. "I'm not even close. There's too much shadow!"

"Wha' if ye throw it high?" O'Malley said.

Tom lowered the cross and launched it up into the sky. It spun in the shadow until it reached the heights above it. For a moment, the sunlight colored the cross's rusted iron nails as they twisted end over end. Then gravity took hold, and the cross retreated toward the ground.

"Catch it, lad!"

Tom shifted - his feet sore inside his wet socks, his lungs and eyes still burning from the smoke - to get under the falling cross. He put his hands out. The dark cross gained speed, rushing at him. It fell faster and faster.

"Don' let it pierce ye!"

Tom reached for the cross. He tried using his fingers. The cross came down hard, intertwining with his digits. The metal slammed into his hand. The connection slowed its speed, but he was unable to hold on. The cross fell onto the moss and the dirt.

"It didn't work," Tom said.

"Did it ge' ye?"

Tom shook his hand to release the pain. "I'm okay."

"Nothin's happenin'," Burns said.

O'Malley said. "Maybe Father Gibson was right. Ye have tae be holdin' it."

"Can we run to the top of the hill?" Tom said.

"Tis tae high, lad. Sun will be down before ye make it."

Tom scanned his surroundings for sunlight. The shadow was everywhere, covering much of the landscape and the water on this side of Loch Ness. The fog had dissipated, its last remaining mist hovering a foot above the water, covering it like a blanket. Several boats sat in the water, unmoving. Smoke drifted into the atmosphere. Beyond the burning boat, another boat floated close to the shore. Three men were on the boat. One waved a crutch.

Sean!

Beyond him, the Thurwick shore was aglow with the final rays of the afternoon sun.

Sean's voice carried over the air. "Did ye find it!"

"We did," Tom shouted back.

Tom pointed across Loch Ness. Thurwick was still aglow in the final daylight before the sun set over the horizon. "There's no sun over here. We need to get across the water!"

"Right!" O'Malley said.

Tom tightened his grip around the cross and ran to Keith Wallace's boat, followed by the others. His feet stung from the cold and the lack of shoes to protect them from the stones and twigs. "Hurry!"

The sun's rays were sinking in the west, casting their last glow of the day upon the town of Thurwick and Saint Michael's Church.

CHAPTER 57

Tom and Burns had blankets over their shoulders. Tom held the blanket and the cross with one hand against his chest while he held onto the railing with the other. The boat bounced over the surface of Loch Ness, passing the empty boats that floated aimlessly upon the water. "How much time do we have?" Tom said as Keith pressed on the gas.

"Five minutes. Ten if we're lucky!" Keith said. He gripped the wheel with white knuckles, his eyes focused on the shore across the loch.

"Well step on it lad. Let's see how fast this boat can fly!" Sean said.

The sunlight was behind the northwestern highland hills, covering the water. The long shadow and the wind chilled Tom. But the daylight remained in the west, sending warm rays across the horizon, giving the old stone buildings in Thurwick a yellow and orange aura and casting long shadows across the green fields and winding roads.

"Look!" Cameron Wallace said. He pointed to the water, and a large black shape appeared and disappeared. It moved like a dolphin, only larger and faster. It dived below the surface in an instant, leaving ripples in the water where it had been.

Burns stood and lifted his pistol. He pulled the trigger, but it misfired, having been submerged in the water of Loch Ness. "It'll ge' us!"

"Hold on," Sean said. He pointed his crutch the other way. "There's another one!"

Keith slowed the boat so he could see, but Tom rose and shouted, "There's no time. The shadow's growing!" He pointed ahead, holding the cross with the other hand. The shadow was rising over the bottom stones of Saint Michael's rectory.

"Ye'll ne'er make it," Stewart said.

Tom had to think.

They were in the shade. The wind was cold.

He had to find sunlight. If he made it to land, he'd have to get high, but where?

Saint Michael's was the tallest structure in Thurwick. Next to the steeple, the bell tower was the highest point of the building. He remembered the stairway he had found when he discovered the crypt.

That was it. He had to get in through the crypt door (which was hopefully still open) and run upstairs as fast as he could. "Take me to the church. I've got to get up the bell tower!"

"Those creatures are tae fast. They'll have ye fur a meal in na time!" Stewart said, his messy hair blowing in the wind.

Tom forced his thoughts to the positive. True, the creatures were fast, faster than the boat. But the boat's bouncing over the surface prevented their attack - if they planned to attack at all. Perhaps the death of the woman at the barn was enough to remove her spell over them. Maybe now they were free. Maybe they'd leave him alone if he left them alone.

Or maybe they want me for lunch!

Tom shook his head, changing his thought. "I have an idea," Tom said.

Keith said, "What's tha'?"

"Keep the engine at full throttle. Speed past the church. When you get near it, I'll jump off and swim to shore."

The men stared at him.

Sean frowned. "I'd go with ye, lad, if I had my leg."

"I know you would."

Stewart, Burns, O'Malley, and Cameron sat still. Their mouths closed.

Saint Michael's approached on the left side. They passed the Thurwick buildings as Keith's boat sped across the water.

"Oh, alrigh'," Burns said. "I'll go with him."

"You believe now, do ye?" Sean said.

"I don' know wha' I believe anymore."

Stewart said to O'Malley, "Ye wan' tae go?"

O'Malley lowered his head. "Canno' swim."

Stewart said, "Alrigh'." He leaned forward and removed his sportscoat. "Ne'er imagined I'd be in th' loch today."

"Ye, tae?" O'Malley said.

"Aye."

Tom said, "Thanks."

Keith leaned forward and pushed the engine to the max. The boat bounced over the waves. "Hang on!"

The wind blew into Tom's ears. The wind blew his hair. His skin was cold. He focused his eyes on the light, the sunlight that was almost gone.

Tom gripped the railing, his rear bouncing up and down on the seat. Sean slipped and fell to the deck. Stewart and O'Malley helped him up.

Burns pointed. "There's a third!"

"More than that!" Tom shouted.

"I'm na sure this is a good idea," O'Malley said.

"Wha' choice do we have?" Sean said. He said to Tom, Burns, and Stewart. "Well play th' decoy. Ye three swim like yer life depends on it, and pray they follow us."

The shadows lengthened, rising up the rectory walls. As Wallace's boat approached the church, the shadow was now covering the door to the crypt and rising.

"Three minutes!" Keith shouted. "I'll veer tae th' sunset. Ye three jump off port side!"

Tom, Burns, and Stewart changed positions, nearing the edge and trying to balance as the boat bounced over the waves. Tom dropped his blanket and held onto the cross. The cold wind chilled his whole body as it blew against his wet clothes and his damp socks.

"Hurry!" Sean said.

"Wha' about them?" Cameron shouted, pointing to the creatures in the water.

Keith said to Cameron, "Be brave, lad, o' I'll make ye jump tae!"

"Keep going. Outrun them!" Tom said.

The boat sped toward the shore, and at the last minute, Keith veered the boat hard to the right. It bounced fast upon Loch Ness, past the cobblestone roads and stone buildings of Thurwick. Several residents stood near the shore, watching with awe as the boat sped over the water. They pointed at the spiraling clouds and the ripples in the water left by breaching and disappearing creatures.

Saint Michael's church approached. Tom hoped they'd be able to make it without the creatures interfering.

Across the loch, the barn still burned, and the smoke of McCulloch's boat still drifted up, spinning into the spiraling clouds. Except now the clouds were drifting away from the barn and over the water. Were the clouds following them? The lightning still flashed within the spirals of the clouds. Tom didn't know what to think of them.

"One minute!"

The Church was a hundred yards away. Tom grasped the cross in his hand and held it close. He whispered a small prayer that what he was trying to do would work, that what the old man in the pub and Father Gibson had said was right. He prayed that Marella was safe, unharmed, and able to be rescued.

He prayed he wouldn't be eaten.

The rays of the sun stretched above them, now reaching the second story of Saint Michael's. The boat kept its pace. "On my count," Keith shouted. "Five . . . Four . . . "

"Distract the creatures!" Tom shouted as he stood and leaned over the edge. Stewart and Burns did the same.

"With wha?" Cameron said.

"Figure it out!" Tom said.

". . . Three . . . Two . . "

"Here we go!" Tom said as he put his socks over the edge.

". . . One . . . Jump!"

Saint Michael's church was in full view in front of him, its steeple reaching the sky, the bell tower next to it, its massive stones lit with sunlight except for the bottom shaded third. Tom leaped feet-first into the air. His stomach heaved with the force of gravity as it took him down, faster and faster through the air. Burns and Stewart fell through the air next to him, waving their arms. The water rushed at him. Everything moved in slow motion. He closed his eyes, sucked in air, closed his mouth, and held onto the cross with both hands while praying he'd survive.

CHAPTER 58

The water hit Tom's legs and he twisted onto his side, knocked over by the forward momentum that carried him on the boat. The ice water pierced him like knives on his skin. He opened his mouth, gasping, and he let out air, that bubbled to the surface. Water filled his mouth, which he closed. His lungs burned and he needed air. He kicked with his legs while making sure he had the cross in his hands. Getting his bearings, he let go of the cross with one hand, held on with the other, and swam upward to the light, away from the darkness, trying to reach the surface. His heart raced as he imagined the plesiosaurs grabbing his legs and pulling him down to the depths.

He kicked with everything he had, stroking his arms and kicking. His head reached the surface. He spat out water and gasped for air.

He shouted "Marella!" to keep his focus. He held the cross. Time was closing in on him.

Burns's and Stewart's heads rose above the dark water, each gasping for breath. Behind them, Wallace's boat, carrying Sean,

O'Malley, and Cameron, motored along the southern shore away from them and toward the setting sun.

Tom hoped the creatures would follow the boat.

"You alright?" Tom said.

"Aye!" Stewart said.

Burns spat out water.

The church was in front of Tom. The shadow rose as the sun lowered.

He didn't have much time. He was in the shadows, a few yards from land. He kicked and stroked, holding the cross, moving his legs, swinging his arms, twisting his head, and breathing when he could.

Burns and Stewart did as well, each working their arms in irregular movements, kicking and stroking.

Tom's hands struck the shore. "Land!" he gasped, hoping it would be the last time he ever had to swim in Loch Ness. He drove his knees forward, crawling through the mud and the muck.

Burns reached the shore, and Stewart was ten yards away.

Tom climbed out of the water on all fours, his clothes still dripping, his body trembling from the cold, his chest heaving with every breath, and his legs wobbly. He coughed up water, holding the cross in his hand while it pressed against the mud. He finished coughing. The shadow was now nearing the top of the rectory. He'd have to run up the stairway of the bell tower and outpace the shadow. He couldn't wait for Stewart or Burns. He lifted his knee and managed to stand.

Then an odor hit his nostrils, the pungent odor of rotting fish.

Tom recognized it.

Burns was still on his hands and knees, recovering from the jump and the swim. Stewart was five yards behind, still stroking when a large head and neck extended from the water.

"Stewart!" Tom shouted, but there was no time.

The eyes of the plesiosaur concentrated on Stewart, examining him like a bird before it thrust its beak into a worm. The head pointed down and struck Stewart with the force of an anvil. Stewart's body dipped below the surface, the neck of the plesiosaur following, and the large torso and fins diving after him in a splash that reminded Tom of a whale breaching the water.

Burns gasped for air. He spun around, half afraid for Stewart, half afraid because he was close to the water. The creature's massive splash rained upon him.

A roar came from their right.

Tom leaped back.

The giant head and neck rose from the water.

Tom's heart leaped, hoping the creature would remain in the water.

But the creature did not stop there. It threw out a mighty fin and it crawled upon the shore, climbing over the rocks with ease, its black body rippling muscles, its power pressing upon the earth with its mighty fins which it used as legs. The Loch Ness monster was the size of a trailer, its neck the length of a giraffe, and its fins the width of truck tires.

It moved at Burns, its eyes fierce, its tongue salivating, its neck lunging, its mouth gaping, and its teeth white and threatening.

Tom stood his ground. Instincts took over. He raised the cross high in his hand and shouted, "Back!"

The creature's eyes focused on Tom and its mouth roared a sound that made his hairs stand on end. The odor of fish filled the air with the creature's roar. Tom squinted and covered his mouth, trying not to breathe the odor. He kept his eyes on the creature, staring him down. Recovering from the roar, Tom glared at the creature and held the cross.

Tom concentrated on the creature's black eyes. They were innocent, emotional, and hungry. This was a creature, a created being with the desire to live. Its eyes held both power and confusion. It knew it had dominance within the water. It wanted to survive in an unfamiliar world and be left alone.

Tom stepped forward. "Back I said. This is no place for you!"

The creature was stunned by Tom's advance. Its head reared back, and its neck retreated.

Tom pressed forward in his socks. "Back. Back!"

The creature retreated into the water. Its neck diving first, its body second. It swam with marvelous ease, its mighty fins splashing one last time before it disappeared into the depths.

Burns sat paralyzed on his rear, his face white with terror, his eyes wide, his hands behind him.

Tom went to him. "You all right?"

Burns babbled something incoherent.

"I gotta run," Tom said. "You might want to get away from the shore."

Burns remained on the shore, unable to speak.

Tom shook his head.

The sun's rays spread overhead. The sunlight was almost gone. He faced the now mostly-shaded Saint Michael's Church. The last vestiges of the day's sunlight shone upon the top of the bell tower.

CHAPTER 59

Tom sprinted to the crypt door, holding the cross with his cold fingers. He ignored the pain of his cold feet upon the sharp rocks and broken twigs as he hurried up the slope to the church. The sunlight was high above, reflecting the outer stones of the old church. He had to get to the light, to hold the cross within its rays. He sprinted forward to the door. It appeared the door was shut. When he arrived he grabbed the handle.

"Please be open," he muttered.

He pressed the latch. The door clicked. He pushed. The door opened right away. "Thank God!" he said. He ran inside relieved the door wasn't locked. The lights were bright, still on from when he had been in there earlier in the day with Liz Stevens. He ran past the wooden pews and avoided stepping on the supposed tomb in the middle of the floor.

He ran into the stairwell.

The spiral staircase circled upward.

He forced his tired knees to lift his legs. His wet socks slipped upon the stone steps. He held the cross tight with his cold hands and bumped the stone sides with his wet shoulders. Darkness consumed him. He lept two to three steps at a time, trying to get past the shadow line somewhere above him, beating the sun. He went up in the spiral, twisting around and around, his leg muscles burning with agony.

He reached the secret doorway where last he had pressed against it to keep the locals from finding him. But the staircase kept going up. He had to reach higher, to go up into the bell tower. He forced his legs to move, going past the secret door of the main church, up toward the bell tower, praying he'd reach the top in time, praying he'd beat the sun. His calves cramped, and so did his feet. He ignored it, stumbling, pulling, pushing with his arms on the old stone bricks as he climbed up the bell tower.

He twisted up the staircase, going around and around.

And then he heard it.

Singing.

His heart sank.

He knew the voice.

It was her.

The caoineag.

She was still alive.

The soft seductive voice came from above, somewhere on the bell tower platform.

I know ye ne'er loved me.
Yer heart still goes elsewhere.
Th' one ye want refused ye.
She doesn' even care.

"That's not true!" Tom shouted, his voice echoing between the stone stairwell. He pushed his legs up the final stairs into the sunlight. The cold air blew into his face.

The beautiful woman sat upon the edge of the bell tower wall, her hood down behind her back, the wind blowing her robe that hung loosely on her body, revealing her cleavage and her slender seductive legs. Sorrow covered her pale face. Her long white hair whipped in the wind.

She showed no concern about falling from the bell tower. The sunlight cast a glow around her frame, her sad eyes aflame with desire.

Tom's chest rose and fell from running up the steps. His wet socks pressed against the stone floor of the bell tower. He held the cross behind his back, hiding it.

The woman licked her lips.

Tom said, "What do you want?"

Her red lips pressed together. Her white hair blew in the wind. "I want everythin'."

"What's this got to do with me?"

She gave an agonizing smile. "We've been joined. Yer mine, Tom. We'll be together . . . furever."

"This is what you call an abusive relationship," Tom said. He faced the sun and pulled the cross from behind his back.

The woman's eyes widened. Then she shut them and she disappeared, cloth and body together. The sound of wings flapping filled the bell tower. Black feathers hung in the air and blew with the wind.

Tom stood still, waiting. The sunlight beat against his face.

An invisible arm suddenly grasped his forearm and pulled it down. A force swatted the cross from his grip, and he dropped it. It fell to the floor. He reached down to pick it up, but it flung as the invisible force kicked it. It slid across the floor and down the stairs. It bounced upon the steps.

Tom lept for it, but the invisible force grasped his legs, pulling him back.

Tom kicked.

Nothing was there except the last fades of sunlight. He crawled to the stairs.

The invisible hand grasped his ankle.

He kicked and rolled and went to the stairs. He clambered upon his belly, shuffling down the steps.

The cross lay on the edge of a step and against the stone wall.

It was within his reach. An invisible foot stepped on his hand. Tom swung at where he imagined the ankle would be. His hand passed through something. He pulled his hand away and reached again at the cross. He grabbed it with both hands.

Something punched his back.

He withstood the blows and twisted. The shadows still covered him. Using his knees and elbows, he crawled up the stairs.

The force grabbed him from behind, like claws digging into his skin. He swung with his elbow, not hitting anything, yet somehow he was released. He fell backward, his rear and shoulder blades falling upon the stone. He almost lost the grip of the cross but he forced himself to hold on. He balanced himself upon the steps.

The bell tower platform was above him. The last rays of sunlight shined overhead. He had to get to them.

He climbed on his belly and crawled to the top of the stairs. He found himself out of the darkness of the stairway and onto the platform. He had reached the top of the bell tower.

The evening shadow had reached the bell tower platform. The sun was seconds away from falling behind the horizon. The bottom of the orange ball was behind the dark-shaded hillside, the last of the sun's rays emanating through the cold windy air.

Tom climbed to his feet, still sore and bruised inside his cold damp socks.

He ran to the edge of the bell tower. He slammed his torso against the railing.

Pressing his belly against the stone, he lifted the cross with both his arms over the open air and into the last bit of sunlight, and he prayed something good would happen.

CHAPTER 60

The cross's rust changed into bright gold. Light shone between his fingers. The iron cross warmed his hands, a welcome relief from the cold wind and wet clothes. The light fell upon Tom's face, and he squinted like he was holding the sun.

The sound of pain and wailing came from behind him. He held the cross with everything he had. The caoineag writhed upon the floor, her body twisting and contorting inside her hooded robe. Her head thrashed from side to side, and her white hair whipped back and forth. Her hands opened and closed while her legs lifted and stretched in a strange seizure of internal agony.

Her mouth opened and closed. Her pupils rotated behind her eyes, showing the back of her eyeballs. Her eyelids fluttered open and shut.

The clouds above Tom flashed with lightning. Thunder echoed across the Loch Ness waters and bounced over the hillsides. The bell in the tower suddenly went back and forth and rang its song, hurting Tom's eardrums.

The caoineag's body grayed, then blackened. She lay still, her hands open, her eyes white, her mouth ajar, her legs twisted.

Strange veins appeared on her skin. Small edges formed over her body. Her skin flaked and fluttered in the wind. A black feather blew from her arm, then her leg. Then another, and another. Her entire body changed into a heap of black feathers.

The wind blew, and her body disappeared as the wind blew the black feathers into the open air. The shape of her body disintegrated with each blown feather. Her robe tore at the seams, leaving trails of thread on the floor of the bell tower platform. Her feathers blew over the stone. The black feathers rolled off the bell tower platform. The wind picked them up and they scattered into the open air, drifting in the atmosphere towards the waters of Loch Ness.

Tom gripped the cross, not sure if he should let it go. The bell stopped ringing. The sound of the wind blowing echoed around the tower. The caoineag was gone, her remains but a few black feathers and threads, catching in the cracks of the platform stones while the rest blew over the landscape.

But what of Marella? How would he save her? Something had to happen.

He had to rescue her!

A strange whirlwind sounded. Next to him, the air swirled. The vision of Thurwick - its city lights and rooftops - blurred and made way for a spiraling portal of light that spun counterclockwise in blue and green mists, interspersed by sparkles of light that glowed purple and orange and yellow and red.

"What the. . . ?" Tom said.

The mist spun. Tom's hair blew wild as the mist formed a circle in a sound of fury. It spun like a whirlpool, opening a hole within its center. The center widened as the mist spun faster and faster.

Through the center of the mist, a different world appeared, a setting Tom had never before imagined. There was a field under the same spiraling flashing clouds. Lightning spread across the horizons, and the wind blew green grass over the hillsides interspersed by cold gray stones.

Tom remembered how Father Gibson had said a door would open. "This has to be it," he said. Holding the cross high, he tried to bring it down.

The cross wouldn't budge. He let go of it, and it hung in the air in the last rays of sunlight.

Tom backed away from the cross.

The door remained open. The sun was setting.

He had to hurry!

He closed his eyes and, with a push of his aching muscles and wet feet, he leaped through the door toward the other world.

A force sucked him in, like a vortex pressing him through. He shouted, not knowing if the sensation would end his life or not. His feet landed on the ground and he tumbled.

He opened his eyes.

He lifted off his belly and climbed to all-fours. His hands and knees pressed against moss and grass.

The wind blew against his side.

The air was cold and sharp. Dark gray stones adorned the hillsides.

In the distance, two large planets hovered over the horizon, the crescent reflection of an unseen light adorning their surfaces. The sun was hidden, and yet there was a dim light like an eternal dusk covering the landscape.

Time stopped in this place. Though the wind blew and the grass swayed, no stars twinkled overhead. There was the constant light of dusk.

In front of him was an old ruin. It could have once been a castle or a cathedral. Its columns stretched several stories high. Another column had fallen over, leaving a cracked and broken obstacle over the grass.

He was on the outside of a stone wall. The wall had a high doorway, and above it were windows that arched at their peaks. More ancient walls surrounded him. Some walls remained standing, others had tumbled. Sporadic stones lay upon the ground where their remains had fallen. The wind howled as it blew through the structures of the open windows and around the edges of the remaining stone walls.

He shouted, "Marella!"

There was no answer. He wasn't sure if she'd be able to hear him over the wind.

"Marella!"

He ran around the wall. There was more grass, more stones, and more dimming light that came from God knew where.

"Marella!"

He ran again, his cold sock-covered feet pressing against the grass, his eyes searching, hoping.

He rounded a hill and, fifty yards away, upon a large boulder sat three figures in white. He ran to them. As he approached he realized he knew them.

Wearing white wedding gowns were Marella, Felicia Morgan, and Liz Stevens. Their dresses and hair blew wild in the wind.

"Marella!" he shouted again.

She did not hear him. Neither did Felicia or Liz. The three women stared straight ahead, their eyes in a trance.

Tom sprinted. When he reached them he bent down in front of Marella. She sat upon the boulder like an elegant princess. Her back was straight. Her red hair had blemished with a white streak that went over her right ear and down her back. Hanging from her ear was one of the four-leaf clover earrings he had given her. The other was inside her father's house. "Marella, it's me, Tom!"

She faced him, but her expression was one of apathy, uncaring, remorse, and sadness.

"Come with me!" he said.

Marella's expression remained neutral, unchanged.

"The door's going to close," he said. "We have to go!" He grabbed her arm and pulled.

She didn't budge.

"Come on!"

Marella focused into the distance, her mind lost within itself. Her green earring shimmered in the light of dusk. Her eyes were on the edge of sadness, her soul close to despair.

"Oh, hell!" He bent down, put his arms under her legs, and lifted her. His cold feet moving inside wet socks, he carried her over the strange landscape, through the wind, around the ruins, and toward the doorway. He pumped his knees, running. The doorway remained open in front of him. On the other side was the fading sunlight over the bell tower platform. He reached the doorway and jumped through it.

He fell when his feet hit the platform. He dropped Marella, but he managed to brace her fall with his arms.

When she landed, her eyes blinked. "Tom?"

He gathered himself next to her.

Her green earring reflected the fading sunlight. Her eyes shifted, examining the setting. "Where am I?"

"Thank God," he said. "You're safe!"

Marella examined her surroundings as she had woken from her trance. "Wha' happened?"

"I came for you."

Marella brought her eyes back toward Tom's as tears fell down her cheeks.

"I told you, you can trust me," Tom said.

She wiped a tear from her eye. She blinked. She pointed at the portal. "There are others."

"Stay here!" He stood up.

The sun was almost gone.

His chest rose as he breathed. He lifted his leg and leaped back through the doorway.

CHAPTER 61

The ruins screamed as the wind and the overhead storm bore down on him. The wind strengthened his second time through. He hurried, his cold feet landing upon the grass and stones.

He sprinted past the corner around the ruins. Felicia and Liz still sat unmoving in their gowns upon the stone, their white dresses blowing in the wind.

He reached the two of them. They remained entranced; neither noticed he was there.

Tom grabbed Felecia's and Liz's arms and pulled. The women sat, expressionless. "Come on you two. I can't carry you both!"

The two women sat upon the stone, their entranced faces gazing at the distant horizon beyond the planets. Both had white streaks running through their hair.

Tom grabbed Felicia's arm and pulled hard. He fell backward as she came off the stone and landed on the ground. She landed upon him. She didn't rise but laid there like a mannequin that had fallen on the floor. Tom scampered out from underneath her.

Liz remained sitting, oblivious to the commotion below her, the white streak in her hair blowing in the wind.

Tom shrugged. "Okay." He bent down, picked Felicia up by the waist, and lifted her over his shoulders. He carried her over the terrain, holding her legs and arms. He rounded the stones and hills, ran through the ruins, and trodded over the grass to the portal.

The doorway appeared to be spinning faster. Beyond the portal, Marella sat on the bell tower floor. Her image was becoming distorted like an image through a glass of water.

He pressed his legs. "Stay open!" he said, pressing his cold feet against the ground.

The mist spun faster and faster. Tom reached the portal and leaped, heaving Felicia through the portal. He fell to the ground with Felicia upon him.

Marella climbed on her knees, the white streak still running down her hair.

"Wha' happened?" Felicia said.

Tom put his hands on his knees. "One more." The portal spun, the mist flowing in erratic circles.

As he said it, the golden cross became rust again. It fell to the ground, clanging as metal does upon stone. It bounced upon the platform until it stayed in place.

The portal door twisted in a contortion, It moved back and forth in strange oscillations.

On the other side of the doorway, Liz Steven's face appeared. She wore her white dress like a woman left at the altar. Her dark hair blew in the wind. Her entranced eyes bled red with sadness.

Her hair grew white; her face turned pale. Tears ran down her cheeks.

Her eyes connected with his. They showed hurt, and anger, and sadness, and vengeance. Tom reached in to grab her, but the portal flashed. The mist closed in around her. Liz Stevens vanished in a whirlwind of swirling air and light.

Tom leaned back and sat next to Marella.

Felicia shook her head and touched her face. "What's goin' on," she asked.

Tom didn't answer.

He focused on breathing.

He had done all he could do. He had saved Marella. He had saved Felicia.

Liz was gone.

The view of the roofs of Thurwick came into view under the shadow of dusk. The clouds overhead dissipated, and the first star appeared in the Eastern sky.

Marella leaned her head against Tom's chest. He put his arms around her to comfort her while she cried.

CHAPTER 62

Tom lifted the suitcase. "This is heavy," he said, trying to be humorous.

Marella didn't laugh. She stared at the wall while she sat on the couch, still confused by the events that happened the day before. She wore her jeans, her corduroy sweater, and her boots. Her beautiful red hair hung over her shoulders, her new white stripe running from her temple over her ear and down her back, her green eyes glistening. She remained still and quiet.

"Are you alright?" Tom said.

Marella broke her trance and raised her eyes. "Huh? Oh. . . sorry. I guess I was jus' thinkin'."

The black feathers spread all over, the claw marks on the wall, the broken kitchen window, and the knives scattered on the floor, Sean Paterson's house was still a disaster. How could one think after all that they had endured?

"I'm tellin' ye, there's proof o' an alternate universe. After all this, that's th' only explanation I can come up with." Sean walked down the hall, using his crutch. With his free arm, he waved his hand. "We can find energy we never knew existed. We can build machines tha' can transform th' world!"

Tom didn't smile. "There's been enough transforming for a while."

"There's power in tha' cross. Maybe we can use it–."

"No," Tom said. "Right now, we get out of here." He lifted the suitcase with his arm and made for the front door.

He passed through the doorway. The wind blew under a sunny Scottish Highland day. Sean's yard windmills spun fast in the wind. The grass leaned, pressed down by the force of the wind. The cold air hit his face. He carried the suitcase to Sean's blue sedan. He set it down by the trunk and went to the driver's door to open the rear.

A car honked behind him, followed by the familiar sound of tires upon gravel.

Tom stood tall under the sky. "It better not be...," he mumbled.

The car engine whirred, then shut off. A dog barked, which surprised him.

Detective Logan O'Malley sat in the car, wearing his fedora. A small cairn terrier sat in the passenger seat, barking and wanting to get out with him. O'Malley opened his car door. He shoved the dog back inside, blocking it from escaping. He climbed out and shut the door. The little dog barked, muffled by the windows.

"I don't want to see you," Tom said.

O'Malley took off his fedora and held it to his chest. His gray hair and beard blew in the wind. "Don' blame ye, lad."

"If you hadn't grabbed me the first time, we'd have been out of here, and none of this would have happened."

O'Malley stood still. The windmills spun with the breeze. "There's authorities tha' wan' tae talk with ye."

"They can find us in London."

"Tha's where yer goin'?"

Tom caught movement back at the house. Marella was standing in the doorway, leaning against the doorframe, her arms crossed, her white streak flowing in her red hair, and her corduroy sweater blowing from the wind.

O'Malley dipped his head. "M' lady."

Marella didn't respond. She disappeared behind the wall.

Tom went to the trunk, lifted the suitcase, and put it inside.

"Ye canno' just leave. Tae many questions still," O'Malley said.

"You're the detective, aren't you? It's your job to answer them."

"Canno' do it withou' yer help."

"Not my problem," Tom said. He stepped toward the house.

"Mr. Wayne," O'Malley said.

Tom stopped. He lowered his head, listening.

"Lives were lost. Lots o' them. People are scared. Hell, over half th' Council is dead o' in jail. And all we have left in th' police force is me and Officer Burns."

"What's that got to do with me?"

"We need answers."

Tom waited. He kept his mouth shut.

"Like, wha' did ye do with th' cross?"

Tom had hidden it under the car seat, intending to take it to Father Gibson. He didn't want O'Malley to know that. Felicia had been on the platform. Tom hoped that she was too confused at the time to know it was even there. "Check the bell tower. It may still be up there," Tom lied.

"Oh?" O'Malley said. "I'll look again."

Tom pursed his lips.

"Do ye know whose it was?"

"No. I think it was Saint Columba's, but can't be sure."

O'Malley put his fedora back on his head. "Wha' do ye think about Nessie?"

Tom chuckled. "There's creatures in the loch. But it's the monsters on land you need to watch."

O'Malley stood still. After a few moments, he dipped his hat. "Thank ye, Mr. Wayne. We'll be in contact with ye. Fur now, good day." O'Malley opened his car door.

"Detective," Tom said.

O'Malley lifted his head.

"Thanks."

O'Malley dipped his fedora and placed his fingers near the brim. The dog barked as he sat in his car and closed the door. The car retreated, and drove down the dirt road back to Thurwick.

"So are ye goin' tae talk?" Marella said.

Tom spun back around toward the front door. She stood in the doorway again, her arms crossed. The wind blew her red hair. Her new white streak ran over her ear, down her scalp to the length of her ends. Her sweater blew in the wind at the hems. She was tired, but still beautiful. He shook his head. "No. We're packed. And we're leaving."

Behind her, Sean came through the door. "And another thin', we can explore th' fusion between energy, find ou' how tae get metals tae bend. Who knows, I may get me a new leg before we're all done – th' nuclear kind!" He went to the sedan, opened the rear door, and climbed inside. Before shutting the door, he said, "Are ye ready?"

"We are," Tom said.

"Alrigh' then. Let's na delay!" Sean said. He shut the door.

Tom watched Marella. She was beautiful as the wind blew her hair. He couldn't comprehend her ordeal, what she was thinking. He wanted to hold her, to help her. But he didn't know if that was what she wanted at the moment. He didn't even know - after all he had done - if she would ever trust him.

He swallowed. "Well, are you ready?"

"Aye," she said.

Tom locked eyes with her for a moment. He went to the passenger door and opened it. He held it for her.

She pulled the front door of the cottage shut, not bothering to lock it. She approached the car. She put her hand on the top of the door and closed it. She leaned in close to Tom. Her earrings sparkled below her ears.

"Thank ye," she said.

Tom smiled.

She leaned up, put her hand on his shoulder, closed her eyes, and kissed Tom on the lips.

Tom's heart melted.

She backed away and smiled.

"You're wearing the earrings I gave you," he said.

"Brought me luck."

Tom opened the car door again and held it steady. She climbed inside. He shut the door and went to the sedan's driver's side and sat in the driver's seat.

"Tis a long drive tae London, about eleven hours, lad. But I've been thinkin', with th' new powers we'll find, maybe we should focus on building individual flyin' machines," Sean said. "Or maybe teleportation. Now wouldn' tha' be somethin'.""

Tom's eyes met Marella's. "Is it going to be this way the whole trip?"

Marella grinned. "Depends on how long ye wan' th' trip tae be." She reached her hand to his and touched it.

Tom smiled, ready for their life together.

THE END

ACKNOWLEDGEMENTS

There are many to thank for the creation of this novel. The people who helped me most either inspired me to push through when things got tough, or they educated me on techniques and tactics in order to create the finished product.

To those who gave me the fuel of inspiration, I thank first those I have spoken with personally. Fellow authors Carolyn Aspenson, Karen White, Emily Giffin, David Frizzell, Linda Sands, Marsha Roush Cornelius, and Haywood Smith, and Rona Simmons each contributed nuggets of wisdom either in person or through phone calls. With their encouragement, whether it was one word of hope or an hour conversation of strategy, they inspired me to push through.

For those who were not authors, but recognized some ability in me to write, especially Father Matthew and Father Patrick from St. Brendan's Catholic Church in Cumming, GA, I thank them. They set me on a path of study that has been invaluable. Their wisdom about story and human nature raises our spirits in ways that expose us to the deeper meanings of life.

For those authors who have written so much about writing, thank you. I've read about thirty books on the subject, and each of you contributed in some way to my growth. But I want to thank especially for this project Dean Wesley Smith. Your book Writing into the Dark changed much for me, and made the process soar.

And thanks to my Beta Readers: Marc Arrington, Kathy Morgan, Dottie Marlan, and Robert Rosner. But a special thank you goes to Wayne Boston. Your recommended changes are so good, I have gotten used to saying, "Yeah, he's right," and I make 99% of all your suggestions. Your comments helped me to strive to be a better writer, to know what I was good at, and to know where I needed work. Your time was invaluable to me, and I'll never forget it.

Thank you to my wonderful wife, RaDonna, who has been so supportive of the time I've spent on this book. Your hope drives me forward. I can't wait to read this one to you.

And thank you to God, and his Son Jesus Christ, for sending me divine help when everything seemed so insurmountable. I know you laughed every time I told you my plans. There definitely is a God, and I'm not him!

ABOUT THE AUTHOR

Matt Kunz is all about the adventure. He has climbed mountains, competed for sports championships, ran for office, and helped lead a city. An Eagle Scout and former walk-on football player at the University of Notre Dame, he spent years contributing to his community as a city councilman and non-profit president in the city of Milton, GA. He learned several insights into team building and human nature during his exploits, many of which can be found inside his books. Whether you pick up a fiction or non-fiction book, you'll find yourself pulled inside the stories, joining with a cast of characters as they experience life's lessons through conflict and suspense. So, don't just sit there. Your journey awaits. Come along, and enjoy the adventure!

www.mattkunzwrites.com

OTHER FICTION BOOKS BY MATT KUNZ

LOCH NESS
REVELATION
FIGHTING HANDS

Coming Soon
ONE NIGHT IN NASSAU

See all of Matt Kunz's books at
www.mattkunzwrites.com

www.ingramcontent.com/pod-product-compliance
Lightning Source LLC
Chambersburg PA
CBHW051316250626
47155CB00007B/2349